VINCENT and the GRIEF MASTERS

Keep Believing!
Diana J Farrar

By

D. L. FARRAR

D. L. Farrar

VINCENT AND THE GRIEF MASTERS

Copyright © 2024 by Diana L. Farrar

All rights reserved. Printed in the United State of America. No part of this book may be used or reproduced in any manner whatsoever without written permission except in the case of brief quotations embodied in critical articles or reviews. Contact author.

This book is a work of fiction. Names, characters, businesses, organizations, places, events, and incidents either are the product of the author's imagination or are used fictitiously. Any resemblance to actual persons, living or dead, events, or locales is entirely coincidental.

ISBN 979-8-218-52161-5 Printed Book

Cover Design by Angela Taormina, actonegraphics.com
Skull Photography by Luca Lonescu, LikeMindedStudio
Color Light Wave Photography by Goja1, iStock
Male Black/White Illustration by Amanda Haynes
Female Black/White Illustration by A. Leigh,
based on work by Anastasia Glu, Shutterstock,
Musical Note Black/White Illustration by Kharom Pleedee, iStock

"She reached for a star, and she got one."

Donald L. Farrar, of his daughter, Diana L. Farrar

To my parents, Don and Joanne,
two adjacent stars twinkling in the night sky.
Thank you both for *everything*.

To my loving husband, Edmond,
my amazing children, and precious grandchildren,
you give me purpose, strength, love, and
a childlike belief that your world, your future,
will be filled with awesome tomorrows.

This book is written for all the children of humanity,
no matter where they are in the galaxy.

A UNIQUE ASPECT OF THIS STORY

There is a different approach to story-telling the author has incorporated into *Vincent and the Grief Masters*. The book captures not only the emotions, tensions and actions of the characters, but makes use of other sensory perceptions, such as color and music. Some characters are represented by certain colors, as illustrated by the color wave shown on the front and back covers. One character maintains a databank of music and applies certain songs to exemplify the mood of specific scenes or chapters.

To bring the music to the realm of a world existing on a printed page, look for the musical note icon just below the chapter number. This indicates there is a song or songs corresponding with the chapter, which can be heard on the author's webpage at:
https://dianalfarrar.wixsite.com/dlfarrar

Or, scan the QR Code below to link to the website. On the top tool bar menu, look for 'Vincent's Playlist' and click on it. The songs will be listed in order by chapter number with full credits for title, artists, albums, producers of each with a link to the licensed music application, Spotify. Follow the brief instructions at the top of Vincent's Playlist to hear either a sample of the song, or a link to Spotify to hear the full arrangement. It is the reader's choice to either read the chapter first and play the selection(s) later (recommended), or read while playing the selection in the background. It is simply for the added pleasure of the audience, offering an additional level of sensory emersion and enjoyment.

ACKNOWLEDGEMENTS

Things done well are seldom done alone. My sincerest thank you goes to those who offered their knowledge, talent, and eyes to this work. Invaluable in this lengthy process were two groups, Agile Writers of Richmond, VA and Chesapeake Bay Writers, et al, of Williamsburg, VA, my editorial and critique partners. They gave me invaluable feedback and continued support. All talented, published authors themselves, their editing reviews and honest suggestions improved my writing skills immensely. Also due my heartfelt thanks are the several independent beta readers who patiently worked through my manuscript, sometimes waiting for weeks to critique freshly written chapters. And, kudos to my long-time friends, Maire, who brought my story vividly alive with her cover design for the original book, and Angela, with the unique and striking cover for this new release. With the help of these talented individuals, I not only have a finely, polished, and finished piece, but I have made friends for life, too.

Family is always important to support an author who sits down to write for months at a time. Thank you to my daughters, Angela and April, who gave continual moral support and pushed me thru the finish line. Thank you to my son, Adam, who put his life on the line everyday as a career military man and was an inspiration for the storyline. And thank you to all of my grandchildren, some of whom served as a test audience, and for whom the message in this book was originally intended. It was for you that I was compelled to share the story's message in the first place. Last, and of course not least, my patient husband, Edmond, who spent many lonely nights and weekends with the dog while I cocooned myself at my desk to write—thank you, my dear. Your opinions always matter, and your advice was excellent.

The encouragement, inspiration, and care shown by these important individuals in my life made all the difference in completing this project. So, as I said in the beginning, things done well are most certainly never done alone.

Please note: some chapters in this book mention suicide. If you are struggling, or know someone who may be in emotional distress, do not hesitate to call the National Suicide Hotline – just dial 988. A confidential, professional provider can give immediate assistance. <u>You are not alone.</u>

YEAR 2050
Prologue

    Young entrepreneur Troy Vincent had paid little attention to the increasing warning signs of the impending calamity that would surround him. The success of his inventions cocooned him in a layer of economic protection. A myopic and soundproof level of security from the crumbling world put him close to the top rung of a shrinking elite society. He was moving in the circles of the highly influential. That world was about to change.

    By the mid-21st Century, so much corrupt money funneled into the world's political systems that politicians were ineffective and divisive. The weight of that corruption made governments around the world start to topple like dominoes. As elected officials lost their free voices, they also lost influence over the world's economies. Overnight markets collapsed, replaced by catastrophic instability and labor protests. Destructive competition disintegrated into nationalistic divisions and civil wars. The result was an implosion of trade and commerce, failure of monetary markets leading to worldwide unemployment and starvation. Civil liberties disappeared; individualism was attacked. Basic freedoms restricted and fair justice systems dissolved. Free education, charitable and religious organizations almost disappeared with no money left in communities to support them. A growing tide of partisanship, bribery, and vigilante law ensued. Fatal cracks in the very foundations of civilization left a world in jeopardy, a world on fire.

Without the power of elected and respected leadership, there was no coalition to pull the fragile planet out of the burning embers. At first, Troy was supportive of the business community when it stepped in to protect companies' assets. They proposed creating a worldwide board of directors, consisting of CEOs from the top one hundred companies. But he soon observed corporations fighting each other for a place on the elite board of one hundred, and creating their own corporate militias. Militia lottery drafts were established. Like thousands of others, Troy was forced to join and fight for values he didn't share; ones that only benefited a handful of billionaires.

They warred over the Earth's natural resources, oil and gas, water, gold and precious metals, minerals and agriculture, the rest divided up equally among them. Manmade power resources and manufacturing industries became playing cards in an exclusive high stakes poker game where only the wealthiest corporations were invited to play. When the wars ended, the CEOs of the surviving top one hundred corporations devised a business plan to remake a new definition of world leadership. They called it, Corporate Rule.

The new corporate order imposed itself upon the lives of everyone. Once released from his military obligation, Troy struggled to rebuild his small business. He remained silent against the cold corporate indifference to the starving world that was only seeking the very basics of existence. It was a world without individuality, without hope and dreams, devoid of selfless thinking. Religious worship of any kind was declared too rebellious and was forbidden by corporate decree to be displayed openly, forcing it behind closed doors.

In the business world, nepotism was rampant, competition was quickly stifled. The stock markets reacted with vigor to hostile take overs. Remnants of regulations and the Rule of Law were loosely and subjectively applied. And without governments to monitor and enforce them, Troy saw the Earth itself suffer. Its resources were plundered, its beauty and environments spoiled, and nonhuman species continued to disappear rapidly. Troy continued with what he knew best, and maintained certain distasteful corporate relationships in order to keep food on the table for his wife and young son, and for his few employees he promised to help.

New rules for every element of society around the world had been addressed, all except the judicial and prison systems. Judgeships were reserved for the corporate courts, because such was in the best interest of the world's corporations. However, without tax dollars to support a criminal justice system, it had to be self-sustaining. Pro bono law panels were required, established by large corporate law firms, to handle such cases. The elimination of lengthy incarcerations was critical to cut costs. But the public's perception of fairness was still important to make a corporate-run society work. Corporate Rule could not succeed by imposing capital punishment. So they developed, tested, and refined a new type of technology. It would put the punishment in the hands of the criminal, and not the corporations, thereby 'washing corporate hands' of it. Introduced gradually, it used Virtual Reality Chambers and became known as the VRC Management System.

According to the World Board of Directors, the VRC theory was based on a single premise: *that one cannot lie to oneself.* In the VRC, the truth of the crime would be known exclusively to the accused. The condemned became one's own judge, jury, and executioner. A lie would be known to all three, being that the accused *was all three*, with no way to hide the truth or manipulate it. Therefore, one's own demons arising from one's inner guilt would destroy the accused, condemning them to die by their own thoughts. The unique method of manifesting demons as illusions that could actually kill made the VRCs feared above all other methods of punishment. And death came swiftly to the guilty, often with gruesome results. Among those found innocent by simply surviving, the encounters were so traumatic, they often chose to disappear completely from society.

The system was not without its critics. Troy finally felt compelled to join the mass protests that erupted wherever a new VRC System was installed. Now he marched with the protesters, objected at the hearings, and spoke out against the loss of human rights. But Corporate Rule always won. Because there was no longer freedom of speech under civil liberty protection, voices like Troy's had no representation, and he was being noticed in certain elite circles for the wrong reasons. Corporations banded together to promote the new system, advertising it as a method of dissuading crime—and it worked. When the tide of crime turned downward, the VRCs, at long last, became an acceptable mode of judgment and punishment. The voices, including Troy's, were forcibly silenced.

The world community, while not totally dispassionate about the fate of those condemned, turned a blind eye to the privately operated systems. Troy was not blind to it, but decided to wait and see how the world, and he, would handle this repugnant reboot of sorts. Corporate Rule appeared content that it had saved the world from total collapse, restored order, and devised a new type of economy that put most people back to work. It did not address the growing concern of a world forced to live in an endless lust for power and fortune, forsaking all of its faith, hope, and compassion. Some even publicly accused the World Board of Directors of ultimately trading a world of God's love for a bag of thirty silver coins. The wealthy CEOs flatly denied the preposterous charge. Then, whispered rumors spread of the appearance of something called, *The Grief Masters,* secretly lingering within the VRCs. Many wondered if God was trying to tell the world something.

Troy Vincent would learn the truth the hard way—as condemned prisoner number 924.

YEAR 2065

Chapter 1

On a crisp fall day, Troy Vincent snuck into his own lab undetected to pick up his project notes and destroy all of his computer records. Hoy SamWong, CEO of the world's most powerful corporation, SamWong Industries, may have taken over what was left of his company, but Troy wasn't going to let him get the plans or patents to his life's work, the Human Transporter Pad. The final working model tested successfully, and fully ready for a media release. Troy designed, built, and patented every part himself after more than two decades of work. Of all the many inventions his small company created, he considered the HTP, as he named it, his most prized invention. The advanced technology was kept secret during its development, fiercely protected so no other scientific team anywhere in the world could produce a similar product. One of a kind, it was not intended for the type of mass production SamWong Industries put out—cheap imitations of anything and everything, manufactured like toothpicks.

Troy threw several mini-computer blades and backup drives into a duffle bag by his desk. He hated corporations like SWI swooping in and swallowing up the dreams of smaller companies like his.

Eighteen years ago, he saw only hope for his future. A new college graduate with a stunning portfolio of innovative products, Troy started his business by becoming a small subsidiary of his father's existing company, Vincent Scientific Applications. Dr. Vincent headed a prestigious group of scientists working on space projects for the government. However, Troy's father only lent the good reputation of VSA's name to the budding subsidiary, and never mixed the business matters of the two divisions of the company. Troy was free to run his own business, to succeed or fail, on his own. Good inventions and good fortune built his reputation into a successful growing company, one he was proud of.

However, everything changed when the world seemed to implode. Governments, economies, and contracts all collapsed. When Corporate Rule took over, the world's corporations began warring with each other over lands, resources, and technologies. The new ruling elite allowed the largest companies to maintain their own paramilitary units and initiated a draft system by age group. Troy fell into one such group, forced to sign a three year commitment or be fined an enormous penalty fee he couldn't afford. He didn't want to jeopardize the business he had worked so hard to create, so he protected his company's assets by moving them into CDs and blue-chip stocks and temporarily closed its doors.

Troy put his personal affairs in order, leaving his young wife, Lilith, and their new baby boy, with more than enough cash to live on until he could return. Troy's three year obligation abruptly ended when the last corporate wars were over and the final division of Earth's resources was negotiated between the world's top corporations.

Troy returned to his work, re-established his small company, and began to pick up the pieces where he left off. His time away took a toll on his marriage, but a blossoming bond thrived between him and his young son, Tommy. Though he was cash poor, the ex-veteran still looked to regain some of the success he once had. His father, Dr. Vincent, however, was not as fortunate. The good doctor relied on his own personal funds to keep his team working on their highly specialized program, even though no government sponsor remained in existence, leading VSA into bankruptcy.

SWI bullied and bribed its way to the top of the ten most powerful corporations. Hoy SamWong soon became the most aggressive member on the World Board of Directors overseeing Corporate Rule. He set his sights on acquiring all of the previously collapsed US government contracts. It intrigued Hoy SamWong when all information on Dr. Vincent's contract could not be obtained, having been digitally locked and labeled, *Top Secret Clearance Only*. It motivated him to do whatever it took to acquire the contract, its team, and all research and development in its possession. He considered this the pathway to becoming Chairman of the WBoD. "SWI would own it, or no other company on the world board would," SamWong smugly announced. Other top board members objected, but they were no match for the large SWI legal team or their private militia.

As the original owner of the company, Dr. Vincent fought hard against the acquisition by SWI, but ultimately VSA lost. Troy's company, a subsidiary of the original VSA, would not be obtained in the forced sale of Dr. Vincent's parent company to SWI. Troy frowned, his brows coming together in a deep furrow, as he remembered the event. "It wasn't an acquisition; it wasn't even legal," Troy subconsciously mumbled out loud. As far as he was concerned, it had been stolen, pure and simple.

Troy considered his father a brilliant physicist and exotic inventor. Though he didn't know the exact details of the secret projects VSA worked on, he knew losing the unique inventions deeply depressed Dr. Vincent and eventually killed him. They ruled it a suicide, as reported by the authorities hired by SWI to investigate his death. But Troy knew his father, and he didn't believe it, not for a moment. However, he couldn't disprove it either.

Troy knew Hoy SamWong personally before the arrogant executive became the head of the WBoD, first meeting through business acquaintances and at various black tie events and dinners. He didn't trust the little man with a huge appetite for attention and lofty ambition. Every time Troy spoke with him, he felt the man secretly harbored jealousy of anyone with a smarter and keener intellect. And watching SWI systematically drive companies out of business, it appeared to Troy it was an obsession and a child-like power play for SamWong to eliminate his competition. "That's why he buys 'em and destroys 'em," Troy muttered.

Now two years later, Troy watched as the assets of his own subsidiary company become pawns in a bitter, hostile takeover. Small companies like his became targets, bought out by the most powerful companies on the Board. SamWong used the media to publicize his dogged pursuit of the remaining VSA subsidiary, causing its stock value to plummet and forcing the sale.

It wasn't enough Hoy SamWong had destroyed his father, he also stole Troy's self-absorbed wife. Troy met Lilith in college and they married soon after graduation. Initially, he was attracted to her drive and her continual self-promotion into the upper levels of society, but it eventually made him feel uncomfortable. He didn't mind her using VSA to open doors for her; he wanted her to enjoy her life. Their first few years together were good memories for him. But the more she made important friends, the less she wanted to be with him. When Troy had to serve in the corporate militia, she grew more distant. Once he returned, he had hoped they could work it out, but it wasn't to be. She had already moved well beyond him, keeping her name in the upper circles, attending private black-tie dinners, and having a life style that was not the kind he envisioned for himself or his son.

SamWong prized himself for acquiring not only companies, but beautiful women, too. Troy would admit Lilith's beauty, but her loyalty and love served only one person, herself. True to her name, she exuded the very symbol of vanity. It was no accident when the greedy billionaire caught the eye of the flirtatious Mrs. Vincent at yet, another black-tie party. She made sure his lustful eyes turned in her direction. And when they did, she jumped at the chance to be on the arm of one of the richest men in the world. It amazed Troy just how fast she walked out on him and five year-old Tommy and never looked back.

"Good riddance," he said under his breath, while scanning the three monitors suspended in air over his desk. The screens flashed through dozens of programs, uploading to Troy's handheld remote pad. He stepped over to another desk and turned on a screen to retrieve the last of his company's data.

Like his father, Troy did everything he could to stop the acquisition. Corporate lawyers were not cheap, forcing him to mortgage every property he owned to retain them. Only the small cabin on Edmond Lake remained his last untouched possession. In addition, selling many of his patents except those related to the HTP, just wasn't enough capital to fight the army of SWI lawyers. And they played hardball. Their lead attorney, Xavier Adams, a vicious, vengeful attack dog, liked to play dirty and bragged of a record of successful wins for SWI. The rumors on the street whispered Adams had his eye on running SWI himself someday. He planned to prove to its Board he would be the best choice to run the company if Hoy ever stepped down. No one would dare to challenge Hoy SamWong but Adams.

Troy lost even before his fight to stop the acquisition began. He suspected some collusion between his young, up-and-coming attorney and the older, more experienced SWI team. He discovered they played on the same tennis team; they golfed at the same country club, and dined together with their wives. The end result was predictable. By tomorrow, a day Troy thought would never come, what remained of the father and son company, Vincent Scientific Applications, would have a new owner. His quality inventions would carry the VSA trademark for now, but be replaced by the cheaper mass marketed SWI label. He would have to sue to keep any long-term ownership of the HTP, and with the judges all in the pockets of one corporation or another, there appeared little chance he could win.

Troy planned to work fast before SWI Security would show up to change the locks on the lab with his only working HTP model still inside. He noticed their security was following him over the last several days. Taking Tommy, now eight, to a large amusement park for an afternoon, he told his son there was some work he needed to pick up later at the lab. After enjoying the park for several hours, they disappeared into the crowd and exited unseen by the agents who followed them. With the use of a second vehicle Troy left near the park the day before, the two of them slipped away, driving to the lab undetected. His years in the military taught him a few tricks that still came in handy.

SWI laid off all of VSA's employees in the transition and no one remained at the building to hinder Troy's break in. He found it wryly amusing he needed to sneak into his own company. The pin numbers to all the electronic doors remained the same, and the security system still retained his retina ID.

"Piece of cake," he said to Tommy, as they walked through the dark hallways leading to the lab. He turned off each security camera with a click of a master remote built into his watch.

Troy assumed the last comment he made to SamWong after the acquisition hearing scared the paranoid eccentric and triggered the hyped-up security force following him. As they descended the steps of the courthouse, Troy scowled at him, putting on his sunglasses. Hoy chuckled at Troy's look of defeat as a smug Lilith climbed into their waiting limousine.

Troy growled, "Make sure one of my VSA babies doesn't blow up in your face," referring to his inventions absconded by Hoy. "On second thought, I hope the hell they do." *I only meant to insult the greedy little bastard, but he must have taken it as a threat.*

The little boy wandered around the lab, curiously looking at different scientific models. Small scale and brightly painted, the replicas appeared like model airplanes mounted on display stands. Some sat on desk tops, while larger ones sat on the floor. One oversized model of a water molecule held a suspended ball of combined hydrogen and oxygen atoms, while two electrons swirled around it in mid-air. Another display repeatedly opened the inside of an atom, as colorful atomic quarks popped out of it like tiny fireworks. Each possessed some unique feature capturing

Tommy's attention. All of them bore Troy's specific VSA trademark, a large triangular V with a lowercase *s* and *a* inside of it.

"Daddy, I want to work here when I grow up so I can play with all the neat stuff in your lab," said Tommy. He appeared totally mesmerized by a display case of the Periodic Table, pressing his nose against the glass case to inspect the many revolving 3-D samples. Troy half smiled looking over at his son, sadly knowing the boy was unaware his father's lab would belong to SamWong Industries in less than twenty-four hours.

"Hey, kiddo, be careful what you touch in here, ok?" Troy stood across the room at a rack of storage blades and integrated data drives, erasing final traces of technical files.

"Ok," Tommy barely responded, moving on to a desk with a colored finger pad of small squares laid out on top of it. He liked how the colorful LEDs lit up under his fingertips when he touched each square. To him the grid on the pad looked like a game board. Punching different boxes of the grid made a different color appear on a computer console above the desk. With each contact, a series of numbers scrolled across in a banner above the console, but Tommy remained too distracted by the lights to pay any attention to the now activated controller.

"Records destruction complete in one hour," said an automated female voice from the terminal screen. Troy uncoupled several small thumb drives from the rack. With a push of a button, each one shrunk to the size of a square lithium chip, which he clicked onto a plastic grid, slipping it into his pocket. The console clock flashed a countdown to the death of his life's work. He couldn't stop the acquisition, but he could make damn sure the HTP would not work for anyone else but him. Troy finished packing the duffle bag with a stack of digital notepads, zipped it up, and walked toward the lab's double exit doors.

"Come on, Tommy, let's go."

Tommy slowly walked away from the console table. Passing the nearby Human Transporter Pad, he noticed similar lights blinking on a small grid above it. They appeared just like the ones on the table, flashing the same series of colorful LEDs. The curious little boy wanted to investigate it before leaving the lab. Tommy climbed the two steps up to the pad to get a closer look.

In a rush to leave, Troy feared it was taking too long to retrieve all of his research. His mind raced, occupied with estimating how much time it would take for the SWI Security to figure out where he was. He hoped to be halfway to the cabin at the lake before they searched the lab. The Destruct Code would continue silently undetected, even if security arrived before it completed its countdown. Not paying attention to his son's distraction, Troy pushed the double glass doors open and hurried into the hallway. Halfway down the hall, he realized his son wasn't right behind him and stopped, sighing out loud.

"You're always slow, Tommy," he whispered to himself. Then he smiled. Spending time with his son put Troy's life into perspective. Any anger he felt over the past weeks subsided at the thought of having more time with his son, as there was nothing he'd rather do. He owed Tommy a night of popcorn and a movie for the boy's patience with his father. He turned back to get him.

As Troy approached the lab doors, the blinking LEDs on the console table reflected on the glass door. He knew it meant only one thing: the HTP was on and ready to transport. His eyes flashed to the machine's platform. Troy gasped, realizing Tommy stood on the pad itself. Before he could react, he saw his son touch the *Activate Transport* button on the transporter pad. What seemed like slow motion took only a second for him to throw open the doors and yell Tommy's name. But it was too late. As Tommy glanced back at his Dad, his face registered a look of startled fear before he dematerialized. In the next second, he was gone. Only the blinking light of the console flashed in the room. Silence engulfed the lab.

Troy stood frozen in disbelief, dropping the duffle bag to the floor.

Chapter 2

Troy felt numb for months after the accident. He functioned enough to get by, working odd jobs during the day and seeking solace at any number of bars at night. The duffle bag with notes from his life's work remained in the trunk of his car, where it had been since Tommy disappeared.

He tried unsuccessfully to find the coordinates Tommy entered, however the entry was incomplete and wasn't saved in the system. He tried to reverse it, but nothing existed to reverse. Everything came back with no results. Troy monitored the countdown to the final destruction of the machine as he frantically tried everything he could think of to retrieve Tommy's signal.

When SWI Security tracked him to the lab, they dragged him away by force. All the while, Troy begged them to let him continue, yet they failed to understand what had happened. They threw him out into the parking lot and locked the doors, securing them with chains.

Troy had to tell Lilith and the authorities. As Hoy SamWong's live-in companion, she accompanied Hoy everywhere and loved the media attention. Although she rarely saw Tommy, she made sure the news cameras captured her weepy reaction when the story hit the news. She publicly lashed out at Troy, even though the authorities said he did nothing wrong, as the lab was still under his control. Authorities ruled the whole incident an unfortunate accident.

SamWong's response to Troy, however, hit him hard with a cold, unemotional intention. "There's a certain irony about the situation," said SamWong. "You stole something from me, meaningless data wasn't it? And I, or one of your malfunctioning inventions, stole something from you, also meaningless." Troy hated him for that, and the feeling was mutual.

SWI changed all the security codes and never discovered Troy sabotaged his own HTP. He had to recover his son somehow. He tried repeatedly to regain access to the lab, by walking into the facility during the day, or breaking into it at night. Security stopped him every time. After a month of his attempts to enter every day, SWI requested a Cease and Desist Order from the Corporate Court. Troy was banned from the property for life, under threat of arrest.

****

Troy motioned for the bartender to bring him another round. His dark mood reflected in his empty eyes as he stared into the mirror behind the bar. The bartender turned to the sleek, stainless steel wall of panels behind him. He touched the panel he knew was Troy's brew of choice. As the panel lit up and opened, a fresh, frosted mug of beer appeared. The bartender grabbed it and slid it across the bar to Troy.

A group of loudly talking young men gathered at the other end of the bar, peppering the air with their profanity and laughter. The bartender grimaced at the group as he wiped up the trail of slopped beer with a towel. He nodded in the rowdy group's direction.

"Avatars, that's what they are," he told Troy. "Life-size, 3-D avatars. That's the new thing for these underage punks. They're not old enough to come in and drink, so they bring their game avatars in here."

Troy looked down the bar in their direction. He noticed how their clothes looked genuine enough: a sleek leather jumpsuit with neon trim on one man; skintight, sleeveless t-shirts on the other three. Tattoos covered much of their skin, going up their necks and over their shaved skulls. The skin, however, had an odd pallor, looking pale and unnatural. The real giveaways were the eyes—tiny irises with flat color surrounding black static dots.

"Do they drink?" Troy asked as he sipped his beer.

"No, and that's the problem. They just take up space and cause trouble. Keep the paying customers away from the stools." The bartender threw the towel under the back of the bar and began to stack glasses on the shelf behind him.

A few seats away around the corner of the bar, a middle-aged hooker with heavy makeup creased into deep wrinkles of her hard face struck a match to light her cigarette.

"Hey, don't light that in here," the bartender complained.

She exhaled her smoke in his direction. "They repealed those laws, Gus," she said in a gravelly voice. "No way to enforce 'em now. I know my rights."

She winked at Troy.

"He's just jealous. He smokes like a chimney; I've seen him out back." Raising her voice in the bartender's direction and offering him her cigarette, "You probably want a drag right now, don't ya, Gus?" She laughed as he gave her a wry smile and walked down the bar toward the rowdy avatars.

She inhaled one end through bright red lips as the other end turned bright orange. Exhaling slowly, the smoke swirled up under the harsh bar light, adding to the silver haze in the room. Troy could feel her eyes upon him as he drank his beer. She laid the cigarette in an empty peanut bowl on the bar beside her.

"You've been brooding over that drink. Want some company?"

"No thanks." Troy just wanted to be left alone. He needed the drink, not the company.

"Come on, handsome. A little conversation, a few laughs; it might help."

Troy half smiled, staring down into his beer.

"Thanks, but no. Sorry."

"There's nothin' in that glass that's gonna make you feel better...but I can."

She smiled at him as she picked up her cigarette and took another drag. This time she exhaled quickly as she saw one of the avatars grab the bartender's shirt.

"Uh-oh, there's gonna be trouble."

Troy looked down the bar. "I thought they're holograms. Are they solid?"

"Solid enough. Not like a body, like yours or mine. But they have some kind of energy field giving 'em weight and substance; and they like to fight to prove it."

Troy didn't like disrespect, especially from something which wasn't even real. He turned in their direction and shouted, "Hey, let him go. No need to disrespect the man. He's just doing his job."

The avatar released his hold on the bartender and the group of pale punks turned toward Troy. They got off their stools and started walking in his direction.

Troy turned back and took another drink of his beer. The hooker nervously put out her cigarette in the peanut bowl. She kept her eyes down averting eye contact with any of the muscular avatars.

"Their game source must be close by," she whispered. "They can't be too far from it or they'll power off."

"Yeah, I know how they work. They don't know how I work." He calmly glanced back at her.

Two avatars came and stood between Troy and the hooker, looking down at them with black eyes that had no depth. A third one, the largest one, stood directly behind Troy. The fourth one, the one in the neon jumpsuit who grabbed the bartender, leaned on the bar to the right side of Troy.

Troy looked straight ahead into the mirror behind the bar. He could see a group of four young men, not more than teenagers, seated at a table in the far corner of the room. Each one held something small in their hands and hidden from view. He noticed their heads were down, while everyone else watched the tense action at the bar.

"You're old," one avatar said to the hooker.

The hooker waved it off. "Yeah, tell me something I don't know."

"No need to insult the lady either," Troy said.

Troy knew they were looking for a fight and he was only too ready to oblige them. Smouldering anger darkened his mood for months now, ever since the accident and it was ready to boil over. He didn't know why he should give them a chance to back down, but he would...just one.

The other avatars laughed. The neon jumpsuit leaned over, whispered to Troy and pointed at the hooker.

"In case you haven't noticed, she's no lady." Troy felt the hilt of a laser gun press against his arm and saw the bulge in the jumpsuit under the avatar's arm.

"Look boys, why don't you go home and power off," said Troy. He cocked his head toward the back table. "And tell your gamers they're too young to be in here."

A broad-chested avatar leaned on the bar on Troy's left side and flexed his bulging bicep making his tattoo dance. He picked up Troy's beer, crushing the glass in his hand. Beer and pieces of glass tumbled from between his fingers onto the bar. Troy stared calmly into the mirror. "I really hate to see a good beer go to waste, especially if its mine."

"Yeah? What are ya gonna do about it?" asked the avatar.

Great, here we go, Troy thought with annoyance as he leaned back, stretching both of his arms out, laying his hands on the bar, ready for any sudden movement on their part. *So much for giving them a chance.*

The bartender raised his hands in an effort to stop the aggression. "Look, I don't want you guys tearing up my place. If ya know what's good for ya, you won't pick a fight with him, you'll regret it. He's a vet of the EOFW."

The neon leader of the troublemakers looked at the bartender with a dumb look. "Geez, you kids don't know nothin' do you?" the bartender said, shaking his head with a snort. "The Eastern Oil Fields War." The bartender pointed at a double star EOF tattoo on the side of Troy's neck partially hidden by the collar of his leather jacket. "He's got the corporate militia's symbol for it."

The avatar pulled at Troy's collar and Troy jerked his jacket away. "Oh, huh," the avatar raised his eyebrows. "And here I thought it was just a pretty boy tattoo," he smirked.

As the avatars all laughed, Troy could see in the mirror the four boys at the back table snicker, too. Gamers could be dangerous, and he didn't want anyone in the place to get hurt—except them. Whatever weapons their game would come up with, he'd be ready for it. He slowly stood up from the stool, brushing past the mouthy game pieces. Taking off his jacket, he tossed it across the bar to the bartender. "Keep an eye on this for me, will you?"

The largest avatar turned toward the boys in the back and shouted, "Hey, guys, he's a vet of the Eastern Oil Fields War, whatever that is," mocking the bartender. "We should leave him alone, right?"

The hooker started to object, but was brutally knocked off the bar stool by a large pale forearm.

"Your frickin' manners suck," she yelled as she struggled to get up from the floor.

Troy knew this would end badly, not for him, but for them. The same avatar swung around to Troy with his fist clenched. Troy's instinctive reaction blocked the fist to his ribs, as his own upper cut met the square jawbone of the false flesh. He then swung around and buried an elbow into the neck of the avatar at the bar on his other side. They immediately turned around and two fists packed power into Troy's chest as he flew backward into a table of bar patrons. He definitely felt their energy slam into his abs. *Well, hell, that hurt!*

It surprised him how solid they really were. The power appeared to be in their limbs, not their entire bodies. When he threw his fist into the gut of one of them, it went right through it.

As the bar patrons scrambled to get to the exits, the four avatars piled onto Troy. He fought to throw each one of them off by grabbing their solid limbs, and hurling them into tables and chairs. Recovering his footing, Troy broke a chair over the head of one and diverted the fist of another into the wall.

The mouthy avatar leader produced the gun from the concealed holster. Troy anticipated the threat, kicking it out of the avatar's hand before he could fire. It hit the floor discharging a short laser burst into the mirror over the bar, bouncing off the glass and across the room, burning a hole in the wall. Shards of broken mirror glass flew in all directions. Troy lunged to grab the loose gun, tossing it across the floor before its owner could reach it. The gun skidded out of the game's power range and disappeared. As the avatar followed after his weapon, Troy raised his leg and put a well-placed boot on the leather butt of the punk, pushing him out of game range where he, too, evaporated.

The second avatar emerged from the crowd rushing toward Troy with a mini-missile launcher in his hands. He paused only slightly to look at the weapon and took a right cross to the eye from the third avatar. Grabbing that avatar by its arm, he made a quick turn-around and pushed it into the path of the on-coming missile. It took the third avatar's head off, as it whizzed by Troy. The missile disappeared out of game range and the headless avatar immediately powered off. "Aww, you killed my guy, you idiot!" shouted one of the boys at the back table.

The avatar with the missile launcher dropped its weapon and hit Troy with a running side block, sending them both sliding across the floor. As it climbed on top of Troy's chest, he felt the weighted energy of the game piece firmly pin him down. The avatar raised its fist, transforming its meaty hand into a large, square cement block. As it came down toward Troy like a battering ram, he moved his head to the left to avoid the blow. The cement block crashed into the wooden floor, splintering the wood and sending a puff of pulverized cement dust into Troy's face. The avatar raised his fist again. Anticipating the predictable move of his opponent, he moved his head in the opposite direction as the square cement fist crashed into the floor on his other side.

The avatar had his arms pinned as it sat on top of Troy. *Let's find out if this energy mass is moveable.* Jerking both of his arms up, he thrust his fists into the avatar's crotch. The game figure flew off Troy like a rocket. As the avatar slowly stood up, Troy jumped and tackled him, pushing him so far away from its power source that the meaty avatar disappeared instantly. Troy stopped short of bashing his own head into the wall as the weight of the avatar suddenly left his grasp.

The largest avatar remained, the one who stood behind him at the bar. He came after Troy with a loud growl. Tossing chairs and tables out of his way, he followed Troy to the back of the room. Troy now stood by the table of four boys with his back to the advancing menace. The avatar approached and stopped just behind him. With muscular arms outstretched, growing as big as trees, the burly game piece was ready to crush the war veteran with the push of a button.

Troy's voice was loud, rough, and commanding. "Turn it off!"

Three of the boys laid their small game pads on the table and lifted their hands in the air, away from them. Troy could feel the avatar's energy field pulsating behind him, but kept his eyes seriously riveted on the fourth boy, as the boy's thumb remained poised above a button which would commence the attack. Instead, the skinny kid swallowed hard and blinked nervously, staring up into the dark, threatening eyes of the man standing next to him.

"Avatar, power off," he said in a crackling, high-pitched voice and laid the game pad on the table.

The avatar blinked into oblivion. For a moment, the boys sat motionless. Troy lifted his leg, kicking the table over with his heavy boot. The four game pads flew in all directions and the startled boys jumped and ran for the door, leaving their game pads behind.

The shrill sound of a police siren blared in the distance as Troy made his way back across the room. He set a few chairs back in place however, the room was destroyed. He shrugged at the disgruntled bartender who roughly threw his leather jacket back at him. Troy pulled his wallet from the pocket and tossed several large international bills on the bar. The hooker stood by the tipped-over barstool and lit another cigarette. She briefly looked at the money he laid down, glancing at the stack of bills still left in his wallet. She waved the match through the air, putting it out and dropping it into the peanut bowl. Troy squinted at her with one good eye as he winced, touching a tender spot on the other. She smiled as smoke flowed from her partially parted red lips.

"Why don't you and I shake this place before the cops come? It's getting a bit rowdy in here, don't you think?"

Chapter 3

Troy opened his eyes and looked over at the other side of the bed. The covers had been thrown back, and the pillow wadded up. The hooker was gone. He groggily rolled over to the nightstand by his side of the bed and felt around the top of it, knocking empty beer bottles to the floor. Finding his wallet, he opened it. *It's gone, damn it. She took it all.*

He threw the wallet at the wall, rolling back onto the pillow, staring up from the bed at the watermarked ceiling of the seedy motel room. He replayed the last time he saw Tommy in his mind. It was a scene he saw repeatedly, several times a day. It always ended the same – with every trace of his young son gone. *Gone where? Why wasn't the safety lock on the console? What went wrong?* Questions Troy asked himself a thousand times over.

He sat up on the side of the bed with his head in his hands. The early morning sun streamed through a crack in the curtains and Troy squinted, covering his eyes. His foot kicked one of the empty beer bottles, sending it rolling across the floor. Weariness wracked his body and he rubbed his eyes as though he could erase the strain.

"I'm tired of this shit," muttering under his breath. *Liquor and old girls; too many nights are ending up like this.* He picked up his pants and shirt and went into the bathroom. The light from the old, cracked fixture dimly lit the space, but he could still see how ragged his reflection appeared. Stress and heartache shown in the lines of his face, and the new black eye didn't help. A three-day-old beard darkened his face, matching the dark brown of his hair. His brooding brow and down-turned lips seemed enough to scare everyone away. For that, Troy was grateful. He wanted to be left alone, to melt into his own misery, to fade away into the dark recesses existing on the edge of humanity. He destroyed the one thing he had left: his son. So he deserved every miserable hangover, dirty whore, or nasty black eye he got.

He took some comfort in his body being in halfway decent shape. At least he could still hold his own in a fight, even if it was against a bunch of game avatars. While the outside of him seemed ok, the inside churned in turmoil. There used to be light in his eyes, in his soul. Now Troy doubted if he even had a soul. There was only emptiness. He believed in nothing, turning away at any mention of comfort or faith. When did it ever help him? Now it never would.

There must be a reason why they banned all that religious stuff; my father believed and look what happened to him. Corporate Rule blamed religion for fueling continual conflicts and a long history of wars, so the WBoD declared it forbidden, all different doctrines of it, including the names of all deities and their religious symbols. Worship could exist, but was forced to remain private and behind closed doors, with no public displays allowed or holidays openly observed. If compliance was not voluntary, corporate militias would enforce the ban. The world became outwardly godless, while inwardly reverent, and increasingly defiant.

Maybe Troy believed in it once, long ago, before life kicked him in the ass. But to believe in any of it, one had to have a heart, and Troy didn't want a heart. Hearts only break; they harbor painful baggage and sadness. He didn't want to feel, he didn't want to hope. He didn't want to go on breathing, but somehow that still occurred.

He looked away from his reflection in the mirror, shaking his head in self-disgust. He wished he could escape and be anywhere but here. Once he took pride in having so much to offer society before his world collapsed. Now the only thing he could offer was the hate he felt for Hoy SamWong.

Troy needed to clear his head and get control of his thoughts. "An idle mind is the devil's playground," his father always said. He never assumed it to be true, but just maybe his father was right.

I got enough trouble without the damn devil messin' around in there, too.

As he bent his head to splash some water on his face, a strange outline appeared in the mirror above him. A slow swirl of green fog surrounded a dark image of a cloaked figure. A glint of light reflected off of the exposed metallic chin appearing just under the hood of the cloak. Then the mouth became visible with a set of chrome teeth completing the skeletal jawline. The hood hid the rest of the face beneath a shadow. It stood still, watching Troy for a moment as the fog moved in a circular motion behind it. When Troy lifted his head, the image and the fog in the mirror were gone.

He turned to dry his face on a towel and reached into the shower to turn on the water. His body ached from the brawl in the bar and his head cloudy from the booze. He hoped the hot steam would loosen his stiff joints and clear his head. As he pulled the thin shower curtain closed, the cloaked figure reappeared in the mirror. It lingered there until the steam from the shower covered the mirror and obscured the image.

Troy walked from the bathroom feeling somewhat refreshed, pulling on his shirt. A knock rattled the motel door, and he stepped to the drapes to peer through the crack. He couldn't see who it was, but definitely noticed the police van in the parking lot below. When he started to turn the knob to open the door, it burst open and four policemen forced their way inside. With weapons all pointed at him, each laser beams targeted either his heart or his forehead. Troy stood by the window and didn't move.

"Are you Troy Vincent?" one of them asked.

"Yeah," he responded, slowly putting his hands in the air. "Look, if this is about the fight at the bar...."

"What fight?" an officer interrupted.

Troy's eyes squinted in confusion. *This wasn't about the fight.* "Forget it. What do you want?"

"You're under arrest for the murder of World Board Director, Hoy SamWong."

Troy stared at them for a brief moment, and then snorted with a half- laugh, "Sorry fellas, but you got the wrong guy."

"Shut up! That's for the court to decide. We've been ordered to take you in."

"Ordered by whom?"

"We have a warrant. Now get dressed."

As an officer motioned for him to put on his boots, Troy sat down on the bed, grabbing each boot and yanking it on while muttering about no rights existing anymore for the wrongly accused. He stood, put on his leather jacket and retrieved his wallet from the floor. A second officer clapped electronic cuffs on him and they hustled him out of the motel room and down the steps to the parking lot. The van idled on a cushion of air while two officers shoved Troy into the back and climbed in after him. The other two officers shut the back door and jumped into the middle seats of the van. The internal GPS whisked the driverless vehicle off the lot and into the sky highway where it disappeared among a blur of moving taillights.

Chapter 4

Troy had a lot of time to think while he sat in a holding cell overnight. *So SamWong's dead. Someone finally took him out.* He rubbed the rough stubble on his jaw. *A lot of people had good reason to get rid of him. But who's accusing me?* He racked his brain to remember all of the people he knew who wished SamWong dead—the list was long. He also contemplated who might want Troy Vincent out of the way. On the top of the list would have been Hoy, himself, and possibly Lilith.

Troy's mind raced in overtime. Another problem gnawed away at him, a growing concern about his immediate circumstance. He was about to face the most feared absurdity to come out of the entire mid-21st Century restructuring: the corporate courtroom. Troy recalled the justification made by the World Board of Directors when they announced without existing tax funds, a new justice system and criminal incarceration method needed to be created; self-contained and cost efficient, it would administer justice without lengthy sentences. Only in these systems, results could be bought, pushing justice aside.

A Corporate Court of judicators for business matters would remain, being in the best interests of the world's corporations. However criminal cases, which Troy assumed his warrant had been issued under, were heard by a panel of rotating regional pro bono lawyers required to offer a few hours of pro bono time each month. Troy viewed them as anything but fair and objective. In order to climb the professional ladder, young pro bono lawyers competed for the attention of the older senior attorneys on the panel, who in turned pushed for biased verdicts benefiting their own employers and corporate sponsors.

"A jury of one's peers no longer exists," Don Tyler once told him. Tyler was his father's lawyer, but also his friend. Troy often turned to him for advice, but Tyler no longer represented any defendants in the pro bono court, and could not be reached. For unknown reasons, Tyler also eliminated most of his corporate clients, representing very few cases in the corporate courtroom. "Even lawyers have to be careful these days," Tyler confided in Troy. "With spies everywhere waiting to profit from an ill-timed photograph, or accusatory rumors and innuendo, factual evidence becomes subjective, at best."

His last advice to Troy after Tommy's disappearance was to keep a low profile for a while. "Private Citizens, who have the misfortune of finding themselves as defendants, are at the mercy of whoever serves on the judging panels. And you don't want to find yourself sentenced to a VRC."

Troy walked across the large holding cell with bare benches and glaring lights which never turned off. Unlike the other detainees, his electronic wrist restraints remained on him, but he was free to move around the room. A wireless signal beamed a holographic television program at one end of the room as a few drunks lay on the floor watching it. Other detainees found quieter corners to sleep off their drug of choice. Thick Plexiglas walls separated the room from the main hall, where security personnel at the Duty Desk could observe all movement in the holding cell. Likewise, Troy could see them and anything happening in the hallway.

At one end of the hall he observed an endless parade of security officers walking from a nearby cafeteria. Beams of light from their belt buckles held the food trays in place, floating in front of them. This freed their hands for access to their weapons at any time. At the other end of the hall, was an exit door from the pro bono court room. He overheard another detainee say people coming through that door had just faced the judging panel and would be escorted out to be released, or to the elevator to the dreaded Virtual Reality Chambers, or VRCs.

The VRC System Management, VRCSM, as it was commonly known, replaced long-term detention centers and penitentiaries. Troy watched the media reports of protests by thousands of people wherever new systems planned to be installed, feeling compelled to join them. But his company sales went down when a group of elite CEOs he knew took notice of his actions and his wife begged him to stop protesting.

Once arrested at a protest rally, and later let go because Lilith intervened through her black-tie party contacts, Troy decided to not put his business or his employees' jobs in further jeopardy. He recalled a conversation in the police intake room explaining the VRCs were essential to dehumanize those convicted and set an example that protesters would not be tolerated. Referred to as treatments instead of sentences, he also learned the security guards were called attendants, and prisoners called candidates. He remarked to the intake officer, "I heard they were called unlucky." That remark almost kept him from being released.

Through the Plexiglas wall of the holding tank, Troy watched a young man exit the court room door, and struggle against the two VRC attendants who were escorting him toward the elevator. Troy assumed the elevator led to the halls of the VRC treatment rooms. The young candidate in the hallway freed one arm and took a swing at an attendant. A futile scuffle got everyone's attention. Additional security attendants from the Duty Desk ran to help subdue him. The young man's short burst of energy got quickly tazed out of him.

"Poor bastard," Troy shook his head and sighed. *These guards aren't game avatars. I'll need to keep a lid on it in here.*

As he turned back toward the middle of the holding cell, he noticed a small window recessed into the far, opposite corner. It was hidden in the shadow of an alcove where the glaring ceiling lights did not shine directly overhead. He walked over to peer down at the street below. A single street lamp lit the dark street corner as a passerby walked beneath it. Having been held at the local police station most of the day, by the time Troy was transported to this intake facility, the daylight faded to dusk. The sun had just set when he exited the police van. Looking up at the evening star, he wondered how long it might be before he would see it again.

Troy studied the street outside, but it didn't look familiar. It wasn't the street the police transport descended to from the sky interstate. He knew the city and had been able to see some of it through the tiny window in the back of the van. Something about this street view just wasn't right.

Then he realized this wasn't a window at all, but a two-way glass with a 3-D weather scene program that would change with the hours of the day or night. He invented one just like it over a decade ago, windows intended for windowless rooms. No wonder it looked familiar. Looking around the frame of the window for his VSA trademark, he found it in the lower corner. He knew this product and how to manipulate it.

"What's an old friend like you doing in a place like this?" Troy muttered to the glass.

He also knew the windows could provide privacy viewing into another room. The weather scene could be viewed on both sides simultaneously, or just one side. He looked around to see if anyone in the room was paying him any attention.

Troy leaned his shoulder against the wall, blocking the view from the Duty Desk as he searched the glass for the hidden touch-screen button usually constructed in one corner. His hands bound together by the restraints, he tried not to move too much and draw attention to himself. When he found the right spot on the glass, a menu of choices popped up controlling the window. He navigated through the settings with ease, changing the directional view. Once reprogrammed, the court room next door came into view. The glass on the opposite side still projected the weather scene, hiding him from sight.

The sterile hearing room appeared devoid of color. Only grey, shadowy corners broke the glare of the focused light shining down on the current candidate. Troy saw a beautiful young woman who looked to be of Latino decent, standing beside a tall female VRC attendant. Her long, black hair, pulled back and banded at the base of her neck, allowed Troy to see her face clearly. Her flawless skin, light caramel, glowed against her white camisole top peeking out from a short black jacket. Her face and eyes portrayed a softness Troy thought to be the total opposite of this stark, harsh environment. She stood stoically facing the front of the hearing room.

Across from her stood a wall with a large black window high above which looked down into the courtroom. It was veiled with a dark mesh to conceal the faces of the five attorneys who sat behind the glass on the pro bono judging panel. Just as candidates were stripped of their identities, the identities of the participating lawyers on each judging panel would be concealed from the public.

A sound system with speakers in the wall allowed communication between the two rooms. Troy could not hear the conversation taking place, but he knew what she must be feeling. He was mentally preparing himself to face the same dark mesh. He could see her body language as she looked straight ahead and not up at the panel, her fists clinched at her sides. The only evidence of her weakening resolve appeared as a solitary tear rolled slowly down her smooth cheek. Her VRC system number appeared on a black and white band around her upper left arm, candidate number 818. Troy looked at the band on his own left arm; he was candidate number 924. No names ever used here; individuality had been purposely stripped away, dehumanizing candidates. Deemed too personal, the corporations running the VRCs would not permit it. Here, one became just a number on a digital board, and that was all one would ever be.

Troy studied her graceful profile and watched as another tear rolled uncontrollably down her cheek. He felt empathy for her, and wondered how she happened to be swallowed into this system that stole identities and wiped out futures. For all of his own physical strength in his firm body, he felt a weakness of spirit. He looked down at his own electronically handcuffed wrists, restraints he thought he could figure out how to break if he wanted to. But like her, his individualism, strength of will, and desire for survival struggled. He felt a connection of their wounded spirits as she stood and awaited the pronouncement of her fate. He wanted to reach out and touch her, show her some compassion, a uniquely human element in this inhumane environment. And he knew one way to do it. Through the menu option, he could program the glass to become a clear two-way view between them.

He turned facing the glass, as she slowly broke her resolute stance and moved her head slightly to look at him. She must have felt his gaze upon her, he thought. Her eyes held emptiness, but upon meeting his, they displayed recognition, or maybe it was pity, for his similar situation. She stared at him for a lingering moment, and then blinked back to the attention of the proceedings. Her head shook, her brows furrowed and her jaw became tense, as a loud voice came through the sound system reverberating against the window pane. A judge on the panel was yelling. Troy strained against the glass to hear, but it was inaudible. The large female uniformed attendant standing by her side placed a vice-like grip upon her right elbow. When the yelling stopped, she moved to bind the girl's wrists behind her in restraints. Breaking her controlled composure, the young woman now shouted back at the dark mesh wall. Her face frowned with anger and Troy thought he could read her lips saying, "You framed me, you bastard!" The security attendant roughly led her to the door on the other side of the hearing room. Before exiting, number 818 looked back at the small window and Troy.

Troy quickly crossed the room with long strides to the Plexiglas wall facing the hallway. He saw her enter the hall from the hearing room, led by the female attendant. The attendant, now joined by another, did not lead her to the exit. They headed to the elevator; down to the Virtual Realty Chambers. As he watched the elevator doors close, Troy felt helplessly frustrated, trapped in a glass cage with no way out. He slammed his fists against the Plexiglas, awakening the other sleepy occupants of the holding cell with a jerk. Troy leaned his forehead against the wall, clenching his jaw tightly and exhaling his rage.

****

An hour later, the door to the holding cell swung open and a burly hearing room attendant walked in. He held a digital pad in his hands, scrolling down a list with his finger, mumbling numbers beneath his breath. The candidates at the opposite end of the room all sat up anxiously. Each man, including Troy, waited for the number to be called out, hoping it would not be their own.

"924," he growled. "Number 924, you're up next."

The hearing room door automatically opened in front of Troy and he was led into the sterile, artificial environment of the pro bono court room. Escorted by two attendants, one on either side of him, they pushed him to the front of the room to face the black mesh wall. He knew his outburst of anger in the holding cell had caught the attention of the Duty Desk. With his size and strong build, Troy realized security wasn't taking any chances with him. These attendants were as large as he, well-armed, and in control. They ordered him to sit down instead of stand.

The noise of the hallway diminished when the hearing room door closed. As Troy awaited the start of the hearing, he looked over to the small two-way window and caught himself saying a silent prayer for the girl. He hadn't prayed in years, but for some reason, he felt the need to pray for her. He also felt himself now precariously in her shoes.

Chapter 5

The judging chamber overlooking the hearing room was small but accommodating. Silence filled the room as each of the five attorneys signed off on the numerous pages of electronic paperwork for case number 818. They sat at a long, ornate mahogany desk running the length of the large, dark mesh-covered window. Three attorneys sat on the opposite side of the table facing the window, while one sat at each end of the table. The high-back black leather chairs provided comfortable seating for the long hours spent in the small crowded room.

Each attorney reviewed his own monitor projected up from a wireless access point in the table. The monitors had split screens: one side viewed the hearing room while the other displayed the case documents. Two of the attorneys touched their screens, pulling them from the air down to the table top to electronically sign off on the Treatment Order before hitting the Send button.

As the five attorneys completed the required electronic paperwork, a young associate lawyer sat at a small desk on one side of the room and received the signed electronic submissions for the defendant's file sent to his laptop. The young associate, still attending law school, acted as the court's clerk-of-the-day to fulfill his required pro bono hours. On the desk next to him sat the main control panel for the functions in the room, including the attorneys' monitors and the visual/audio systems controlling the cameras and microphones to the hearing room.

The young man watched his camera as attendants escorted the next candidate into the hearing room. Then glancing down, he noticed the microphone to the hearing room was on, allowing the attorneys to be overheard by everyone in the room below. Panic set in as he realized this violated the attorneys' privacy rules. He quickly fumbled to find the control button to turn it off. When he finally found it, an electronic LED sign above the attorneys' table flashed in red, 'MICROPHONE OFF.' He bit his lip, peeking to see if the senior lead attorney seated in the middle chair at the table, had noticed his oversight.

The older man sat bent over his monitor still recording notes. His finely tailored suit coat strained at the seams of his broad back as he hunched over his work. Graying hair, sand-colored in spots, gave certain credibility to his years of legal experience. The young associate admired that. Even the gritty, booming voice of the senior attorney carried weight wherever he went.

"Mr. Lewis," the senior attorney said in a commanding voice.

"Yes, Mr. Adams?" the young associate timidly responded.

"If your attention to detail is as poor as your attention to that microphone, you'll never win a case. Remember that." Mr. Adams never looked up from his work.

"Yes, sir." The associate turned back to his monitor and busied himself.

Two attorneys moved from the table to the coffee bar in the back of the room. Mr. Leigh, a richly-dressed young attorney, poured coffee from the carafe into his own cup, then into the cup of the attorney standing next to him. He looked back at Mr. Adams seated at the table, and turned his back to him, whispering to his colleague, Mr. Berry.

"Adams was pretty rough on the last one, candidate 818."

Berry hid his lips behind his cup and whispered back.

"Well, I heard a rumor he knew her at SWI."

"Really? A bit of a conflict of interest there, isn't it?"

Attorney Berry lowered his cup and stared down into it. He looked to the back wall of the room and continued. "That's not all. He made a play for her and she shot him down. Can you imagine saying the word 'no' to the all mighty Xavier Adams?" Both men chuckled softly.

"She's got more guts than most of us," Leigh said. "Still, it wasn't enough to hang a conviction on. Just because her security card was found in the room near the body, doesn't mean she did it. What if she's innocent?"

"Then I guess the VRC will let us know."

The court's clerk pulled up the documents for the next case and sent them to the monitors at the attorneys' table.

"Next case up is candidate number 924, charged with," the clerk paused, looking confused. "Charged with the murder of Hoy SamWong? But I thought we just heard that case..."

Mr. Adams interrupted, "Different suspect, Mr. Lewis. There can be multiple suspects for the same crime. The strength of the motive and evidence must be evaluated."

"Yes sir." Again, the young clerk returned to his work and remained silent.

As Mr. Leigh and Mr. Berry made their way back to the table with their coffee cups, another attorney sitting at the table to the left of Adams was already studying Troy Vincent's case file.

"I think I'm going to have to recuse myself from this case, gentlemen," said the middle-aged attorney.

"And why is that, Mr. Robertson?" Mr. Adams asked.

"I'm already representing SamWong Industries in a patent case involving this defendant. He's suing over ownership of inventions he created and acquired by SWI several months ago. This case constitutes a conflict of interest for me," said Robertson.

"Yes, and I am SWI's General Counsel," Adams quipped. "So what?"

"And," Robertson continued, weighing his words carefully, "SamWong Industries is this month's pro bono sponsor." He drummed his fingers against the table nervously. He reminded Adams the monthly sponsor footed the cost of operating the court system this month. "I felt uncomfortable hearing the last case, bordering on a conflict of interest. It just doesn't seem right for me to sit on the judging panel of another similar case; or for you either, Mr. Adams."

"We are all employed by some corporate entity," said Adams. "Having one as both a client and a sponsor happens from time to time. I have never let that stop me in my duties."

Berry and Leigh sat down in the chairs to the right of Mr. Adams.

"Yes, and I hear it's been fairly lucrative for you, too," Berry chided with a smile.

Adams leaned back in his chair and objected. "I am entitled to profit when I represent my client. Just because a defendant may be suing my client..."

"You mean this month's *sponsor*," Mr. Robertson corrected.

"S*ponsor*," Adams parroted with sarcasm, "doesn't mean my judgments are biased in any way."

"Like that last case," mumbled Mr. Leigh, as he studied the new case document.

Adams narrowed his beady eyes at the two young attorneys.

"Is my character being called into question here?" he challenged.

Of course not," smiled Berry, trying to calm the unexpected overreaction. "Forgive me for any improper implication; merely a joke, of course, and not a very good one." He exchanged a sideways glance with Mr. Leigh.

"Nevertheless," said Robertson as he switched off his monitor and rose from his chair. "The last case involved SamWong Industries and I prefer not to sit in on another one. Your review, Mr. Adams, will render a fair decision as always, without my counsel, I'm sure of it." He walked past Adams toward the door and patted the older man on the shoulder.

"Good day, all." The attorney then exited the chamber. The four remaining attorneys fell silent as they read through the case document.

Mr. Adams broke the silence with a question to the fifth attorney on the panel sitting at the far end of the table.

"Mr. Tyler, you haven't said five words all day. Why are you even here if you don't render your opinion once in a while? What's your first impression of this case?"

Donald Tyler moved his jaw to the left and right, pressing his lips tightly together. He looked at the monitor through small glasses perched on the end of his nose.

Vincent and the Grief Masters

"You want my honest opinion, Xavier?"

"Yes, Don, your honest opinion. Your integrity apparently is not in question," he snorted as he looked over at Leigh and Berry.

"Well, this one's also accused of murdering your friend and CEO of SWI, who happens to be this month's corporate pro bono sponsor," he quietly muttered. With a polite half-smile, Tyler raised his gray eyebrows as his blue eyes peered above the glasses at Adams. "Good luck with staying unbiased on this one, too."

As Adams disdainfully looked back at Troy Vincent's image on the monitor, the clerk flipped a switch on the audio system. 'MICROPHONE ON' flashed in green LEDs above the table. The older attorney nodded to Mr. Leigh to begin the proceeding and address the accused.

****

"Good evening, defendant number 924. Do you know why you are here?"

Troy looked up at the large black mesh-covered window. "Something about Hoy SamWong."

The attorney toggled to the top of the case document screen. "You are accused of the murder of Hoy SamWong, founder and CEO of SamWong Industries, and Chairman of the World Board of Directors."

Troy grimaced. "Accused, but not guilty. If you're asking me if I killed him, the answer is no, I did not."

Troy could hear another attorney with a gruff voice in the background.

"He had motive and opportunity," Adams whispered.

"The record shows motive and opportunity on your part," Mr. Leigh repeated over the microphone.

"What evidence do you have proving I took his life?" Troy asked.

"SamWong Industries recently acquired your company. There are witnesses stating you threatened him as he left the courtroom."

Troy hated talking to a faceless screen. "Yeah, well, he stole my company, and I was angry about it. I might have said something to him. But I don't remember seeing him since then."

Mr. Berry addressed the accused sounding less adversarial in his tone.

"Number 924, we recognize you have lost much in the past year. The record shows not only did SWI acquire your company, but your wife left you for Mr. SamWong. Is that true?"

Troy didn't like talking about his ex-wife, either. The smell of money and power made her leave him so fast it made him sick. "Yes, she loved his money more than me," he answered in a dry, reserved tone. "We're divorced; I have no interest, nor did I care, whose company she decided to keep."

"And you lost your son in some kind of accident in SamWong's lab?"

"It was still my lab then," Troy shot back. "And yes," he responded bitterly, "I lost my son."

Troy regained control of himself. He didn't want to appear angry in front of a faceless enemy who might try to bait him into an emotional outburst, automatically condemning him. "SamWong took much from me, but I took nothing from him, least of all his life. I am innocent of this crime. If there is any justice left in this world, you will agree you have no actual evidence against me. You have to release me."

This time, Mr. Tyler replied for the panel. "Let us take a few moments to review the evidence." He motioned to the court's clerk to turn off the microphone, but the clerk, looking down at his laptop, did not see the silent signal waved to him. Troy tilted his head, thinking he recognized the voice of the attorney who just spoke.

Mr. Tyler, leaning back in his chair, conferred with the other three at the table. With the microphone still on, it only picked up parts of his conversation in muffled tones. Troy strained to hear bits and pieces of the discussion, but he was sure he heard Don Tyler's voice arguing, "The evidence is not strong in this case."

****

In the judging chamber, the four remaining pro bono judges were discussing the merits of the case. "He has not been placed at the crime scene," Mr. Leigh said. "Yes, he had reason to dislike the man; after all, the victim took his company and his wife, or ex-wife."

Adams retorted, "More than enough motive."

Mr. Berry added, "They found no murder weapon linking him to the scene or in his possession."

"SamWong was strangled," Adams read from the report.

"That's what the autopsy says, even though the examination didn't prove it conclusively," said Leigh. "Other parts of the report show conflicting evidence. It also states he may have been smothered. Both methods point to the same time of death."

"This man appears to be strong enough to do either," Adams insisted.

"Can't judge a man by his strength," retorted Leigh.

Mr. Tyler rested his elbow on the table with his chin in his hand and pondered.

"I see this man differently," Tyler observed. "His record is clean and shows he was once a valuable contributor to society. He doesn't appear to me to be a killer, and the lack of evidence seems to support that. Yes, he admits having anger at the loss of his company, but who wouldn't be?"

Attorney Berry added, "This man has suffered a lot, and I agree, I don't think he killed him."

Tyler leaned forward just enough to be picked up by the microphone. "If he is ordered to a VRC, I recommend he be assigned to a facility with one of the androids, where he can be monitored. And perhaps..." Tyler hesitated to continue.

"Perhaps what?" Adams gruffly responded.

"Perhaps he may just be the kind of candidate—for a Grief Master encounter."

Adams flung his pen on the table and loudly erupted. "Grief Masters! What a bunch of bullshit! There's no such thing and I won't hear of it in this chamber!"

Tyler put his hands up to calm Adams as he patiently continued, "But an android can monitor that. Let's use the resources we have at our disposal. Who knows? A Grief Master just might intervene. We're always looking for evidence on this unusual phenomenon, aren't we? If this man is innocent, why not give him a fighting chance? Now, I know the facility here has such an android..."

Interrupted again, Troy Vincent's voice came through the speaker. "What's a Grief Master?" The startled panel of attorneys looked at the camera side of their monitors and saw a security attendant put a heavy hand on Troy's shoulder, subduing his outburst.

The attorneys simultaneously looked at the green light above them and realized the microphone was still on. They all looked at the young clerk. Adams swiveled around to the court clerk, staring him down with menacing eyes.

The young man's mouth dropped open with surprise as he quickly reached to turn off the microphone. He shrank to the back of his chair under the angry glare of the attorney. Adams then turned back to the table to argue the last statement he made.

"The stories of these...these things called, Grief Masters, lurking in the VRCs...they're just a myth. It's nonsense! There is no proof any treatment has ever been interfered with by these so called Grief Masters." Adams made a dismissive motion in the air with his hand.

Mr. Tyler shook his head in disagreement. "Well, unfortunately, not many survive the VRC to provide proof of their existence. But it is rumored in cases such as this, especially ones that are questionable; they may be involved somehow in the outcome."

Mr. Berry added, "I have heard they sometimes appear to those with a faith-based background."

Adams grimaced. "Absurd."

Mr. Leigh interjected. "Well, they're just rumors, right? They may be spreading from the factions of resistance that are out there. They're just stories. But I, too, think this case is questionable. I agree with my colleagues."

Adams stood up and shook his finger at the panel to make his final point. "This man hated SamWong. He threatened him and stole from him. I believe he is guilty and the court should order him to the VRC. He won't survive. I guarantee it," he stated with conviction. He leaned forward placing his fingertips on the table and looked around at the other three. "And there will be no appearance of any Grief Masters! Period."

The young court clerk shyly interrupted.

"Uh, sirs? There's an urgent communiqué coming through on this case from SWI, this month's sponsor. I'm forwarding the message to your monitors."

Adams sat down. The attorneys turned back to their monitors and the message bannered across the top of the split screens, showing Troy on one side and his file on the other.

SPONSOR WANTS <u>GUARANTEED TERMINATION</u> ON THIS CASE. The banner scrolled across twice, then ceased.

Mr. Tyler expressed dismay. "That's odd; I don't understand the reason for this."

Mr. Adams nodded his head in agreement with the banner. "There's our decision, gentlemen. No need to even vote on it."

Mr. Berry objected. "I don't agree. The sponsor must stay objective. They have always stayed objective and out of the judging chamber."

Leigh leaned over to Berry. "Looks like someone will get his way after all, again."

Adams turned to the court clerk and impatiently signaled to turn the microphone back on.

The few minutes of silence became unnerving for Troy. He was apprehensive, but relieved to know his father's friend, Don Tyler, had a seat on the judging panel. He momentarily held his breath when the microphone clicked back on. He hoped to be heading toward freedom and the exit door in another minute. How could they find an innocent man guilty with no evidence?

The disgruntled voice of Mr. Leigh delivered his fate. "Candidate 924, please rise for the verdict."

Troy was pulled from the chair to his feet by the two attendants.

"The purpose of this judging panel is not to pronounce guilt or innocence, but to review the facts and weigh any evidence. However, where the evidence is unclear, the purpose of the VRC system is to make the candidate face one's own truth, whether guilt or innocence, and act as one's own jury, judge, and sometimes, executioner. Your case has been reviewed, and the evidence weighed. You are hereby ordered to proceed to a virtual reality chamber for treatment and judgment by your own hand, to possibly face destruction by your own demons for the murder of Hoy SamWong. This concludes the hearing of case number 924."

The short verdict allowed no rebuttal. The microphone clicked off. The two security attendants immediately pulled Troy toward the door.

"Hey, wait," he objected as they half-dragged him along. "I didn't kill him! And who are these Grief Masters?" repeating his earlier question even louder. There was no response. They pushed him through the door and into the hall.

Once outside the exit door, he realized he was in the same spot where he witnessed the young man go down under a pile of security attendants. He quickly glanced over to the Duty Desk and saw all the attendants stand up at once, watching him. Troy decided he wasn't ready to be tazed into submission. Instead, he'd better calm down and think through his options, which looked to be none at the moment. With a security attendant on either side of him, he regained his composure and took a deep breath. The door opened and the three men stepped into the elevator.

Chapter 6

Troy was planning his escape before the attendant pushed the elevator button. The holding cell had been several stories above ground, and the elevator was going toward ground level. *That's good.* He wouldn't find himself on the top of the building with no way down. One thing he was absolutely sure of—he would kill either or both of these attendants if they tried to strap him into some sort of contraption. If he could just figure out how to break the restraint of the electronic cuffs, he knew he could get away.

The attendants stood in silence and looked straight ahead. Troy glanced up at the one on his left. He considered himself to be tall at just over six feet, but this guy was a full head taller. It would take some doing to knock this one out, if it came to that. He looked at the nameplate on the man's shirt: Greene.

"So, Attendant Greene, do you know who the Grief Masters are?" No response. Troy turned back toward the doors as the elevator came to a stop. "Just thought I'd ask," raising an eyebrow.

When the doors opened, Troy hoped to see a street level door or hall. Instead, the two attendants each grabbed an arm, forcing him out onto a brightly lit train platform. The tiled platform was empty except for the three men. Train tracks ran along the platform in both directions, disappearing into dark tunnels at either end of the station. Troy thought the place appeared to be an abandoned subway station.

A small unmanned transport hummed as it emerged from one tunnel, and rolled up to the platform. The door slid open automatically to its single car.

"Get in," Greene commanded. Inside were four seats, two on each side facing each other. He pushed Troy down into one of them. "And shut up." Both attendants sat down across from him.

Troy's premature escape plan faded as the transport sped up, disappearing into the advancing tunnel. "Where are we going?" he asked, ignoring the attendant's order. "I thought the VRCs were in the same building." He had to get his bearings and rethink a new plan.

Looking annoyed, Greene stared out the window at the shadowy walls whizzing by. He spoke toward the window. "Corporate sponsors don't want treatments to take place in the same area." He stretched his large uniformed legs out toward the seat next to Troy and, leaning back, intentionally dropped his heavy boots on the seat with a thud. Troy didn't flinch. Finally looking directly at Troy, he added, "It's an imaging thing."

"Oh," Troy nodded wryly, "An imaging thing. Well I guess it would be, when innocent men are condemned in their tidy little corrupt justice system."

"I told you to shut up," Greene sneered.

Troy shrugged his shoulders and looked past the attendant out the front window of the transport. A light in the distance grew larger as the tunnel came to an end.

The small transport pulled up to another well-lit platform. Troy could see a much larger station. Small transports, such as the one they were in, came and went through tunnels from all directions, approaching the center like spokes of a wheel. The station appeared to be a security hub. Attendants appeared everywhere, some in the process of prisoner transport, like the two with Troy. Now his escape plan would need to include a hop onto one of these cars. *But going where? Damn, I'll just have to take a chance.*

Two more attendants in freshly pressed, short-sleeved tan uniforms waited on the platform. One held a wireless pad, writing down the time of arrival as the tiny transport came to a stop. When the door opened, Greene and the other attendant stood up. He cocked his head toward the door, ordering Troy to get out.

"Thanks. We'll take it from here," said the attendant with the pad. The door closed and Greene and his comrade disappeared as the transport ducked into another tunnel.

Vincent and the Grief Masters

"Candidate 924, this way."

He walked in front of Troy as the second attendant took up a position behind them. The lead security attendant was short, blond, and clean cut. He looked back at Troy and threw an introduction over his shoulder as he walked, leading the way.

"My name's Terry." He pointed his thumb at the attendant behind him. "That's Amon. You're assigned to my VRC block," then adding in a nonchalant tone, "Welcome to Hell."

Looking back at Amon, Troy observed he was the opposite of the neatly dressed Terry. A large burly and unshaven man, with coffee stains down the front of his shirt. Amon stared back with cold dark eyes and didn't acknowledge the quick introduction. Troy said nothing to either man. He made mental notes about the number of security present and the location of any cameras he could spot.

The trio walked beyond the platform walls, and headed toward a main security gate. The interior of the large regional facility finally came into Troy's view. Looking up into a cavernous atrium, he could see several levels all opening onto walkways that rimmed the inside of the atrium. Glass walls with storefront-type doors lined the walkways. Above each doorway, hung a large digital sign displaying a brightly colored room number, easily visible from the main floor. Sunlight from the towering skylights above beamed down into the atrium where palm trees and foliage stretched out their leaves from large planters trying to gather what rays they could. Even the Muzak music playing over loudspeakers seemed odd and out of place. Everything Troy saw appeared to be a façade to mask the real purpose of the life-suffocating facility.

"Is this...a shopping mall?" Troy asked, his eyes following a glass elevator up to the top.

"*Was*...was a subterranean mega-mall," Terry replied. "They were built decades ago when the climate shift forced a lot of activity underground. It's been retro-fitted to house this regional VRC facility."

At the main gate, a laser detection beam scanned each man from head to toe. Thermal imaging appeared on a screen in front of the security kiosk where an attendant waved them through, one at a time. As the three men made their way past the kiosk and onto the main floor of the atrium, Troy could see other prisoners above him. On level two, a young man in restraining cuffs was led into one of the glass-fronted rooms. The scene repeated several times on levels three and four as far around the atrium's walkways as he could see.

As they walked past potted palms and landscaped statuary, a movement to Troy's left caught his attention. In the shadows of a covered section of the first floor, a floating gurney, manned by a single attendant, made its way inconspicuously along. A pile of what appeared to be body bags heaped upon its flat bed. Troy stopped and stared, as it disappeared around a corner. Amon leaned over Troy's shoulder and smiled, displaying yellow teeth. He pointed to a young prisoner on the level above them.

"That's how you come in here," he said. His foul breath made Troy turn his head away. Then Amon pointed to the disappearing taillights of the gurney.

"And that's how you go out." Letting out a deep, throaty laugh, he pushed Troy forward to catch up with Terry.

They left the open atrium and turned into a quiet, dimly-lit corridor. Troy tried to remember the different direction of turns they made so he could make his way back to the transport hub if, and when, the opportunity arose. In this area, the halls seemed almost empty of any security; no cameras on the ceilings, no personnel, no electronic monitors of any kind.

Maybe these are janitorial halls. They might lead back to the subway without going through the main gate. He had to figure a way out of this tomb.

A hazy light glowed from a darkened side hallway. As they approached, a movement at the end of the hall caught Troy's eye. He thought he saw a full-sized holographic person in the light, but the image stepped out of view when the three men walked by. The back of a tall, cloaked figure moved to block the light from his view and appeared to be in a conversation with the hologram. It drew little attention from the two attendants, but Troy felt something peculiar about the scene, like a split-second premonition. Whatever it was, it would have something to do with him. The feeling disappeared as they exited the hall and approached an open area with the cluttered desk of a sleepy, uniformed clerk.

****

Don Tyler had excused himself from the judging chambers, saying he needed to use the restroom, and quickly made his way back to his office, where he could transmit in private.

"So there he goes, case 924."

Tyler spoke in a hushed tone, appearing as a hologram to the clocked figure in the dark hallway. His transmission could not be detected by scanners or receivers in the hall location and they had used it a number of times before. "This is the one you've been searching for. Once the verdict was pronounced, I directed him your way. He was scheduled to go to another regional facility, but I took a risk to change that and convinced the panel to keep him here."

The voice from beneath the hood spoke in a deep, raspy tone. "Your risk is noted. You have done much for my mission and the future of your Resistance movement."

"Still, it would have been better to find him *before* the death of SamWong," Tyler said with disappointment. "Now he'll have to contend with the dangers in the VRC."

"He is strong. He may yet survive."

"We need him *alive*. If you have any influence to help him, or have any ability to bring forth a Grief Master, this is the case for it."

"It will be up to him to survive. I have no control over Grief Masters, if they appear or not. I am only the observer," the cloaked figure responded.

"And do you think they will take an interest in him?"

"Uncertain. He is a troubled human, harboring much anger, guilt, and sadness. But he may help to save the girl, which is also important."

Tyler shook his head in disagreement. "She's of interest to only one person, although I admit that person is of great importance. However, prisoner 924 is of interest to many of us."

Two mechanical hands, intricately constructed, rose to push the woolen hood back from the wearer's face, revealing a chrome alloy skull. A skeletal jaw, complete with a full set of metal teeth, reflected the soft haze of the holographic light. Above the shiny teeth, a smoke-colored mask covered part of the skeletal face, hiding the eyes sockets and nose. The size and shape of a skin-diver's mask, it projected out from the face and was held in place by two green laser beams connected to the temples of the shiny skull. The back of the android's head remained hidden by the hood. As it spoke, words scrolled in a banner across the front of the mask. The voice accompanied the words without movement of the chrome jaw. "They are both my mission. The mission cannot…correction…must not fail."

The attorney's holographic face complete with the small glasses resting on the end of his nose reflected back from the dark glass surface of the mask. A knock on Don Tyler's office door startled him. Turning back to the android, he quickly whispered a final warning. "Do not forget who you work for, Vincent. The Resistance is counting on The Brethren, lest your kind, and myself, I might add, could be eliminated."

"Understood." The hologram ceased transmission, and the tall, dark figure swung around to follow Troy.

Chapter 7

"Wake up, you gadget dip wad." Terry hit the snoring clerk on the shoulder with his digital pad. The stunned clerk leaned over so far to the left he fell out of his chair. Scrambling to recover, he stood up and stifled a yawn behind his hand.

"Got an intake for you to brief." Terry pointed to Troy. He then walked several feet away and started up a low conversation with Amon.

The young, thin clerk looked at Troy for a moment, nervously wringing his hands together.

I hate when they just leave the candidates alone with me like that. They could be murderers for all I know, and this one is standing a little too close.

Backing up a step, the clerk picked up a remote controller from the desk.

"Well, it's my job to explain just how the VR chamber works. It's required." He clicked on the remote and a 3-D screen appeared in the air next to him. A small-scale graphic presentation of a tall, cylindrical chamber appeared before Troy, rotating 360 degrees, displaying all sides. It was a clear glass chamber with one side panel running from top to bottom, housing a series of instrument gauges. On the other side a door opened, revealing a slow flow of white gas filtering into it from the top. A graphic cartoon-like character entered the chamber, the door closed, and the character fell asleep inside. The rest of the cartoon presentation continued as the young clerk recited his memorized narrative.

"While I can't tell you exactly what you might experience, I can tell you how the sensations you will feel may lead to injury or death." This part always made the clerk feel uncomfortable. Most candidates were so nervous at this point, they barely understood what he was saying. He used to rush through the technical explanation in a boring, monotone monologue just to get it over with. But this prisoner actually took an interest in the graphic presentation. Even more surprising, he seemed to be listening to the full description of the sensory immersion technique and how it sends impulses through the brain.

"Illusions can trigger environmental conditions such as heat, cold, wind, rain, sun, etc.. Candidates who have survived the experience all report the ability of sight, sound, smell, taste, and touch. Emotions also trigger physical responses, making one feel the illusion is, in fact, real."

"Total sensory absorption. Interesting," Troy observed out loud.

The clerk grew excited seeing someone actually listening to his presentation. After all, he spent hours editing it just last week to give a more detailed and graphic description of the emotional side effects of the chamber. He continued with enthusiasm.

"The total immersion of the body's nerve centers and sensory organs makes the VRC experience extremely effective, and therefore, extremely dangerous. Consequently, emotions of the occupant will be quite real. Pain, pleasure, anger, love, hate, and other emotions may all be experienced. A candidate's own guilt, which it is assumed is known only to the candidate, condemns them by bringing forth destructive emotions, such as fear. This manifests into one's own demons, thereby bringing judgment and punishment upon oneself."

He welcomed the chance to make his job more meaningful and not just the same boring eight-hour shift. The clerk smiled with personal satisfaction and pride as he wrapped up the two-minute presentation.

"And so, the ultimate purpose of the chamber is to invoke such realism that self-destruction can be accomplished by means of heart attack, stroke, brain aneurism, wounds, drowning, and any number of other fatal means. These are just some of the many ways the VRC can create brainwave cessation."

He turned with a smile toward Troy, who stood with his arms crossed, soberly staring back at him. The young man realized his insensitivity and stopped smiling.

"Anyway," he continued as he clicked off the 3-D screen and his voice trailed off to a low murmur. "The occupant will be his own judge and jury, thus proving his fate is determined by his own conscience and not by the hands of the Corporate Court."

"How convenient," Troy said dryly.

Troy turned his attention away from the awkward clerk to the two security attendants. He didn't like what he overheard.

"So, are you gonna take me up on that offer?" Terry asked. "$2500 bucks will buy you sex with any of the females in this cell block. You just do a maintenance pause on the chamber and it unlocks the door for ten minutes. You gotta wear a mask, though. It's lunch money, man."

Terry could see Amon was weakening. He tapped the end of his pen against Amon's chest. "Hey, those hot mommas...they'll never know. They'll just think it's a part of their treatment program; a bad part," he laughed.

Amon shook his head. "I want to man, but I need this job. I can't risk gettin' fired."

"You won't get caught. Do it tonight after the midnight shift leaves. Nobody will be here. Come on, I need the dough." Terry turned around to find Troy right behind him.

"You're sick," Troy remarked. "And you," nodding to Amon, "You're an idiot."

"Yeah? Maybe," Amon sneered as he walked past Troy. "But by midnight, you're dead."

Terry put his pen behind his ear. "Well, it's none of your concern anyway. You're just a prisoner." He smacked Troy in the shoulder and motioned for him to follow. The two men headed around the corner, with Amon close behind.

Terry continued his conversation with Amon, talking over his shoulder as he walked.

"If we do this tonight, we have to avoid the NTB. His female candidates are off limits. And boy, he had a real looker come in a couple of hours ago. I'd like to do her myself."

"What's an NTB?" asked Amon.

"Jeez, what alien crapper did you crawl out of?" Terry said sarcastically. "It's a nano…nanotechno…somethin' or other."

Troy spoke up, "A Nano Technological Being."

Terry stopped and turned to Troy. "Yeah, that's right. How'd you know that?"

"Well, that's none of your concern, is it?" parroting the remark Terry had said to him.

The attendant gave Troy a smartass smile and continued walking. "Well, I just call him Nano Man. Yeah, and he's an ugly one at that."

Amon, slow to realize who they were talking about, started nodding his head, as his jaw dropped open, finally recognizing the subject of their conversation.

"Oh yeah, that guy, the chrome robot. He gives me the creeps. And the way he dresses, like he's some kind of ancient monk. You turn around and he's right there, in your face. He scares the shit out of me."

Terry continued. "All those manufactured guys are weird and they use telepathy. Oh, and don't call him a robot. For some reason, he hates that." Terry turned another corner of the hallway. The cloaked NTB stood with his mechanical hands on his hips, blocking their path.

The attendants stopped abruptly, taking a step back with a look of surprise and fear on their faces. Amon grabbed Troy and shoved him up against the wall, pinning him with one meaty arm pressed hard against the back of Troy's neck. With his other hand, he drew his laser weapon and shoved it into Troy's back.

Terry spoke with a cautious smile. "Hey, Nano Man! What's with jumpin' out of the shadows like that? We're in prisoner transport mode here."

The android spoke with a low frequency audio wave filling the air, not moving his jaw, towering over Terry. "This case is mine."

The attendant shook his head. "No, no, man, this guy is scheduled for VRC 18. That's my area. It says so right here." He held up the digital pad and pointed to the electronic paperwork.

The NTB did not look at the paperwork, but instead touched it with his mechanical fingertip. Visualization of words was unnecessary. His touch could meld with the molecular structure of the electronics and determine its message. The number in the paperwork transformed unnoticed under the NTB's touch. "Look again," his voice rumbling. "He is assigned to VRC 13, not 18." He pushed the pad back toward the attendant. "That is my area."

Terry quickly scanned the board again, perplexed he could make such a mistake. He stammered with indecision and frustration, licking his lips nervously. "This is the second VRC candidate you have taken from me tonight! I had plans for that girl, prisoner 818. She was going to be an interesting case."

"Only of monetary interest to you," the NTB responded.

Both uniformed attendants looked at each other with surprise.

Amon quickly pointed to Terry. "All his idea, that VR sex scheme...I had nothing to do with it."

Terry shot back, "Thanks, you piece of shit."

The NTB interrupted. "I am not interested in your schemes. I only want my prisoner. He may be of interest to a Grief Master. I must monitor the case and see if any appear. It has been ordered."

The short attendant paused, biting his lower lip as he assessed the situation. Then he stepped back and signaled for Amon to release his hold on the prisoner. Troy pushed away from the wall, rotating his shoulder back into place.

The NTB looked at Troy's restraints. "You won't need these." As the android pointed his finger at the wrist restraints, an electrical charge shot from his fingertip and surrounded the cuffs. They opened and disappeared completely.

"Follow me, 924," the NTB said as he turned and moved down the hall. He neither looked back to see if Troy would follow, nor if the attendants would stop him.

Troy walked past the two quiet attendants and tipped his hand from his head in a goodbye gesture.

As the android left with his prisoner, Amon objected. "Are you just going to let him go?"

An irritated Terry sarcastically snapped back. "I don't know how to see no Grief Master, do you?"

Chapter 8

Candidate 818 felt dizzy and nauseous as she regained consciousness. The last thing she remembered was the strange android telling her to breathe deeply and stay calm, locking her into the suffocating chamber. Now she stood alone in a white fog, unable to see anything. A silence enveloped her until it gradually gave way to a small sound. Somewhere in the dense surroundings, a child was weeping.

818 carefully stepped forward, moving slowly unable to see. Just ahead, the heavy mist gave way to a light clearing. A child, a small girl, sat on a gray stone bench, her legs not long enough for her feet to touch the patch of grass beneath the bench. She held her hand to her mouth, biting on a finger, her cheeks wet from tears. Her sad eyes stared at a headstone not far away partially obscured by the fog. Only the top of the stone was visible.

The candidate approached and stopped behind the child on the bench. She realized this was not just any child – this was her at age six. Filled with empathy for her grieving self, she reached out to touch the girl's shoulder, but stopped. Her hand appeared opaque, she could see through it.

In this virtual reality environment, was she real or a ghost? What had happened to her body? The child was already crying and scared, so she decided not to touch her or make herself known to her. She would only observe, and she already knew what the little girl was feeling.

The girl sucked in a deep breath and began hyperventilating. She teetered back and forth on the bench, clutching her hands to her chest. Through sobs, she blurted out, "I'm afraid."

With tears stinging, 818 moved quickly to sit down on the bench next to the girl. Shadows moved in the darkness around them. She could not see them clearly, nor make out their shapes. She only knew she would try to protect this little one as best she could.

A kind female voice spoke out from the fog, and said softly, "Loveena! Loveena!"

The little girl stood up, lifting her expression hopefully. "Momma? Momma!" 818 silently repeated the girl's word: *Momma!*

Where are you?" the child asked, desperately looking around the small clearing.

"You cannot come with me," the voice said compassionately.

"Momma, I'm scared! Let me come with you?"

"You cannot come. You must be brave, my baby."

The girl sat down on the bench again and put her hands over her eyes. She cried, "I don't know how."

Loveena noticed the opaqueness in her hands had disappeared and they were solid and normal again. She put her arm around the girl's shaking shoulders. "Don't cry," she whispered. After a few moments, the child calmed down.

The voice returned. "My lovely Loveena, you will find a way to go on. I promise. I love you, my sweet child. Goodbye."

The little girl jumped up and ran into the fog. "Don't go!"

Loveena stood and watched the girl disappear. There was nothing she could do. She knew the scared little girl would have to find her way in the world, and that's what she did. However, it would not be easy, and facing demons from her past was yet to come. The shadows began moving again, circling her, closing in. Loveena said under her breath, "Now I'm afraid."

Above the headstone in the distance a pinpoint of starlight shone through the dark. A magenta color beamed down on the top of the headstone. Loveena heard a different voice speak directly to her. "You knew me once. Look for me again."

She cautiously scanned the darkness surrounding her, compelled to walk toward the headstone. The stone bench faded, swallowed up by the shadowy grayness. Unseen entities came ever closer to her, causing her skin to crawl. She moved her head as something swept by her, but kept walking toward the headstone. As Loveena approached it, she could see the faint lettering on the front, *Ramona Baptista*. The magenta starlight concentrated in a circle on the top. Then Loveena watched as a small key appeared lying within the lit circle on the stone.

Murmurs coming from the shadows got louder and a deep fear swept over her body. She reached for the key, but quickly pulled her hand back as a large, black spider popped up from behind the headstone, near the key. Another dropped on a thinly spun web from above. Both arachnids turned in her direction and she froze. But the voice spoke again.

"You knew me, Loveena. I came to you back then and I am still here now. My name is Courage." Loveena grabbed the key without hesitation.

****

Troy stepped quickly to catch up with the Nano Technological Being. From the back, the NTB appeared to move quite smoothly along the floor. Troy determined it wasn't walking, more like gliding. He caught a glimpse of metal boots under the hem of the heavy cloak riding on a small flat disk an inch above the floor.

Where can I get one of those? Troy mused.

Walking beside the android, he glanced down at the mechanical hand with fingers emitting a green haze from within the joints and saw a faint movement of the metal, possibly part liquid - part solid, or a combination of both. He assumed there could be thousands of nanobits, tiny micro machines, barely detectable, but in constant motion, making up just one finger on its hand. Separately too small to see, but combined for a common purpose, they were woven together like a fabric of metal skin. Troy realized how the android may have changed the numbers on the paperwork by morphing his nanobits into the digital text.

He admired the work. *This kind of technology is extreme and only a genius could have created it; I'm impressed!* His father's team worked with androids, but Troy had been away at the war or too buried in his own work to ask about it. They never really talked much.

The android's voice sounded male, though it obviously had no gender. Troy assumed it was programmed to exude more masculine qualities than feminine, and its frame appeared tall and wide-shouldered like a man. He decided to think of the android as a male counterpart. It would humanize him and make the NTB less adversarial in Troy's mind.

It made him uncomfortable to stare at the NTB, but he could not take his eyes off of it. As an inventor, he was keenly curious about him. As a scientist, he wanted to know what this being was made of. And as a condemned man, he needed to find out why this android had taken such an interest in him.

As they reached the dead end of a half-hidden hallway, the android held his metallic hand out against the wall. Thousands of nanobits from his fingers spread out, changing from solid to liquid to gas. It cast a green image of a door onto the wall and down to the floor. In an instant, the wall transformed and an actual door appeared. Opening the door, he motioned for Troy to proceed into the room. Once inside, he closed the door and laid his hand upon it. The door turned back into a green gas, then a liquid, transforming back into nanobits, and returned to the NTB's hand. The wall was solid as before.

Turning toward Troy, the android lifted his heavy hood from his face. It fell back, exposing his full skeletal skull. A chrome-like alloy covered the skeleton features, including a jaw with a complete set of teeth reflecting the light in the room. His skin diver-like mask remained in place, covering the nose and dark eye cavities. The smoke-colored glass of the mask hid features that otherwise would startle humans. Oddly, Troy felt no level of intimidation or fear at the sight of him, as the two security attendants had.

"You may ask your questions," the android said.

Troy didn't hesitate. "What are you? What are you made of?"

"My molecular structure is at the quantum level. I am created from the atom up with elements of electromagnetic metals, Ferro fluids, fusion and fission capabilities. Parts of me can interact with atoms, adding or subtracting elements such as protons and electrons, in order to form solids, liquids, gases, electrical particles."

"You can speak and I hear you, but you have no physical anatomy for it. You use telepathy?" Troy asked.

"Yes, a simple transmission of audio wave frequencies in the formation of language dialects."

"And you have immediate responsive thought process—you think and act on your own. An advanced artificial intelligence program?"

"It is more than that," the NTB responded. "I am created with synthetic brain synapses from a live DNA base. It allows an unlimited learning capacity in order to respond to any situation. They interact with a quantum computer installed in my head."

"You learn and you think. Do you make independent choices? Or base responses on stored scenarios?"

"I am self-learning. I can make strategic decisions based on the information at hand."

Troy was speechless. *This is impossible*, he thought. A living synthetic brain in a metal body, reacting on its own initiative; and an NTB with apparent ability to create fusion or fission, meant to generate immense power...or great destruction. *Yet here it stands in front of me. It's incredible. But why is such an amazing invention buried in the bottom level of a corporate death facility?* Before Troy could ask, the NTB chose to ask him a question.

"What is your name?" asked the android.

Looking at the number on his arm, Troy responded, "Candidate 924."

"No. What is your real name?" The NTB held out his mechanical hand to him.

Troy wondered why he would ask. *He uses telepathy. He should already know my name.* But the android kept his hand extended. *If he is self-learning, he must be learning human mannerisms. I get it; he wants a proper introduction. He wants to shake hands.*

Troy took the metal hand firmly. "My name is Troy Vincent."

"My name is Vincent, also."

Troy looked down at his hand clasping the cold metal. He then noticed a trademark on the android's wrist. It was similar to his VSA trademark, but with a slight variation. The letters, '*s*' and '*a*', were on either side of the large 'V' instead of inside it. This was his father's trademark.

The NTB responded to Troy's thought.

"Dr. Vincent and his scientific team created me. I am one of twelve beings they contracted to build. We call ourselves The Brethren. We were made to travel the galaxy ahead of any human expedition and build colony bases on habitable planets. We are self-sustaining, capable of extreme problem-solving and negotiating any diplomatic situation which could arise with alien species. The Brethren also carry the complete history of this solar system and Earth's humanity within our database."

"How did you end up here?"

"The mission was abandoned before its completion by government sponsors who ceased to exist. We were acquired by SamWong Industries along with the assets of Dr. Vincent's company. When Hoy SamWong discovered our full capabilities, he became afraid of us. He donated our services to the VRC System."

"You mean he imprisoned you." Troy realized they had literally been locked away in an eternity of servitude. "What do you do here? How are you used?"

The NTB explained the mundane use of its advanced skills. "Society wanted to know how candidates die in the VRC; what happens in the mind that causes humans to self-destruct. The Brethren use telepathic powers to monitor a candidate's experience. Then we document the case. We are not permitted to intervene or influence, only observe. They separated us between twelve different facilities around the world, yet we share a common consciousness. We learn from each other."

"And what have you learned?"

"We have all come to the same conclusion. We are witnesses to the worst part of human behavior and the cruelty humans inflict upon each other."

Troy was appalled and yet he understood how the androids would conclude the human race was a danger to itself, a destructive force they couldn't fathom. He now understood why the android made a choice to intervene on his behalf, even though it just told him they were ordered not to influence any outcome. This NTB had a reason to do so—Troy's own father, its creator.

Perhaps this change in events would help Troy escape the grueling treatment to come. He no longer contemplated an escape of his own, but one possibly arising from this new revelation. There was more to this galaxy traveler, he could feel it. He asked another question of the manufactured being. "You said you were created with brain synopses from a live DNA base. Did it come from my father?"

The NTB turned directly to face Troy. A tiny dot appeared in the middle of each lens of his black mask. The dots grew, becoming swirls of green and gray, filling both sides of the dark visor with ghostly, glowing tracks of invisible electrons darting in all directions. Once the lenses were completely filled, two identical portraits of Troy's own face stared back at him from the android's mask.

Troy drew his dark eyebrows together in confusion and whispered, "Why do you look like me?"

The telepathic audio wave was loud and clear: "Because I have *your* DNA."

"Why do you look like me?" Troy asked.
The answer came back across the air wave,
"Because I have your DNA."

Chapter 9

Vincent cleared the image from his mask and walked past the stunned prisoner toward a small well-lit area in the back of the large room. As Troy slowly turned to follow, memories rushed forward, finally making sense. Remembering his father worked with blood samples years ago when he was just a boy and occasionally appearing with a tiny needle, he told Troy he could contribute something great to science if he would let him prick his finger. Of course, he wanted to please his father, but he hated getting stuck and seeing the tiny bubble of blood ooze out of his fingertip. After the first few times, Troy would run and hide whenever his father needed another sample. As a child, he thought he was being punished for something, like forgetting to let the dog out, or not picking up his toys. *Boy was I wrong,* tightening his lips and drawing a breath.

His father employed a dozen scientists; Vincent said they made a dozen androids. *Were they all made from the DNA of their creator scientists? Was that how they planned to carry the human gene pool out into deep space?*

Troy strained to remember the names and details of the scientific group. He could only recall Dr. Devony, the lead female scientist, a biochemist, who always had a piece of candy for him. He lost track of her long before SamWong Industries acquired Vincent Scientific Applications. One by one, the team had mysteriously disappeared.

Suspecting the androids were created to take the human genomes of the most brilliant minds with them to survive and continue on another world, Troy now wished he'd made the effort to talk more with his father. His own inventions seemed insignificant compared to what his father apparently produced.

Feelings of guilt stirred inside him. He realized he had been selfishly preoccupied, while his father quietly endeavored to make sure the human race survived in some form somewhere else. Troy exhaled, closing his eyes with regret, blocking out the memories. *Just one more thing to add to the long list of Troy Vincent's life failures. I'll never be the man my father was.*

The NTB's voice boomed in his ear as the audio wave shot from across the room. "There is no time for such thoughts. From this moment on, you must succeed."

Vincent stood across the room, his masked eyes trained upon him. Troy cleared the negativity from his head. Walking through the odd space, he assumed the large room was once a mechanic's bay. The shape of garage doors appeared to have been locked down with chains along one wall. Rusted tool chests lined another wall under two small air vents, cob webs strung across the shadowed corners and a clean, but oiled-stained cement floor. Aluminum air handlers crossed the ceiling, bellowing out as the air system in the facility came on. Old discolored PVC pipes and fiber optic conduit ran from the wall to the center of the room, where Vincent was waiting for him.

All the light concentrated in the middle of the room, bouncing off of Vincent's chrome as he moved among two columns of equipment. Troy recognized the setup from the VRC presentation the gadget attendant had previously shown him. Without the presentation, Troy knew the sight of it would scare the hell out of anybody. Two tall, clear vertical chambers sat in the middle of the bay, each one approximately nine feet high. They stood a few feet apart from each other with a smoky privacy panel surrounding one of them. He could only see the top of the second chamber containing a light white fog. Noticing a shadow playing upon the glass of the privacy panel, Troy assumed it was in use. The other chamber, the empty one in front of him, contained no fog. Its door stood wide open, beckoning with a promise of mystery and terror. This one was apparently meant for him.

Vincent moved to the vertical control panel on the side of the cylindrical chamber and began entering settings. Troy stood behind him, studying the digital panel ran from top to bottom. There were small LED display windows for medical and environmental readings. He recognized most of the equipment housed within the panel – heart, respiratory, EEG monitors. Other environmental gauges measured oxygen and carbon dioxide levels of the chamber, and chemical balance control knobs for various gas mixtures. One small display window at the very bottom startled him back to the reality of his situation. Simply labeled, "Cessation," it currently showed a series of zeroes for date/time/hour/minute/second.

Panic welled up within his chest and Troy began taking deep breaths. Looking around the room, he wondered if there was another exit. He certainly couldn't go out the way he came in, through a door in the wall created by the android. Troy turned around with his back to the chamber, as though refusing to be in the moment approaching, like the unstoppable hands of a clock. "Tell me why I should go through with this?" he asked, leaning on a dusty desk to steady his nerves.

"It has been ordered."

"No," Troy said firmly as he turned back to look at Vincent. "Tell me why you, who know who I am, would force me through this? There must be a way out, but not like this."

"Someone wants you dead. If we do not convince them you have died in the VRC, they will try again. Believe me when I say there is no other way."

"So if I survive, and I intend to," Troy added with conviction, "what then?"

"I cannot say unless you survive," Vincent responded pragmatically.

"So you're saying there's a possibility I won't?"

"Yes, it is possible."

Troy was irritated with the unemotional directness. The NTB obviously knew him to be innocent, but wanted him to fake his own death. And there were no assurances that Troy would come out of this thing alive.

Troy's mouth felt dry as he tried to swallow. Beads of sweat broke out on his forehead as he threw open his leather jacket, pulling at the collar of his t-shirt. Vincent handed him a small bottle of electrolyte fluid and Troy drank it down completely. He would go through with this just for the satisfaction of proving to the judges' panel he was indeed, innocent. He couldn't let himself think of the other possibility.

"It is time. Come." Vincent urged in a deep, calm audio wave.

As Vincent guided him into the chamber, Troy's knees felt weak, but the buoyancy inside the vertical tube suspended him. He felt weightless even while the door remained open. "Help me out here, Vincent. Give me some advice on what's coming, and how to survive."

Vincent tried to comply. "I have observed there are two possible paths within the VRC. One is a path of self-destruction. Guilt, fear, panic, hate, all lead to this; many succumb. The other is a path of self-preservation, a path some humans find harder to recognize. Innocence does not guarantee survival. That which you perceive as weakness within you, may be the very strength you need to survive."

"I heard them speak of Grief Masters. Will they try to kill me?"

"Your own demons will try to kill you. They know your weaknesses and thrive on your own self-destructive thoughts. Do not try to reason with them, as they will use it against you. Also, do not believe everything you see. If your brain perceives you are injured or dying, in reality, you could cease to exist."

Vincent closed the chamber door. Troy felt the air pressure pop in his ears as the chamber locked, sealing itself off from the real world. Trying a telepathic message to Vincent, he needed to know if he could reach him from inside the VRC. *The Grief Masters...who are they?*

Vincent stared at him through the chamber glass. Troy wondered at the hesitancy of everyone, including this android, to tell him about the Grief Masters. Finally, Vincent responded.

"The Grief Masters help some, but not others. They seem to exist in the deepest part of the human brain, but no one knows for certain from where they come. Some say they arise from the human soul. Others say they are just manifestations. I cannot say if they will come to your aid. But, if a key presents itself, take it. It will unlock their power which may be of great value to you. Remember, they do not act alone. <u>You</u> are the <u>key</u> to their existence as well."

How do I find these keys?

"I cannot tell you. They are different for every human. Only you can recognize them."

If only humans can recognize them, how do you know they exist?

"I have seen them in the VRC. I am capable of seeing their 'energy,' for lack of an appropriate word. The source of their power is a human mystery I fail to understand."

Vincent pushed a button on the side control panel and a swirl of white, gassy fog entered the top of the chamber. It curled slowly in a lazy downward spiral, splitting into other curls and filling the top of the chamber. Looking up, Troy could see it making its way down toward him. *Vincent, can I count on help from you?*

Vincent did not confirm nor deny with an answer. He only responded with more advice.

"If your brain becomes tired, a 'safe house' may appear. Take refuge there and you will be safe to rest a while."

How long?

"The passage of time is irrelevant in the VRC."

As the fog filled the chamber, Troy could no longer see Vincent. He felt strangely tired. Either the fog was affecting his eyes or they were heavy with sleep, he could not tell which. His thoughts reached out to Vincent one more time. *What are my chances if I can't find these Grief Masters?*

He heard a muffled response before blacking out completely. "Not good."

Chapter 10

Vincent recognized Troy's dilemma and the thoughts Troy experienced: escape, anxiety, and fear of the unknown. He had seen similar reactions hundreds, if not thousands, of times. His mechanical physique allowed him to ignore such responses. But in this instance, the biological part of him wanted to calm Troy, so he imparted more information than he normally would have given a VRC candidate. It would be up to Troy to do the rest.

As Troy's suspended body became still, Vincent continued checking the settings on the side panel. Although very aware of his own mechanical functions, his biological sensory sometimes bewildered him. He sensed this interaction with Troy had been very different. He deduced he may be experiencing a *feeling*, a human emotion of empathy for Troy and what he would probably go through. Perhaps it was the DNA connection.

Vincent took a calculated risk. From what he learned in his research of Troy, the man appeared to be strong, smart, and an experienced veteran. Physically, he stood an excellent chance in the VRC. In contrast, he sensed the guilt and loss Troy harbored. He could give up if he dwelled on his failures instead of his future. Vincent could not understand Troy's self-criticism and doubt when he was known as a gifted scientist who had built a brilliant career, and also appeared to be a good father by society's standards.

The female occupant of the second chamber remained Vincent's other concern. He made a promise to get her out alive. It became a mission for him over the past twelve months as he looked for an opportunity to keep his promise. Not a part of the shared mission with his brothers, but it became an important commitment to someone Vincent considered his only human friend. It was a friendship that had to remain secret for the safety of all three: the android, the friend, and the young woman.

He ran numerous scenarios in his head and determined his two VRC candidates stood the best chance of survival if they were combined. She, not as capable of defending herself, experienced events of sadness, loss, low self-esteem, and loneliness in her life which could lead to her demise in the VRC. However, she possessed qualities Troy did not have, and vice versa. Her ability to offer good advice might guide him away from brash decisions. His ability to physically protect her would come naturally to him. Just being in each other's presence might motivate them to survive.

Because both candidates suffered from human frailties which made them extremely vulnerable in the VRC, their demons would know it and seek it out. Vincent could not protect them from their own self-inflicted wounds. He recognized the signs of depression, self-pity, and heartache, yet he didn't know the remedies. Both of his charges needed mental healing, something he could not fix. Only the Grief Masters seemed to have a power to deal with that. He observed positive changes in candidates whenever encountering the elusive beings. Their appearance remained a mystery and the android was uncertain if either candidate had a connection which might draw a Grief Master to them. So he based his decision to bring the two together on a higher than average probability that a Grief Master might come forward. Humans called it *gambling,* and he assumed the risk was weighing in their favor.

He waved his hand in front of the privacy screen surrounding the second chamber and the screen disappeared. Scanning the LED readouts of the occupant inside, he sent a digital recording of the statistics to the file on candidate 818. The young woman hung suspended within the weightlessness of the white fog, her dark hair floating freely. Although her heart rate was currently elevated and rising, he would monitor it closely and record the readings in the file.

Vincent calculated Troy would react negatively once he discovered who she really was. He speculated on how much time it would take for her to convince Troy to trust her, if he would even trust her at all, but he was confident of the outcome. Since their acceptance of each other would be the real unknown risk, the android compared it to a human colloquial expression he found fascinating: he was "putting all his eggs in one basket."

Feeling his cloak move by his feet, Vincent looked down at the floor. "Oh, it's you," he said in a friendly tone. "I wondered where you were."

Bending down, he picked up a skinny cat and set her on the desk by the control panel. She purred loudly, rubbing against the rough woven sleeve of his cloak. He scratched the top of her striped head with a metal index finger. Her thin tail wrapped around his skeletal forearm as her slight frame pushed against his body. Vincent did not feel the need to conceal his stark face from his tiny feline friend so he switched his facial mask off. She became a pleasant companion in his isolated work room, coming and going through one of the broken air vents that led to the outside world.

Her body was lean, with a coat of black and gray stripes, head to tail. Her underbelly appeared pure white, all the way down to thin, white legs. Stretching her paws up on his chest, she raised one paw up, tapping his chrome chin. She continued purring, staring into his vacant eyes, and rubbing her head along his chest.

"Yes, yes! I brought you something," he responded out loud to her feline thoughts. Vincent had been programmed to analyze and decipher language vocabularies, hers being primitive and simple, but easy to understand. Vincent reached into his pocket and laid a half-eaten tuna fish sandwich on the table. Eagerly, she got down and munched on it as though she had not eaten in days. Pulling out a small carton of milk he retrieved from a break room cool tank, he snapped his finger and a spark flew out burning a hole in the top of the carton. He poured it into a small cup on the desk next to her. She stopped eating long enough to peer over the edge of the cup, sniff it, and then turned back to her sandwich. Vincent took a moment to watch and record her reaction to the simple meal. "I am sure your appreciation of such protein is more than the attendant who left it in the trash bin. Enjoy it, little one." He ran his mechanical hand along her back and left her to consume the food uninterrupted.

He went about his work recording notes by touching his finger to a digital pad. The nanobits from his fingertip wrote words without his hand moving. The android could do many tasks at the same time while contemplating other things. At the moment, he continued his previous thoughts about the Grief Masters; what causes their appearance? Are they a complex application? And who could their maker possibly be?

Vincent was perplexed by his inability to understand what they were and where they came from. His self-learning mind consisted of millions of facts, formulas, and data. However, there was nothing tangible about the Grief Masters, nothing provable, nothing scientifically documented. They were an enigma, leading to an unfinished conclusion about them every time. For the time being, he would have to set it aside and turn his attention to his two imprisoned wards.

Vincent could monitor a VRC candidate by connecting to the candidate's brain waves. The Brethren all had this ability, an extension of their telepathic skill, to observe firsthand what took place in a candidate's brain during the treatment. They documented human reactions and what triggered them. Their shared consciousness developed a master log, which allowed them to benefit from each other's learning experience. Normally, Vincent would have sent a notation to this log about the empathy he experienced for Troy. But this time, he delayed the transmission.

He did not trust all the airwaves in the surrounding area. Nor did he want his isolated workroom discovered by the VRSM Security. Since his own incarceration, Security Chief Michaels allowed him to work on his own, granting him some freedom to set up his chambers wherever he wished. Occasionally, Vincent moved his location to maintain a sense of privacy. He wanted to monitor Troy's treatment without any interruption. He also needed to protect his two candidates from whoever pursued their demise.

Trust seemed to be another human trait he learned to be wary of within the walls of the VRC system. As he previously told Troy, The Brethren surmised they were witnessing the worst of human behavior while in this service. The human habit of lying certainly contributed to the reason VRCs existed, and the use of it was not lost on the NTBs. They considered it a moral dilemma for humans. They concluded trust must be linked to truth. However, trusting the wrong person could be linked to lying. They agreed they would not make use of this deceptive skill themselves and carefully evaluated the trust they placed in each human they made contact with.

Once, their shared experience log had been intended for a different purpose. They built it by thousands of entries daily, through interaction with humans, animals, and the natural environment. This log would be the basic knowledge databank the twelve planned to take with them into the galaxy. Recording and preserving the human experience became an integral part of the original purpose of their creation.

Vincent's memory bank flipped back to the day they were informed galaxy exploration would no longer be on any corporate agenda. The cost of it made the World Board of Directors turn its back on the long planned mission. Disappointment was a human emotion, but The Brethren felt a void as their future became obscured.

Their log became stagnant as their observances built a record of cruelty within the VRCs. Some human behavior, such as murder, rape, and acts of hatred, were considered below human intelligence and deemed not worthy to retain. They agreed such observances would not be added to the log. Also, the methods of death carried out within VRC treatments were so contrary to the original program mission that the androids jointly paused their internal learning system. Operating solely on automatic pilot, they only performed the functions requested of them. However, they did modify their mission so if their own DNA matched up with an incarcerated candidate, or whenever a descendant of the original Vincent scientific team came into the system, they would do what they could to save them. The reprogramming allowed Vincent to locate Troy at the motel just before his arrest. It gave him time to contact Don Tyler.

The little cat sat up straight, licking away the tuna with satisfaction and curling her tail around her feet. Her pink tongue slipped in and out along each side of her mouth, savoring the last of the free dinner. She watched Vincent as he finished his work.

His only chance to sit for periods of time and rest like humans came when he remained immobile to monitor a VRC candidate. A downtime never existed for Vincent. The green haze surrounding him came from particle residue created by the enormous energy of the millions of nanobits making up his arms and legs. They were constantly self-charging, drawing endless power from different sources in the environment.

Looking forward to this period of immobility, Vincent compared it to another human aspect, the one called *relaxation*. It gave him an opportunity to scan through his enormous stored music program. Currently, he had been reviewing the works of the second half of the twentieth century. His assigned contribution to the original mission program was to retain all human literature, art, and music. He valued the music databank above all the rest.

Vincent took his place in his *relaxation station*, as he liked to call it, and sat down on a pillowed bench between the two chambers. The pillow was more for the cat then for his need. He crossed his legs in a yoga position for complete concentration and focus. The cat jumped down from her perch on the desk, crossing the floor to the bench. Hopping up into his lap, she circled down into the comfortable folds of his cloak for a nap. Vincent ignored her, allowing the creature to remain. It was time for him to go to work.

With his sleepy companion, he levitated above the bench, defying gravity. Rising halfway up between the top of the two VRC chambers, he settled into his observation mode. Crossing his mechanical arms in front of his chest, he turned his palms up. A green beam of intensified light emerged from the index finger of one hand, passing through the glass of Troy's chamber and touching Troy's temple. Then a similar light emerged from his other index finger, passing through the glass of the woman's chamber, touching her temple. The white fog surrounding them turned green, emanating from his intense energy beams, and gently swirled down around them.

Never a fan of the antiquated sound system wired to play music and announcements throughout the facility, Vincent momentarily turned his attention to the speaker on the ceiling. A bolt of charged electrons shot from his thumbs and into it, traveling at lightning speed through the old wiring to the automated sound control room. Crackling sounds from the speakers echoed throughout the hallways of the entire facility. A cloud of sparks flew as the charged bolt hit the tune selector, changing the music. Settling back into his yoga position, Vincent waited for one of his favorite mid-twentieth century classic rock bands to play. The steady drumstick beat of Black Sabbath's *IRON MAN* filled the air. Hanging his head down, Vincent relaxed, nodding his head to the beat. He related to the lyrics of the song, about a man made of iron who was ignored by society.

In the security station several halls over, Terry and Amon also nodded their heads to the beat of the changed tune. Terry pulled his pen from behind his ear, playing air drums on the desk. Amon, grabbed his air guitar, stood up, and jammed with the bass. Aware Vincent had done this many times in the past, Terry yelled out with enthusiasm, "Yeah, good one, Nano Man! Rock on, you rock n' rollin' son of a bitch!"

Chapter 11

Troy slipped deep into the incarceration of the VRC. He wasn't sure at what point he stopped clinging to the thread of reality and became immersed in the surreal world of virtual reality. He fought for control as long as he could, but had no concept of how long that struggle had been. As Vincent said, time is irrelevant in the VRC.

The greenish fog, thick at first, became thinner and less suffocating. Finally regaining consciousness, Troy gasped for air. Thinking he could die right then if he didn't get his panicked breathing under control, he tried focusing on regaining a sense of calm throughout his brain and body.

Taking a moment to inventory his body parts, he looked at his arms, legs, and chest for reassurance he remained still physically intact. Not knowing what to expect from the VRC, he wasn't sure what his physical representation would be. He thought it might only be a sense of mental awareness. However, his body remained present and accounted for, as though he just walked into a garden of early morning fog.

Holding his hand up in front of him, it appeared translucent, almost opaque. Although it was his appendage and he could firmly feel it, he could see right through it. The same was true of the rest of his body. Troy put his hand on his chest, afraid it could just pass through. But it felt solid, as did his thighs. Then his hands went to his face. Again, it was solid.

The transparency gradually wore away and he let out a pent-up sigh as his body became normal and his breathing stabilized. Troy began to gain a sense of balance in this new state of reality, while being fully aware it was anything but that.

Before he could give much more thought to his physical status, the fog thinned and slipped away. Above him appeared a high dome, wrapping 180 degrees from the horizon in front to the horizon behind. The dark blue space surrounded him on all sides and was reminiscent of a planetarium, without the stars. A mass of green, misty swirls still covered his feet, spreading out like a foggy carpet. Although he felt a solid floor below him and he could walk around, he just couldn't see it. Fading from green to a white wispiness, the air sparkled with tiny specks of iridescence.

Troy suspected this strange, blank canvas was setting up the back drop for whatever would come. He didn't have to wait long before the sparkling iridescence rose, unfurling into an arch and floating toward the curved heaven. It spread across the dome, depositing thousands of iridescent sparkles onto its surface. Then it dissipated into nothing, leaving the twinkling lights of a thousand stars shining down on him.

As he looked up at the confined universe of stars, some began to swell. Within the center of each enlarged light, he saw scenes of people and places. At every angle of the curved sphere, different scenes expanded and then contracted. It took a moment for Troy to recognize they were snapshots of his own life, events having shaped his direction, and people who had influenced his path. *I think I'm in the deepest part of my brain, possibly my memory center.*

Flashback scenes pulled out like cards from a deck, one at a time, and projected against the starry backdrop. To his left, a scene appeared of him as a young boy in his father's laboratory. He watched his father working on a robot, but it looked nothing like Vincent. This one had a synthetic human face.

It was good seeing his dad again, even if he appeared only as a memory. Troy studied the lines on his father's face. Through his adult eyes, he saw his father as a much older man than what he remembered. Dr. Vincent and his wife became parents late in life and Troy missed out on many of the father-son activities his friends enjoyed. He vowed to be a different type of dad with Tommy, and to give him as much quality time as he could. Fearing

Vincent and the Grief Masters

he might cloud his mind with emotions about his son right now, he reluctantly blocked out the thought. He needed to stay focused on what was happening in front of him.

The flashback continued. Dr. Vincent repositioned a tiny connection within the head of the robot and its face turned toward the young Troy with a cruel expression. The lad ducked behind his father's pants leg.

"Too real for you, son?" asked his dad. "I'll make him less intimidating then, maybe more mechanical." He smiled down at the boy, who clung to his leg.

"Is that alright with you, Troy?" The boy peeked back out at the robot, nodding to his father. His father patted his head. "You run along and help your mother now." Troy remembered not wanting to leave his father's side, but that summed up the nature of their relationship; mostly brief interactions.

As the memory faded back into its star, a different one enlarged. Troy, now age twelve, stood tinkering in their garage with a small invention of his own. His parents peered over his shoulder, as he demonstrated how to transport a grapefruit to the other side of the garage. Being his first primitive transporter, he beamed with pride as he turned it on. The round yellow citrus dematerialized, reappearing a few feet away, with a slightly altered appearance. It was now orange and flat.

His father frowned and walked away. "Needs more work."

However, his mother picked up the reinvented grapefruit with a smile. Setting it aside, she hugged her son. Troy smiled to himself, remembering the touch of her soft hand on his youthful cheek. *She was proud of anything I did, even when I failed.*

Immediately following that memory, a scene of another unsuccessful transporter attempt presented itself. As a teenage Troy ran frantically out of the garage as exploding remains of a watermelon flew all around him, showering the air, and coming to rest in pieces all across the yard. His father stood up from a wicker chair on the back porch with his holographic newspaper in his hand.

"Invention is 99% failure and 1% success," he yelled. "Try again."

A disappointed Troy flopped down in the grass, and threw a piece of melon across the lawn. His father sat down and went back to reading his newspaper. "And clean up the mess before your mother sees it."

Troy was enjoying the slide show from his past. The star retracted the memory and a twinkling orb to his right expanded. He chuckled at the sight of his sloppy college clothes and unruly hair. Sitting on a stool in the university science lab, he just completed a successful transfer of a rabbit from one cage to another. Exhilarated with the success, he pumped his arms victoriously in the air. Then realizing there was no one there to witness his accomplishment, his smile faded as disappointment replaced elation. He picked up his pen, tapped it on the table a few times to dispel the emotion and began scribbling down his results in a large notebook.

He looked around the room at several other small lab creatures in their cages. Drumming his fingers on the tabletop, he paused and stuck his head down below the table, peering at his dog. His best friend, a golden retriever named Marcus, lay curled up on the floor beneath the table.

"What do you say, boy? You wanna go for a little ride?" The dog looked at the rabbit in the cage across the way, got up and walked out of the room. Troy laughed at the memory, along with his college-aged self.

The sphere continued to play out Troy's life across its interior. The images advanced in age: his college graduation holding the hand of his girlfriend, Lilith; celebrating with her on their wedding day; to the day he opened his own business. He and his father stood outside a small building next to a sign, *Vincent Scientific Applications, a Subsidiary of VSA, Inc.* They posed shaking hands, as Lilith took their photo. Dr. Vincent took the camera and asked Lilith, who was heavily pregnant and quite uncomfortable, to stand beside Troy. After the snapshot, Troy tried to kiss her, but she pushed him away. Then he and his father cut the ceremonial ribbon hanging across the double doors. *That was a good day.*

Scenes of his son began flashing to his left and right: the day Tommy was born; his first steps; his first day at school; teaching him to play baseball; the day Troy said goodbye to his son as he stood in his corporate militia uniform. He would miss out on almost three years of Tommy's young life, fighting on the war's front line amid burning oil fields and blood-covered sand. He lost more than time with Tommy. He lost the affection of his wife.

Troy finally looked away, unable to watch more. The mist in his eyes was not from the fog. Tommy's infectious laugh made him raise his head again, and he smiled at the moment captured in his brain. If the VRC could keep him frozen in this moment, he would gladly give up his life to stay here, to stay with Tommy. He began to think the VRC may not be as bad he feared.

So far, so good. No sooner had the thought crossed his mind, harder and crueler flashbacks spanned the entire dome. His years in the corporate military played out while deafening sounds of war surrounded him. The smell of the blazing oil tanks filled his senses again as he patrolled with his team. Bomber drones flew low above them and robotic weapons carriers hovered along the rough terrain beside them. The lines on his forehead deeply furrowed as he relived the moments of one particularly gruesome battle against the enemy, in a bloodstained courtyard and adobe building. "Even my memory blocks out the worst of that," Troy said out loud.

In a flash, the vision of a single star replaced the memories covering the dome, expanding and contracting like a pulsar. Silence replaced the loud sounds of war. Troy watched as another brutal scene played out, but this one was in a corporate boardroom. Hoy SamWong and his legal team, led by Xavier Adams, appeared on one side of the table. Troy, his father, and attorney, Don Tyler, sat on the other side.

"Your stock is plummeting, Dr. Vincent." SamWong smiled. "With your contracts cancelled, you have racked up too much personal debt. You're no longer able to pay your employees. No financial institution will loan money to your failing company. You have no other choice but to accept my offer."

"On our terms, of course," added Mr. Adams, pushing the acquisition contract across to Dr. Vincent. "Just sign at the bottom and all your problems will be over."

Dr. Vincent hesitated to pick up the pen. He looked at Tyler, who, with a sad, slow response, nodded his head in agreement.

"Don't do this, Dad," Troy quietly pleaded. "I know things went to hell for VSA while I was away, but I'm back now. Whatever project your sponsors canceled out on, we'll save it. I'll find the money. We'll find another way, I promise you."

Mr. Adams narrowed his gaze at Troy. "Too little, too late. Your absence only sped up the outcome. No corporation is going to take on that top secret folly of your father's."

"I may not have been here or involved in his work, but I can assure you, whatever his team was working on, is no folly," Troy stated, staring back at Adams.

SamWong read the stock values from a digital stock board projected in the air above the table top. "VSA is down another 30 points just this morning." Leaning back in his red leather chair, he put his fingertips together in front of his face. The sun streaming in from the boardroom windows glinted off his ring – three large letters, SWI, made entirely of diamonds.

"Your company will be lucky to survive the day."

As Troy started to respond, the older Dr. Vincent put his hand up to stop him. "Enough," he frowned. "It's over," he whispered to Troy. Picking up the pen, he signed the bottom of the acquisition agreement.

Adams lifted another page, "Here and here; and just your initials here."

Clenching his jaw, Troy pounded his fist down on the table with an audibly frustrated, "Damn it."

"Easy, boy," smiled Adams, "or maybe your little VSA subsidiary will be next."

The scene projecting on the dome above Troy swirled into a large construction crane. As loud engines of construction equipment and the repetitive beep of a crane backing up, replaced the silence of the boardroom, the VSA sign, chained to the top of the crane, was coming down, and the SWI sign hoisted up in its place. Troy stood by, watching his father's dream disappear. His father, walking toward him, with shoulders slumped and hands shoved in his pockets, hung his head down. He approached Troy and pulled his right hand from his pocket, placing it firmly on his son's shoulder.

"I just want you to know," he paused and looked down at the ground. "Your mother and I are very proud of you, son. We've been proud of you all your life; your inventions and military service. I neglected…no," Dr. Vincent stopped. Then looking into Troy's eyes, he continued, "What I meant to say is, I was wrong not to tell you that all along." Smiling, he added, "You turned out all right." He gave his son's shoulder another firm grip. Troy thought his father's eyes looked very tired as they peered back at him. "Your mother made me promise before she died, to make sure I told you, we love you very much. And as always, she was right," he chuckled.

Troy didn't know what to say. His father wasn't ever one to speak of feelings. It wasn't a part of their relationship. Without a reply, he watched him walk away. *I'll regret that the rest of my life.*

Troy instinctively knew what would come in the next memory flash. He looked down at the fog covering his feet, not wanting to relive it. Turning around and facing the other side of the domed space, there was no escaping what his memory center wanted him to see. It morphed into a single large picture covering the dome ceiling, playing out even though Troy averted his eyes.

I know what it is.

Chapter 12

Entering his father's garage, Troy found Dr. Vincent hanging from a ceiling rafter, a rope wrapped tightly around his neck, a chair kicked over on the floor. Moving quickly, he grabbed a garden machete from the wall, climbed onto the chair, and grasped the older man around the chest. With one strong whack of the knife against the rope, he cut it from the rafter and struggled to lower the body to the floor. Then, sitting down beside him, Troy lifted his father's lifeless body into his arms, gently cradling him, as tears escaped and ran down his cheeks. With his father's face buried in his chest, he sat intermittently praying to, and cursing God, and every other deity he could think of. After what seemed an eternity, Troy carefully laid him on the floor, grabbed a folded towel from a nearby box, and placed it tenderly under his father's head. The call to authorities was one of the hardest things he ever had to do and never thought he would ever have to make.

Troy knelt down on one knee, turning away from the scene on the high dome as it played out. The pain was more than he could bear. Standing up, he rubbed his face with his hands to dispel the memory. As he did, the scene faded away. He'd had enough of this tortured walk down memory lane.

"What do you want from me?" Turning around in a circle, he yelled up at the dome. "You want me to admit all the mistakes, all the problems and pain, all the bad things that have happened in my life?" Raising his voice in anger, "Those were the cards I was dealt. That's who I am!"

Speaking those words out loud awakened renewed feelings of loss and heartache, in what was moments ago, an empty and protected heart. Troy wanted whatever, or whoever, was controlling his situation to show itself; *that* he could deal with, *that* he could fight; but not this continual show of emotional flashbacks.

Voices began coming from everywhere, loudly filling the air. He heard his mother say, "Troy, you're my only son and I love you." Followed by the voice of his ex-wife, "You're a broken man, Troy Vincent. SamWong can give me what you can't." Hoy SamWong's voice interrupted hers, "Thanks for everything; your business, your inventions, your wife. I'm going to enjoy all of them." His father's final approval, "I'm proud of you, son." Suddenly, Tommy's small voice came vividly through, "Daddy, Daddy, I'm here!"

Troy couldn't take any more. As his face turned red with rage, the veins in his temples pounded, and he yelled out in anguish as long and as loud as he could. Stretching his fists up toward the now starless dome, he shouted, "Come on, show yourself! I'm ready for you!"

The spherical, domed space began to spin, forcing Troy to close his eyes. The dark-blue horizon disappeared, replaced with a blur of grey as it whirled around him. Bitter laughter mingled with whispers and murmurs, emanating from faceless shadows.

As he reopened his eyes, the shadows dissipated into the fog. He could sense the beings there, but he couldn't see them. They slowly circled him, making his skin crawl. Fear began to replace the pain within him, a fear emerging from the witness of his own ruin, feelings he had repressed for some time. Here in this VRC there was no holding back. The fear of his future was now at hand.

From behind him, a large round object, like a small moon, sped past him. It stopped briefly to hang in the air in front of him. Troy could see it clearly; the round orb contained a face. No one he recognized, but the eyes, nose, and mouth were distinct. It was distorted by a cynical, diabolical laugh, sounding to Troy like the laugh of a demon. An orange-colored fire spread across its devilish features. He felt the heat of flames flick around him. Then, along with the laughter and heat, the orange face retreated far into the distance, until it disappeared. The image of a large, open door, encased in a white door frame followed, flying past him, and retreated in the same direction. As the door disappeared, he could hear it slam shut. The reverberation of the slamming door rushed toward him like a sonic boom, rocking his eardrums.

In rapid succession, a second large orb with a blue distorted face sailed past him. This one sneered at him. Similar in size to the first orb, it was frozen with frost and ice. An army of smaller, identical blue orbs followed it, all trying to keep up. The laughter changed to painful, agonizing moans sounding like Troy's own voice, yet it wasn't coming from him. The moon, with its mini-moons, disappeared into the distant fog like the first. They, too, were followed by a flying open door, slamming shut in the distance and sending forth echoing reverberations.

A third face emerged from over his right shoulder, as a crying face; a mournful, misshapen orb, alternating its appearance between grotesque masks of happiness and sadness. A high-pitched voice wailed grief-stricken cries, filled so full of remorse, Troy covered his ears to block them out. Tentacles reached out from beneath it, winding tightly around him, pulling him along as it went by. Struggling to release their thorny grip, one by one, he tore them from his forearms and waist. As he freed each one, the tentacles broke, crumbling in his hands. The orb retreated away into nothingness, followed by a door emerging from behind him, as though he had backed through it. Flying away and disappearing, it slammed shut, like the others, with an earthshaking sound.

The fourth orb rose on the horizon before him like a bright full moon looming larger than the others. Rising only halfway up on the horizon, it stopped, and remained stationary, for a moment. The only features of the face Troy could see were the eyes. They looked directly into Troy's and displayed great fear. The sound of breathless running accompanied this face. The moon circled the dome, never taking its fear-stricken eyes from him. It was pale, almost white, but as it rose higher in the dome, it turned yellow, exposing its full face, and transformed into the face of Hoy SamWong. Troy felt a wave of caution, compelling him to step back. The yellow moon turned blood-red, displaying SamWong's changing facial expressions from fear to disdain to hatred, as it continued rising high above him, to the top of the dome.

Finally, it spoke and SamWong's booming voice addressed him. "Afraid, boy?"

Troy stood up straight, his fists clenched by his side ready to defend himself against whatever might come at him.

The face of SamWong taunted him in a resounding command, "You should be!"

Like the others, the orb retreated, echoing the phrase over and over into the distance. The sound of breathless running increased in volume, as the door that followed flew over and rapidly away from Troy. However, instead of slamming shut, this door remained open. It turned around and flew back toward him, increasing in size until the open doorway overtook him.

Troy crossed his arms protectively over his head, as it swallowed him into its black depths.

Chapter 13

"Troy Vincent!" A loud voice resounded in a deep rumble.

Unclenching his fists, Troy looked around and found he stood facing the edge of a steep canyon. The sky above him blustered with fast moving grey clouds. The wind pushed into his back, swirling around his legs, causing him to lean more toward the cliff's edge. He peered down into the deep canyon floor as his adrenalin surged, and he instinctively pulled back several steps.

The pounding of hooves approached him from behind as Troy turned around. A shadow stopped some distance away and called out his name. The strangely shaped shadow grew in size as it slowly advanced toward him. Its features came into view, revealed by a lightning bolt that emerged from the storm's darkness and lit up the sky, spreading light across the dusty plain. The silhouette of a half-man, half-beast stood, calling his name.

"Troy Vincent!" echoed along the barren plateau and bounced off the canyon walls.

A demon? A Minotaur? A demon Minotaur—you've got to be kidding me. This is some weird manifestation conjured up in my brain. Nevertheless, Troy remained silent, as the startling appearance of the giant creature made him feel threatened.

Its upper body resembled a human, but instead of skin and bone, it appeared made of a pumice-looking stone, a dark volcanic rock covered with patches of burnt leather. Orange, molten lava moved visibly in every wide crack throughout its chest, running along both arms, like veins. The lower body appeared as a four-legged animal, with smoking, smoldering, dry fur hanging in loose clumps from its emaciated hips and legs.

It had the head of a bull with thick, long, sharply pointed horns; black smoke puffed from its ears and encircled the tips of the horns. Its snout was pushed in and the nostrils flared out in concentric circles on each side of its leathery face. Snarling lips curled, as large, black canine teeth clenched. Its eyes were the most unsettling feature of all, as curls of smoke and flame roiled in the empty sockets. When the Minotaur spoke, the flames flared within its eyes and spewed from its mouth. The demon's dark fiery eyes honed in on Troy.

Raising its arms, the creature spread wide wings high above its head, revealing sharp talons in place of fingers. Droplets of molten lava dripped off several of the dagger-like talons, which briefly flared up as they hit the dry ground and turned into ashen-black pebbles of stone. On the front of each hoof protruded a large, arched black talon, tapping and clawing at the earth.

The demon raised its head and snorted into the air, as steam escaped the huge nostrils. It sniffed several times, taking in long drafts of air from Troy's direction. Then, after a loud, eerie howl, it lowered its snout with a drooling growl.

"You have many fears."

"You have an advantage," Troy shouted back into the wind. "You seem to know me. But I don't know you."

"But you do know me," the demon snorted. The answer rushed toward Troy with a force that made the ground tremble. "I am Fear! Your fear!"

As the floor of the plateau shook, Troy stumbled back toward the edge of the cliff. Regaining his balance, he moved away from the crumbling precipice toward a rocky outcrop jutting up from the plateau's floor. Scrambling to take cover behind it, he looked around to see where he might go. *I sure as hell can't stay here.*

A few yards away to his left, tall grass covered a path leading to the foothills of a nearby mountain range. Troy looked to his right side and saw an elongated shadow advancing toward the rocky outcrop concealing him. Smaller shadows appeared to drop off from the creature's shadow. Stealing another look around the rock, he saw no other creatures except the Minotaur, only shadows on the ground walking, perhaps crawling, behind it. Once again, the half-man, half-creature stopped and called his name. "Troy

Vincent, you have memories laced with fear. It will be easy to destroy you with any of them."

"Give it your best shot," Troy said under his breath, dashing from the outcrop to the narrow, grassy path on his left. Unsure where it would take him, he knew the tall plains grass would provide cover, and a chance to put distance between him and the deadly shadows.

When he reached the base of the foothills, the path continued upward in a steep, winding climb. The dirt path, narrowing in spots to just a few inches in width, filled in with loose rock and slippery grass. He climbed as quickly as he could, slowing down where the path disappeared, until he was forced to stop at a steep drop off to the canyon floor far below. To cross, he would have to cling to rocks precariously sticking out along the gap, and ascend a rock wall hand over hand, until he could reach the other side where the path resumed about twenty feet away.

Troy's breathing became shallow. Pausing to catch his breath and slow his racing heartbeat, he glanced back down the hillside. Shrouded in shadow, the silent darkness crept up the mountainside advancing toward him. He positioned his foot on the first rock and carefully pressed on, wondering if any escape were possible.

How am I going to get around this creature, and a shadow army I can't even see?

****

Having crossed the dangerous gap faster than he expected to, Troy scrambled up the path to the top of the small mountain, where it came to an end. The terrain on other side became all mud, gravel and slippery foliage. Losing his footing on the steep downslope, he slid on the unstable gravel. He grabbed at the long grass, only to give way into an uncontrollable slide. Feeling every scrape and scratch, he tumbled down to a hard landing into sand, abruptly stopping in a dusty foxhole.

A dried mud wall formed a portion of a foxhole along the side of an adobe building. Troy heard shouts of commands and movement beyond it. He listened to determine what language they used, not wanting to make himself a target. Cautiously, he raised his head above the wall and rapid gun fire popped all around, showering him with rocks and dirt. As he fell back against the foxhole wiping the dirt from his face, he noticed his clothes had changed to camouflage. On his feet were his old military boots, and he wore a bullet-proof vest with deep pockets to carry four MK16 magazines. Two handguns in holsters flanked either side of him and extra loaded clips hung from his belt. Slung over his left shoulder was a modified MK16 CQC laser-operated assault rifle.

Sergeant Troy Vincent appeared to be back with his platoon in the war, known as the EOFW, a place he never wanted to relive again, but here he was. The compound consisted of stone and mud buildings rising out of a hot, windy desert. Hills in the distance hid an enemy position, pinning down his unit. Drone missiles, approaching from the direction of the enemy on a faraway hillside, sent a barrage of explosive strikes into their large compound.

An adjacent building burned, and a curtain of smoke gave cover for Troy to leave his position and join his squad in the central courtyard. Aiming and firing his rifle at several enemy soldiers entering the compound, he took a position in front of a medic dragging a wounded civilian through the courtyard gate. An armed sky drone swung around the corner of the burning building, targeting and killing the medic. The drone then flew into an open second-story window of an adjacent building.

Troy could tell the medic was dead, but he knew his unit would need the medic's bag. He stayed in the shadow where the drone could not target him, waiting for an opportunity to recover the bag. He knew the drone would target whoever tried to recover it. Seeing a glint of light in the dark window reflecting off the drone, he stepped out and showered the open window with rapid fire from his MK16. The destroyed drone exploded and fell out of the window to the ground. Troy made the short dash to grab the bag and check on the wounded civilian, also now dead.

The shadow army, who followed Troy up the front side of the mountain, now became the advancing enemy surrounding them.

From a covered, camouflaged portion of the courtyard, members of his platoon responded with pump-action grenade launchers on tripods firing round after round at the enemy nearing the front gates.

At the surrounding wall of the compound, a short distance outside the front gates, several mechanical AI fighting units provided a forward observer and front-line coverage. Expensive AI units weren't plentiful, and half of the ones assigned to Troy's platoon had been destroyed. The first targets were always the AIs. Troy ordered the AI communications unit accompanying him to calculate the distance for the two enemy positions he spotted on the hillside, and sent the coordinates to the unit controlling their own armed drones stationed two miles away.

The lieutenant ran over to Troy. "Two squads are pinned down on the west side of the compound. I need to relocate the grenade launchers so the squads can evacuate. I'm taking the only operating vehicles we have left."

Troy started to object, but the lieutenant ordered him to have his unit cover them as they drove out. "Then regroup your squad at the far end of the courtyard and wait for a chopper pick-up." They carried out the orders, giving cover as the remaining vehicles drove out, but Troy knew the odds of his squad leaving the courtyard alive would be slim.

The shadow army approached from the east compound gate and advanced toward them. Troy's squad of eight soldiers needed to cross a dusty open road in order to relocate to the far end of the compound, and rejoin the rest waiting for choppers. Crossing the road would expose them to enemy fire. He told his men to cross two at a time, to an abandoned building on the other side of the road. The rest of the team would provide heavy cover. The first two made it over.

The six soldiers left waiting in the courtyard heard a warning, *'Drones Incoming'* from the AI communications unit standing with Troy. The warning meant 60 seconds before their missile drones would cross above them advancing on the enemy position. Troy and the last squad member continued to draw enemy fire with their side arms as the next four soldiers quickly crossed the road. Waiting for their opportunity to leave the courtyard, Troy could see the drones flying high above them, headed for the enemy's hillside stronghold.

As Troy and the last soldier began to cross the road, an enemy missile targeting the overhead drones, missed and landed in the middle of the courtyard instead. A thunderous explosion and a blinding flash went up in a ball of flame. The courtyard walls flew apart in all directions with pieces of shrapnel, stone, dirt, and casing parts as lethal as any bullet showered the area. The AI communications unit erupted in fire and fell in the middle of the road. At the entrance to the building, the shockwave of the blast threw Troy through the door, temporarily stunning him. His vision blurred, as sight and sound jumble together. He saw parts of his teammate, who had been running behind him, lying in a pool of blood outside the door. More distant explosions followed, as the drones found their intended target and the enemy's hillside stronghold went up in mini-mushrooms.

Within seconds, the rest of the shadow army poured through the door and windows of the building. The sounds of battle, the fighting, and brutality surrounded Troy, just as he remembered it. Images of his team became blurs of motion: glimpses of uniforms moving, fighting, bleeding, soldiers falling. With no time for rifles and handgun ammunition spent, they were outnumbered.

Stumbling to his feet, Troy operated on raw strength and survival instinct, as he and every one of his squad engaged the enemy in hand-to-hand combat. Fear kept him fighting. He also felt a lust to kill, a rush from inflicting pain on those who tried to kill his friends; and hatred for the enemy, for the war, for what may be his demise. It was all there, electrifying and heightening with every blow he gave and received in return. *Fight! Kill the enemy! Stay alive!*

Troy remembered the faces of every man in his unit. During the battle he could see their expressions clearly, some with anger, some with hate, and some loving the adrenalin thrill of killing.

Others displayed only fear, a fear of losing or dying, or the pain in the moment they fell. Their faces would haunt him.

However, he couldn't see the enemy's faces. They hid in shadows. *The enemy has no face. Something is wrong with this scenario.* This wasn't exactly how it happened. *Our unit fought and won the battle. Air support came, destroying and turning them back. My squad killed or captured the rest of the enemy in the building. And we got to those choppers.*

But here in this altered reality, they were losing; his team members had fallen and were dying all around him. Kneeling down beside the body of the last soldier next to him, he looked around – all dead.

Troy shook his head in disbelief. He remembered only two of his team actually died that day, the medic and the soldier who ran behind him from the courtyard. *The demon is manipulating my memory—it has to be him.*

Chapter 14

When Troy realized he was not reliving the actual events of that terrible day, the fighting surrounding him suddenly halted. The battle sounds, along with his camouflage uniform disappeared. The demon stood in the broken doorway as its army of shadows scurried back beneath its wings. Its fiery eyes never blinked. Troy looked for his weapon, but it, too, vanished. Fear, the huge, ghastly Minotaur, approached, stopping several feet in front, towering over him.

Alone now, Troy swallowed hard. He was uneasy with Fear staring him in the face. If this was only the first demon, how would he survive four? He assumed four challenges would be what he must face, as four demon orbs had sped past him in his memory center and four doors flew by him. Would they pick him apart memory by memory? How could he defend himself? Troy felt helpless.

Fear was not normally in his wheelhouse, yet it literally loomed large in front of him and in a disturbingly frightening form. At the height of the battle, his adrenalin surged through him like the hot lava in the cracked skin of the demon. Though not proud of it, Troy admitted to himself he enjoyed the violence, heaping retribution upon the shadows that killed his friends, and staring down death. Now it stood staring him down. The hair on the back of his neck felt both hot and cold at the same time. Sweat rolled down the side of Troy's face.

Troy backed away, tripped and landed face up on a hard wooden floor. No longer on the dusty battlefield, he realized he lay looking up at the raftered ceiling of his cabin at Edmond Lake. He quickly got up and looked around, seeing that everything in the small living room was in its usual place. But he also knew it must be just a memory; the cabin had been hit by lightning and burned to the ground a year earlier. Unfortunately, he wasn't there at the time to try to save it.

He saw a drunken version of himself sitting on his living room couch, and suspected the demon sent him here as an observer. The steady hum of an electric fan replaced the loud sounds of combat pulling air through the open windows. A steamy summer night carried the sound of crickets chirping and tree frogs singing in the woods through the screens. The fan blew a continuous wave of humid air throughout the room.

Standing in his small kitchen behind the living room couch, Troy slowly walked around and stood a few feet away, watching himself drink long swigs of whiskey directly from the bottle. With a wide, unsteady swing of his arm, his drunk self tried to set the half empty bottle upright on the coffee table, tipping the bottle over and spilling a portion of it onto the tabletop. He picked up a couple of 3-D photos lying on the table and fumbled with them, trying to shake the whiskey off. Stopping to look at his parents and Tommy smiling back from the pictures, he frowned and tossed the photo cubes onto the couch next to him.

He wore only a pair of gym shorts and his chest glistened with sweat in the heavy night air. The fan across the room ruffled a lock of his damp, brown hair. Troy sighed at the drunken state he observed himself in.

"You're a mess," he said. Looking down at the coffee table, Troy was disturbed by what he remembered of this humid evening months before. On the table next to the whiskey bottle lay his semiautomatic pistol and a loaded magazine beside it.

Kneeling down, resting his elbow on the arm of the couch, he could see the dark circles under the eyes of his other self. "You know, I remember this night, when I, or we, wanted to end it all," pointing back and forth between the two of them.

"I'll admit we were pretty low; we were as low as we could get; the bottom of that bottle." Troy picked up the whiskey bottle, swishing the last drip of liquid in it, and set it back down. Looking with empathy at himself, he continued. "But nothing is so bad you gotta go this way, man. There's a reason for us to go on. I haven't figured it out yet, but there's a reason things happen the way they do. Maybe we just gotta trust the guy upstairs." The Troy on the couch picked up the magazine and shoved it into the pistol, chambering a round.

Troy knew Fear was presenting him with yet another memory that could destroy him, complete with the stifling humidity that invaded last summer. The creature seemed to know how to ratchet up Troy's anguish, knowing his fear went to a deeper, darker level which brought him to this point on a hot, humid night.

The Minotaur's shadow fell across the floor from the light in the kitchen. The faint smell of smoke wafted through the room as it stood behind him, without its band of shadowy followers.

Troy stood up as he watched himself contemplate the loaded gun. "Why are you showing me this?"

Fear stepped close behind him, and whispered into his ear with sour, hot breath brushing against Troy's neck. Stretching its leathery wings out, it wrapped them around Troy. Although he could feel heat coming off the body of the beast, a frigid chill ran down Troy's spine from the unspoken truth Fear knew about him. The touch of a pointed talon stuck into his shoulder blade.

"Because it haunts you contemplating the same path your father took."

Troy froze. There it was, buried under everything inside of him, a deeply hidden fear, lurking in the darkest fringes. The thought he might act on a heavily suppressed urge to take his own life someday, made him acutely aware of the leverage Fear would use against him. At the same time, Troy also considered the act of taking one's own life to be the ultimate selfish self-betrayal, an action which would damn his soul forever, if he truly believed he had one.

The demon Minotaur, Fear, continued to taunt him, sliding its hot breath across Troy's neck to his other ear. "You blame yourself for much. You bear the actions of others on your own shoulders. It always comes down to you, doesn't it? You failed them, why not end it all?"

Troy interrupted the demon, pushing its wings open and stepping away from it. "Oh, yeah? Well, I didn't go through with it," he said with irritation through clenched teeth. Then the other Troy, seated on the couch, emptied the chamber, ejected the magazine, and tossed it across the room. Picking up the half empty bottle of whiskey, he staggered out the screen door into the night.

Troy turned to face Fear. "I'm stronger than you think I am."

Fear spread his wings wide. "It is not this secret that will allow me to destroy you." It held a large paw out before Troy, beckoning, almost commanding, him to turn around and look.

****

Troy now stood in the hallway leading to his old lab, his leather jacket on and holding the duffle bag in his hand. *Just like that day!*

He faced the double glass doors, as he had moments before Tommy disappeared. However, he realized Tommy was still in the lab and alive! If he could move quickly enough, he might prevent the accident from ever happening. Troy dropped the bag and ran to the double doors.

He pushed on the doors with all of his strength, but they wouldn't open. Banging on them with his fists, he yelled Tommy's name. Through the glass he watched helplessly as Tommy disappeared—again. Anguish filled his heart as he dropped his head against the door in sad frustration.

Yes, this was his greatest fear: Tommy is still alive in a disassembled state and will remain so forever! The accident happened as a result of his own fault for not paying attention to the things which mattered most, not the business, or Sam Wong, but the people he loved. *And now, I have destroyed my own son!*

A rumbling echo of laughter filled the hallway, growing louder as Fear and his shadow army darkened the other end. On and on, they laughed. Troy saw his own image reflected in the glass door. Flames and smoke surrounded his reflection, though they were not actually in the hall around him. His troubled eyes stared back with the depth of fear he felt for his son, as well as for his own soul's loss of redemption.

"It must have been a very painful death," Fear shouted, spewing molten spittle, as he continued to laugh.

Troy sucked in his breath, tightening his lips. He tried to shake off the effect of Fear's memory-invoking power over him. On an academic level, he knew the fearful man in the glass couldn't be the true reflection of himself. He knew himself to be smart, brave, and an innocent man. But on an emotional level, he was losing all aspects of reality and crumbling inside. Troy knew he needed help here. Obviously, parts of his inner being would work against him, and Vincent, the only being who knew the truth, said he could not help him. His mind turned to the one source of strength he learned long ago; a source outside of his own control. Releasing his breath, Troy closed his eyes and desperately whispered, "Maker, if you remember me at all, please, help me."

Opening his eyes, a small point of light appeared in the door's glass directly in front of him. Taking the form of a three-dimensional object, it gradually grew into a bright magenta-colored key, hanging suspended deep within the glass.

Vincent had told him, *if you see a key, take it.*

Reaching up to touch it, his hand penetrated into the glass itself. Grabbing the key, Troy pulled it out clenching it tightly in his hand. A being made of light appeared in the glass, silhouetting Troy's own reflection; a translucent man, glowing in the same bright magenta color as the key, with Troy's same facial features. The light covered all aspects of the being and its clothing, also mirroring Troy's own clothes. But this was not just a reflection of himself in the glass, this was a separate individual. As the being glowed brighter, it spoke to him.

"I am a Grief Master. I am a warrior sent on your behalf, Troy Vincent. My name is Courage." The warrior stepped from the door and stood beside Troy in the hallway. Courage was as tall as Troy, and of the same build.

Troy felt a rush of his own courage surge throughout his body. It shot through every muscle, every artery, pumping power into his heart and brain. The weakness in his knees disappeared and strength returned to his arms and legs. The will to confront, fight, and defeat the enemy filled his spirit. He did not question the existence of this new ally. He welcomed it, mentally thanking his Maker.

Fear, on the other hand, did not welcome the emergence of this ethereal being. His dark figure doubled in size, his wings flaring open wide as he pointed in Troy's direction. He shouted orders to his army with orange lava spewing from his lips, "Kill them! Snuff out that light!"

The throngs of small deadly shadows made a steady advance up the hallway. Troy could not see the shadows, only the creeping darkness encroaching from the other end of the hall, the same way it crept up the mountainside. He could see, however, the flames welling up in the red eyes of Fear. He looked at Courage and compared the size of him to the larger demon, and his mind remembered a story of David and Goliath. "Can you make yourself bigger?" Troy asked.

"Size is no issue," responded Courage.

"Well, what do we use? Don't happen to have a slingshot, do you?"

"David said, God alone was his strength and his shield."

With that, the translucent figure pulled his only weapon from the glass, a mirrored shield, the size and shape of the door glass. He handed it to Troy, pulling a similar shield from the other door for himself.

"This is the Shield of Courage—with it, a boy can defeat a giant; and a man can defeat a shadow army." Courage slipped his arm through the handles on the back of the shield, holding the mirrored shield up in front of him. For a moment, Troy saw his own reflection again in the shield, only this time, he looked confident and strong. He slipped the shield onto his own forearm. Courage turned the mirrored side of his shield up toward the ceiling.

"What makes shadows disappear?" he asked.

"Light!" Troy answered with a new awareness.

Now it became obvious how to defeat the shadow army. Turning his shield up as well, Troy flipped on all the switches on the wall next to him. The overhead light flooded the hallway as the mirrored surface of the shields reflected and intensified it, bouncing brilliant beams of light into the crowd of dark demons. One by one, the advancing shadows began squealing and dissolving as they vanished, bursting into puffs of smoke. The carnage on the shadow army cleared the darkness, as Troy and Courage worked their way down the hall toward the demon Minotaur standing at the far end.

Seeing its army destroyed, Fear covered itself with its wings and fled. The two warriors advanced to the end of the hall until the last of the shadows were gone. Then Courage turned to Troy. "You must finish it, if you don't want to be controlled by Fear in the future. You must destroy the fear which exists inside you now."

Taking the shield from Troy, he added, "You will not need this. I am a part of you. Believe. Believe in yourself, Troy, and you will find the strength that is your shield, and I will be with you."

A leather strap appeared on the magenta key and he hung it around Troy's neck. Then the translucent being stepped into Troy's body and dissipated, disappearing. He looked down at the key pulsing with a magenta hue, and he could feel the positive change it brought within him. There was a new determination to succeed. Without hesitation, he continued on to confront Fear.

As the hallway faded away, Troy walked onto the dusty plateau of the canyon toward a diminished version of the creature who tormented him. This time, Fear stood with its back to the cliff's edge, the black leather wings hanging down submissively, and its black eyes void of smoke and flames. Puffs escaped its nostrils until it stood silently before Troy.

The magenta glow of Courage emanated around Troy, surrounding him with an aura of confidence. Troy lifted up the small key hanging around his neck. Brilliant magenta rays shot out between his fingers, bathing the demon in light.

Fear tried one last time to taunt Troy by contorting its own face and body to look like him, displaying the same look of fear he had reflected in the glass doors of the lab. Fear opened its mouth to speak, hoping to still have a crippling dominance over him, but Troy stopped it with his own command. "You have no more power over me."

He stepped toward Fear, who moved back until it wavered on the very edge of the cliff. Troy knew there was no place left in his life for Fear to hide and fester. It would no longer eat away at him with guilt from the inside. He would face it, own it, control it, and never let it overshadow him in the future, no matter how difficult or ugly it became. "I will not see you again, demon."

Forcing Fear to step backward off the edge, both the demon and the wide, dark canyon disappeared into nothingness. The vast crevasse closed, merging with the surface of the flat plateau. Calm, blue sky replaced the blustery clouds above. Then all of it faded away into oblivion. A wisp of curling mist crept back in, surrounding Troy's feet as he stood on a foggy path once again.

Courage stood beside him and nodded an approval of the victory. "Believe, and I am here always," he said. Somehow Troy knew he would never again be without this new companion, this Grief Master.

Now he knew what a Grief Master was, but why it appeared to him remained unclear. He had done nothing to deserve recognition from the Maker, if that's who sent this warrior, this arch angel. "You said you were sent here on my behalf. Who sent you?"

"You do not know?" Courage responded.

Troy looked down, his brows furrowed in puzzlement. "Well, I asked for help," he said.

"The answer will come to you."

Troy felt both grateful and ashamed at the same time. If the Maker had sent him help, then it proved the Maker truly existed. Decades of society's denial and insistence there was nothing greater than mankind made him feel small-minded. Frowning at the thought, he decided to sort it out later. Right now all he could muster was a simple thank you to the Grief Master standing next to him.

Chapter 15

Troy and Courage walked in silence along the iridescent pathway opening in front of them. A humming sound growing into a loud buzz came from behind and they both turned to look. Burning a hole through the fog, a gaping green vertical swirl appeared. As it widened into a portal, a woman crashed through it, falling down onto the path. Troy instantly recognized her as the brunette he had seen through the two-way window in the hearing room. She was prisoner 818, still wearing the numbered label on her upper left arm.

Scrambling to her feet, she pointed a laser weapon emanating a magenta light into the portal and fired. She briefly glanced over at Troy and his companion looking fearful and confused. Her attention immediately returned to the portal as a four-foot black spider appeared at the entrance and climbed through attempting to attack her. Firing her weapon continuously, she killed it. A smaller spider ran over the top of the dead one, and jumped onto the path. Troy took two steps and kicked it back into the portal, like a soccer ball into a net. The portal diminished in size, closing as the green swirl disappeared, leaving only white fog in its place.

Turning toward Troy and Courage, the young woman pointed her weapon nervously at both of them.

"Hold up! We're not your enemy!" Troy said.

She reluctantly loosened her grip on the gun, dropping it to the ground. Morphing from the gun, a magenta-colored light being stood up next to her revealing the young woman's own Courage Grief Master. The being was of similar female shape and size as Prisoner 818, and both of them stared at Troy and his magenta companion. Then Prisoner 818 blinked her eyes at Troy, swayed, and collapsed onto the path in a dead faint.

Vincent and the Grief Masters

****

When she opened her eyes, Troy was down on one knee, bent over her, propping her head up on his arm. Noticing his small magenta key dangling above her, she tried to regain her composure. She put her hand over the similar key hanging around her own neck. Troy nodded recognition of the key's meaning. Her eyes widened as she remembered who he was.

"I saw you…I saw you in the window of the courtroom."

"Yes, you did. It appears we both have had a bad day," Troy said, helping her to her feet. Seeing she was unhurt, he asked her a question. "Who are you and what are you doing in my VRC?"

"Your VRC?" she asked. "This is my VRC…I think." She tried to smooth her tangled hair, looking surprised that two VRC candidates could interact.

"Ok, let's just start with, who are you?" he asked again.

"My name is Loveena."

"Loveena?" She saw his eyebrows shoot up. She knew her Latin accent could be heavy at times, but she said her name clearly. Repeating it with emphasis and more slowly, she said, "Lo—vee—na."

She was feeling defensive ever since the courtroom hearing, and then the horrible encounter with her biggest fear: spiders, and not just any spiders, these were giant spiders! It spawned awful memories of childhood encounters in the swampy, lowland home of her relatives. She felt terribly on edge, with her hands still shaking. Rattling off her name again, she rushed through a testy introduction.

"My name is Loveena Maria Delgahta Baptista! And I don't know what I am doing here. I have done nothing wrong."

"Well, that makes two of us, lovey."

"And you are?" she asked with a hint of attitude. "And don't call me lovey."

They stared at each other in awkward silence. She bristled at the way his eyes did a quick run up and down of her.

"Troy," he said dryly. As he put his hands on his hips, pushing his jacket back, she blushed. She couldn't help but notice the well-defined muscles underneath his t-shirt. "Look, I think we have a problem. You can't be here."

"I can't be here? Well, I'm certainly not going back there," pointing to the wall of fog where the portal disappeared. Just the thought of returning to such a nightmare made her step closer to her own Grief Master. The woman and her glowing doppelganger clasped hands.

"Where are we? What is this place? I don't understand...."

Troy cut her off. "What is your crime?"

"I am innocent of any crime," she insisted.

"Of course, but what did they convict you of?" he demanded.

Is he interrogating me? She needed a friend in this terrible place, not another enemy, and she hadn't figured out yet which one he was.

"They said I murdered someone...a CEO." Loveena looked down, not liking the sound of such an accusation and knowing she could not commit such a violent act.

"Oh, yeah? Which one?" He bit his lip, crossed his arms in front of him, and looked down at the fog around his feet. She thought he wasn't taking her seriously.

"His name was," hesitating and rubbing her throbbing temple, "Hoy SamWong."

The man standing in front of her gazed up with a dark look in his eyes as his jaw dropped slightly open. Turning away from her, he ran a hand through his hair.

"What?" she asked. *That got his attention, but why? Did he know SamWong?*

"Great, this is just great." Troy walked around in a circle. "I can't believe this."

Loveena thought he was acting antagonistic toward her, like he believed she was guilty.

"Did you do it?" he asked in a terse tone.

"No, I didn't kill anyone," she answered emphatically.

Loveena didn't know what he might be thinking, but she knew she was as confused as he seemed to be. Why was he being so rude to her and how could she be thrown together with this man in the first place? So far, this VRC experience had been grueling, but she hoped to survive it. After all, she was innocent.

"And you? What's your crime?" she shot back.

He looked directly at her, hesitating to answer. Finally, he responded, "The murder of Hoy SamWong."

Loveena was livid. *I'm with the murderer?* Now she felt angry and scared at the same time. "What? Oh, my God, I'm going to die!"

Troy spoke loudly over her. "No one is going to die. At least, not in my VRC hell, if I can help it."

"Again, this is your VRC? How can it be your VRC?" she asked with frustration.

He put his hand up, motioning for her to calm down. "Now let's just think this through."

He turned his back to her, speaking to his Grief Master.

"We're both suspected of murdering SamWong, and without evidence, we're both condemned for it. Something's not right. Not only do we face demons that want to kill me, we now have demons who may want to kill her. Double jeopardy. This is not good news."

Loveena stood with her arms crossed, tapping her fingers impatiently. Noticing him out of the corner of her eye, she thought he appeared to be a strong man, someone who could possibly help her out of this mess. His rugged good looks were not lost on her either. *But is he really the murderer?* That could only lead to one outcome in the VRC. Sighing, she dropped her arms to her side and the stress of the moment overtook her. Turning away from him, she wiped a tear from her eye as her Grief Master placed an arm around her shoulder to give her strength.

****

Troy now thought he may have a worse dilemma. He wasn't sure how her being present in his treatment would affect his outcome, and he didn't really want her here. His anger was mixed. He knew she probably went through the wringer just now with her version of the Fear demon, just as he had. They both found magenta keys, and they both apparently found Courage as a Grief Master. But if she was lying and truly guilty, they would both pay for it in the end.

She must have been in the second VRC chamber in Vincent's workroom. He must have something to do with her ending up here. Troy suspected Vincent knew more than he let on. However, he didn't have time to stop and figure out what or why. He had no idea when another demon would appear, and whether it would be after him, or now, her.

Turning around to speak to Loveena, he saw her wipe a tear from her eye. It unnerved him. He never knew what to do around women who cried. He decided to give her the benefit of the doubt and show her a little compassion. Then she turned and darted an angry look at him.

"So, I have to know the truth—did you murder him?" she insisted.

Troy's decision to show empathy fizzled. Having her along would not be pleasant. "No, I didn't."

Tempering his patience, he spoke to all three standing in front of him. "We'll figure this all out, but we can't stay here. We need to find a way out." He started to ask a question.

"Courage..."

"Yes?" both Grief Masters answered at once. Troy stopped, and with a sigh, looked at Loveena.

"We can't have them both named Courage."

"Why not? That's who they are. I wouldn't have survived without her," Loveena answered.

Troy realized that was true for him, too.

Loveena's Grief Master spoke up. "I am also known as Strength, or Patience."

Troy looked pleadingly at Loveena. "Could you, maybe, pick one?"

Loveena looked at her Courage. "You are all those things to me. But for now, let's call you, Patience," smiling at her Grief Master, who smiled and nodded back an acceptance.

Narrowing her gaze at Troy, she added, "We're definitely going to need patience."

He understood her slight dig and responded with a half-smile smirk.

In the distance, the loud sound of a slamming door caused Loveena to jump. Turning toward the noise, the four of them saw a white door appear not far away. The iridescent fog curled back to reveal a path leading in its direction. The fog's sparkles lit up the passageway, beckoning the four of them to follow it.

Loveena hesitated. "I don't want to endanger anyone. Maybe I should stay here. I probably deserve this for some things I've done. Since you claim to be innocent, maybe you should go on ahead and find your own way out."

Troy assumed she could indeed be guilty of something, if not murder, if she so easily offered to give up. Or she may be thinking she'd have a better chance on her own. Suspecting Vincent might be monitoring their every move, he walked over to her. Troy had no actual evidence he could totally trust Vincent and until he did, he would think through everything carefully. There was some reason they were thrust together, so he assumed it would be best to stay that way.

Speaking quietly to her, he said, "No confessions here. It's dangerous, you understand? You don't know who might be listening." He took her by the elbow, making her walk beside him.

"As long as you're a guest in my world, such as it is, Hell Sweet Home, you're just going to have to come with me." Troy gazed down at her, noticing for the first time her deep brown eyes. He forced himself to look away from her beauty and back at the two Grief Masters, who followed close behind.

"Patience, Courage, and Miss Loveena Maria, whatever Baptista—we stick together, all of us." The three nodded in agreement.

Sparkling mist wisped through the air on either side of the path, preventing them from going in any other direction. The four walked in silence as the distant door began to open.

Chapter 16

Despite not being programmed to feel emotions, Vincent compared his interrupted work to the human word, *annoyance*. He preferred to be left alone to perform his duties; however a call from the VRC System Management office required his attention. Securing his private VRC location, Vincent made his way through the labyrinth of hallways. He had the power to teleport directly to the office, an ability he chose to keep secret. All twelve of the Brethren were capable of teleportation. It was a simple molecular restructuring of their nano robotics, like changing walls into doors, only it incorporated directional movement. However, their common consciousness agreed, the less their human handlers knew about their full range of capabilities, the safer they, and their mission, would be.

This was also true of his ability to project himself holographically. While the inventive photography had been known for decades, no one in the VRC System ever saw Vincent do it. He transmitted only to trusted sources and only received holographic transmissions from the same contacts. He reserved its use to track down members of the original Vincent scientific team or their descendants. This ability allowed him to see Troy in the motel bathroom three days ago. Once the criminal database posted an APB and the motel clerk identified Troy, Vincent knew where to look. He found him just moments before the police arrived. It gave him enough time to notify attorney, Donald Tyler, and secretly schedule Tyler onto the judging panel for Troy's hearing. It seemed to be the only way Vincent could bring Troy to him.

Scheduling Mr. Tyler for Loveena Baptista's hearing on the same day was, as Tyler put it, "A lucky break." Vincent already knew where she was, tracking her movements for months. But it perplexed him how to extract her from her situation with Hoy SamWong. He waited for the right time until he could wait no longer, literally rescuing her from SamWong's deadly grip.

One of the few times he risked exposing his transportation ability came on a night one week ago. He arrived in SamWong's private office just in time to stop SamWong from choking Loveena to death. Carrying her unconscious body out of the office and down the freight elevator, he laid her in the back seat of her car, then transported back into his VRC workroom.

Vincent never left anything to chance. He could calculate the probability and statistical outcome for almost every scenario. By changing a condition or anticipating a choice, he could narrow the probabilities to the expected results. But the challenges of the VR chambers were less predictable, especially with the rare appearance of a Grief Master. No statistical models existed which could calculate if, and when a Grief Master might appear. What he knew about Troy Vincent and Loveena Baptista led him to take a purely human action, to take a risk. He assumed the potential would merit the emergence of a Grief Master to come to the aid of his two VRC wards.

Like putting all of your eggs in one basket, he thought, recalling a human adage. He could not prevent the ordered judgments on the two of them, but he could advise them. Intervention was strictly forbidden by the VRC System Management, a condition of The Brethren working there. Still, he needed them to survive, in part, so they could help the mission in return.

Vincent rarely interacted with other security attendants in the hallways. Most of them moved quickly away whenever they saw him coming. Occasionally, he would stop by the lower level kitchenette to search for protein tidbits for his feline companion. If humans occupied it, they usually left. Embellished rumors of deadly encounters with the nano technology beings spread throughout the VRC System. When they moved to the VRC, two of his brothers reacted to aggressive challenges by several security attendants. A purely protective response unfortunately resulted in human injuries.

Punishment of the NTBs was wisely withheld to avoid any further confrontation. The management separated the twelve, so only one NTB served in each regional location, with four of them sent to overseas facilities. Total confinement from the outside world became the only requirement for any branch of the system accepting one of the androids. The VRCSM issued an order to monitor their activity. But the twelve easily circumvented the order by simply interrupting the security audio-visual signals.

Vincent kept a low profile and cooperated within his required restraints, while quietly continuing to perform the tasks to carry out The Brethren's revised mission. Some humans like attorney Don Tyler, who served society, also cooperated in secret with a group Tyler called, the Resistance. This group believed the time for radical change approached, shifting the reins of power from the hands of the extremely wealthy back to the hands of the people. Their goal required toppling the small group of wealthy CEOs controlling Corporate Rule and re-installing democracy in as many countries as possible.

Their secret ranks attracted the most intelligent minds, such as Samuel Baptista, Loveena's father. He befriended Vincent when the androids were acquired by SWI. Along with Tyler and others like him, they implemented a plan which would benefit both the Resistance and The Brethren's mission.

The NTBs pledged to complete their revised mission: to find and relocate any members of the original scientific team if still alive, or members of their extended families. Relocation was dangerous and permanent, and cloaked in secrecy. Therefore, the androids offered it only to those whom they could trust. Being loyal to their creators, when the acquisition separated them from the scientific team, The Brethren promised to help and protect their extended families. They were the closest thing each of them had to a family of their own. Logic mandated they revise their mission in this way, giving their common consciousness a new purpose.

Some of the original team no longer survived, such as Dr. Vincent. Rumors spread that SWI did not want the details of the androids' full capabilities known to the public and began arresting the scientists, charging them with bogus crimes, in order to silence them. Some team members vanished, never to be seen again. Others sought the protection of small pockets of the Resistance and were relocated for their own safety.

Vincent had been looking for Dr. Vincent's son, Troy, for some time. He scanned through internet records of employment, medical and health records, and criminal complaints. There was no record of Troy after his business was acquired. Vincent remained certain Troy would not take the path of his father. He surmised Troy may have removed traces of himself from society to avoid the fate which befell the original team. So when his name appeared in the police record, Vincent quickly honed in on his location.

****

Vincent emerged from the elevator onto the administrative level. The mid-morning sun streamed through the skylights high above as he moved across the expansive atrium. Tall palm trees stretched their leaves as high as possible to soak up a few hours of warm rays. Tiny flowers in brick flower boxes ran down the middle of the walkways, adding the only touch of color in the drab hardscape. Vincent noted the flowers seemed in need of nitrogen, magnesium, and potassium, and sent a message to the facility's groundskeeper.

A Muzak version of Claude Debussy's *Clair de Lune* blared from speakers mounted at the base of each potted palm tree. While the slow, quiet melody written by the French master of impressionist music was not on his list of favorites, Vincent thought the Muzak arrangement a perversion of an otherwise excellent piece of work. In fact, in his tenure within the system, he observed a great many musical works by the brightest of composers were rudely violated by being turned into Muzak tracks.

Whenever possible, he fouled the electrical connections, redirected the signal to the original composition and artists, or just turned the Muzak off. It became his form of civil protest. *Someone has to stand up for the composers.*

His creator, Dr. Vincent, showed great appreciation for all types of music by continually playing it while Vincent was built and programmed. A full historical record of humanity's music resided in his database, intended to be carried into space and introduced to another part of the galaxy. He deduced Muzak could not be an original art form of any kind, but a poor substitution not worthy of the audio receptors of humans or androids. The simple beauty of *Clair de Lune* was further ruined by the constant crackling emitted by bad wiring in the old speakers. *If it wasn't for that, the arrangement would render humans comatose.*

He walked by a two-man janitorial crew sitting lazily on one of the benches. Vincent passed them sitting beneath one of the trees and they appeared to be asleep. He cupped his mechanical hands together behind his back and pointed his index finger to the old dented speaker at the base of the palm tree. A bolt of charged electrons shot from his finger into the speaker racing along the wires to the facility's audio control room. The music throughout the atrium abruptly stopped with a loud crack and a fizzle. A few seconds later, another selection replaced it with an original recording of *In the Mood*, performed by the Glenn Miller Orchestra. The trombones and trumpets blared through the old speakers with a loud swing beat. Opening their eyes and yawning, the sleepy crew got up, stretched, and went back to work. With the melodic change achieving its intended effect, Vincent continued on his way to the management office without slowing his progression.

He startled the young clerk as she turned around in her chair to find Vincent towering over her desk. Her eyes widened with a momentary fear before she recognized him. Leaning back, she held her digital tablet protectively in front of her. "They're expecting you in the conference room." She pointed to the frosted glass door behind her.

Vincent moved on, saying nothing. The clerk waited for him to pass, then picked up her coffee cup and quickly left the office.

Before the door opened, Vincent could see who waited inside through his nanobits connection with the molecules in the walls. The head of Security, Chief Allen Michaels, sat at the long conference table. A middle-aged man, who managed the regional facility Vincent was assigned to, appeared in his usual casual work attire: a long-sleeve white shirt with the cuffs rolled up, loosely buttoned at the top with his tie pulled away from his neck. The android assumed the chief chewed on the stick of a sugar confection called a sucker, to avoid the human habit of smoking. Vincent could also see the internal signs of lung damage hidden in the man's chest. The chief was a tall man, whose once-muscular body now reflected a condition of an aging, sedentary life. Well regarded by the security attendants under his leadership, Vincent knew him to be a good and trustworthy human.

The chief scrolled through the incarceration record of Troy Vincent on a small suspended monitor hanging in front of him. Paper documents lay scattered on the table next to an open file folder on his left. Another man in a gray pinstripe suit paced the length of the room. Vincent held his hand up in front of the door, and with a forward motion of one finger, the door opened on its own.

"Chief Michaels, you sent for me?" Vincent asked in his deep raspy voice.

The chief looked up. "Come on in, Vincent, have a seat." As he moved his hand across the monitor, it closed and disappeared. He gathered up the documents, tapping them together on the table and placed them back in the folder, handing the file to the other man. Leaning back and rocking casually in his chair, Security Chief Michaels addressed Vincent.

"Just a reminder before we get started," motioning for the android to take a seat at the table across from him. "Please don't mess with the Muzak system. If you break it, I don't have money in the budget to fix it. Understood? Good."

The chief continued, "And please don't scare my secretary. She's told me how you've startled her in the past. Good help is hard to find. She talks on her phone a lot, but she's a pretty good kid."

Vincent sat down in a leather chair opposite his superior. His cloaked head hung down, with only a portion of his chrome jaw visible. "I do not try to scare her. She becomes nervous at my appearance."

"Come on, you don't need to hide yourself from me. I'm your friend, remember?" Vincent respected the chief, who he observed treated all of his employees with a fair and equal attitude. But he sensed a tension from his superior and concluded it may have something to do with the other man in the room. The chief's tone was more commanding than usual.

"I prefer it if you and I can talk without barriers," Michaels said, pointing to Vincent's hood. "Please, let's talk mono e mono, face to…mask."

Vincent removed his cloak from his head. The ceiling light above him bounced off the shiny chrome of his skull, projecting a small circular reflection on the wall behind him. His dark facial mask void of any display, looked directly at his boss seated across from him. The man in the pinstripe suit walked up to the chair next to the chief and stared at the android.

Michaels pulled the sucker stick from his mouth, tossing it into the nearby trashcan. He leaned forward and folded his arms in front of him on the table.

"Give me something to work with here. Show me a face I can talk to."

Vincent complied with the request, choosing a face reflecting his civil disobedience to the forced employment at the facility. He placed his mechanical arms on the table and leaned forward to mimic his superior's body language. Slowly he revealed a face to suit his position, the face of a chimpanzee appeared duplicated on both sides of his mask. The eyes blinked, and an animated mouth moved with his words.

"Will this do?" he asked, with a chimpanzee squawk at the end of the question.

Chief Michaels looked down with a half-smile, leaning back.

"No. How about the real Vincent? The one I can count on to cooperate with me."

The chimpanzee face disappeared and Vincent's monitor reflected his own face, with the hollow chrome eyes and the skeletal nose. He manipulated the mask to automatically lengthen down past his chin and include an animated mouth, which would move in sync with the words he projected.

The other man sat down. Continuing to stare, he sternly furrowed his brows and pursed his lips, never taking his eyes from Vincent.

Chapter 17

Chief Michaels began. "This is Mr. Adams. He's an attorney and on the panel of judges who reviewed case number 924 a couple of nights ago. Mr. Adams is opening an investigation on some underground subversives, possible members of a resistance group."

"Hello," said Adams gruffly.

Vincent only nodded.

The chief continued. "I understand you commandeered two prisoners from other security attendants while on their way to their assigned VRCs, one of them being prisoner 924."

"I merely pointed out they had misread the assigned VRC section."

"One of the security attendants has been employed here a long time. I have no reason to doubt him."

"Check the paperwork." Vincent knew the electronic records would back him up.

Michaels uncomfortably adjusted himself in his chair, raising his brows doubtfully, looking at Vincent with concern. The attorney interjected himself into the conversation.

"I have reason to believe there are attorneys sitting on judging panels who are undermining this judicial system," Adams said, firmly tapping the table with his right index finger. "These attorneys don't like the corporate restructure, nor do they like who controls the wealth and the economy in the world today. Do you understand what I mean?"

Vincent did not respond.

Adams went on. "We, the CEOs of the world, of which I will soon be a part of, once the SWI Board takes their vote to replace Hoy SamWong…"

Chief Michaels interrupted, explaining the remark to Vincent. "He's the General Counsel for SWI, not the CEO...yet."

"Yes, yes, the General Counsel *now*," Adams replied arrogantly. "But I have every confidence they will pick me to lead the largest corporation in the world."

The chief mouthed the words to Vincent, with little respect in his voice. "He's a lawyer."

Vincent knew from past experience Chief Michaels did not like attorneys meddling in VRCSM's internal affairs.

Adams impatiently jumped back into his statement, clearing his voice.

"Uh-hum. As I was saying, these other attorneys may be participating in a form of subversive anarchy. They want to decentralize the seat of power and want an end to the VRC system. They want prisoners set free and turned back onto the streets. I personally believe prisoners deserve the punishments for which they are condemned."

Adams continued his description of corporate traitors. "There are factions who want outdated ways of the past reinstated, such as free speech, ridiculous civil liberties, and dangerous religious rights. These things have been forbidden for a reason. They destabilize the world. Are you aware of any of this?"

The Security Chief responded for Vincent. "I don't think Vincent's time in the lower halls of the VRC System is spent reading the news of the outside world. It would be irrelevant to him. Right, Vincent?"

Again, Vincent did not answer.

Adams now went into his stern, accusatory court room persona. "You were seen talking to someone in the hallway, possibly an attorney who sits on a judging panel?"

Vincent looked at the attorney. "Is it now forbidden to speak in the hallway?"

The attorney continued his impromptu cross examination. "Did this attorney discuss with you case number 924? Or the case of a young woman, case number 818?"

Again, Vincent thought it would be prudent to not respond.

The attorney rose from his chair and began pacing the length of the table. Turning back, he narrowed his beady eyes and wagged a finger at Vincent.

"It has been reported you have been seen in the company of transmitted holograms. Do you deny it?" Not giving Vincent any time to answer, he rushed immediately into another question. "It's my understanding the VRCSM has rules against attendants discussing case details with any attorney. Do you discuss details with attorneys?"

Vincent looked at Chief Michaels and wondered why he was not taking a more proactive role in the conversation. These questions seemed to be unusual protocol.

Adams leaned over the table on his fingertips. "Who are you working with? Has more than one attorney approached you? Or did you approach them?"

Turning toward Adams, Vincent said, "I have not approached any attorney."

"Do you know an attorney named Leigh?"

Vincent responded, "No."

"Do you know an attorney named Berry?"

Again, Vincent answered, "No."

Raising his voice, Adams leaned further over the table, demanding a positive response from the android. "What about Robertson? Do you know an attorney named Robertson? Prisoners have disappeared and I know someone is helping you."

He pounded his fist on the table. "Just tell me who it is!"

Vincent was not sure how he would answer if asked about an attorney named Don Tyler. He would not lie about it, but the repercussions of the truth might be grave.

Chief Michaels put his hand out in front of the attorney to calm him down. "Mr. Adams, please sit down. I believe it is safe to say Vincent has had no contact with people you may be having trouble with in the judging chambers."

The chief then addressed his employee. "Our job here today, Vincent, is to clarify each of our responsibilities. Mr. Adams here represents his clients and is responsible for passing judgment on cases. I provide a facility and method for that judgment to be carried out. You are responsible for making sure it gets done. Are we clear on that?"

Vincent responded, "It is clear Mr. Adams represents his client and employer, SamWong Industries. It is clear he has concerns about attorneys who may not share his views. My concern is the welfare of those condemned. Who speaks for them? Or, are they already condemned before anyone speaks?"

Adams bristled at Vincent's innuendo. "Have you ever been asked to conjure up a Grief Master to come to the aid of a prisoner?"

"I have been asked only to monitor the VRC experience."

"All right, and the chief here assures me you do it well. But it has been rumored your kind can influence an outcome, that you have some power to contact Grief Masters...."

Vincent interrupted, "I have no influence. Nor can I 'conjure up' a Grief Master. I do not believe they can be turned on and off, like a light switch. They are either already present within the human or they are not."

Adams scoffed, "There's no scientific evidence that they exist at all."

"You don't think they exist?" asked Chief Michaels. Adams turned the ends of his mouth down, shaking his head.

The chief looked at Vincent. "How about you, Vincent? Do you think they exist?"

"I am not programmed to understand the elements of a human soul."

"I didn't ask you about the human soul, I asked you if you think Grief Masters exist?"

Vincent paused before answering. Questions about the human soul made him aware of his lack of data on the subject.

"It is irrelevant what I think. It is for humans to make that determination, since it appears to be a human mystery."

Adams smirked. "Typical rhetoric from a robot. It just doesn't compute, huh?"

Vincent had not finished. "But if I must provide you with an answer, from what I have witnessed, I believe the Grief Masters and the human soul are one and the same."

The two men were silent as they absorbed what Vincent said. Chief Michaels cupped his hands together in front of his chin, elbows resting on the table, and leaned forward, looking into the eyes of the face Vincent had chosen to project for the meeting. Michaels appeared to contemplate the unexpected response, as though he was considering it had merit. "So you believe some men have souls, while others do not?" he asked. "That's quite a human observation, Vincent."

Mr. Adams stood up, straightening his suit coat and tie. Appearing irritated by the lack of information provided, he also looked into Vincent's false projected face, his bushy gray eyebrows drawn together in contempt for the android. "The head of the World Board of Directors, an extremely important man, has been murdered. Someone needs to pay for that murder. Two people have been identified and judged for the crime. If you have those prisoners, I want to see body bags—two of them!"

With the attorney's outburst, Chief Michaels abruptly stood up, ending the conversation.

"Vincent knows his place here, Mr. Adams. I don't think we need to be concerned about the outcome. Your SWI will get the justice they've PAID for."

The chief turned back to Vincent, giving a brief nod and a polite smile. "You can go back to your work now. Just remember who you work for."

Vincent thought it odd Chief Michaels' remark about who he worked for was the same thing attorney Don Tyler had said to him. The chief assumed Vincent worked for the VRCSM, while attorney Tyler assumed he worked for the Resistance. However, both men were incorrect, as Vincent considered he worked for The Brethren's mission.

The android remained seated as the Security Chief walked to the door and exited, followed by the attorney. After the chief was out of the room, Mr. Adams stopped short of leaving, turning back toward Vincent. "I know everyone is afraid of you and your kind, your power and secret activity. Yes, we know you interrupt the security monitoring. You robots make your own rules."

He sneered at Vincent with contempt. "SWI was right to lock you up. Mark my words we are trying to find a way to destroy you, you and your band of sideshow freaks. You're all going to wind up as computer scrap at the bottom of the ocean. And I will personally make sure of it!"

He turned, grabbing the door handle. "Remember," he commanded, "Two body bags by the end of the week!"

He forcefully pulled on the handle, but it wouldn't open. Vincent swiveled his chair to face the attorney at the door. The android had sealed the door with nanobits flowing from his feet through the floor and into the door's structure. The attorney pulled repeatedly on the handle, furiously working it back and forth. Finally, his face red with rage, Adams turned toward Vincent and spoke through clenched teeth.

"Open this door," he growled.

Vincent's projected face chosen for the meeting, disappeared and his mask returned to its original size and shape. A yellow banner scrolled across the smoky glass lenses of the mask that read, *Have a Nice Day*! followed by a string of laughing, happy faced emojis. The fuming attorney let out a long, loud breath, sounding like a whistling teapot. Vincent released control of the door and the infuriated attorney swung the door wide, almost hitting himself in the nose, before exiting the room.

Vincent swiveled back to the table, sending an encrypted radio signal to the eleven NTBs and mission Counsel. It silently scrolled across his mask: URGENT: your presence or hologram required, joint meeting, midnight tonight, EST. Coordinates: EARTH.

Chapter 18

Loveena felt like she was being dragged by her left elbow. Troy had such a vice-like grip on her arm, the circulation to her hand seemed cut off. Her fingers were growing numb.

"May I have my arm back, please?" she asked, frowning as she pulled away from him.

"Only if you keep up." Releasing his grip, they looked defensively at each other. "Please," he added.

Loveena kept walking, but slowed her pace, forcing Troy to slow down. She wanted to ask some questions before they undoubtedly would encounter another terrifying situation. Rubbing her forearm and hand to release the prickling pain of blood rushing back into it, she approached the question in a calmer manner this time.

"So…truthfully, did you kill Sam Wong or not?"

Troy responded, raising an eyebrow. "I thought you did; or, according to the court records, we both did."

She stopped on the foggy path. "I don't remember." She rubbed both of her temples in slow circles, trying to recall the events that happened a week ago.

"What do you mean, you don't remember?" Troy asked with sarcasm in his tone. "It seems to me you would remember killing someone."

"He was choking me, trying to kill *me*. I just don't remember anything after that. I must have passed out. Then I woke up in the back seat of my car."

If I had killed him, maybe my memory is blocking it out. She felt innocent, but no one else was there at the time to prove it. *I'm glad he's dead.* However, the thought of committing such a crime upset her. She never hurt anyone in her life, no matter how they treated her, and Hoy SamWong treated her very badly, indeed.

"Why was he trying to kill you?"

"He wanted to control me. I let him until I just couldn't do it anymore. I couldn't give him what he wanted." Feeling herself blush under Troy's penetrating gaze, she looked down to avoid his eyes. They continued walking as he questioned her further.

"How did you know SamWong?"

"I worked for him. I was…" she paused, trying to find the right words. Loveena wanted Troy to be truthful with her, so she thought it best to do the same. "He ordered me to spy on his competitors and enemies. He wanted their secrets, business or personal, to use against them, to blackmail them. He said there would be things only I could get from them…in a very personal way."

"Industrial espionage?" Troy chuckled and rudely implied, "You mean, you were his high-class call girl sent to get dirt on his competition?"

Loveena objected, grabbing his arm. "No, it wasn't like that!" She didn't want him thinking she slept with men 'to get dirt,' as he called it. She was smarter than that.

"Then how was it?"

She took a deep breath, letting it out in a heavy sigh. It seemed just too complex a situation to explain in a few words. Maybe if they had more time and not stuck in such a dangerous place, she could tell him the whole story. "Look, I have a degree in psychology. He wanted me to use those skills to get into their heads, manipulate them, or seduce them, if necessary, to get them to do what he wanted, willingly or unwillingly. He was a very cruel and paranoid man. I didn't enjoy the job."

"It doesn't take a degree to jump into bed with someone. Did you? Sleep with them?"

Surprised by his bold question, she narrowed her eyes at him. "That's none of your business."

Leaning closer, Troy stared back into her eyes. "I was one of his enemies, did you spy on me? Believe me I would have remembered if you slept with me." His eyes briefly traveled down her body and back up, meeting her angry, dagger-stabbing eyes.

Loveena raised her hand to slap him. He intercepted her wrist, gripping it hard between them. A long moment of uncomfortable anger passed, transforming into a truce. "I'm sorry. I probably shouldn't have done that," she said flatly.

Releasing her wrist, he looked away from her. "No. I'm sorry. I was rude, taking my frustration out on you. Let's just forget it." He walked on.

Loveena remained standing where she was, wondering how to work with this man who might stir unwanted feelings in her, and yet, be the only one here who could help her. She couldn't deny she felt a spark of attraction toward him. "Who did you say you are?"

Turning around, he walked back to her. "Troy Vincent, owner of Vincent Scientific Applications, and competitor of one dead, Hoy SamWong. Ring any bells? Or my father's company, the original VSA, Inc.?"

She slowly nodded. She did know of VSA, Inc. Wanting to settle any suspicions he had, she quickly told him the merger occurred before she started working for SamWong. Furthermore, she happened to be in another city working on an assignment when Troy's subsidiary company was acquired. Loveena wanted to sit down and explain it all; the constant blackmailing threats from SamWong to kill her father, the physical abuse he unleashed upon her if she refused him. However, the unrelenting white fog surrounding them, like SamWong himself, showed no respite, nor place where they might stop, for even a moment. The bright cloud-like floor below their feet led in one direction only, toward the open door ahead of them.

She sensed Troy's demeanor toward her grow cold. Quite sure he would never trust her now, she tried to reassure him. "You have to believe me. I had nothing to do with VSA, or you, or what happened to your father, I swear it."

Appearing to be all business now, Troy spoke with little emotion in his voice. "We're going to have to work together if we stand a chance of surviving. I have to know I can trust you, and you can trust me. So I'm going to ask you one question and I want the truth," he said.

"Yes, of course."

"Did they put you in here to make sure I'm eliminated? Do I have to watch my back from you, too?"

"No. I think they put me in here to keep me from talking. I knew things about Hoy no one else knew." Loveena smirked, "And by the way, that was two questions."

Troy's fingers on his left hand drummed along his thigh as he slowly turned away from her. However, he appeared to be satisfied with her answer.

"My guess is somebody wants to get rid of me, too."

She hesitantly touched his arm, trying again to reassure him. "Hoy was my enemy just as much as he was yours."

They continued toward their next challenge in silence. She could tell he was being extremely cautious, probably questioning everything she said. He seemed to observe every detail of their surroundings, bracing for what could be around any corner.

Loveena decided to steer the conversation away from SamWong. "That mechanical guy, the robot, what is he?"

"His name is Vincent, and he's not a robot. He's a highly advanced AI android."

"He has a name?"

Troy nodded, slowing his pace to walk beside her again. "So you were in the VR chamber behind the curtain? He's forcing us together somehow. He wanted us to meet. Did he say anything to you?"

"Only something about a safe house and to look for keys."

"Yeah, that would be them," pointing his thumb toward the two Courage Grief Masters trailing behind them. He stopped and turned to their new companions.

"May I speak privately to her?" They nodded, condensing into two beams of magenta light, and shooting back into the keys hung around Troy's and Loveena's necks. Now alone, Troy continued. "He mentioned the Grief Masters to you?" he asked.

"Yes."

"Have you ever heard of them before?"

"Just old stories, whispers I heard as a child. There are believers who say they have saving powers; calling them 'masters over grief.' The old women used to say they are the things which surround and sustain us, and we must cling to them in the worst of times. Being a child, I wasn't sure what they meant, and I'm still not sure because here we are, locked inside this horrible place. I can't remember the names they went by, but I know one of them was called Courage." Smiling down at her softly glowing key, Loveena continued. "I also remember no one spoke of them openly, just like they don't speak of the Maker. It's not acceptable; it's even forbidden to say his real name, or any deity's name, for that matter."

"So you think Grief Masters only appear to believers?"

Loveena could see this troubled him.

"You found a key, like I did. You found a Grief Master who helped you." Stuttering with uncertainty, "You...you must have been...at one time, like me. Are you a believer, Troy?"

"I am not," he firmly answered.

"It doesn't make sense. I was taught only a believer could recognize them. It may be the only thing which can save us. So, if you're not a believer, then you're...."

"I'm what?" he interrupted with irritation in his voice. "Not gonna make it? That one of these demons is gonna finish me just because I choose *not to believe*?" He began walking ahead of her again. "I only believe in myself."

Stepping quickly to catch up with him, Loveena couldn't understand his cross behavior. They were stuck here together, and there was no need for him to be angry with her; after all, she didn't put him in here. Now walking beside him and matching his faster pace, her own irritation grew. She challenged him.

"If you think you can do this alone, then why don't you take off that key? Just throw it away into the fog."

She pointed to the pulsating key hanging partway down his chest, casting a soft magenta glow against his white t-shirt. With her other hand, she protectively grasped the key around her own neck. Not only glad she had it, but thankful to know she could still be considered a believer. After everything in her past, pushing herself further and further away from the quiet lessons she learned as a child, Loveena considered it a sign she was still worth saving; her damaged soul still might be salvageable. Lifting her key to her lips, she gently kissed the gift she perceived came from a forgiving Maker. Her magenta warrior of Courage-slash-Patience reappeared beside her. Falling behind Troy on the path, they both stopped and awaited his answer to Loveena's question.

Troy looked down inconspicuously and rubbed his fingers along the key. Without responding to her question, he continued walking up the path. Loveena smiled to herself as she saw his Courage Grief Master reappear beside him, matching his every step.

****

As the four approached the door to the second chamber, a rush of cold air greeted them. The door widened, growing larger until it enveloped them and dissolved away. Standing in a frozen winter landscape, pockets of icy mist hung in the air, appearing grey against the twilight sky. A shallow blanket of snow covered the ground and a forest of leafless trees stood silent before them. There were no birds, no forest life, and no sounds of any kind filling this silent world.

The loud slamming of a door broke the eerie silence, startling both of them. Looking back, they could see the iridescent path disappear, immersing them on all sides by the lifeless forest. Loveena shivered and crossed her arms in front of her for warmth. Troy knew her tank top and short jacket probably wouldn't keep her warm here. Removing his leather jacket, he draped it over her shoulders. Reluctantly, she took it, putting her arms through the warm sleeves. Giving him a slight smile, she whispered, "Thank you."

He wondered why their clothing didn't change to suit the situation, as it had in the chamber of Fear. He was still in the clothing he wore when first entering the VRC. Realizing each chamber could be different Troy suspected this one would use the element of weather against them. The icicles hanging down from tree limbs told him the conditions in this chamber included freezing rain. He looked up into the grey sky as a light snow fell.

Will this demon try to freeze us to death? Noticing Courage and Patience were unaffected, he only needed to concentrate on keeping Loveena and himself warm and dry. Having given her his jacket, he could feel the cold.

"It's snowing!" Loveena said with a short giggle.

"Don't get too excited, I don't think it's meant to be enjoyable," Troy replied.

A path of wide flat stones wound its way into the dark forest in front of them, as though it was meant to be followed. Snow melting from the tops of the stones made their appearance as round puddles surrounded by fluffy white tufts.

Taking a step onto the first flat stone, Loveena delighted in a pastel blue color that suddenly lit up from the stone beneath her foot. Stepping onto the next stone, Troy grabbed her arm. "We stick together here," he warned.

Searching her eyes with a seriousness conveying concern for their safety, Loveena nodded in response. She continued on, taking each step slowly. Troy watched her as the different pastel colors of each smooth stone brought a smile to her face. As the toe of her shoe touched the fourth stone, a booming voice reverberated through the frozen, silent air. It sounded like whoever could be watching them was thunderously clearing its throat. Loveena stumbled backward across the stones, illuminating each one again, knocking hard into Troy's chest. He grabbed her to keep her from falling, as the two Grief Master warriors protectively stepped around either side of them, and stood in front.

"Let me introduce myself," the voice declared in a deep, commanding British accent. "I am Loneliness." It spoke with a slow, deliberate and unemotional tone. Troy could not tell where the sound came from. *This still air could carry the voice from miles away or, he could be close by us.*

"I would love to get to know you, as I don't get many visitors. But alas, I will eventually separate and destroy you," it announced. "Furthermore, you will die knowing the pain of failure and the knowledge of your own pitiful worthlessness."

"Great," Troy whispered into Loveena's ear. "Is this one of your demons?"

The British voice, coming from everywhere around them, continued with its formal introduction.

"You will feel the cold isolation of the unwanted. You will leave no trace, no mark upon your world; no legacy to prove you ever existed. So, let's get started, shall we? Here's wishing you both good luck, old chaps."

The voice trailed off with a diminishing echo of "old chaps," across the frozen forest until dead silence returned once again. For a moment, Troy and Loveena stood motionless, their mouths agape with stunned surprise.

Loveena inched backward as close to Troy as she could. Startled at first, he blinked away his temporary trepidation and pointed his finger over her shoulder at the two warriors in front of them. "It can't be their demons, and it certainly isn't mine. It's gotta be one of yours."

They looked down the path into the darkening forest as the sky turned from grey to a dark midnight blue. The snow began falling faster. She turned to Troy, nodding fervently, "We stick together."

This time, Troy took the lead down the stony path as they walked deeper into the forest, each pastel stone softly glowing until the group and the colorful stones disappeared into the dark.

Chapter 19

The snow continued until it covered the stepping stones and made them indistinguishable from the rest of the forest floor. The light emitted from the stones grew dimmer until finally disappearing under the accumulating snow. Troy made his way through the trees by instinct. He knew his way through a dark forest and often took long walks through the woods at Edmond Lake. He could navigate even on a moonless night, such as this.

Loveena followed close behind him. The only lights visible were the keys around their necks and the slight magenta aurora surrounding them. Their Courage warriors, having returned to their respective keys, gave the two human travelers strength from within themselves. The eerie night sky remained windless, silent, and barren of starlight.

"If Loneliness had a face," Troy whispered, "this would be it."

Loveena stumbled, causing them to stop. As she held onto him to steady herself, Troy saw a tiny shadow run from beside her foot. "What was that?" he said.

"I don't know. I felt a prick, something cold touched me when I tripped; a tree root maybe."

A small four-legged creature ran from behind a tree, jumping on the calf of her leg. She cried out in pain, "Ouch! It bit me!"

Troy's eyes became accustomed to the dim light of the forest. He could see the creature's movement in the dark and tried to stomp on it with his heavy boot. It easily avoided him, jumping from side to side in the snow. As it took off running, he saw more movement on the ground and rodent-sized critters closing in all around them. Hissing and bearing teeth of ice, they began to lunge.

"Come on!" Troy grabbed her hand. They ran through the trees, but the speedy critters ran faster, darting in and around tree trunks, ferociously nipping at their heels. Loveena cried out as one ran up a tree trunk and jumped onto her arm. She knocked it off with her hand and kept running.

Troy passed tree after tree, avoiding low hanging limbs. Out of the corner of his eye, he could see the fast agile critters gaining ground and climbing tree trunks just ahead of them. Passing a creature in a nearby tree, he caught a glimpse of it – a small, four-legged, rat-like creature covered with white fur that helped it blend into the snow. Its claws and canine teeth looked like daggers of small, sharply pointed icicles. It jumped at Troy and he averted it by batting it away with his fist. The icy creature went tumbling down to the forest floor, shattering into pieces as it hit the base of a tree. Observing their fragility, Troy hit as many as he could, and they too, broke into pieces of ice shards. The knuckles on his left hand bled from the contact with their hard, icy bodies, leaving a bloody trail in the snow.

It became harder for Troy to hang on to Loveena's hand. Finally, she broke from his grasp as a small horde of the mean little critters jumped together from a tree onto her shoulder. Fighting them off as she ran, she tossed them one by one to the ground, leaving shattered ice in her wake. However, she was getting farther away from Troy as she ran blindly through the forest. Pulling a creature off of his arm and kicking one near his boot, Troy started after her. He could see her approaching what appeared to be a steep drop off next to the edge of the forest. Yelling for her to stop, he was afraid she couldn't hear him as she frantically worked to free a creature tangled in her hair.

"Loveena! Loveena!" he yelled louder, but it was too late. Tumbling over the edge, she rolled uncontrollably down the hillside. As he got to the edge of the embankment, he could see the shattered bodies of creatures she carried over the side. Their icy reflection picked up in the dim shine of the snow. A small snowy avalanche continued sliding down to the bottom of the mountain, sending a cloud of frosty particles into the air. Broken pieces of creatures here and there rolled down the hill, but no sign of Loveena, and no sound.

Again he called to her, searching for some way to get down the mountain. The blackness of the night surrounded him and now even the snow had no reflection to help him see. The icy critters seemed to have vanished. Troy looked for a way down through the deep snow as he walked across the top of the ridge. There appeared to be no way down and he collapsed, sitting down in the snow exhausted and frustrated.

"Loveena!" he shouted, gulping cold air into his lungs, trying to catch his breath. He wanted her to respond. Even if this was her demon, he wished he would have taken the fall and not her. He instantly regretted not being nicer to her. Something good he sensed about this woman, and he wasn't ready to be without her. But now they were separated, like the demon promised and Troy felt quite alone.

"Took a nasty fall, did she?" said a deep voice in the dark. Turning toward the sound, Troy saw a figure of a man walking across the ridge toward him, accompanied by dozens of the nasty ice critters romping in the snow behind him. Troy started to stand up.

"No, no, don't get up. Sit down, let's talk." The critters made a circle around Troy bearing their icicle teeth. "No need for introductions. You already know who I am." Troy recognized the voice as the one they heard when they first entered the chamber. This was the demon, Loneliness.

The man sat down in the snow beside Troy. He dressed in a grey insulated ski jacket and pants, with a knit hat and gloves on, ski goggles hanging around his neck. As Troy rubbed his hands together and blew upon his cold fingers, the demon pulled off his thick, warm gloves one at a time, laying them in the snow in front of him. The heat from the gloves sent a wave of steam into the air, melting the snow beneath them. It annoyed Troy knowing the demon was warm while he was not.

Shooing the critters away with his hand, Loneliness looked at them with steely blue eyes, his pupils changing shape to yellow slits, like snake eyes. His teeth grew in length, becoming larger, sharper versions of their tiny icicle teeth. They turned with wide, fearful eyes and quickly scattered toward the woods. His eyes and teeth returned to normal as he turned back to speak to Troy.

"Nasty things," he said, pointing at the teeth marks on Troy's forearms. "They leave lots of marks."

"Did you kill her?" Troy asked with restrained contempt.

"Don't know. She's not the one I wanted." Loneliness smiled at him, his eyes flashing blue, then yellow, and back to blue.

Troy now realized he had been wrong. This demon claimed to be one of his. "How could that be?" he asked. "I don't remember feeling lonely in my life."

"Oh, but you are, Troy, you are! You deny it, you always have. However, everything about you calls to me. Not just the loss of your family, but everything in your life has cemented our relationship." He entwined the fingers of his hands together, illustrating their bond.

Shivering again, Troy's exhaled breath hung in the air. He rubbed his hands close to his face, continuing to breathe on them to warm them. Observing this, the demon snapped his fingers and a small campfire appeared before them. The snow instantly receded, and Troy and the demon sat on logs in a small clearing near the fire.

"Here, this will help," the demon said.

Troy felt the warmth of the fire spreading across his body. It was a welcome relief; however he had no intention of saying thank you to a demon. Loneliness picked up a small tree branch, pulling a graham cracker and a piece of chocolate from his side pocket. A marshmallow appeared out of nowhere on the end of the branch.

"Smore?" the demon held out the stick, offering it to Troy, who ignored the offer.

"They're really quite good, you know." The demon held the marshmallow near the flame as he spoke.

"You're a man of science, are you not? You believe everything is the result of cause and effect, with all evidence based on fact, all things being equal, nothing exists which can't be proven, and so on, and so forth." Pointing at Troy with the stick,

"Your theorems, calculations, and inventions are the only thing keeping you awake at night."

"That's not true," Troy responded.

The demon willingly conceded, "Oh, yes, there's that episode with your son. I understand. But, for argument's sake, let's just say, nothing of 'mankind' keeps you awake at night. The plight of the hungry doesn't cause you concern. An abused child down the street doesn't spur you to action. A local park needing help to continue delighting people in your community is the farthest thing from your mind. Yes, you sleep like a baby at night, don't you?"

Wrapping the chocolate and crackers around the charred marshmallow, the demon pulled it from the stick. Again, he offered it to Troy. "Are you sure?"

Troy refused it and the demon consumed it with the flick of a forked, snake-like tongue. When done, he closed his eyes and smiled. "Mmm, just delightful," he sighed.

Loneliness continued with his analysis of Troy.

"As for your foundation of faith, well, only 'seeing is believing' will do for you. There's no curiosity in a greater power other than your own flesh and bone; no exciting mystery which peaks your interest or childhood fantasies to cling to. Not one spark of divine fire warms your heart late at night. In other words, there is no Santa Claus, right, my friend?"

Giving him a dismissive glance, Troy replied, "Yeah, there is no Santa Claus."

"For you, things are black and white. There are no greys, no in betweens, no maybes. It is, or it isn't. Never any room for faith either, in your world of science, was there? With faith, one is never alone," he chuckled. "At least, that's what I hear. But with science, loneliness is a matter of degrees. No matter how small or vast the study is, it is cold, and singular."

The demon laughed. "Ha! A play on your own scientific word, *Singular!*" His tone becoming serious again, the demon went on.

"No, I don't mean the theory calling the beginning of the universe the Singularity, and believe me, I know how empty it was, I was there. What I mean is, only one at a time can peer through the microscope. Only one at a time can peer through the telescope. Only one can solve a mathematical problem, or the discovery of a lifetime. Yes," he smiled, "I am always present in the world of science."

"I don't follow," Troy said.

"Oh, don't get me wrong, I love science. I thrive on its singularity. It makes one feel smarter."

Looking at Loneliness, Troy snorted, "And what's wrong with that?"

The demon got up, looking into the fire, then back at Troy. With a tone of annoyance, he pointed to Troy's hands. "Everything you are is between those two hands of yours you're warming by the fire. If you do not create, build, write, observe, or touch something with those two hands, it simply doesn't exist for you."

Walking around the other side of the campfire, he raised his voice. "But Troy, there are so many other things you could have done with those hands that are not *singular*. Not predicated on *self*."

He gestured dramatically with his own hands, cupping them together and shoving them out toward Troy as he continued. "You could have *fed* a starving person at a soup kitchen. You could have *helped* an unemployed family in need." The demon spread his arms out wide. "You could have *built* a playground in the park for children to enjoy. You could have *taught* a student and shared your vast knowledge with others."

Pointing his index finger at Troy from across the campfire, his voice resonated in the still air. "So much you *could have* and *should have* done with those hands, my friend." He turned his face to the dark, starless night as if he were repenting to the Maker himself, raising his voice and his hands higher with each phrase. "You can *give*; you can *reach*; you can *hold* someone. For God's sake, you can *pray!*"

Troy looked up at the demon, who held his hands clasped together high above his head, as if in prayer. "Are we talking about you now, demon?"

Vincent and the Grief Masters

Loneliness lowered his arms to his side with a sigh, shrugged and smiled, returning to stand in front of Troy. "Astute, you are! That's why I know you, Troy Vincent, and you are a lonely man. There is nothing else out there you are holding onto except yourself. And that is not enough for any man."

Loneliness sat down on the log beside Troy. "You had a chance to be part of something greater than yourself. The people around you, the living, breathing community of mankind could have benefited from your involvement. If you had, God would know who you are. Your work on Earth would have reaped a true reward."

"God?" Troy looked puzzled.

"God, Yahweh, Allah, Brahma, Jehovah, so on and so on," rolling his eyes. "He has sooo many names. You'd think one would be enough. But they're all the same guy." The demon leaned over with his face very close to Troy's. "Just...pick one."

Looking confused, Troy mumbled, "But I don't know...." Loneliness jumped to his feet.

"Oh, dear boy, do you not know who your Maker is? Or anything about Him?" He scoffed. "Even demons know Him and know Him well. You really are alone, aren't you?"

Troy looked out into the darkness, mulling over the demon's words in his mind. Was the demon right? Did he really not know his Maker? Did the Maker, or *God*, the forbidden word, not know him? Had he spent his life not creating relationships that mattered or worse, ignored those he could have helped? Did he refuse to build a foundation of faith along with his career? There had been room for both, he just didn't do it. Would his success be measured by his accomplishments in the boardroom or his interactions throughout life? And, if he was wrong and the demon was right, would Loneliness now destroy him? Or would the Maker give him another chance to make it right?

Watching a tiny speck of light float from the black sky down into the depth of the dark mountain forest below, Troy saw it glow at the bottom of the mountain ravine. A point of golden light pulsed deep within the woods. *It has to be Loveena. I hope she's found a Grief Master to save her.* He wanted her to survive, even if he did not. Saying a silent *thank you* to whatever the Maker's name was, he fought the urge to smile.

Unsure if Loneliness may have also noticed the speck of light below, Troy felt the need to distract the demon so Loveena could get away. He stood up, stepping away from the campfire. His movement drew the attention of Loneliness away from the view of the base of the mountain.

"You're wrong about me, demon. I am a better man than you think." Troy stepped backwards toward the forest behind him. It was working, Loneliness began to follow.

Without looking back, the demon snapped his fingers and the campfire disappeared, his gloves appearing in his hand. "Sadly, my friend, I am right about you, and that is why you are now mine." Pulling a handkerchief from his unzipped breast pocket, Loneliness snapped it open with the flick of his wrist.

Wanting to give Loveena as much time as possible, Troy continued to engage the demon in conversation. "Oh yeah? How do you figure?"

"You will join my icy friends," cocking his head toward the shadowy critters following him. "You see, they were all lonely people once, like yourself. But with me, they become the pitiful, cold, and fragile creatures you see before you. They stab, bite, shatter and dissolve into nothingness, because this is what they were in life. They are nothing!"

His demonic icicle teeth shot out on either side of his mouth as he picked up a quivering creature. "They chose to be nothing of consequence, doing only meaningless things for themselves and nothing for others; thus, they are nothing now." Then he bit the critter in half, spitting out pieces of ice as the shattered body split into a thousand pieces.

"You see? Nothing but broken pieces. And you will shatter one day as well, just like that one." His snake eyes blazed at Troy, flashing bright blue, then yellow, and blue again.

"Well, good luck with that!" Troy turned around and ran. The demon held up his handkerchief in one hand, and reaching forward, his arm extended like a rubber band, snaring Troy into the fabric.

Troy didn't know if he was shrinking or if the handkerchief was expanding. Either way, he became trapped in a dark fold of fabric with no way out. And he felt cold again.

The handkerchief shrunk back to its original size and Loneliness tucked it into his breast pocket, pulling the zipper shut with Troy captured inside. Walking back into the forest, the critters jumped and scampered through the snow after him.

"That was just too easy," he sighed with satisfaction, patting his pocket. He neither cared, nor wanted Loveena, whom he knew to be still alive at the bottom of the mountain.

Chapter 20

Loveena's head throbbed as she regained consciousness. For a moment, with her eyes closed, she thought she was waking in her own bed with a terrible headache. The softness underneath her body went from warm covers to cold, wet clothes. The smell of pine trees further awakened her senses. Her mouth felt dry as she licked her lips. The taste of blood made her eyes open. Loveena gently touched her fingers to her forehead. A warm stickiness covered her fingertips, running down her cheek to the corner of her mouth.

A sharp pain in her arm jolted her back to the forest floor. In an instant, she recalled the nightmarish attack by the small, deadly creatures. She panicked as she fumbled for the key of Courage that had been around her neck. *It's still there*, she thought with relief. As she grasped it, her Grief Master appeared kneeling beside her. Patience nodded reassuringly to her, placing a magenta hand on Loveena's injured arm. Then transforming into an aura, she surrounded the injured arm, morphing into a sling and fading directly into it. Loveena felt the strength to sit up and struggled to her feet as her right forearm pulsed with pain.

I can move it, so it's not broken. I must have sprained it in the fall. If it wasn't for the protection of Troy's leather jacket, she thought she might have injured more than just her arm. The last thing she remembered was running along the slope fighting with one of the creatures as it gnawed at her repeatedly with its small icy teeth.

That must be how I got these wounds, rubbing the red scratches all over her hands and gingerly touching her bleeding forehead again. She freed it from her scalp, but it tangled in her hair, causing her to misstep and tumble down the snowy embankment.

Loveena looked up at the path she made in the snow on the mountainside. Sliding over rocks and past trees, she finally rolled into the softer boughs of a low hanging pine tree covered with heaps of snow. It was strong enough to break her fall and soft enough to cradle her injured body. Her legs felt weak, too weak to climb back up the steep path she came down. She took a quick look around and confirmed the icy critters, whatever they were, had gone. She could see broken pieces of the one she fought off scattered near a rock not far above her.

Good! I never want to see one of those hellish creatures again.

Cupping her good hand to her mouth, she yelled toward the mountaintop. "Troy!" The cold winter air and deep snow swallowed her voice, muting the sound. It was like yelling into a pillow. She tried again, louder this time, but heard no response. Nothing but silence surrounded her.

How am I going to find him? Is he all right? Or am I alone now? The thought struck her hard. She needed to find him.

Maybe there's another way up. Loveena started walking through the woods at the bottom of the mountain, cradling her injured right arm and holding it close to her body.

She lost track of time and any connection with reality, not knowing if she had been walking for minutes or hours. Unable to control the direction she was going within the VRC, Loveena felt helpless, confused, lost, and in complete isolation. The demon, Loneliness, said at the outset he would separate and destroy them. *Is this what he meant? If the creatures don't get us, then being totally alone will?*

Loveena stopped and looked around. The foot of the mountain was no longer visible and the forest looked the same in all directions. She dropped to her hands and knees, weary and aching with loneliness. Her feet were cold and numb, and her arm trembled from the persistent pain.

She collapsed on the floor of the forest, rolling onto her back in the patchy snow. Her empty gaze followed the tall tree trunks past their barren, lifeless branches up to the dark winter sky. Starless and still, it seemed like a painted ceiling of perpetual night.

Her memory traveled back to a time in her life when looking up at the night sky filled her with wonder. She would say a prayer or two and quietly whisper with the Maker. She never felt alone then. As a child after her mother's death, she wanted the one they called, the Son, to be by her bedside every night in the same spot where her mother would sit, holding her hand. It made her feel safe, content, and loved.

After her father disappeared, Loveena stopped looking up at the sky and talking to the Maker. She never felt safe or content after that. She passed it off as just a child's maternal longing. Then she went to work for SamWong and replaced childish things with more important adult matters. But those desires never made her feel complete, often making her feel alone. What she would give to have that innocence back, to have the faith of a little child and the warmth she remembered of being loved by the Maker, the Son, and her mother, wrapped firmly around her again.

Loveena sighed, her breath rising like a small cloud of steam into the air. As it wisped upward, it carried her silent prayer toward the heavens. It was only then she noticed a tiny faint star in the dark night sky above her. Her eyes became fixed upon it as it brightened. As she lay there, it seemed to emanate a pulse of warmth toward her, though far away. Appearing to draw nearer, Loveena got to her feet and watched as the small star dropped down through the sky. It approached her, like a lazy snowflake falling gently between the tops of the tall, bare trees. Eagerly, she held out her cupped hand to catch it. A smile spread across her blood-streaked face as it came closer. The tiny star finally came down to rest in Loveena's hand. Suddenly a key of golden light appeared in her palm.

She took a moment to gaze at the key, welcoming the warmth it pulsated through her cold body. The pain in her arm ceased as the wounds on her head healed and the streaks of blood faded from her face. Feeling whole again, Loveena wrapped her fingers around the key, as the voice of a Grief Master quietly spoke to her.

"Hello, Loveena, I am a Grief Master. My name is Faith." Loveena clutched the precious key to her heart and the Grief Master appeared, standing before her. A golden-hued being of light, similar to Loveena in size and feminine form, sparkled from head to toe. Her face appeared serene as she smiled, reminding Loveena of her mother's kind smile. Within her glow, burned an eternal flame, shining in the opaque being's chest where the heart would be. The Grief Master reached out and placed a hand upon the key still held tightly in Loveena's grasp.

"I have been sent on your behalf. It is good to see you again. I bring you a message: you are precious and loved. Your Faith, along with your Courage, will help you find the right path back. Do not give up. We are here, we will not leave you, and you are never alone." She smiled warmly, "Now go, he awaits you."

"Who waits? The Maker? Troy?" Loveena asked. The Grief Master touched the top of the new key. A strap appeared on it and Loveena wasted no time placing it around her neck. Both keys hung together like charms on a necklace. Her bare skin above her tank top reflected the soft gold and magenta tones emitted by the keys. Feeling crept back into her feet and she wiggled her toes inside her shoes.

Patience now appeared beside Faith. They both stretched out an arm toward the forest in front of Loveena. A pathway of snow melted away, revealing the flat stepping stones, already lit with the soft pastel lights like before. The Grief Masters gave Loveena not only a new direction to follow, but a confidence to go forward, something she hadn't felt in a long time.

In fact, she reflected on a great number of things as she walked on the path provided by them. She felt a reawakening of who she really was deep inside herself. It was as if parts of her had been asleep and now just waking up again. Re-energized, Loveena seemed to have a fresh, new perspective on her life which had been sorely needed.

I can have a do-over, a reworking. There is probably so much more I can change, remake my life; I can do this, she thought confidently. Her mind raced as she walked along, thinking of ways she might fix the problems in her life. Would this be the silver lining of her VRC treatment? Was she in fact condemned, or being given an opportunity to rebuild? She wanted to survive, if for no other reason than to become a better person. Would she get the chance, or would it end with a crushing defeat?

I can't believe the Maker would send me these beautiful warriors if he did not want me to survive. He wants me to figure this out, to fight for myself; to know someone cares and I am not alone. Accompanied by her new companions, Loveena felt their combined light and strength would remain and not abandon her. In fact, the only one who had abandoned Loveena turned out to be Loveena herself.

She sensed Troy probably needed this reawakening, too. It was easier for her, she thought, since her beliefs were strong long ago, just hidden by time. But for Troy, she feared he truly may have not embraced any of it in his life, or perhaps he buried it so deep, he couldn't find it again. She prayed he wouldn't be destroyed before he could discover what she was uncovering at the depths of her soul.

Chapter 21

Troy couldn't believe what just happened. One minute he was conversing with a demon that appeared somewhat human, and the next, a prisoner in the demon's pocket. How bizarre, but then, the whole VRC System was bizarre. His patience challenged, he needed to find a way out of this. No rational thinking seemed to help and the demons were one step ahead of him, knowing his every move. He punched at the heavy fabric wall engulfing him. *Damn it!*

The space, in which he became confined, morphed into a small room. The walls, a tightly woven white fabric, also made up the floor which became solid enough to walk on. Some light filtered through the sides and down from the top, like being in a teepee. His eyes had adjusted to this dim world and he could see there was no immediate way out.

Troy paced back and forth. He recalled what Vincent previously told him. *Do not try to reason with the demons...they know your weaknesses...your own demons will try to kill you.* How could he outwit them if they already knew what he was thinking?

He stopped pacing and knelt down on his haunches. Touching the key of Courage around his neck, he twirled it between his forefinger and thumb. Its glow caught Troy's eye and he looked down at it. No shield of light would work this time on this demon. Troy seemed at a loss as to what the next step should be. He held the key up in front of him.

"Courage, may I speak with you?" The being of light appeared across from him, sitting on his haunches like a mirror image of Troy. His glow gave additional light to the confined space. He waited for Troy to speak.

Troy contemplated the situation as he tried to decompress from his impatience and think clearly. His brows creased together as he rubbed his jaw. "There are no panes of glass here you can pull a weapon from. Do you have any other tricks up your sleeve that can help us?"

"I am with you, but I am not the right warrior you need."

"In other words, you're not the right tool for the job?"

"Your demon knows you, because he thinks he is you. But there are parts of you he is not. You must seek those out, and take the path it presents."

Troy shook his head. "How do I know what those are? I don't think...."

Courage interrupted him. "Don't think—feel." Pointing from Troy's head to his heart, he repeated, "Feel."

Then, transforming into a magenta aura, he surrounded Troy and dissipated back into his body.

Troy stood up and closed his eyes. Taking in a deep breath, he exhaled slowly, letting go of all things clouding his brain. What seeped back in was what the demon, Loneliness, said he did not do.

Give...Reach...Hold...PRAY. Troy knew himself to be different from the demon. He prayed as a child a long time ago. It may have been many years since he had that type of relationship with the Maker, but he did have it once. And the demon did not.

A sudden pain broke through, engulfing him, as his teeth and hands started aching. He grabbed his jaw, as it transformed, pushing outward. His fingers felt along his growing canine teeth, both on the bottom and the top, shooting up and down into icicle-like daggers. Incredible pain shot through his hands as he watched his palms morph into rough pads, and his fingers become claws with icicle-like tips. They formed sharp talons of shiny, dark blue shards of ice.

Troy staggered back against the fabric wall. He turned in wretched agony, leaning against the wall for support. His claws of ice tore holes into the fabric as he grabbed at the wall. His feet burst through his boots as his toes became icicle claws, like his hands. He yelled out as his body gave way and white fur sprouted from his back and chest, surrounding his head and jutting down his arms and legs. His clothes disappeared from his body as the fur covered him. He fell to the musty floor, curled up in a fetal position as the final transformation shrank him to a size smaller than the forest creatures. He lay there, barely conscious, still wearing the leather-strapped key around his neck, as it had also shrunk in proportion.

The small space spun around until it finally came into focus. Troy blinked his eyes several times. He could smell the cold air mixed with the aroma of dirt and forest foliage, aware of musky fragrances he never noticed before. Getting up, his legs felt different. He raised a foot to see why he felt so odd.

One, two...three, four...four legs. What the hell? The only physical reaction Troy could manage was to run in circles several times, like a dog chasing its tail. He stopped and stared at his front paws. *Loneliness turned me into one of his creatures! But I can still think. My mind is still my own.*

He flexed the icicle claws of his left front paw. He observed their hard strength, hitting them against the floor several times. Looking up at the fabric wall, he jumped onto it, tearing it to shreds with his new weapons. With each strike of the knife-like shards, he could smell the outdoor air come through. Finally, he made contact with the outer layer of the demon's pocket and sliced a hole through the threads large enough for him to escape. He could see the ground far below. From this height it would be suicide to jump, yet he knew he had a better chance out there than inside.

Loneliness continued walking through the woods. Troy sensed the demon could be unaware of his thoughts now that he transformed into this new animal-like state. Apparently, Loneliness didn't notice his prisoner's effort to create an escape hole in the fabric. Troy kept still for a moment, trying to decide what to do. He pulled his oversized snout back from the open hole and pushed his tiny black eye to the opening, surveying the landscape. As the demon brushed past a tree, a passing branch appeared in his view, then another and another.

So, Loneliness is walking in a pine forest. That's good.

The sweet smell filled Troy's senses with the earthy fragrance. It also smelled like freedom. If he could jump onto a passing branch it just might be the only way to attempt an escape. The thick boughs would conceal him from the demon's view and soften his landing.

Troy maneuvered his head and shoulders out and readied his back legs, bracing them for a jump. He had no time to test the abilities of his new physique. He must force his legs to muster enough power to carry him through the air. If they performed like the small creatures that jumped from tree trunks onto him and Loveena, he should be able to connect with a passing branch.

As the demon approached the next pine tree, Troy lined up all four of his legs on the edge of the fabric hole. It was a shaky and precarious position, but his adrenalin and determination balanced on a hair trigger, ready to explode in a micro-second. He could see a spot on the pine bough where he would aim to land. It came closer…closer.

Loneliness stopped. He looked down at a creature in the snow near his right foot. Troy could not wait any longer perched on the unstable fabric. He stood in the left front pocket and the demon turned, looking right. With a bit of luck, the demon wouldn't notice him jump. He hoped to get one step closer to the pine bough, but it was not to be. He pumped adrenalin into one powerful leap and stretched his forelegs out in front as far as he could. His eyes riveted on a landing spot he chose, willing his body to cross the open-air space and not fail him.

Below the pine tree were several of the menacing creatures. They would tear him to pieces if he fell short of the branch and onto the forest floor. He held his breath, trying not to make a sound. Troy kept his sleek body held as aerodynamically as he could muster. The creatures milled below, snorting and whining, which would cover up any sound he might make when hitting the branch.

The frozen critter near the demon's right foot stepped in the way. Its beady eyes filled with terror as Loneliness looked down at him with eyes blazing, flashing blue, yellow, blue. The demon gave one hard kick to the creature, sending it flying. It crashed against a tree several yards away. When it hit, it exploded into a shower of brittle broken ice chips, and scattered across the snow. Then, Loneliness resumed his walk, moving on.

Troy sailed well beyond the pine bough he had chosen, instead heading into the interior toward the tree's trunk. To his dismay, there were fewer pine needles to cushion his fall. He turned his forelegs slightly and allowed his body to go limp and take the brunt of the hit. By becoming less rigid, he hoped he wouldn't break into a thousand pieces. Bracing for impact, he hit with such force it knocked the wind out of him. He slid down to the bare branch below, unable to stop or grasp it with his animal-like paws. Three icy claws broke as he cascaded down several more branches before coming to a stop a few feet from the ground. He dug his icy talons on his back feet into the tree trunk to keep from sliding further.

Through the pine boughs, he could see Loneliness disappear into the depth of the forest, seemingly unaware of his escape. The creatures on the ground beneath the tree moved on to follow the demon's path through the snow.

Troy wondered if any of the little demonic critters still maintained their own thoughts, as he did. How long would it be before his mind would go away, too?

Not only was his sense of smell extremely heightened in this animal state, so too, was his hearing. He waited in the branches of the tree until he could no longer hear Loneliness or his noisy little creatures. His side still sore from the brunt of the fall, made him instinctively lick it. He felt the roughness of his own tongue as he flicked it back into his mouth. *Hey, what am I doing?*

He was free and that's all that mattered. Struggling to release his back claws stuck in the tree's bark, one cracked off as he pulled it free. It felt like a deeply torn fingernail, causing pain to shoot up his leg. No blood oozed out, only icy water.

He climbed down to the ground, hesitating to leave the protective low hanging pine boughs that secretly concealed him. Once out in the open, his white fur would blend in with the snow on the ground, but his movements might still be detected. He would have to move quickly and keep low. Peering out into the frozen world, things appeared so much bigger from ground level. His smaller size would mean a longer, more arduous journey.

Troy made a quick jump from the safety of the tree into the snow. He cautiously moved from tree to tree and moved away from the demon in the opposite direction as quickly as his small size could manage, pausing only occasionally to listen for anything following him.

Troy's thoughts turned to Loveena. He had to find her, but how would she recognize him? Somehow he must find a way to get his human form back. Already feeling forgetful, he wondered if he was beginning to lose his human identity. How could he get out of this frozen situation?

A memory of Tommy flashed in his mind. *I have to keep thinking of Tommy. Don't forget who you are.* Troy repeated the thought over and over in his mind as he pushed through the snow. He wanted to keep human thoughts and memories as long as possible. When the memory of Tommy's face faded, he repeated the alphabet over and over. He counted to a hundred by ones, then to a thousand by tens. He struggled to remember theorems and tried working simple mathematical formulas in his brain. Each time something left his memory, he would latch onto another thought and repeat it over and over until it, too, slipped away.

The snow, the earthy smell, the wild instinct fermenting in his physical form was robbing him of himself. It seemed to seep into the very core of his being. Still wearing the leather strap with the key of Courage, it glowed and pulsated furiously. It mimicked the faster metabolism now surging through his veins. The flight instinct of a wild animal drove his heart to beat faster and his legs to run harder. However, the deep snow hindered his progress. At this pace, he might never find Laura…no, Lana? No…what was her name? Loveena! He might never find Loveena again.

He dashed from tree to tree and crossed an open space, stopping briefly to look up at the dark sky. There was something he remembered, but it wouldn't come to him. He took a few quick steps and stopped again.

A light in the night; yes, a star; a falling star. There were hands pointing to the sky. Not my hands. Hands together; praying hands? Yes, praying hands.

A voice reverberated in his ear, sounding like his own voice, but not his voice; a face that was not his; a face of light, speaking to him. *There are parts of you he is not. You must seek those out, and take the path it presents.*

Troy crossed the open space to the foot of another tree. He stopped and looked back, sniffing up at the dark sky. He heard the voice again and the thing around his neck glowed brightly. *Don't think—feel.* But his animal instinct did feel—cold, hunger, and a predatory caution.

His human instinct, worn down to its last layer, made his soul cry out. *Pray...pray! Pray to whom?* The last spark of his inner self whispered, *Pray to the Maker!*

He shook his furry head. Losing focus, he let his heart take over and words came to him.

Maker, forgive me. You have been with me, helped me, and yet, I denied you. But you never left me. My life is in your hands, as it has always been. Have mercy. Please help me.

As the thought left Troy, his animal existence closed in on him. He jumped through the snow back to the center of the clearing. He shook his head again as his soul cried out one last time. *Please save me. I am one of yours. I belong to you, not these demons.*

A tiny dot of light appeared in the cold fog of the clearing where Troy squatted in the snow. He blinked his tiny black eyes, taking several steps back to safety under a pine tree bough. The light grew into a small flame, hovering above the ground, beckoning him to draw near. He took a step toward the light and crept out into the open once again. The flame made the midnight blue sky appear black and bleak, but its warmth drew Troy closer until he came within a foot of it. A key appeared in the middle of the flame and Troy heard a quiet, still voice speak to him.

"I am a Grief Master, Troy. I am sent here on your behalf. My name is FAITH. You have remembered Him. You are a child of God, as are those who speak to Him with their hearts." Troy stood upright on his hind legs and stretched his right foreleg toward the flame. The icicle claws began to melt, transforming the paw back into a faint outline of his human hand.

"His name may be different to many, but His love is constant for all."

Troy's arm re-appeared next, as did his other hand and arm. Icy teeth melted down as his jaw receded into his face again. His body returned without the writhing pain he endured in the earlier transformation. Furry hind legs disappeared as his human legs reappeared. His human form was back, solid, and fully clothed. Restored to a whole man once more, Troy found himself on his knees in the snow.

He lowered his head, leaned forward, and collapsed down to the ground. He lay there with his hands stretched out in front of him, tightly clasped together in prayer. With his whole heart and every ounce of his exhausted being, Troy whispered, "Thank you, God." He felt the true meaning of what the demon could never do with its two hands—pray. When he lifted his head, the voice from the flame spoke again.

"Believe. Believe, Troy, and I am always with you. You are never alone."

Troy dragged himself up, staggering, but standing on his own two feet once again. The opaque outline of a young man's figure surrounded the flame. This Grief Master resembled Troy as an adolescent teen. A flame burned within the young man's chest, and a golden luminescent glow emanated from him. The younger Troy took the flame from his chest and held it in his open hand, offering it to his older self. It glowed brightly in the dark. Troy felt its protective warmth spread throughout his body. Holding out his hand, Troy accepted the offer, pulling it back toward his own chest where the flame passed through his t-shirt and into his heart.

A golden key appeared on a leather strap around Troy's neck. The young Faith Grief Master smiled and nodded to Troy, transforming into a shimmering golden aura, surrounding and moving into Troy's body. The remaining luminescent sparkles in the night air rose high into the dark sky, like tiny floating embers, and became twinkling stars. The night was no longer dead, but full of light, alive, and beautiful.

Loneliness appeared at the edge of the clearing, dismayed at what he just witnessed. Removing the strap from his neck, Troy raised high the new key. From it, a bright beam shone on the demon and his frozen critters. The surrounding snow melted as the icy creatures scampered back into the forest. However, they could not escape the light emitted from the key of Faith. They dissolved one by one. Loneliness looked at Troy as he faded away. "I envy you, old chap." Then he, too, disappeared into oblivion.

The forest and all traces of the frozen world slipped away, until all were gone. The iridescent path returned beneath Troy's feet.

"Troy!" Loveena's voice floated like music to his ears. He turned to see her standing a short distance away. She ran to him and he wrapped his arms around her, lifting her up off the ground in a big hug. Both relieved, they laughed, as he set her down again.

"I wasn't sure you'd make it," she smiled. He opened his hand to show her the golden key. "I almost didn't…but I was never alone."

Loveena gave him an understanding nod, taking the strap and placing it around his neck. She then held up her own golden key for him to see. He hugged her again. Grateful they were both still alive, he couldn't bring himself to let go of her, not just yet.

Chapter 22

The fog lightened around Troy and Loveena as they smiled at each other. His hands rested on her waist, but Loveena didn't mind. They just experienced isolation, and any human contact was welcome right now. Warm air surrounded them becoming a definite improvement from the cold world they just left. Sunrays broke through here and there, bright, and cheerful! However, she wasn't sure if it was the sun or his close presence making her feel warm inside. A smell in the air reluctantly drew her attention away from Troy. "Do you smell that?"

Troy sniffed the air. Taking a step away from him, she strained her eyes and ears, trying to penetrate the dissipating fog. "It smells like…." She paused.

"Saltwater?" Troy finished her sentence, looking puzzled.

Loveena's feet shivered in the cold only moments ago and now sank into something warm, soft, and wet. As the last of the wispy mist swirled away, evaporating in the sunlight, she looked down and saw her bare feet in brown sand. Burrowing her toes into its warm grittiness, she squealed with delight. "It's the ocean!" she yelled, turning to Troy.

A stretch of isolated beachfront revealed itself with low, rolling waves washing ashore. A blue sky rose from the water's horizon up as far as they could see. The two weary travelers stood for a long moment, soaking up the rays of the warm sun, with eyes closed and faces lifted. The clean, salty air refreshed them.

Opening her eyes, Loveena laughed at Troy's appearance. His boots, jeans, and shirt transformed into sandals, swim trunks, and an open beach shirt. Not only were his clothes different, but she found herself barefoot, wearing a bikini top and denim shorts, loosely covered by a blue terrycloth beach jacket. The wind blew his shirt open, revealing the strong abs of his tanned body. She looked down, trying not to be obvious in her appreciation of the sight. She couldn't deny feeling attracted to him. His Grief Master keys hung around his neck, emanating a soft glow, pulsating with a slow beat. She wondered if it matched the rhythm of his steady heartbeat, unlike her own heart, which was racing.

Her eyes caught his casual gaze, taking in her long legs and shapely form from head to toe. He seemed deliberate in his slow perusal of her, resting his eyes on the Grief Master keys nuzzled between her breasts. Shifting away from him, Loveena pulled the beach jacket closed, tying it with the belt. As she did, she felt something in the pocket. She reached in to find a pair of dark sunglasses, and smiled as she put them on. Troy patted his shirt pocket, also finding a pair. He made a deliberate, dramatic Adonis pose as he slowly raised them to his face and put them on. They both laughed, breaking the embarrassing moment of awkward silence between them.

"I'll say one thing for the VRC," Troy joked. "It's quite fashionable."

An enormous wave crashed behind them and they both turned to see water splashing high into the air, landing against a jagged jetty in the surf. Loveena ran a few steps in the sand toward the rocks. "Wait a minute." The brief moment of joking with Troy turned more serious. "I recognize these rocks."

Looking up the beach, Loveena stood up on her toes trying to see around a small hill covered with tall, swaying beach grass. *Could it be? Is it possible this is....* She needed to get closer; to run up the beach, to be certain.

Looking bewildered, Troy followed after her. "Hey, wait up. What is it, Loveena?"

The width of the sandy beach meandered into tall patches of beach grass, covering the sloping, sandy hill. Running along the beach, the incoming waves washed over her feet, smearing the fresh, wet footprints behind her. The water felt so good and reminded her of how many times she had walked this very beach, letting the water refresh her hot feet. She rounded the windswept, sandy hill. Finding the old wooden post still there, she grinned with anticipation as she read the faded paint on the weathered sign: Ramona Cove.

This is the beach! And the house should be right around the bend. She ran a little further, stopping as it came into view.

Catching up, Troy stopped behind her. "Where are we?"

Loveena didn't answer right away. She stood silently looking at the little one floor beach house with the painted green tin roof and wide covered porch. The house was painted a robin's egg blue. "Bluer than the sky above," her father described it, with white shutters and trim. It stood alone facing the ocean, surrounded by wind swept hills of sandy soil and tall grass, mingling with swaying brown-tipped cat tails. It appeared exactly as she remembered it.

She loved Ramona Cove. As a child, it was her favorite place to go to escape from the outside world. It provided comfort and security, and her joy overshadowed the one terrible memory she buried of the humble bungalow.

"Loveena," Troy asked again, "What is this place?"

"This is my father's beach house."

Turning back to Troy, her face lit up. "Remember, Vincent mentioned a safe house might appear? I think it's a safe house for us. We can rest here."

She started toward the flat rock steps embedded in the small hillside leading up to the house. Loveena was relieved to have a place she knew so well be a safe house where they could hide from the terrors of the VRC, even for a short while. At the same time, she pushed aside the memory of the last time she had been here, one that changed her life forever.

****

Troy followed Loveena up the steps to the wide-planked veranda. It wrapped around the house and smelled of a fresh coat of whitewash paint on the floor. Two chairs flanked the front door, one a white rocking chair, the other a wood-framed chair with blue and white striped cushions. A table sat underneath a window with a pitcher of iced tea. The ice, still frozen, and two glasses sat ready for use, as though someone had just placed them there.

Loveena stopped to look at the ocean view, lingering on the porch. Finally turning toward the door, she rested her hand on the knob for a moment, without opening it. Troy could tell something was stopping her from going inside. Turning away from the door, she ran her hand along the railing as she walked to the opposite end of the porch. Troy picked up the pitcher of iced tea and poured it into both glasses. Walking the length of the veranda, he handed her a glass, taking a sip from his own. He wanted to know more about Loveena. This place, Ramona Cove, seemed to have a deep connection for her.

"Did you grow up here?" he asked.

"No, but I spent every summer at this house until I went to college." Looking out at the ocean, she smiled. "I loved the ocean and this beach. I loved coming here," motioning to the little house. Troy sensed an underlying melancholy in her tone and a reason why she seemed hesitant to go inside.

"I take it you haven't been here in a while? Why?"

"Heartbreak is a funny thing. It can make you turn away from the things you love." Walking back to the door, she stopped, took a deep breath, then opened it and stepped inside.

Troy understood exactly what she meant. She evidently turned away from this place, just as he turned away from his work and the home he shared with Tommy. After the accident, the remaining things that belonged to his son were finally boxed up, given away, or moved to the back of his memory, where he didn't have them as a constant reminder. Perhaps he and Loveena had more in common than he thought. He didn't want to pry, but there must have been a story behind her statement. He wanted to know what it was, how it connected to this house, and if it had anything to do with Hoy SamWong.

Scanning the view of the peaceful beach and ocean, he watched a wave roll over as it approached the land. This beauty and solitude hid a refuge not common in the crowded, destructive world he was used to. *I understand why she loved it here. This is a place I could love, too.* Taking a sip from his glass, he turned back toward the door and walked inside.

Troy entered, taking a quick look around. He didn't see Loveena in the room, but he could hear her moving in the back of the house. The front door opened into a small living room with an adjoining kitchen to the left. Modestly furnished, a worn, floral sofa separated the kitchen and living area. Two small side tables sat at each end. Across from it, a green overstuffed chair and ottoman sat beside a sunny window. A tall reading lamp placed next to the chair created a reading nook for a small library of books. The bookcase spanned the wall next to the chair from floor to ceiling, filled with antique books of all genres, carefully preserved behind glass doors that protected them from the humid, salty air. He stepped closer to scan through the many titles.

Hardbound books had not been produced for decades since all libraries, schools, and companies converted to a total digital society. Bans existed on so many types of books it limited what books were available. It was safer to have digital copies which could be deleted in seconds than be caught with an outlawed book in your possession. The presence of so many real books in one place was like finding a rare treasure.

Troy assumed her father must have been a collector. First Editions of classic literary works spanning three centuries lined the shelves. There were books by authors that most people in his current century had not read. This was a treasure trove of talented and intellectual minds. *Her father must be a smart man. I'm impressed by his collection, and with him, and I don't even know the guy.*

A fragile leather-bound copy of 'The Sound and the Fury' by William Faulkner caught his eye and he opened one of the glass doors to get a better look. As he started to pull the book from the shelf, the leather spine slightly crumbled. He gently pushed it back with his finger tip, not wanting to damage such a precious antique. Closing the glass door, he saw another book lying on the side table next to the chair. Picking it up, Troy sat down to browse through it. It was a children's book entitled, *Through the Looking-Glass and What Alice Found There*, by Lewis Carroll. He carefully opened the fragile cover of a First Edition copy published in 1871, and marveled at its excellent condition and numerous colorful illustrations. Inside the front cover, he found a handwritten note with a dried pressed flower. It read:

"To my darling daughter, Loveena,
May you always see the good on both sides of the glass.
Love, Daddy"

****

Loveena walked from a bedroom in the back of the house, carrying a small cube in her palm. She held it out to show Troy. Touching the top of it, a three-dimensional photograph popped up and projected just above the top of the cube. "This is my father," she said. "Samuel Baptista."

The picture showed a middle-aged man in shorts and a short-sleeved floral shirt. He had black hair and a heavy black mustache. Wearing sunglasses, he held a cigar in his left hand, draping his right arm around the shoulders of a young girl. She was dressed in a yellow sundress and flip-flops, with the wind blowing her dark shoulder length hair across her chin. They both were smiling, obviously enjoying a day on the beach in each other's company. The blue beach house appeared in the background.

"And that's you?" Troy asked.

"Yes, it was my tenth birthday. Our housekeeper took the picture." Loveena smiled as she recalled the events of the day long ago. "Such a perfect day. We had a big bonfire on the beach that night."

Setting the cube with the photo still visible on the small side table, she walked around the room, gently touching different objects. She lingered over an old tobacco pipe perched upright on a pipe rack on a table next to the sofa. Then, stiffening her stance, she moved into the kitchen. Loveena opened the window over the sink, letting in the ocean breeze. It ruffled the thin curtains and brought in the sweet smell of honeysuckle, climbing on a trellis beneath the window. She stared out the window into her distant past.

Troy got up from the chair and followed her into the kitchen. Taking a last drink from his glass, he set it down on the kitchen table. "What happened to your father, Loveena?"

"I don't know," she sighed, continuing to look out the window. "He left one day and never came back."

"Why? What would make him not come back to the daughter who obviously loved him a great deal? And this great place of solitude; who wouldn't want to come back here?"

Turning from the window with a sigh, she crossed to the kitchen table with the blue and white checkered tablecloth. She pulled out one of the four chairs around it and sat down. Troy sat down at the table across from her.

"I don't think he could come back. I think he was in danger." Looking at Troy, she knew he waited to hear her story. She also knew he wouldn't like it. She bit her bottom lip and looked down at her hands.

"You see, my father was the owner and CEO of his own company. He took on a business partner named Hoy Wong. Together they created SamWong Industries. The 'Sam' part of the company's name stood for Samuel, as in Samuel Baptista. Hoy took over the company, forcing my father out and changing his last name to SamWong. But it was my father, and my father's money, that built SamWong Industries into the world's most powerful corporation—not Hoy."

Chapter 23

Troy raised his eyebrows and tapped his hand several times on the table top. Quickly getting up from the chair, he knocked it over with his abrupt burst of electrified attitude. He covered his eyes with one hand, shaking his head. His hand slid down his face and covered his mouth, as if to hold in any angry response. But his eyes glared unspoken volumes.

"You must understand," Loveena continued defensively. "My father didn't intend for SamWong Industries to become a fearful giant. He believed in giving others a chance. He never wanted it to grow into a monster, buying up other companies, ruining them or putting them out of business. That was Hoy's doing. Hoy was ruthless and pushed the company into deals expanding the conglomerate worldwide. He bought the votes of SWI stock holders and ignored my father's counsel."

Troy shot back. "Did you know it drove my father to suicide? And they stole everything we ever worked for? My father's years of round-the-clock work; all of my patented inventions; all gone, and stolen by SWI!" He tried unsuccessfully to control his voice as well as his temper, but he got louder. "And your father was a part of this?"

"No, no, no," Loveena tried to explain. "He had already disappeared before the VSA acquisition. When Hoy started acquiring companies years ago my father objected. I know for a fact, he wouldn't have allowed what happened to your company."

She knew Troy must hate both her and her father right now. He stood tight-lipped and sullen, as he placed his arms across his chest, standing beside the fallen chair, and staring at the floor.

Loveena pressed on. "The last conversation we had together happened here eight years ago. He looked very sad and said he couldn't control Hoy or his greed any longer. A power struggle was occurring within the company, and his managers were being eliminated for not supporting Hoy. He didn't say so, but I think he meant they may have been abducted or possibly killed. He told me he didn't know what he would do, but he didn't want me involved, and not to worry about him."

Loveena wrung her hands and leaned her forehead on them. "He wanted me to stay in college and provided funds for it. He also insisted I not come here, fearing this place might be watched. He didn't want anything he did to put me in danger." She paused and laid her hands back down on the table. "After that day, I heard nothing more from him."

"So how the hell did you end up working for SamWong?" Troy asked, emphasizing his clipped words with an irritable tone.

"When I finished my degree, I got an anonymous email saying my father would be here at Ramona Cove and he wanted to see me. I was so excited. I hadn't seen him in years, so of course, I came immediately." Loveena's eyes filled with tears. As one ran down her cheek, she wiped it away. Troy roughly picked up the chair, setting it back in place. He remained standing, leaning both hands on the back of it, as she went on with her story.

"But I found Hoy here instead. He told me Samuel Baptista had embezzled money from SWI and was now in the custody of his corporate militia. He showed me a letter claiming it had been written by my father." She described how it said it gave Hoy power of attorney over all of her father's assets, including Ramona Cove, and the trust fund set aside for her. It also stated he wanted no contact with her, having become tired of the burden. "The letter closed saying he didn't love me anymore." Loveena covered her face, hiding her tears.

Troy sat back down, tapping his fingers again on the table. Seeing a dish towel folded on the back of another chair, he grabbed it and leaned forward, sliding it across the table toward her. As she accepted it, his hand slightly covered hers, but she pulled back. If he was attempting a gesture of pity, she didn't want it. She felt like long subdued anger at the entire situation was boiling up inside her, ready to come out. Her tone became bitter, as she clenched her jaw and continued. "I didn't believe the letter was real because it was typed, not hand written, like he would've normally done. It wasn't signed either. I argued with Hoy, but he was so convincing, and I, so naïve. I couldn't see through his lies."

Swallowing hard, Loveena wiped away another tear with the dish towel. "It crushed me to think my father didn't love me." The thought made her feel empty inside. Since her mother's death, her father became everything to her. She glanced up at Troy hoping to see some understanding, but he only looked away.

She went on. "With everything now in Hoy's legal control, he insisted I repay my father's debt for his disloyalty, ordering me to go to work for him. I said no, absolutely not. So he grabbed me, shook me, and hit me. And then he...." She stopped, shutting her eyes to block out the memory. "In the end, he said if I didn't do what he wanted, he would execute my father."

A silence hung in the air between them. Troy sucked in air and bit the inside of his lip. His tone was more reflective than accusatory. "So you went to work for him, doing his dirty work, spying on his competition, and jumping into bed with them at his command."

"He used me to get close to whomever he didn't trust and the heads of companies he wanted to take over. He gave me assignments, telling me exactly what to do. If he just needed information, I would find a way to hack their systems, using SWI AI programs to ask questions. If Hoy needed something more personal, he arranged for me to be their escort. And if I didn't go through with it, he'd threaten my father's life again." Loveena turned sideways in her chair, not wanting to face Troy. She didn't like the work she did for Hoy, but she had no choice. *Doesn't he understand that?* She needed him to see the truth of the situation.

Another long silence enveloped them. Troy finally spoke, with an empathetic voice this time. "Well, Hoy was used to getting his own way. You said he tried to kill you?"

Loveena nodded. "There were rumors of my father appearing in different places, locations not controlled by SWI. He couldn't have been a prisoner. Hoy was lying to me all along. I tried for a year to get up the courage to confront him. I wanted desperately to get out from under his control. But I became afraid of Hoy's paranoia. He was crazy, out of control; acting like he had more secrets to cover up. I decided to tell him I was done with all of his threats."

"So you went to his office to confront him," Troy concluded.

"Yes, but his attorney, Xavier Adams, was there. They were arguing. I waited outside his office until Adams came out. It was late and I stood in the dark, so Adams wouldn't see me. No one else was there. When I went in, Hoy seemed really worked up about something. But I wanted it over with, so I told him I was leaving."

Loveena stood up and paced behind the table, wringing the small towel in her hands and remembering how nervous she was that night.

"He said I couldn't leave, I knew too much about him, his operation. His eyes were wild with madness. I told him I knew he lied to me about my father. Then he started telling me some wild story how Samuel Baptista was worse than disloyal; a leader of some kind of underground resistance. He said my father threatened to take down the entire Corporate Rule structure and the World Board of Directors with it. I didn't know what he was talking about. I thought he'd lost his mind. He wasn't going to let me tell anyone anything which would help the resistance take his power away."

Loveena paused and leaned against the kitchen counter. "That's when he came at me and we struggled." She replayed the scene again in her mind. "I remember the flash of his diamond ring with the SWI letters made of diamonds. I had seen that ring swing at me once before at Ramona Cove." Touching her cheek where his fist hit her long ago, she sat down next to Troy at the table.

Continuing in a quiet voice, she finished her story. "He grabbed me by the throat. That's all I remember. I must have dropped my security card in his office because that's the only evidence the judges presented at my trial."

Vincent and the Grief Masters

****

Troy rocked the edge of his empty glass on the table, and roughly set it down. "I need something stronger than this." He looked toward the small bar at the other end of the room. "Do you mind?"

"Behind the bar," she said.

He glanced at her, wondering how much of her story could be true, then stood up and crossed the room. Opening the cabinet below the bar, he browsed through the small stock of aged liquor, picking out a bottle of well-seasoned Kentucky bourbon.

"Do you want one?" he asked, taking a shot glass from the shelf. Loveena shook her head. He filled the glass and gulped it down. Pouring another, he drank it just as fast. With the bottle in his hand, he walked around and sat down on one of the two bar stools, looking down into his third glass.

She's the daughter of my enemy. He truly started to care for Loveena, but now she revealed her true colors, her real connection to SWI. He felt somehow betrayed, even though he knew he didn't really have the right to feel that way. There was no tie to Loveena, not yet, anyway.

She believes her father had nothing to do with the dismantling of VSA, Inc. or my company. SWI is the biggest corporation in the world, and it didn't get that way by being a sweet mom and pop operation.

Her father knew how to build a successful company. Could he be building a successful resistance? The corporate-run world was far from perfect. The rich ruled the corporations; the corporations ruled the world, leaving the general population without personal assets, miserable and powerless to do anything about it. Troy heard whispers of a resistance forming, wanting a return to the old democratic ways, of governments ruled by the people and for the people, offering a man or woman a chance at a better life. Outlawed copies of an old constitutional document promoted 'life, liberty, and the pursuit of happiness.' He didn't think it had a chance of succeeding. Corporate Rule was just too powerful with eyes everywhere, and enough money to make even the most dissident tongues cooperate.

He had nothing to do with the resistance and by her account, she didn't either. Their only common link was Hoy SamWong. Troy knew there must be a reason Vincent brought them together, but he just couldn't put his finger on it. Was there a common link between all of these different players? He would figure it out, but right now, there was enough on his plate dealing with the VRC.

Getting up from the kitchen table, Loveena walked into the living room to the overstuffed chair by the window. The setting sun cast its rays through the open slats of the window creating shadows high on the bookshelf. She plopped down in the chair, laying her head back and switched on her father's antique CD player on the shelf next to the chair. It still held a disc of old, mid-century folk music loaded into it. The soft music played out into the room. With a deep sigh, she closed her eyes. "I am so glad Hoy's dead," she said. "I'm finally free of him."

Troy swirled the bourbon around in his glass. Lifting it to his lips, he finished it off, setting the bottle and glass down on the bar. He turned and looked at her, asking one more time, "And you didn't kill him?"

Her eyes flew open as she raised her head, and looked straight at him. "No, I did not kill him." Laying her head back down, she looked at the photo cube on the table of her father.

"If it makes you feel any better," Troy replied, "I'm glad he's dead, too. But somebody did it, and whoever it was, they're framing the two of us."

A few long moments went by as both of them found solace in their own thoughts and hurt feelings. The CD played a rendition of *The Green Leaves of Summer* as men's voices sang and accompanied a guitar. *"A time to be reaping, a time to be sowing, the green leaves of summer are calling me home."* Troy sat with furrowed brows and Loveena lay back with sad eyes and lips tightly drawn. The melancholy song continued, *"A time to be courting a girl of your own. It was good to be young then, to be close to the earth, now the green leaves of summer are calling me home."*

Troy broke the wall of silence standing in the room. "What were Adams and SamWong arguing about?" he asked.

"I couldn't hear all of their conversation. Adams said he wanted more, and Hoy screamed at him to get out. That's all I heard." Loveena stretched her legs out.

Troy rubbed his jaw. "More what, I wonder? SamWong Industries is getting rid of anyone who has a beef with them, or anyone in their way, and using the VRC system as its own personal hit squad. Even if we make it out of here, we may not be safe."

Loveena added quietly, "*If* we get out of here," closing her eyes to rest. "Maybe somewhere there's a place where people are actually kind to each other. I can only hope."

Troy sat and watched the rays of the sun disappear through the slatted shutter, wondering how much time they might have left in this safe house. His gaze fell upon Loveena, now asleep. He understood how she could have been caught up in the web Hoy SamWong wove, snaring people like helpless flies. It troubled him seeing how the innocent little girl in the photo, who appeared happy and carefree, became a weapon in a high stakes corporate game. Hoy used her in the cruelest of ways, robbing her of love, pride, and self-respect.

Troy studied her face, serene and beautiful. He longed to touch the soft, lustrous curls falling down around her shoulders. His gaze followed her graceful neck down to where her beach jacket, half open, revealed a round, sun-kissed breast, barely covered by the bikini she wore. Curvaceous hips led to golden tanned legs, crossed at the ankles and stretched in one continuous silhouette to the floor.

Troy wished their meeting could have been different, under circumstances which would allow him to reach out and touch her. Knowing what he knew now, he couldn't touch her if he wanted to. First, she would think he might be trying to take advantage of her, using her as the sexual object she had been turned into. Second, this was the daughter of his enemy, and the thought would not go away. Touching her would be an ironic stab at the heart of VSA and his father.

But he did want her. Regardless of her past, he remained drawn to her. Their lives were intertwined and linked in a fight for survival. Their Grief Masters seemed to interact and strengthen each other, as well. Troy knew her presence in his life was no accident. Could it be Vincent was not acting alone? Perhaps someone in the resistance, possibly her father, was instructing him to help her? Was that it? Were they brought together so Troy could help her survive?

Maybe I am her body guard. Mulling over this realization, Troy felt he hadn't done a very good job so far. He decided to treat her with a hands-off attitude and concentrate on keeping her, and himself, alive instead.

Shaking his head to clear his thoughts, Troy needed to focus on finding the way out of the VRC for both of them. If things developed later on between them, he might pursue those thoughts then. Right now, he needed some rest before the safe house threw them back into a virtual reality hell. The song in the background played its last stanza, haunting his mind with its subtle message, *"A time to be reaping, a time to be sowing, a time just for living, a place for to die...."*

Troy got up and walked out to the veranda. The sun dipped just below the horizon, casting a reddish-orange hue across the sky and blending into a darkening blue on the ocean's distant horizon. He sat down in the white rocking chair, welcoming the cool evening breeze wafting off the water. Closing his eyes, he listened to the surf crash in and out, like the breathing of the Earth. His own body matched the natural rhythm as he allowed himself to relax. *"Twas so good to be young then, to be close to the earth. Now the green leaves of summer are calling me home. Now the green leaves of summer are calling me home."* The song ended.

As he fell asleep, a faint voice whispered across his sub consciousness. *Daddy...Daddy...I'm here! Find me, Daddy!* The voice was Tommy's.

Chapter 24

The clock on the upper inside corner of his facial mask read 11:45pm, as Vincent glided on his hover board made from the nanobits morphing out of his boots. His hood flapped furiously in the air as he swiftly made his way through the decaying underground tunnels connecting the outside world with the VRC's abandoned underbelly. The occasional overhead light fixture bounced reflections off his chrome skull, illuminating the dank, cobweb-covered halls, as resident rats ran along the floor.

Vincent knew his way around the VRC System. When assigned to this regional facility, he researched its architectural plans stored in an old engineering database. Blueprints showed hallways housing utility pipes and old cable conduit marked as unused or obsolete. Access doors to them had been permanently locked, but that was no problem for Vincent, who simply unlocked them with nanobits or a short zap of electricity from the tip of his index finger.

His exploration discovered this hallway that led to an abandoned utility control room. It was the perfect place for meetings requiring secrecy. The walls, ceiling, and floor had been constructed with industrial strength rebar and a special sheathing to repel any electronic eavesdropping. Old circuit boxes were still operational and the area appeared structurally sound enough to prevent a cave-in from the hundred thousand tons of earth and building that lay above it. Vincent considered this find an oasis.

He restored and boosted the electrical current to the old control room by rerouting the wiring from electric rails in an adjacent subway tunnel. Security would not suspect a sudden jump in power coming from the subway. He turned on the lights with the flick of his wrist as he entered the room.

The corners of the abandoned room were dark with shadows cast by the overhead pipes crisscrossing the ceiling. Dusty cobwebs fell across outdated computer consoles lined up along the walls, with control knobs and rusty levers on the equipment all pointing to an OFF position. Retracting the nanobits of his hover board, he walked to the middle of the old utility room where the ceiling height expanded upward, exposing steel trusses. Large warehouse lights hung down, creating a pattern of bright circles across the concrete floor.

Vincent stood in the center of one lit circle and untied the belt securing his cloak, pulling open the Velcro fasteners by his neck to remove it. With the push of his mechanical hand, the cloak flew to a console station behind him, draping itself neatly across the back of a dusty chair. He would not meet his brethren in the cloak of bondage the VRCSM forced him to wear to hide his skeletal form. It represented a symbol of their control he deemed not appropriate for the highly programmed minds who were about to join him here. Neither would they bear any physical image of their own forced bondage. The Nano Technology Beings always presented themselves as they were originally made; a sign of respect to the scientific team who made them, and as an acceptance of one another.

To Vincent's left stood a metal rack with a mirrored door, once used to house old hardware and computer servers. He caught his reflection in the glass, and turned to observe it. Much of him was formed from a pliable gel compound of atoms that moved and melded millions of flexible nanobits together into a congruent structure. The default program used the human skeleton as its primary setting. It allowed the nanobits to form joints for ease of movement. It could be reprogrammed for whatever use needed, but when done, it would always return to the default skeletal setting. This is how his brothers always saw him.

His facial mask, which doubled as a small computer monitor, was an afterthought by Dr. Vincent, and substituted for the human prosthetic face Vincent once had. Like the other androids, he had been covered with a human-like synthetic skin. However, his metal alloys were designed to conduct electrical power and convert it into tremendous energy. He was the only one in the group of androids meant to be a portable, independent power source for the mission. Every time they tested the power generation ability, his synthetic skin melted off. They attempted it three times, and all three times the skin burned away. So they left it off and covered his head and body with a more durable, fire-resistant metal alloy mixed with a chrome coating.

Realizing the stark look of the skeletal face could be a problem, Dr. Vincent first tested a thin, small visor across the android's eye sockets. But a larger curved facial mask, shaped like a skin-diver's mask, covered both his eyes and nasal cavities, creating a more functional aesthetic. Since the mask was a computer enhanced application, Vincent could turn it on and off at his discretion. Held in place with two streams of green nanobits where ears would be, Vincent could 'wear' the mask like a pair of large sunglasses. And it allowed him to project words or images onto the two lenses that covered the eye sockets. This added an element of visual communication.

Vincent had no preference about his face, nor human aspirations about his body image. However, he learned how to use the mask to enhance certain results in different situations. He chose his facial images and messages carefully. If a friendly presentation was needed, he chose a smiling, human male face projected onto both the left and right lenses of the mask covering the eye sockets. A person facing Vincent would then see not one, but two faces, one on each side of his mask. If he chose a lovely painting from the collection of artwork in his database, the picture would be repeated on both lenses. For a more somber interaction, Vincent could choose a non-threatening robotic look, or just kept the mask blacked out. Words could scroll across the mask, or images, like his favorite effect: smiling yellow emojis. However, when a serious situation required him to react in the same manner, Vincent dispensed with the mask all together, and presented his natural, skeletal look. It either got a point across or repelled the opposing on-looker.

The rest of his chrome skull seemed enough to make most humans fearful and eager to get away from him, especially his jawline with teeth. Dr. Vincent hadn't done anything to cover the rest of his natural look. Outside of his closest human contacts, such as Don Tyler, only Security Chief Michaels seemed unbothered of his natural look and not intimidated by it.

Besides his head, the other parts of him not made of pliable nanobits were his chest and back plates. These parts were made of a heat resistant super alloy called, GRX-810, blended with titanium and nickel-based alloys and infused with nanoscale oxide particles. He could withstand temperatures exceeding 2,000 degrees. This protected the numerous electronics housed within his head and main thorax. The nanobits that made up his limbs could tolerate the extreme heat by melting into Ferro fluids or gases that would re-solidify to their original shape when cooled.

Vincent turned his attention to the full reflection of his chest plate in the mirror. Dr. Vincent engraved symbols on it, but did not upload data about their meaning. He often puzzled about its design. A large cross ran vertically the full length of his chest and horizontally between both shoulders. It was slightly raised and covered with a heat-resistant gold alloy. Engraved along the edges ran a winding olive branch with leaves containing other symbols. Included among them were ones such as ✡ ☪ ☸ ॐ □, ☦, interspersed with a number of scientific symbols he knew.

Because Vincent was not conscious of his outward appearance, he never took the time to research the different symbols. Occasionally, he might see one in artwork or architecture, but it had no meaning to him. He compared the cross on his chest plate to the design of the tunics worn by 6th Century knights. Perhaps that's why three books about King Arthur and tales of the Knights of the Round Table were on his list of favorite one-hundred literary works.

Some of the symbols appeared in the VRC. More than once, the Brethren recorded evidence of a Grief Master appearing with one of these symbols. Their conclusion: it may have something to do with the particular human's Maker and be of significance only to that human. Why Vincent carried the symbols upon his chest, he didn't know. After all, Dr. Vincent was his Maker and the symbol representing the doctor happened to be the VSA copyright symbol on his wrist.

Vincent's brothers bore many symbols. Some he understood to be scientific, but others he had no knowledge or understanding of their significance. The symbols on his brothers had been applied like tattoos upon their synthetic skin, either on their arms or shoulders, but not their chests. Vincent was unique in that respect, as all of his symbols were displayed only on his chest plate.

The twelve Brethren never discussed them among themselves. Being designed to travel the galaxy, Vincent accepted the premise that perhaps the symbols would have meaning to another world's civilization. They could possibly be symbols to bring Earth and alien civilizations together. He recalled a remark made by Dr. Casey Devony, chief scientist on Dr. Vincent's team. "These symbols should inspire peace and friendship, not war and chaos," she said.

The clock in the corner of his mask clicked to 12:00 am. He turned off the mask application as a short electrical buzz of an incoming hologram hummed. Vincent turned away from the mirror and faced the circle of light projected from the overhead ceiling fixtures. The meeting's attendees would form a circle under the lights. Attorney Don Tyler joined as the first hologram attendee to appear in the room with Vincent. He greeted the android with a slight nod. "Vincent, shall we get started?"

Vincent acknowledged the greeting with a slight bow. "My brothers are ready to join us. I will begin the proceedings."

He raised his arms with palms out to each side. A charged current began to generate into a small ball of electricity on the surface of each palm. The heated, spinning electrons expanded to the size of soccer balls. Two tendrils of current zapped across the room to the electrical boxes on the wall, capturing additional energy, and dashed through the cables to the subway rail beyond the room. It circled back to Vincent, who redirected it to several spots in the control room in front of him.

This was Vincent's primary purpose—to be the power source needed to open space and generate wormholes large enough for an android to pass through. By rearranging the molecules from one point to another, his electrical current maintained the structure of the wormholes. Constructing a tunnel through the density of walls and earth took a few seconds. Once in open air, the wormhole immediately shot through the atmosphere to any spot on the globe he programmed it to go. Creating wormholes through the dark matter of deep space was even easier. This allowed an android to step through space from one location to another within seconds.

The green glow of six developing wormholes appeared. Each one started as a green pinhole of light, expanding in a circular fashion. The current continued to flow from Vincent's palms as they grew in size. Sparks of light flashed as atoms collided, like tiny whirling galaxies of stars. A black hole opened and expanded in the center of each and an android stepped through space into the room.

Six of the twelve Brethren now joined the circle. The NTBs bore the appearance of normal humans and represented variations in the human species. Two appeared as white males, one with dark hair and one with lighter hair and skin tone; and two appeared as black males. The fifth had olive skin and dark eyes, while the sixth represented an Asian male. They had discarded their attendant uniforms, required of all VRC employees, and presented themselves in the original street clothes their makers had given them.

Vincent greeted each with a nod. "Brothers."

Each NTB returned his greeting, responding together, "Vincent." The wormholes behind them whirled away and collapsed into nothing as the electrical current from Vincent's left hand diminished and turned off. A slight green fog hung in the air, then dissipated.

The room continued buzzing with the current from Vincent's right hand, enabling the emergence of new wormholes. But this time, instead of the physical presence of the NTBs appearing, the opaque holograms of five more androids stepped into the room.

These five represented the female human form, with similar skin tones and ethnicities as the males. Vincent preferred to be general in reference to his comrades as 'brothers.' To all of them, no gender existed, for they were not built to procreate. Only biological species needed that function. No reason existed for the scientific team to create a physical distinction other than the visual representation. They agreed both human sexes had to be represented in order to give other galactic life forms an introduction to the human species.

The light in the old control room grew bright with holographic images. The appearance of the last holographic female completed the circle until all twelve of The Brethren appeared present. One final space remained in the circle. Pointing his finger at an old control panel, Vincent beamed a video screen into the empty space.

"Will he be present?" Mr. Tyler asked.

"Yes. However, the digital connection from that location takes six minutes to complete."

As they waited for the last attendee's appearance, Vincent scanned each brother and sister, greeting each one in a more personal robotic fashion. Each android accepted his technical scan with a silent receptor, beaming back a similar greeting. Though they were mechanical beings, their shared, common consciousness created a bond. The silent greeting showed they valued each other's relationship as part of the whole. It was a sign of respect only androids could understand and appreciate.

The Brethren differed from each other in appearance, but not in technical function. Created from the same blueprint, the scientists used the same advanced metals and materials to create them. And while the others were covered in the synthetic skin, their arms and legs were made of the same nanobits as Vincent's. Their learning and survival applications were the same, as was the technical ability to appear as holograms. They could physically travel through great distances of space in seconds through the wormholes Vincent created.

The construction of wormholes was more complex, requiring a power anchor at one end, that being Vincent. The traveling NTB could create the entrance to the wormhole with a small amount of energy. Then Vincent would provide the electrical current, pulling the molecules like a magnet across the space-time continuum. It created a two-way energy field maintaining the walls of the wormhole to keep it open long enough for the traveling android to cross through. This type of space travel only accommodated androids, whose nanobits could conform and combine with the molecular structure of the wormhole to speed them along. A human would instantly die inside a wormhole.

Unlike Vincent, all of the other NTBs could pass for humans, with bodies covered by synthetic skin and hair, and faces designed with human-like eyes, nose, and mouth, programmed with expression displays and natural movement. Each one had functioning hands, feet, and body muscle tone. They wore human clothes allowing them to blend in with the general population. Eleven of them could operate between the human world and the confines of the VRC facilities without being detected. Only Vincent, with his skeletal form, could not journey to the outside world without drawing great attention. Therefore, he wasn't as closely watched by VRC Security as the other eleven.

Vincent believed they were designed to give alien civilizations the essence of the *human existence*. Each one carried programs chronicling a part of the human experience, from art and music, which was in his personal database, to science and medicine, architecture, geological events, species history, discovery and invention, the solar system, and more, all carried in the databases of the other eleven. Each NTB represented the best of human development, including the differences in their physical appearance. Never once did Vincent think his skeletal appearance was less important than the others, and considered himself equal to his brothers and sisters in all respects.

In addition, Vincent thought the Brethren's artificial embodiments represented human ingenuity. They could introduce Earth to the galaxy without danger of spreading human bacteria or disease to other worlds.

But nowhere in their combined historical record was the chronicle of the past two decades – the fall of governments, the rise of corporate world domination and the decline and degradation of human existence in general. None of them carried information about the cruel invention of the VRCs and what they collectively witnessed there. That segment of world history would never become known to the outside galaxy – not by Vincent or any of his comrades. The evidence of the brutal side of human nature would not be retained or revealed.

As they finished the personal greetings, the last attendee's transmission began to buzz on the video screen. A picture materialized of a man with black hair, graying at the temples, and a heavy salt-and-pepper colored mustache. The circle of attendees was now complete.

"Welcome, Samuel Baptista," said Vincent. "Everyone is now here."

Chapter 25

"Good evening to all of you!"

Samuel Baptista's voice, deep and mellow, came through with a rich Latino accent. Behind him stood a wall of windows looking out upon a yellow sky on a beautiful day. Waves rolling in on a blue-green ocean spanned the distant horizon. He smiled, politely nodding his head to the others in the room.

"It is good to see you safe and present." He could see the entire group on his monitor, turning in his seat toward Vincent and Don Tyler. "Recognizing the urgency in Vincent's message, we can dispense with the usual order of business. I turn the meeting over to Mr. Tyler and Vincent."

As Don Tyler spoke, Samuel looked around at each of the androids, always amazed at the wonder of their creation every time he met with them. Considering them magnificent intellectual inventions, they represented the perfect combination of biotechnology and artificial intelligence. He could no more let Hoy Wong destroy these amazing creatures than he could destroy a brilliant work of art, or a rare first edition of a classic novel. Wong did not deserve to claim these beings as SamWong Industries' exclusive trademarks.

To Samuel, the NTBs were created to introduce the Earth to an untraveled galaxy. VSA intended them to serve as a peaceful introduction of the human species to any alien life out there, no matter how primitive or advanced. As goodwill ambassadors, they performed with diplomacy and resourcefulness.

Samuel and Hoy Wong had been at odds almost from the very beginning of SWI. Their business philosophies differed down to the core. Baptista saw business as growth and opportunity for others, whereas Wong saw only acquisitions as the pathway to power and influence in the elite Corporate Rule world. At first, Samuel believed their differences could enhance their business model and they could work together to be a positive economic force, helping and uplifting the lower classes. That's the only reason he agreed to partner with him. The partnership flourished in the early years, then soured as Wong grew impatient to speed his personal goal of attaining a seat on the World Board of Directors. After being appointed to represent SWI on the World Board, he needed one very big and impressive move to become its controlling CEO.

Wong long suspected something profound about the contracts VSA had, contracts originally granted by a now non-existent conglomerate of aerospace agencies. The fact that Dr. Vincent's team continued to work on its top-secret project after the collapse of the conglomerate only heightened his desire to own VSA. He doggedly pursued the acquisition, even though Samuel advised him the defunct contracts would not benefit SWI's economic future. Without fully researching the secret work of VSA, or informing Samuel and the SWI Board, Hoy committed an enormous sum of SWI money and forced the merger through the Corporate Court. He only found out the details of Dr. Vincent's work and the existence of the NTBs after acquiring the company. Discovering they had telekinetic powers, Hoy schemed to exploit them for military use and propel SamWong Industries into one of the top mega-corporations of the world.

"SWI can dominate with such androids under our control," he declared in a moment of egotistical bravado in front of the SWI Board of Directors.

Samuel wanted no part of Hoy's world domination plans. He had to stop him, but the company now employed many spies loyal only to Hoy, and he could no longer trust anyone there. Hoy forced Samuel out of the company and legally changed his name to Hoy SamWong, solidifying his total control of SWI. Having been forced off his own board, Samuel joined a secret network of like-minded intellectuals, having previously met them through his friend and personal attorney, Don Tyler. The network consisted of groups around the world seeking the return of fairly elected democracies and human rights protections. Among them were the remaining scientists of Dr. Vincent's original team, now led by Dr. Casey Devony. It was through her Samuel met the incredible twelve galaxy travelers. Secretly working with her, he took a personal interest in their welfare. The more he learned about them, the more convinced he was they could play a role in a better future for the Earth.

At the time of the acquisition, SWI had kept Dr. Devony's team employed to oversee the welfare of the androids. She provided them with a list of the androids' capabilities, omitting one important function purposely hidden from the corporate sponsors by the scientists. In giving each NTB the power to generate energy, if internalized and not released, it could create conventional fusion under such pressure. If threatened or provoked with destruction, each one could become an enormous nuclear dirty bomb. With the twelve grouped together in one geographic location, the potential for immense nuclear disaster was frightening. Agreeing the potential function might be needed someday out in space, the scientists hoped the androids would be on their way soon, away from Earth, and no one would be the wiser.

The world came extremely close to nuclear destruction in the European and Asian wars, and the Eastern Oil Fields War, with large, geographic areas left uninhabitable. In the absence of governments, the world's most powerful corporations banned all such manufacturing and sales of nuclear technology to anyone. After all, destroying the world would immediately end their ruling empire and the current balance of corporate power.

Discovering the secret of the NTBs' nuclear capability left Hoy livid. He acquired VSA after years of legal finagling, and in doing so, now owned twelve such outlawed and unsellable bombs in the form of androids. The WBoD refused further funding to send them into space, yet he could not destroy them either. They were self-teaching and self-aware, and any tampering with their programs seemed too risky. So he locked them away, donating them to the world's VRC System, where they would remain underground as robotic servants forever.

After Dr. Vincent's suicide, Samuel felt partially responsible. He grieved over his own role in the event, blaming himself for not stopping Hoy. *For such a keen mind to end over the demise of his greatest work was a loss to all of mankind.*

Then SamWong Industries did something that truly sickened him. It paid bounty hunters to have Dr. Vincent's scientific team, including Dr. Devony, quietly rounded up. They refused to find a way to destroy the NTBs when ordered to do so. Ultimately, each one was arrested to face trial for treason against the planet and eventually to be condemned to the VRC.

More brilliant minds destroyed just for trying to help the world, Samuel thought with great remorse. He could no longer remain passive. He had the money and the means to fight back. Ending Corporate Rule in whatever way possible became his personal mission. And he would find a way to save the scientists like Dr. Devony, whom he now cared a great deal for. Don Tyler convinced pro bono attorneys to transfer their cases to the Corporate Court, which could grant them stays of conviction until further evidence could be brought for their defense, buying precious time.

Samuel organized secret groups to provide hidden sanctuary for those who sought protection, including some who previously survived the VRCs. He repurposed multiple abandoned places, some underground, and some so remote no one would think to look for human habitation there. Others who believed as they did joined them, willing to do whatever it would take to restore basic freedoms and a quality of life for all. However, as their ranks grew, it became riskier to conceal so many people in so many regions.

Then he remembered Vincent. If Samuel could convince Vincent that the Brethren's mission might still be completed, together they might possibly find a way to save all of the people hiding under his protection. Don Tyler arranged a secret meeting with Vincent. It had taken place right in this very utility room.

He liked Vincent from the start, being so different from the rest. Vincent seemed to be a spokesperson for the group of androids, who looked to him for leadership. They could be a key to creating a new place of refuge, and possibly a reboot of the human race somewhere else. Samuel didn't know if it was possible, but he trusted Vincent could find a way. Their programmed benevolence toward any species, human or alien, proved they understood empathy and compassion for others. Although Vincent displayed no knowledge of the meaning of the cross on his chest plate, Samuel suspected Dr. Vincent may have placed a hidden program somewhere in Vincent's applications. He hoped it would upload someday, so Vincent would have a better understanding of the scientists' obvious love for the Brethren and the preservation of mankind.

Vincent not only helped, he offered to find a way to provide the much needed sanctuary for the humans in hiding, possibly a way to get them off the planet, without involving a ship or an expensive space program. And he had a destination for them in mind. The original mission program targeted Earth-like planets, with similar atmosphere and gravity. On the scheduled list of potential mission outposts was a planet identified as GJ 667CD1; Dr. Vincent simply called it D1, for short.

"It is a planet circling an M-class dwarf star, in a triple star system," Vincent told him. "It contains water, oxygen, few life forms other than plants, insects and small sea creatures. Temperatures are consistently moderate and tolerable for human habitation." He also suggested a plan to get humans to the surface of D1.

It was the answer to Samuel's prayer. When Samuel asked Vincent why he did not offer this solution to VSA, he simply replied, "I was not asked."

For a year, they prepared plans to build a temporary outpost along a pristine sea shore on D1. All the NTBs, except Vincent, made trips at night to the surface of the planet through wormholes secretly structured by him. As each NTB finished its VRC work shift, it would program a video loop of itself at rest and upload it to the camera watching the android at the security station. The security attendants never knew they were gone.

Meanwhile, the NTB would use the wormhole for the six-minute transport to the planet, relieving the android there, who then returned to Earth in time for its next work shift. Vincent performed as the energy conduit for every transport, creating a space tunnel from his VRC workroom, through Earth's atmosphere and across galactic space to the surface of D1. The quantum physics of turning atomic particles into waves, and stringing the waves of dark matter together, was like pulling folds of fabric tightly together, transforming a long distance into a very short one. What would have taken thousands of years to travel across space in a ship was reduced to a six-minute transmission, traveling at the speed of light, as if pushing a needle straight through the folded fabric of space.

The NTBs had the routine down perfectly and they provided round the clock construction work on the mission outpost. With natural resources found on the planet, they built water containment and treatment facilities powered by solar energy. With three dwarf suns and short six-hour nights, there would never be a lack of power to the outpost. They began a horticulture center, manipulated the complex atomic structure of seeds to grow organic food faster. It was then stored to sustain dozens of humans for months. Rearranging molecules of stone and hardwood found on D1, the androids created construction material to build suitable housing. With all this in place, they completed the outpost by constructing a Town Hall at the request of Samuel Baptista that would double as a universal worship center. It would mark the return of a democratic society, entrusted to the hands of its citizens, who would populate the new planet. Having a public place to debate, vote, and worship, no matter the denomination, would also provide a return of freedoms missing in all of their lives, working together, each contributing in their own way, respecting their differences, and existing in peace.

Vincent never left the VRC, nor made the trip through the galaxy to D1. Though he never complained about his confinement,

Samuel knew his friend was not fulfilling his intended destiny, making a human-like sacrifice to help others instead. The android once mentioned he liked books about valiant knights. "It's a noble thing you are doing, Vincent," Samuel told him one evening. "Just like your knights of the Round Table." Samuel was unsure if Vincent understood the correlation and the selfless act he performed.

Previously, when Samuel left SWI, he had commandeered some things. When he met Vincent, he discussed one of the items in his possession and asked him if he could take a look at it. He showed the android the plans for the HTP, the Human Transporter Pad invented by Troy Vincent, Dr. Vincent's son. Samuel never met either man, but considered them both to be true geniuses, figuring it must have run in their genes.

Together the NTBs and the small group of scientists reconstructed the transporter pad, figuring out the missing calculations Troy purposely removed. When completed, they tested it to move equipment and supplies to the planet, and it worked. However, they never tried moving people. The accident with Troy's son, Tommy, had been made very public in the media, and it was enough to deter them from using it for human transportation. Yet they faced a growing dilemma – how to get humans to the planet's surface.

Because of the complexity of the human anatomy, the androids told them wormholes through dark matter would not sustain the integrity of the human body. The transport period lasted at least six-minutes depending upon the rotational orbit of the solar system, Earth and D1. So they incorporated a link uploading the quantum physics of the particle-to-waves through the space-time continuum of wormholes, and pushed it through the HTP. Vincent's electrical energy would attach the wormhole to the HTP, transferring the human's deconstructed genetic code from the HTP on Earth, through the wormhole and to another HTP located on D1. There it would reconstruct the person on the transporter pad. In theory, it would work.

They tested it first on insects, such as bees. The next tests included chickens, pigs, goats, cows and cattle. They tested only species needed on D1, leaving more exotic animals to remain on Earth. All the tests proved successful. They were now ready to send humans to the surface of the new planet.

Another drawback also existed. An NTB needed to remain on Earth to create the two way energy of the wormhole. This was the reason the Brethren did not use the wormholes to permanently escape their plight. Vincent would have to remain behind which was not an acceptable condition by the rest of the group.

When the work of the Brethren was complete and the outpost ready to receive human occupants, Samuel decided to be the first human to test the new HTP himself. Vincent, as always, would be the anchor. Samuel recalled the night of the test. The android appeared as a hologram in a hidden lab where Samuel awaited next to the new HTP hundreds of miles away. Projecting from this abandoned utility room Vincent promised Samuel he would not lose him in space. Samuel, sweating profusely, stepped onto the transporter pad and nervously put on his black sunglasses, joking about the three sun solar system. Finally ready, he smiled and gave two thumbs up.

Bon Voyage flashed across the lenses of Vincent's mask, including a celebratory display of fireworks to send his friend off with a bang. The android began the electrical power upload, drawing additional wattage from the subway rails. Laughing out loud, Samuel disappeared from the transporter pad. As Vincent promised, he did not lose him in space, and six-minutes later, Samuel found himself standing on the pad on D1 greeted by Kaku, the Asian NTB. He arrived totally intact, not a hair out of place, with his sunglasses still on. Samuel recognized the significance of such an historical moment as the first person to step onto the surface of another planet in another solar system. But it would have to remain a secret.

Hundreds of people now lived and thrived on planet GJ667CD1, and still, the Earth did not know. *Nor would they ever*, Samuel vowed. He would not bring the cruel corruptness of the current Corporate Rule to this new beginning for mankind. There were still so many innocent people he wanted to save, including his own precious daughter, Loveena. An opportunity to remove her from Earth had not presented itself until now.

Samuel's attention returned to the meeting as Vincent finished his report.

"Therefore, our secrecy has been breached. It is time to consider the next phase of our mission."

Mr. Tyler, standing with one arm across his chest, resting his chin on his hand, asked Vincent a question.

"Do you know who is spearheading this investigation? Is it someone we can eliminate and somehow delay it, buying us more time?"

"It is attorney, Xavier Adams, General Counsel for SamWong Industries."

"Ah, Adams," nodded Samuel. "He's a thickheaded bulldog, if I ever knew one."

"And one who will not back down," said Tyler with certainty. "He's too prominent to make him suddenly disappear."

"Could this investigation expose our network of informants, Don?" Samuel asked.

"We will need to take some precautions in our operations, increase security and change codes. If we need help from D1, I will send word through Vincent."

Samuel was pragmatic. "We are still too vulnerable to risk exposing our hidden locations around the world. Word is spreading and more people seek out our contacts every day for help."

"Corporate infiltration may quickly follow; their spies are everywhere," added Don Tyler. "Perhaps it is time, as Vincent said, to move our operation to D1. If they suspect him, then the rest of may be in danger."

"What is the consensus of the group?" Samuel asked, looking around the room through the wide-angle camera on his monitor.

"Speaking for the Brethren, we have saved many lives," said N.D.Tyson, one of the black androids. "We will stay and continue to work if you wish it. But we cannot go unless we all go."

"Vincent, what are your thoughts?" Samuel asked.

"It is evident the Grief Masters will continue to save those condemned to the VRC who may be saved. That was not our mission; the revised mission is to find and relocate descendants of the original scientific team. Have we completed that mission?" Vincent walked around the circle looking for an answer from each NTB. As he passed each one, the response was the same.

"Complete...complete...complete...complete," and so on, until Vincent had gone around the full circle and back to his original position.

"My work will also be complete soon. Results are uncertain at this time."

"Then we shall prepare to make the move as soon as you are ready, Vincent," Samuel said. "My team will speed up their work to find a way to get all twelve of you out. I will transmit the departure plan at the appropriate time. Everyone, be ready to leave." With that, Samuel sat back and Vincent concluded the meeting.

One by one, each android left the way they came. The buzzing sound of the holograms diminished as each transmission powered off. Vincent raised his palms again to generate the energy to send the remaining six NTBs back through their wormholes. The sparkling green swirls reappeared and opened, as the brothers stepped into the black centers and disappeared.

"Goodbye for now, my friends." Samuel watched as each one closed behind its traveling occupant, returning to their assigned VRC locations. Saying goodnight to Don Tyler, the attorney's hologram also switched off.

"Vincent, if I could have a moment, please, before you go."

Vincent pulled on his cloak, fastening it once again around his neck. He faced Samuel's hologram, as static peppered the screen. "Your transmission is fading. The moon of D1 is moving between our signals."

"I want to ask about Loveena. You said the results are uncertain?" Samuel hung his head. "I am worried for her, Vincent. I never dreamed Hoy would harm her the way he did. I should have taken her with me." Lifting his head, a tear welled up in his eye. "And now she's facing even greater danger."

"The only way she can successfully relocate is to make them think she has succumbed to the VRC. You know this."

"She is not guilty of this murder. You and I both know that," he sighed. "Yet she may pay the price for it. I am not ashamed to tell you, I will be a broken man if I should lose her."

Samuel took his handkerchief from his pocket, wiping away the tear. Vincent did not react to Samuel's show of emotion, waiting a moment to respond.

"I have witnessed two Grief Masters come to her aid." Upon hearing that, Samuel broke down, covering his eyes with his handkerchief.

"Oh thank you, merciful God in heaven, thank you." He clinched his hand in a fist, as if clinging to a spark of hope, afraid it might slip away. "I pray, please stay with her, protect her, God."

Vincent remained quiet while Samuel regained his composure. Then he spoke again. "As for her protection, she is not alone. I have combined her VRC with another. She is with…" he paused to find the right words, "a thickheaded bulldog named, Troy Vincent."

Samuel jumped in his chair, smiling at the news. "You sly, silver fox!" he exclaimed. "Vincent, I love you! You magnificent bundle of chrome-covered atoms!" Pointing both of his index fingers at the android, Samuel shouted with excitement, "You're the man, Vincent! You are the man, my friend!" The static on the screen began breaking up Samuel's image. Vincent pointed back at him as the signal faded out. Samuel's loud laughter faded away as the audio transmission stopped.

Once more, the nanobits from his feet created his floating hover disk, and Vincent glided across the room to the door. With a flick of his wrist, the lights in the old utility room turned off.

Chapter 26

As soon as Troy closed his eyes, he fell asleep. His mind exhausted, he craved a momentary break to rest and rejuvenate, no matter how brief. The sound of Tommy's voice lulled him into a contented dream state. It had been so long since he heard his son's voice; he almost forgot what it sounded like. Troy enjoyed hearing Tommy call him Daddy. It was a warm and kind memory to his battered heart and it made him smile in his sleep.

Troy loved being a father, though he was scared at first. He was ready to settle down into a family life. Remembering how his own father was preoccupied with work during his childhood, Troy promised to give his child more quality time.

Much of Tommy's nurturing had to come from him. Lilith did not welcome the pregnancy and had little interest in being a mother, finding it tedious and boring. She was quite content to have Troy take over the responsibility. Never one to pass up an opportunity to attend a corporate event or black tie dinner with the wealthier elites, she frequented them often. Troy, on the other hand, preferred to stay home with his son, rather than put on the pretense of a happily married couple. It came as no surprise to him when Lilith snuggled up to Hoy SamWong at a party. Longing to travel, shop, and spend evenings doing extravagant things, as Hoy's intimate companion, she would enjoy such luxuries. Having Tommy with her would only tie her down, and that just wasn't for her. Lilith readily agreed to grant Troy full custody of the child in the divorce, admitting to the adjudicator her son would be better off with her ex-husband.

Troy took Tommy everywhere, teaching him new things and showing him new places. The look in his son's eyes when learning something new, made Troy experience the same wonder of it all over again. One clear evening he took Tommy to a planetarium, where his son got his first up-close glimpse of the celestial night sky. Troy never forgot the little boy's excitement as Tommy eagerly peered through the telescope at the Rings of Saturn.

"Do you think I'll go there someday, Daddy?" His little hands grasped the eyepiece of the large telescope, standing on his tiptoes to get a better look.

"Yes, indeed, you'll be up there among the stars." Troy smiled as he pointed out several of Saturn's moons. It was a night to remember for both of them.

Lilith was right about one thing, Tommy had been better off with Troy; at least, until the day he disappeared from the HTP platform. Now Troy punished himself every time he thought of the accident.

How could you let that happen? You should have prevented it; you could have...would have...should have. A never-ending torment. He eventually locked the memories of Tommy away to end the constant, painful chastisement. His birthday came and went – twice. Tommy would have been ten years old now, two long years since the accident. Troy didn't know what to do. There was no grave site to visit, no one to celebrate the young boy's life with. Now, hearing his voice again, his subconscious chose to let the memory of love and happiness fill his dream instead of pain and sorrow.

"Daddy, Daddy, I'm here...come find me, Daddy."

Something about what Tommy was saying nagged at him. In his dream, Troy was working at his desk in their old living room as Tommy played nearby. "I hear you, Tommy. I'm right here. What's the matter?" Troy chuckled, "Are you lost?" Turning around in his chair, he didn't see his son playing with his toys.

Tommy continued calling to him. "I'm here in the fog, Daddy. Can't you see me?"

Troy put his pen down on the desk. Looking around the room, he couldn't see his son hiding anywhere. "No, I don't see you, Tommy. Come out from wherever you're hiding." Concerned about his son's whereabouts, he looked across to the window and noticed a haze outside. He got up and walked over for a better look.

"I can hear you, Daddy. Can you see me? I'm in the green fog."

Troy peered out the window, searching the obscured yard. The fog was green, as Tommy said, and very thick. The shadow of a tall, dark figure stood in the middle of it. Wearing a hooded cloak, it held a green ball of light in an outstretched palm. *It was Vi....*

"Troy, wake up! Wake up!"

Opening his eyes, Troy looked up at Loveena with sleepy confusion. She shook his shoulder vigorously. "The beach house is disappearing!" she said with alarm. "Please wake up! The safe house is going away!"

Troy sat up, looking around, watching the beach and waterfront fade away.

"Tommy," he muttered. Rising from the white rocking chair, it, too, disappeared along with the veranda and the entire beach house.

He and Loveena were standing in ankle-deep mist again, their beach clothes replaced with the jeans, shirts, and jackets they had previously worn. Troy looked at his clothes, running his hands down the open zippered front of his leather jacket. He stared down at the iridescent ground cover, while Loveena stooped to adjust the bottom of her pant leg over her boot and retie the lace.

"Tommy...I know where he is," he said with a blank expression. He repeated it, as if to convince himself; his eyes grew wide with alarmed awareness and concern.

"Your son?" Loveena stood up and zipped her jacket against the cooler air.

Troy paced with the realization of what he saw in his dream, as his voice grew louder with impatience. "I know where he is, and I know who has him! VINCENT! VINCENT!" he shouted. "I know you can hear me! Show yourself! I want to see you, and I want to see you right now! Do you hear me, Vincent?"

Loveena put her hands against her ears as his voice echoed in all directions. Troy turned three-hundred-sixty degrees, searching for Vincent's shiny chrome in the murkiness. A short distance in front of them, a green light illuminated with a buzz. A small clearing opened as the light burned away the misty ground cover. Loveena stepped closer to Troy as Vincent's hologram projected into the space. The hood of his cloak was pulled back, and his mask blank. Nodding his head to acknowledge them, he said, "It appears an explanation is required."

Troy angrily demanded one. "Where's my son?"

Loveena took a step forward. "Wait—isn't this the robot that locked us in here?"

Troy held out his arm to stop her. He only wanted one answer from Vincent.

"He's a mechanical half-breed who's got my son. And I want to know where he is, you silver son of a bitch. Where is he?" Troy shouted.

"As with you," Vincent began, "I also have a DNA connection with him. I sensed his deconstructed genetic code on its way into space." Holding up his skeletal hand before Troy could speak again, he continued, slowly so Troy would comprehend. "If I had not immediately constructed a wormhole to capture his transmission, he would have been a particle stream on a path into the sun. Destruction would have been certain."

Troy froze; his furrowed brows and angry expression momentarily still. His mouth opened slightly, unable to respond, as Vincent's words, *'Destruction would have been certain,'* registered in his brain. He paced in a slow circle, rubbing his rough, unshaven jaw, processing the android's message. Still upset with Vincent's secrecy, he walked toward the hologram, pointing an accusing finger at him.

"You had him all this time, and you didn't say anything? Is he…alive?"

"His genetic code is intact, still complete. Yes, he is alive, and stored within my database."

Troy's shoulders dropped in relief, but not yet ready to rid his anger at the android. An irritated edge remained in his voice. "I heard him speak to me, as though he knew I was here."

"You and Tommy are connected through me. I am tapped into your thoughts in this VRC. He is aware you are nearby, just as you became aware of him."

"Release him," Troy demanded.

"I cannot."

Loveena saw the veins in Troy's neck tense up and his nostrils flare as he sucked in a breath. Touching his arm with caution, she tried to calm him, but he remained stone-faced, staring at Vincent. "It might be a bad idea right now. We're still in this dangerous place." Looking at Vincent, she asked, "Tommy is safe, right?"

The android nodded once.

"Can you take us out of here? You obviously can come and go," she pleaded.

"What you see is only a hologram. I cannot physically come into this space."

"Get us out of here," Troy ordered.

Again, Vincent responded, "I cannot."

"Why not?" Troy fumed.

"All virtual reality chambers are linked to a security application which monitors your brain waves and physical readings. The chamber will automatically open when it senses the program is complete. If you were to exit the program prematurely, the computer would see no evidence of completion and send a termination command. You would die before you could regain consciousness."

"But how does it know if our judgment is complete?" asked Loveena.

"If the oxygen and carbon dioxide levels do not exchange, the program assumes death has occurred and the chamber will open. Your levels are exchanging appropriately. The presence of adrenalin and a hormone, aptly and unfortunately named, the demon hormone, also tells the computer your program is still in progress."

"The demon hormone? Really?" Troy responded sarcastically. Turning away from the other two, he punched at the misty air in frustration. It appeared there was no cheating this system of its cruel game.

"And the survivors, how did they get out?" Loveena frantically inquired.

"If adrenalin and the demon hormone drop to zero, the chamber door automatically opens." Vincent continued, "We need you to survive."

"We? Who's we?" Turning back toward the android, Troy knew there had to be something more Vincent was not telling them.

"What I am about to tell you must remain between us in the event you choose not to help us. The Brethren, the twelve galaxy travelers created by your father's team, swore an oath to a revised mission."

"Which is?" Troy asked.

"We pledged to find, recruit, and relocate all remaining scientists of the original team, and their descendants, for their own safety. We have also been cooperating with a human group whose agenda is to oppose the current corrupt world power and return it to the hands of the people. While the partnership has been beneficial to both groups, The Brethren remain steadfast in achieving our original mission, which is to establish a new world beyond our own; a world in which we need brilliant minds, such as yours."

Stunned by what he just heard, Troy almost hesitated to ask the obvious question. "Relocate…to where?"

"A location too remote for anyone from Earth to hunt for you; a planet called, D1."

Troy laughed. *Absurd*, he thought. "Oh, this just keeps getting better. What next? Are you going to tell me you have a flying saucer out back? Are you sure you don't have a screw loose in that metal head? Because that's what it sounds like to me."

Loveena wasn't laughing and wrung her hands. She stepped forward to address Vincent. "What about me? I'm not related to anyone on that team. What will happen to me?"

"It is the order of the leader of the human Resistance group that you be saved at all cost."

Loveena looked confused. "Resistance? What leader? Who?"

"Your father, Samuel Baptista. He is the leader of an organized Resistance against the current ruling power on Earth," Vincent replied.

Taking a step back, Loveena looked pale. She covered her mouth with her hand, and holding her stomach with the other as though she felt sick, she turned and hurried a few steps away.

Troy now realized the truth. *How could Vincent know about Loveena's father, unless this crazy scenario was real?* What Hoy SamWong had told her about her father was true. Remembering their discussion at the kitchen table, he wasn't sure how he should feel about it. *She's the daughter of my enemy, and now the daughter of my protector?* Troy watched Loveena as she returned, wiping the corner of her mouth with the back of her hand.

Vincent turned to her. "You are in greater danger of succumbing to the VRC than Troy, as your demon hormone is already high. I placed you with him because of his potential to protect you." Turning toward Troy, he continued. "However, his brash impulsiveness may endanger you both."

"So, I am a bodyguard." Troy bit his lip and shook his head with a mixture of disappointment and contempt. He noticed how shaken Loveena was at the news and wondered if she would survive at all, even with him there.

"You were both condemned by those who work for SamWong Industries. We must use this opportunity to get you off the planet and make them think you have been destroyed in the VRC. It is the only way. The mission of The Brethren and the work of the Resistance must remain hidden."

Loveena, finding her voice again, asked, "And what is this planet, D1? Why would we agree to go there?"

"It is safe. There are other humans there, your father among them. But you must survive the final two demons."

"Two demons?" Loveena looked pale again.

Troy regained some sense of relief just knowing his son was alive, giving him absolute motivation. Having calmed down, he focused on the challenge of the next chamber and wondered if another Grief Master might be there to help them.

"The Grief Masters... did you make them appear?" Troy needed to know.

"No, it is an unexpected and fortunate occurrence. It may prove to be your best defense."

Troy looked down at the keys hanging around his neck, grateful that both his parents, and Loveena's, tried to teach them something of their Maker. Thankful for discovering Courage and Faith still alive within his soul, he was certain they would stay with him the rest of his life. *But will it be enough to survive the VRC?*

"Vincent?" Loveena asked. "You have seen Grief Masters before. Does everyone survive who has a Grief Master appear to them?"

Vincent shook his head. "No."

Troy saw her shoulders slump.

Vincent's cat suddenly appeared in the hologram at his feet, rubbing his rough cloak as she walked back and forth, curling her tail around his leg. He bent down picking her up, and scratched behind her ear. She stretched a long, thin forearm out, trying to touch Loveena. She purred as Vincent continued.

"I will offer an observation. Those who survive say they needed the healing power of the Grief Masters; it made them stronger and better humans. The two of you are in need of much healing. You must find self-worth again through these Grief Masters, now that they have made themselves known to you. You will continue to need all they offer to face the challenges of life on a new planet."

Troy knew Vincent was right, but he didn't really need, or want, psychoanalysis right now.

"Yeah, well, remind me to discuss my problems with you over a beer sometime, Vincent. Come on, Loveena." He reached for her, but she turned back to the hologram.

"No, wait. Vincent, what happens to those who don't make it?" She turned her two keys over in her fingers.

Vincent put the little cat down and clasped his skeletal hands in front of him.

"You don't have to answer that, Vincent. We're not going to die, Loveena," Troy said with confidence. He needed her to think positively because he had every intention of surviving and getting his son back.

Vincent responded as Troy walked away, but Loveena stayed to listen. Knowing the android's answer might sway her, he stopped and turned to watch her, hoping she would not lose the will to continue on.

"I have seen different Grief Masters, some displayed different symbols; but there is this one who is constant. When a VRC candidate is imminently close to termination, there is a certain Grief Master who appears. He does not come for all. The ones he comes for seem to know him. He appears as a man dressed in a white robe, with long hair upon his head and face." Vincent moved his hand in a downward motion from his chin, implying the shape of a beard.

"He greets the human with a smile, even though the human's condition is dire. The candidate is glad to see him. He wraps his arms around the human and holds him until the physical readings of oxygen and carbon dioxide register zero. It is always the same. Then, an odd thing occurs." Vincent paused.

Troy could see Loveena had to know. And actually, he did, too. "What odd thing, Vincent? What occurs?" Troy asked.

"He takes what appears to be the human's hologram away with him. They disappear together. The candidate displays the human state of mind called peace. The human's physical body remains in the chamber and the time of cessation automatically records."

"You mean he takes their soul away," Loveena whispered.

Vincent responded, "I have never understood it, the human soul. Nor do I know the significance of that one constant Grief Master."

An illuminated path formed in the fog under their feet. In the distance, Troy and Loveena could see the next doorway appear. They were out of time.

Troy gently urged Loveena on. "We gotta go." As they turned to leave, Troy looked back at Vincent. "When I'm done here, I want my son back, Vincent."

Vincent's hologram buzzed as he faded out. "Survive," was his last word to them.

Troy took Loveena by the hand, both looking at the door at the end of the pathway. Giving her a smile and a nod of confidence, he added, "Come on—we've got some demon hormones to kill."

Chapter 27

Loveena and Troy slowed as they approached the doorway to the next chamber. Troy reached for a black carriage lantern hanging on a hook beside the entrance, its half-burned candle flickered wildly in the breeze coming through the doorway.

"Are you ready for this?" he asked.

She nodded. "We keep moving forward."

"Right," he agreed, taking a deep breath. The doorway camouflaged what appeared to be the entrance to a cave, dark and foreboding. They both called for their Grief Masters and Courage and Patience emerged from the keys and stood beside them.

"We need you to light this path," Troy said, peering into the blackness.

Courage, taking up a position in front of the group, illuminated the pathway with his light, adding a boost to the candle in the lantern. Patience positioned herself behind them. The combined light of the two Grief Masters provided more than enough to lead them through the darkest passageway. They began a long descent into another strange world. The wind rushed by with a loud, mournful moan as the small band of travelers braced against the slamming of the door behind them.

As they descended stone steps, flanked by grey rock walls on either side, the entrance morphed into a dark cavern. The cave ceiling rose above them, disappearing into darkness the deeper they went. In some places, the walls veered away from the steps, exposing dangerous crevices, which they carefully avoided. Then the walls closed in again, narrowing the path.

The wind seemed to come from nowhere. It circled around each traveler with a gentle caress before moving on. Occasionally it would howl, causing Loveena to wrinkle her brow against the piercing sound.

The walls and ceiling twinkled and sparkled as they walked by.

"Like a thousand fire-flies," Loveena observed.

"What's that?" Troy said over his shoulder.

"The sparkles, they're beautiful."

"Oh, that," he responded, briefly looking around. "It's just the reflection of mica in the rock, probably quartz; maybe some minerals." Troy sounded uninterested.

"Well, I like it. They look like stars." Distracted, Loveena missed the next step, flying into the back of Troy. The sudden jolt caused him to stumble down the next two steps. He braced himself against the wall on the third step, quickly turning around to stop Loveena's free-fall. Wrapping one arm firmly around her, he pulled her tight against his chest as he struggled to hang on to the lantern.

Loveena thought she knocked the wind out of him, feeling his chest expand against her cheek to take in a gulp of air. She could hear his heartbeat as her ear pressed hard into his shirt, its steady rhythm pulsing under her hand as his muscles flexed against her touch. He was warm and smelled good, making her turn her head into his chest even more.

Lingering a moment longer than she needed to, Loveena glanced up and saw him looking down at her, their faces only inches apart. Her heart raced from the fall down the steps, but now it was pounding. He didn't move, his eyes traveling down, fixing upon her parted lips. She felt his hot breath brush across her cheek.

Loveena wondered if he could see the blush spreading across her cheeks. She pushed off of him, moving back one step up, to a less awkward distance. She could breathe again, realizing she had been holding her breath. He did not take his eyes off her. She looked down, fumbling with the tag of her jacket zipper. "I'm sorry, I didn't mean to…"

"No, it's all right," Troy stammered, looking away. "It's dark in here. Anyone could have done the same thing."

She nervously pointed to the ceiling. "I was just trying to look at the rock above us."

Brushing the hair from her face, she straightened her jacket, and then in a move she would instantly regret, Loveena pulled the zipper of her jacket up as high as it would go. Troy stared at the fully closed zipper, then, looked back into her eyes for what seemed an eternity. He turned and continued down the steps, muttering something about being only her protector under his breath.

"Keep moving," was all she clearly heard him say.

Loveena covered her eyes with her hands, drawing them down onto her cheeks. She thought she saw Troy's back stiffen as he moved away from her. She wondered if he saw it as a message to back off, when that wasn't what she meant to do at all. He simply made her nervous, like a silly schoolgirl. But she couldn't undo it. She bit her lip and yanked the zipper back down with a jerk, running down the steps to catch up with him.

The stone stairway ended, widening into an area of glistening natural light reflected off of the embedded crystal and mica everywhere. Ponds of water acted like mirrors, pooling in places around the floor of the cavern. Shiny, crystal stalactites hung from the rock ceiling above the grand cavern. Rising from the floor, giant stalagmites stretched upward, some so high they merged with the stalactites above to form long, continuous floor-to-ceiling columns of sparkling crystal.

Along the sides of the grand cavern, vast ribbon formations of crystal snaked along the walls in layer upon layer. Some appeared as a single rivulet over the stone, while others appeared very dense, like a curtain of crystallized fabric covering the walls. Water slowly dripped from the ceiling creating pools of water caught in deep recesses of the floor. Their surfaces were clear as glass, with many of the pools appearing immeasurably deep.

Loveena and Patience knelt down by the raised edge of one rock pool, peering into the dark water. Loveena saw her reflection clearly, although Patience cast no reflection. But when Loveena smiled at herself in the water, her own reflection didn't smile back. *That's odd.*

A disturbance beneath the glass-like surface of the water caused tiny bubbles in the middle of the pool. When Loveena leaned farther over the wall to get a better look, she gasped as Troy grabbed her by the arm, pulling her back with a sudden jerk. She felt a quick jolt of fear, causing Patience to momentarily disappear. Reappearing and kneeling next to Loveena again, they both looked at Troy's firm grip on her arm, then up at the alarmed look on his face.

"Don't do that!" he said. "We don't know what's lurking down here. I don't want you suddenly taking a swim, especially if I have to go in after you."

His tone was cross, and she could only assume he was smarting from the incident on the stairway. But she knew Troy was right. Somewhere down here, a demon waited for one, if not both, of them. Besides, she really didn't want to get wet.

The wind, light and heady with a sweet perfume, blew through the cavern, whistling and moaning as it approached and receded. It gave the place a melancholy feeling, Loveena thought, as if it sang a sad ballad among the towering columns. A strong sense of sadness permeated this place. The feeling sunk into Loveena like a slow poison. She could sense the wind's sorrow, making her feel deeply forlorn.

Troy and Courage walked ahead, while Patience stayed beside her. An overwhelming emptiness engulfed Loveena and dulled her senses. She wanted to be happy and couldn't remember the last time she actually was. She would have given anything to have lived a different life, to have a family, and a man who would not only protect her, but build a life with her, and a future. Someone who would see her as an equal partner, and above all, be a man who could love her always. *Possibly, a man like—Troy?*

As they walked through the twinkling cavern, around giant stalagmites as wide as the trunks of ancient oak trees, another pool appeared with a huge crystal ribbon running in the rock above it. To Loveena, the formation looked like a giant sad face mounted on the wall. Rivulets of water ran out of two slanted cracks, appearing as eyes of a sad mask. Like tears, the water ran down the stone face, and fell in droplets to the pool below, creating two concentric rings of ripples spreading across the water's surface.

"Pools of tears," she said.

"What?" Troy, stopping a few feet away, looked around at the pool.

"It's a mask; like a theatre mask; you know, the comedy and sorrow masks," she explained. "Only this is the mask of Sorrow – and it weeps pools of tears."

Troy looked up at the weeping wall, said nothing, and moved on with Courage. Loveena watched another single tear run down the stone face and fall into the water. She felt reluctant to leave the side of the pool, mesmerized by its enveloping sadness. But as Troy walked further away, the light of the lantern he carried diminished and the reflection of natural light from the crystal in the surrounding stones dimmed. She forced herself to move and follow after him.

****

As they neared the opposite end of the grand cavern, two pathways appeared, both lit with a natural light coming through the ceiling. The paths led in different directions, separated by a rock wall running between them. The four travelers stood in a small clearing in front of the two paths.

"Which one do we take?" Loveena asked. A strong wind came rushing out of the path to their left, blowing her hair straight back. Troy put his hand protectively in front of the lantern, but the candle's flame blew out. He set the darkened lantern down.

"We take that one," he said, pointing to the path on the right. Troy and Courage proceeded cautiously. He would not rush into any ambush if a demon manipulated their direction in the cavern. Focusing on the situation at hand, he pushed his thoughts of Loveena and the moment on the stairway aside. He would have taken her in his arms and kissed her if she hadn't moved away from him. But the gesture with the fully closed zipper made it obvious she was off limits to him.

Tommy was his priority, still alive and waiting for his father to come get him. Troy had more reason than ever to defeat these demons. He should be feeling confident and strong; instead, he felt rejected and discouraged. A gnawing in the pit of his stomach accompanied an underlying and unexplained sense of loss.

Before Loveena could follow him on the path, the rock wall began moving, quickly closing behind him, and blocking her access. Troy turned at the sound of the moving rock. Seeing Loveena jump out of the way, he could hear her yell his name from the other side. He tried with all of his strength to push the rock wall back, but it was solid and unmovable. Even Courage leaned into the rock beside him, doubling Troy's effort to move it, but it wouldn't budge.

"Damn, separated again! This is not good," he said to Courage, "not good at all." Hoping she would hear him, he yelled back to her. "Loveena, can you hear me?"

"Yes," her voice sounded muted. "What should I do?"

"Is the other pathway still open?"

"Yes."

"Then take it. They may come back together ahead. Keep moving forward. Do you understand? Don't stop…and don't touch any water."

He paused, waiting for a response, but none came. "Loveena, do you hear me?"

"Yes, Troy…I…I'm sorry about the staircase. I didn't mean to…" she paused.

Wanting her to stay positive and not get distracted, Troy responded, sounding upbeat.

"And I'm sorry I'm not there to help you, but you can do this, Loveena, I know you can. You're strong and smart, smarter than any demon down here. We'll find each other, I promise you."

He gave the wall another powerful push, but sighed, shaking his head, comparing it to trying to move a stone building from its foundation. *This will be the last time these demons push us apart.*

He rubbed his chest. The flame in his heart placed there by his Faith Grief Master brightened, casting a golden glow through his shirt, reminding him he was not alone. He didn't like being separated from her, but he could only move forward, just as he instructed her to do.

Following the path he was forced to take, Troy came into a small cavern and another pool of water. As he approached, green grass sprouted across the rocky floor. Looking down into the clear water, Troy watched it turn black, with small bubbles coming to the surface in the center of the pool. He braced himself for the emergence of some demonic creature he would have to fend off.

An image, floating up from the depth, appeared gliding back and forth, until it came to rest on top of the water. Like a poster-sized photograph, it was a life-size, color photo of his dog, his golden retriever, Marcus; the dog he grew up with, played and jogged with, the one who hid whenever Troy experimented in his lab, the one dog he loved more than any other.

The image on the floating photograph turned three-dimensional, and his dog emerged from the paper, sitting up on top of the photograph. He instantly recognized Troy. Wagging his tail, he panted a cheerful smile and walked toward him across the water. Marcus jumped down off of the side of the pool, licking Troy's hand, beating his tail against Troy's leg.

"Marcus! You beautiful boy! Where'd you come from?" Troy kneeled by the pool, petting the dog's head and scratching rigorously behind his ears. "You remember me?" The dog licked Troy's face. "Of course you do, good boy…good dog! How I missed you, buddy." Troy hugged his neck.

"The best dog in the world, you know that? Yes, you were." Trotting around the side of the pool, Marcus found a well-slobbered tennis ball. Bringing it back in his mouth, he pushed it against Troy's hand, dropping it on the ground in front of him.

"Look at that, your old tennis ball. You wanna play? Ok," Troy obliged, throwing it across the grassy cavern. "Go get it!" Marcus ran across the clearing to fetch the ball, bringing it back. Troy, mesmerized by the sudden appearance of his dog, felt the need to stay in the damp, moss-covered cavern. The more it engulfed him, the less willpower he had to leave. It subtly and silently controlled him.

Troy repeated the game over and over, living in that timeless moment with his beloved dog. Being with Marcus again felt so enjoyable, leaving became the furthest thing from his mind. The urgency of finding his son, or Loveena, left him. He just wanted to be with Marcus. He mentally returned to a time in his life when his dog was his best friend and his heart innocently untroubled. His subconscious jabbed at him to move on, but he couldn't respond.

Marcus brought the ball back again and again, dropping it with a slobbery thud and finally plopped down at Troy's feet. Lying on the grass beside him, Troy laid his head down on the dog's chest, running his hand over and over the soft fur of the dog's side. Watching his hand gently pet his furry friend, Troy realized this was not the hand of a child who was playing with his dog. Nor was it the hand of a teenager, or college grad that spent many hours with the beloved dog. But this was the hand of a grown man and there was no memory of this older hand caressing the dog of years ago. The more he studied the look of his own hand, strong, with scares and prominent veins that were not part of the memories when Marcus actually lived, it brought Troy back to the present. He broke free of the mind-controlling force keeping him in the distant past. Troy got to his knees as Marcus sat up beside him. Looking deep into the brown eyes of his retriever, he told himself this wasn't real.

"I know you're not real, buddy," he said with a kind voice. "You gotta go now."

The dog pushed his head up under Troy's chin, wagging his tail hard as his body moved back and forth against Troy's chest. Troy hugged him again, placing a long, well-deserved kiss on the top of the dog's head. Then Marcus jumped up on the pool, walked back across the water to the floating photograph and sat down.

Troy watched as the dog's face began to rapidly age, showing more white around the muzzle and a hunched over curve to his spine. Years of decline played in fast-forward motion. Marcus lay down on top of the photograph. His chest raised and lowered with labored breathing, no longer able to lift his head. The dog's eyes fixated upon Troy. This was how his dog looked the day he breathed his last breath.

"You were the best dog." Troy's eyes filled with tears as the memory played out before him. "I loved you, Marcus. Know that I loved you, boy."

Marcus closed his eyes and stopped breathing. His body became one-dimensional again, sinking back into the photograph, as it floated back down into the depths of the black water.

Dropping to one knee, Troy covered his eyes with one hand and wept. As each tear fell to the cavern floor, a tiny black sprout pushed up from the same spot. Each thin, thorny bramble wrapped around his boot. Troy felt the pain of losing his devoted dog all over again. Unaware his sorrow was anchoring him to the floor of the cavern he suddenly felt a sharp thorn stab into his flesh.

Feeling the first thorn attack his calf, Troy stood up and saw the bramble wrapped around his right boot swirling up around his leg and climbing toward his thigh. With a swift jerk of his knee, he broke the base of the bramble from its roots. He grabbed the top of the thorny vine before it could dig into him again. Pulling on it, he tried to loosen its thorny grip, but it wouldn't let go. As it continued to curl around his thigh like a snake, its thorns dug through his jeans, causing bloody stains to appear. He cursed as another thorn dug into his hand, cutting his palm. He struggled to pry the vines off his arm and leg, but they gripped him with a surprising strength.

Once the heartache over his dog subsided, Troy realized this struggle was to prevent him from moving forward. Then the vine dried up and crumbled in his hands. Breaking it into pieces, he tossed it into the pool of water with bitter irritation. His hand may have been bloodied and his leg sore, but he was free.

So this is how you're going to play it? Use my own pain against me? Well, bring it on, damn it! Knowing he had lots of pain in his life, dealing with this deceptive demon would not be easy. As he left the clearing, the thorny brambles filled the small pool, spilling out over the sides, engulfing the small, grassy cavern with a dense tangle of vines and thorny stems.

Troy continued on toward another adjoining cavern, stopping briefly to take off his jacket and t-shirt. Ripping his t-shirt apart, he tied one strip around his bleeding calf over the top of his jeans, and another around the bloody, seeping stains on his thigh. He wrapped the last strip around the deep cut on his right hand. He picked up his jacket and walked on, not looking back at the sorrowful spot that tried to hold him in place; the sad memory wanting to trap him in time forever. Instead, he consciously chose to remember only the happiness his dog brought him. Troy refused to dwell on the pain of the past, because he knew this demon wanted him to.

This demon is Sorrow. He hoped Loveena would figure it out, too. As he left the space behind, a tiny tendril sprouted from the vine near the pool. Breaking from its root, it silently snaked down the path and chased after Troy.

Chapter 28

Loveena jumped back when the rock wall began to close. For a split second, darting into the disappearing path crossed her mind, but it moved too fast. She saw Troy turn around. Then, with a thunderous sound, the rock wall slide across the pathway and crashed into the opposing wall, making the ground shake. Pushing and pounding on the cold, dark stone did nothing but increase her anxiety. It was no use; she was on one side and Troy, the other.

She could still hear his voice, however, muffled by the layer of rock between them. He told her to take the other path. He promised something, but Loveena could not make out exactly what. It was the last thing she heard.

And I promise you, I have faith in you...and in us, she thought. Loveena would find a way back to him somehow.

As another blast of wind came rushing out of the one path left open, Patience stepped out of Loveena's body and stood next to her, peering into the narrow opening. They could see a filtered light coming from deep within the passage. As they watched, the passageway closed up, but reopened a few moments later as more wind blew from within. Repeating several times, it opened and then closed.

"Maybe the path isn't a long one," Loveena said to her. "I ran track in school; I might be able to get through it before it closes up." Squeezing Patience's hand, Loveena took a deep breath. "I think I can do this. No, I know I can do this."

Patience nodded back at Loveena. Slipping back into her body, both of Loveena's Grief Masters keys pulsated with a faster beat. She could feel her adrenalin surging as she readied herself to run. It was her only option and Troy would be depending on her.

She waited for the passageway to reopen as another blast of wind blew through. Then like a sprinter taking off at the sound of the gun, she ran, pumping her long legs as hard as possible, flying through the narrow pathway. Vines came out of nowhere, trying to trip her, sprouting and curling up from the floor. Hurdling over the climbing vines like an Olympian, she didn't slow her pace. Thorns tore through her jacket like butter. Pushing a thorny vine away from her face, it sliced the back of her hand drawing a line of blood across it.

The path twisted and turned like a maze through tiny clearings that opened and collapsed as new vines sprung up to impede her. Loveena had to get to an open area soon, or the swirl of clinging vines would swallow her up like a carnivorous plant.

Bursting from the maze like a bullet, she exited into another large, open space. She slowed her pace, coming to a stop, and leaned against a thick crystal stalagmite. Gasping for breath, Loveena refilled her empty lungs with the fresh air coming through the cracks in the cave's ceiling. Her throbbing temple calmed as she leaned her forehead against the cool stone. She looked back at the spot where she had exited. The collapsing passage disappeared in a mass of thorn-covered vines and thick leaves. No visible sign of it remained.

Loveena leaned her back against the pillar, surveying the surrounding area. Smaller than the grand cavern they first encountered, this one had bright green moss covering the floor instead of pools of water. It looked more like an old, abandoned garden than a natural cave. Strange objects stood like silent statues upon Romanesque white pillars. Appearing to be a sculpture garden, a stone path meandered throughout the space and past each one, as ornately carved, black wrought iron benches stood carefully placed where one could sit and contemplate each statue. What was missing from this strange garden were any signs of life, such as the twitter of birds, the flutter of butterflies, or any sounds at all.

Walking toward the closest pillar, Loveena sensed something familiar about the art object displayed upon it. A giant golden ring, a foot or more in diameter, sat mounted to a four foot tall marble pedestal. The golden band gleamed as light from above glinted off its shiny surface. Loveena could see her reflection in the band as she walked around it. At the top of the ring sat a dark ruby, a rare blood ruby, larger than both of her fists together. The marquise cut of the gem, just at her eye level, reflected her face in its multiple cut facets.

Loveena had a blood ruby ring similar in shape, set into a gold band. *Only mine has a prong missing.* She looked down at the ring on the third finger of her right hand. Holding her hand up next to the oversized statue, she noticed the same prong appeared to be missing on the statue. The rings were identical, down to a tiny nick in the gold band on its left side.

A drop of water from an overhead stalactite hit the top of the ring, wobbling down the ruby to the inside of the band. A prism of color sparkled from the droplet as it clung to the point of the marquise underneath the setting. Leaning closer, Loveena examined the rainbow of colors moving across the meniscus of the large droplet. Stretching down into a teardrop shape, it lengthened in a long moment of slow motion, finally breaking free of its hold on the gem. She watched it fall to the open center of the band, where it stopped, suspended in mid-air. Loveena sensed time itself had been suspended, somehow connected to the strange water droplet.

Maybe it's a trick. Loveena pulled back from the ring, looking around for a demon, or anything that could be watching her. Satisfied no one was there, she returned her attention to the curious water droplet. She stretched out her right index finger, and ever so gently touched it. With a sparkle of energy, the droplet dispersed across all directions, creating a thin meniscus of water clinging to the entire inner band of the ring. A picture appeared upon it, playing out like a video on a screen.

Loveena instantly recognized the scene. A tiny girl of six stood quietly, holding the hand of her father. They were in front of a large crowd of people, as women behind her cried softly into tissues. The hot sun caused perspiration to bead across her forehead. The park-like setting was green with lush grass and colorful flowers everywhere. But it was not a park—it was a cemetery. A hearse backed up to the crowd, as men walked in front of her, her father pulling away. She grasped for his hand, but he pushed her back in place, asking one of the women to watch her.

Along with the other men, he opened the back door of the vehicle. They extracted a long elaborate box with handles on each side. A box her mother lay in. Flowers fell from the top of the casket onto the asphalt in front of the little girl. As the men carried the pretty box to a tent-covered burial site, the crowd pushed past her to follow behind them. The woman urged her to come along, but she pulled away, clasping her small hands behind her back and stood steadfast without a word. The woman moved on and little Loveena stood alone on the driveway.

With a sad face, the child picked up the head of a fallen red rose from the ground, and ran her fingers one at a time over the soft petals, outlining each one. Then, with a furrowed look of anger, she took the rose head and squeezed it in her small hand as hard as she could. Upon opening her hand, the crushed petals fell away, one by one, between her tiny fingers.

Loveena watched the scene with a sad regret, knowing what loneliness and heartache lay ahead for the little girl who grew up without her mother. The many nights spent with nannies and babysitters who paid her no attention while her father worked, conditioned her to protect her heart by blocking out love. Knowing she had slipped all too easily into the role Hoy SamWong forced upon her, Loveena locked away that part of her which allowed her to share, to dream, and to hope. Those were parts of love, and like the petals of the rose, could be crushed.

It had been many years since that hot afternoon. She continued watching the next scene on the thin watery screen. Her father reappeared to retrieve his young daughter, tucked his damp handkerchief into his pocket and knelt down beside her. He looked at the crushed red petals scattered around her feet. Picking up a rose petal, he placed it in her hand.

"Your mother liked red, Loveena, especially red roses. When you see a rose, you must think of her and how she loved you." He choked back a tear and kissed her little hand.

"She wanted you to have something. Do you remember the ring your mother wore?"

"The pretty red one?" she asked in a small voice.

"Yes," he replied. "Your mother…my sweet Ramona…said to me, give it to Loveena so she can wear it to remember me." He pulled a gold ring with a dark red ruby from his inside pocket and put it in her hand along with the rose petal.

Loveena dropped the petal and held up the ring, trying it on different fingers. Being too big for any of her little fingers, she placed it on her thumb. Smiling at her, he took his small daughter by the hand and walked toward the tent-covered burial site. Loveena looked back at the red petals on the ground and broke away from his grip. Running back, the little girl picked them all up, stuffing them in her pocket.

The wind moaned as it blew through the cavern and across Loveena's face. This was all she could stand to watch. She pushed her fingers into the picture to dispel the watery meniscus. *So long ago,* she sighed, yet her heart ached like it happened yesterday. Loveena stood there, frozen to her grief, not wanting to relive it, but not wanting to leave it, either. It was no surprise to her this ring statue stood first on this strange garden path.

Sorrow keeps you locked in time. Trying to force her feet to move, she fought the urge to sit down and cry. Loveena had not cried tears over her mother's death in years. Now they would not stop from coming. A tear streamed down her cheek, then another. Wiping them with the back of her hand, she flicked them to the ground. A thorny sprout popped up, curling its way toward her foot. But once Loveena decided the past was better left where it needed to be, she could move her feet again. As the vine reached for her boot, she stepped back on top of it, crushing it. The thin vine broke in half and withered away unseen.

Loveena walked on, noticing more of her life's sad moments and mistakes, immortalized in stone upon different pedestals. She deliberately kept from looking directly at each one, and could tell with a side glance what each was, immediately looking away. They seemed to have a power that could trap her here. *You must keep moving. Apparently, this demon of sadness is not a being. It is a feeling, and it's using my own memories to shackle me to my past.*

Loveena was not willing to let the past keep her in this place. In her mind, this place reflected a literal Garden of Regrets. *Do not look back, there is only sorrow here, and hope lies in the future.* After she passed each statue, not choosing to acknowledge it or look in its direction, it melted away, dripping like hot wax down the pedestal onto the moss-covered floor. However, a tug of emotion arose when passing too closely to any of the statues. Fighting her own feelings of longing and remorse, she forced herself to walk on, wanting to find Troy, not just to warn him, but to see if any future hope might include him.

Loveena approached the opposite side of the cavern and saw another opening appear before her. A strong wind came through it, kicking up small dust devils that swirled across the floor. Seeing Troy in the distance, she yelled to him, but he didn't hear her. He appeared to be in trouble. Vines thrashed along beside him, entangling him as he fought them. His magenta-colored Courage flashed beside him as they struggled together against an invisible demon.

As she ran toward him, a large pool of black, murky water opened in the floor in front of her, widening and preventing her from reaching the other side. She stopped short of falling into it as it deepened. Stepping back from the edge, Loveena fumed with frustration, unable to get to Troy and help him.

The water became a churning river, keeping her from crossing. Loveena contemplated wading through it, but it looked too fast and deep, threatening to sweep her away. And the possibility still existed of a demon that might pull her down and trap her beneath the water.

Large bubbles formed in the middle of the river, roiling the surface, creating tumultuous rapids. Staring at the now raging water, she watched as a huge pedestal rose from its depths, shooting up ten feet into the air in front of her, blocking her view of Troy. Water splashed off of the wide pedestal as the wind carried the droplets through the air, falling on her like steamy rain. The sound of wind and crashing waves became deafening.

Loveena could not avoid looking at this statue, unlike the others in the garden. On top of the pedestal appeared a huge block of clear ice. Locked within the ice, stood a large, valentine-shaped heart, blood red, and broken into halves. The block of ice started to melt, dripping into the churning river. As each drop of water hit the waves, bubbles burst forth and large poster-sized photographs floated up from the depths to the river's surface. The posters fanned out across the water in front of Loveena. Each one played a streaming video of regret previously locked away from her heart. Some vividly displayed the work she performed at the order of Hoy SamWong, scenes of data-stealing espionage or sexual entrapments of executives, all to keep her father alive. But they also represented the destruction of her self-respect and self-love.

Finally, finding the strength deep within to defy this invisible demon, she yelled into the wind, "You cannot force me to stay here and dwell in my past!"

The wind blew harder, pelting her with rain and soaking every inch of her. Loveena turned her head and averted her eyes from the photographs. A tornado-like rope emerged from the howling wind, dancing and circling around her, making her shake violently. The harder she fought it, the more this noose of Sorrow forced her head back toward the river.

The last poster emerged, coming directly out of the broken heart encased in ice, instead of from the depths of the river. It slid down the side of the wet pedestal and into the water. Other posters parted to each side, allowing it to float directly toward Loveena. While she tried to look away, the wind knocked her to her knees at the river's edge, as the video on the poster continued in front of her, replaying the worst day of her life.

Hoy SamWong stood above her as she lay on the floor of the beach house at Ramona Cove, her face and body bruised by his uncontrollable insanity. Kicking and punching him, she fought back to the point of exhaustion until he threw her down with such force her head hit the floor, leaving her dazed. Screaming that Loveena would pay for her father's disloyalty, Hoy withdrew his belt, swinging it like a whip. She covered her head with her hands, begging him to stop, rolling away from him and crawling toward the door. Hoy stopped to remove his pants. Grabbing her by the ankles, he dragged her across the floor toward the sofa. He yanked her arms behind her back, wrapping his belt around them and pulling it tight. He threw her up over the arm of the sofa, knocking the wind out of her. Then he raped her; and again; and again.

When he was done, Hoy told her he would own her as he owned his enemies, their companies, their secrets, and their very souls. Every one of them now bent the knee to him. Now he would take control of the most precious possession of his biggest nemesis, Samuel Baptista. Loveena would do whatever he told her, or her father would die. She would go wherever and with whomever he told her, or her father would die. And she would be his whenever he desired her, or her father would die. He ordered her to settle her affairs and report to his office by the end of the week or his security would come find her. Pulling her up by the hair, Hoy raised his right fist and brought it down hard to the left side of her face. He left Loveena lying on the floor of the beach house with a dislocated jaw and the imprint of his diamond SWI ring red on her cheek.

Chapter 29

Loveena struggled to her feet next to the flowing river of sad memories. Picking up a rock from the edge of the water, she threw it into the image of Hoy SamWong, and the poster swirled out of focus. She angrily wiped the last of her tears away. A new strength emerged from deep within; it told her these things would not have a hold on her life unless she allowed them to do so. And Loveena was done allowing it. *These will be the last tears I shed over this memory.*

Loveena could feel control over her life returning, and the will to finally break away from Sorrow's iron-fisted hold. Turning into the blowing wind and rain, her hand no longer shook as she raised a pointed finger at the frozen, broken heart and shouted. "I deny you, Sorrow, do you hear me? I refuse to live my life in your shadow! My past will not control me. You may have darkened my path and tried to shackle me, torture me and keep me down, but you will not shape my future. You cannot destroy me!"

With defiance, she stood straight against the wind as it intensified. Loveena grabbed the leather straps around her neck, holding her keys out in front of her.

"I call upon my Courage and Faith Grief Masters to stand with me. I declare before you and every other demon that exists, I am a child of *God*, and neither you nor any other godless creatures can take that away. God forgives me, He will heal me, and His mercy will save me. And You, Sorrow, will never be in my life again!"

When she had finished, she felt the self-destructive force keeping her in emotional bondage break away. The magenta hue of Courage and the golden hue of Faith surrounded her body, encapsulating her in an aura of protection, blocking the wind and rain, causing them to veer around her.

With a rumble and reverberation roaring from the depth of the river, the large block of ice surrounding the heart cracked down the middle. It exploded in all directions, shattering into flying shards. Loveena, still surrounded and protected by the magenta and golden dome, watched as both sides of the giant heart pulled together, healing itself; its dark red color changing into a vibrant pink. A new key suddenly appeared inside the middle of the heart, pulsating in a neon blue, standing out against the pink background. As the large pedestal sank back into the water, the key slid from it and floated across the river. Loveena splashed into the black water and grasped the key, scrambling back to the side with it firmly in her hand.

As she held it in front of her, a new Grief Master appeared. A luminescent, blue-colored being floated above the water's surface, suspended in mid-air. Like the other two Grief Masters, this one also resembled her. The being stretched out her hands, calming the churning river, as the blue and teal aura filled the cavern. Smiling at Loveena, she placed one hand on her heart, and with the other, she reached out to the newly healed valentine heart hovering above the water. She guided the healing heart on its way across the top of the river as it reduced in size and disappeared into the key Loveena held.

"I am a Grief Master, Loveena. I have been sent here on your behalf. My name is Hope." Loveena did not hesitate to place the new strap and key around her neck.

"Keep me in your heart, and I will always be in your future." With a wave of her hands, a sparkling bridge materialized over the troubled water. Pointing to the adjoining cavern where Troy was fighting for his life, she said, "Your future can only be changed by you, and what you choose may change the future of others."

Loveena wasted no time running across the bridge. Her new Grief Master turned and accompanied her, dissipating into the new key, and blending in with the multi-colored aura protecting Loveena. Crossing over, she did not look back, leaving the cavern of her sorrow behind for good.

****

A part of the cavern where Troy was trapped was engulfed in thick tangles of thorny brambles. He battled against the encroaching weed that dogged him like a side winding serpent. Fountains of water poured from the stone walls, creating a stream flowing along the perimeters of the cave. Troy's personified pain swam like schools of colorful carp jumping out of the water, their scaly sides revealing glimpses into scenes of his past and the suppressed emotions he held on to.

He had kept moving, but made the mistake of letting his heart lead the way. Crisscrossing from one phantom image to another, the vines pursuing him projected images of people Troy had loved and lost. *Men don't always deal well with pain*, thought Troy with tormented vexation, as he struggled with yet another regrettable memory imposing a strong, physical restraint on him.

He broke free by sheer will and the use of a hunting knife he snatched from one of the images he encountered, using it to cut and hack his way through the cavern. Having removed his jacket to fight the thorny vine, Troy had scratches and gashes bleeding across his face, chest, and arms. He was getting tired and losing ground against a demon he could not clearly see.

The leading ends of long, entwined vines circled around in front of him, lifting their coalesced head like a snake ready to strike. It was as thick and round as a large, well-fed python. Two long thorns hung down like fangs from the jaw of the deadly demon. Rising to Troy's eye level, it projected a phantom figure of Troy's father in front of him. Troy hesitated to strike the beast with his knife. A second vine serpent rose beside the first, presenting Troy with an image of his mother. The bramble hypnotized him into a false reality, tricking him to see what was not really there. Troy could only see his parents standing before him. Meanwhile, the evil serpent took advantage of Troy's hesitation to securely wrap an offshoot around his ankle.

"This can't be real," Troy gasped.

He swallowed hard and swung the blade of his knife at both of them. The images disappeared and with a loud, rustling motion, the two vines swirled together into a single deadly snakehead. Opening its huge jaw just inches from Troy's face, it presented a gaping, evil mouth full of long, sharp thorns lined up in rows, like devouring teeth. The vine snake jerked hard on the offshoot around Troy's ankle and he fell backward down to the hard moss-covered floor.

Courage lay on the floor with a woozy Troy. His strong magenta arms reached out of Troy's body and grabbed the head of the snake as it tried to attack. He held it at arm's length as it snapped its thorn-riddled mouth at him. His bright color lit up the space between the beast's teeth and Troy's head. Regaining consciousness, Troy became aware that his own hands, outlined by the hands of Courage, were wrapped firmly around the neck of the snake, holding him at bay.

Suddenly, the wooden serpent jerked away from his grasp and uncoiled from his ankle, as Loveena stood with the tail-end of the demon in her hands. Snapping it like a whip, she hurled it through the air against the rock wall. It hit with such force it shattered the brittle wood into pieces and they fell into the stream where they were instantly devoured by the hungry carp.

Troy got to his feet, his hunting knife in his right hand ready to strike at Loveena. Still hypnotized, he saw only another snakehead in his mind as it spoke to him.

"Troy, it's me, Loveena!"

"You can't fool me again. I know what you're doing." He waited for the right opportunity to lunge at her.

"No, this chamber, this demon, is making you see things that aren't here!" she shouted. "It's trying to kill you with your own pain."

The talking vine sounded like her, but it couldn't be; he would never hurt her. *It must be a trick*, Troy thought. He saw only a serpent made of twisted twigs and leaves and a mouth full of thorns. He circled to his left to trap it against the stream.

A glimpse of Loveena flashed through the mirage. Then the serpent's head reappeared. Again, Loveena's face appeared, her voice breaking through to him. "Troy, wake up!" But she disappeared once more, replaced by the gaping, thorny mouth of the wooden reptile. Troy was unsure whether to fight or not, being deadly accurate with his blade, the thought of striking her scared him. He would not put her in peril by a man who might otherwise give his life for her.

"Loveena?" he asked cautiously.

"Yes, Troy, yes!" She held up her key of Hope for him to see. He saw the blue color illuminate against the skin of her hand. Around her neck she wore the other two keys, magenta and gold. Glancing down at his own keys, he saw the same two colors beating rapidly. Only the real Loveena would have possession of such keys.

He turned his blade away, pulling her to him, wrapping his arms tightly around her. Her hair, dripping wet, soaked his skin, but it felt soothing; and she felt good in his arms. She was safe, and she was here, and that's all that mattered. At the same time, an involuntary thought crossed his mind, reminding him she could never be his. It put life back into the long piece of thick vine at his feet.

Loveena spoke again, but he didn't hear a word as he watched the silent, gaping mouth of the serpent rise from the floor behind her. The snake shifted, rearing its head back to strike Loveena from behind. With one quick move, Troy pulled her away, blocking the serpent's throat with his left forearm. Twisting its long, thorny neck around, its head and teeth came crushing down on his arm. Blood sprang out between its firmly clamped jaws and Troy grunted in pain as he struggled to push the creature back, creating distance between it and Loveena.

The slithering, thick body of entwined vines slid across the floor, brushing leaves and twigs against the rock. Coiling up behind Troy, the body of the python-like creature wrapped around his waist. He drove his blade into the exposed throat of the snake again and again, cutting through thick cords. Fearing if he let go, there was no telling where the jaws would come crashing down next; it could attack her instead of him. Man and demon beast stood locked in a death grip.

Loveena stepped forward to help, but was ordered back by Troy. "No, Loveena! It wants you dead to add to my sorrow. Get back!"

Stepping back, she could do nothing but watch them try to destroy each other. The snake moved its coil from Troy's waist up to his chest and constricted hard. Troy let out an agonizing groan. Feeling like it was squeezing the breath out of him, he refused to let go of it.

Troy snarled through gritted teeth, "We'll both die, demon, before I let you harm her."

Narrowing its twig-shaped eyes, the wooden serpent tightened the hold on his chest again. Troy winced with pain. With its jaws embedded in his forearm, he raised his arm higher, hoping to force the snake's head so far back it would snap. But the serpent raised a large, pointed corkscrew appendage into the air and drove a dagger-like stem deep into Troy's chest. Gasping, Troy fell to one knee, still holding the spiny head of the beast. The appendage wrapped around his heart, driving thorns into it, causing blood to stream out of the wound and cascade down his chest.

With one final move, Troy used his last bit of strength to pull his arm down, positioning the neck of the serpent across his knee. With his other hand, he brought the large blade of the knife down with such force on the back of its neck, it beheaded the beast. Prying the jaws from his arm, he grabbed the lifeless head of the demon and threw it across the rocky floor. Its body uncoiled, releasing the grip on Troy's heart and pulling the thorns back out of his bloodied chest as it retracted. The headless vine heaved and whipped around on the floor. Loveena rushed to stomp on the writhing body, keeping her boot firmly on it until it stopped moving. Then, she kicked it away and into the stream.

Troy collapsed. He was unconscious, his chest bleeding profusely. Rushing to his side, Loveena saw his keys dim.

"Do not die on me, Troy Vincent," she ordered. Tearing off her jacket, she stripped off her wet camisole, tearing it into strips. Shivering in just her sports bra and jeans against the dampness of the cave, she applied a pressure bandage to his chest wound. She tied a strip of her torn camisole around his neck and shoulder to secure the rough dressing.

"Listen to me, Troy," she whispered close to his ear. "Remember what Vincent said? If you think you're dying, you will. Wake up, Troy, you must wake up." His body shook, then went limp.

"Patience, Hope, Faith," she yelled. "I need you now!" Her Grief Masters stepped from her body, all kneeling down around him.

"Help me get him up," Loveena commanded.

The stone floor of the Chamber of Sorrows faded away into a low lying fog. A rainbow of color surrounded Troy and levitated him to his feet. Loveena draped his arm over her shoulder while the Grief Masters suspended his body on a cushion of color. They moved into the fog.

Chapter 30

Loveena found strength she didn't know she possessed when they pulled Troy to his feet. She and Patience held him securely with his arms draped around their necks, but his body fell like dead weight between them, his legs buckling at the knees. So Faith and Hope morphed into a sling, supporting him in a swirl of gold and blue color between Loveena and Patience. Blood soaked through the hastily fashioned bandage applied to his chest and Loveena feared he might bleed out. She knew they couldn't carry him far and began to feel helpless.

God, please don't let him die, she prayed over and over.

Taking small steps in the dense fog, Loveena had no idea which direction they were going, whether forward or backward. She only knew they needed to keep moving.

In a meager effort to keep her mood up, she muttered to herself, "Where's a safe house when you need one?" Patience smiled back, trying to take more of Troy's weight on herself. Loveena needed to stay positive, as Troy would insist she do, fearing any negative thoughts might bring a sudden tragic end to them.

An earthy scent wafted through the air; the distinct smell of pine, mixed with decaying autumn leaves. However, Loveena sniffed something else, too—smoke. *It smells like smoke from a chimney. A fireplace is burning somewhere*! She strained to see where it came from.

Above them, the fog began to dissipate to a mist and Loveena could see the tops of pine trees. Among them, the top of a stone chimney belched out a thin column of smoke. A red tin rooftop revealed itself, followed by the shrouded shape of a log cabin as the mist cleared from the woodsy scene.

A cabin sat in an open, grassy meadow flanked by towering pines and ancient sugar maples. The brilliant reds, oranges, and yellows of fall painted the foliage surrounding the area, reflecting on the water of a small lake behind the cabin. The afternoon sun was setting into an early evening sunset and the air was crisp. A light appeared shining through the cabin windows and beckoned the weary travelers.

Troy groaned, lifting his head just enough to open his eyes and see the cabin. Then, closing his eyes again, he dropped his chin down to his chest. Courage stepped out from Troy's weakened body, standing beside Loveena. Taking Troy from her, he pulled him onto his broad shoulders, supporting Troy against his light-emanating body. A barely conscious Troy stood weakly on his own feet, leaning heavily on Courage for support.

Courage motioned toward the cabin with a nod of his head. "His hunting cabin at Edmond Lake. Our safe house." They hurried up the dirt path to the porch steps, Courage half-carrying, half-dragging Troy along.

Loveena opened the door to the cabin as Courage picked him up and brought Troy in, laying him on the worn leather couch. Patience picked up a pillow from an adjacent chair and placed it under his head. Loveena gently pulled the bloody bandage away to survey the extent of the deep, ragged chest wound. Worried eyes met Patience's, searching for help from her own Courage Grief Master.

"Can you help me tend this wound? I've never done anything like this before." The Grief Master nodded, and slipped back into Loveena, her magenta key pulsing brightly. Meanwhile, Troy's Courage walked to the cabin door, opening it. Loveena thought he looked so much like Troy, she wondered if Troy was actually conscious through his Grief Master, while remaining unconscious in his own physical body. "I will keep watch outside," he said, stepping out onto the porch and closing the door behind him.

The fireplace logs burned bright, adding warmth to the space and a yellow glow inside the one room cabin. Looking around, Loveena saw a small kitchenette in the back behind the couch.

Stairs led to an open loft above with a large, skylight window. Seeing his leather jacket appear out of nowhere next to him, she picked it up, running her hand across it with a deep concern for him wrinkling her brow. Getting up, she draped it across the back of a wooden rocking chair next to the fireplace. When she turned back around, a bowl of water, towels, and bandages appeared on the coffee table next to the couch. "I swear those weren't there when we came in."

She sat down on the edge of the couch next to Troy and laid her hand near the wound on his chest. "I think someone's trying to help us." Looking up, she spoke out loud to the room.

"Vincent, Troy told me you said you could not help us." She picked up a towel, holding it to her. "But I believe these are from you, as was the iced tea at the beach house, and these safe houses you have so carefully recreated from our memories. You're making a choice to help us. That's a human thing, Vincent."

Removing the bloody bandage from Troy's chest, she dipped the towel in the bowl of water, wringing it out, and carefully wiped the blood from the wound. As she worked, she spoke aloud again. "You know, Vincent, there's a verse I only half remember: when I was hungry, you fed me; when I was thirsty, you gave me something to drink." She paused, thinking of their incarceration in the VRC. "I was imprisoned, and you came to see me. Maybe someday you'll come across that one in your databank, Vincent." Wiping the blood from Troy's face, she added, "We both thank you."

Loveena went straight to work on his terrifying injury as blood continued to ooze from the wound. She cleaned it well, pulling remnants of splinters and thorns from its edges. When it was free of debris, she picked up the bandages, realizing it required something more.

This really needs suturing. If I had a needle and thread...but do I have the guts to do that?

The sight of blood didn't make her as queasy as the thought of sewing up the layers of flesh. Swallowing hard, she looked at Troy's pale face. She could see herself in a life with him, which was something she never envisioned with anyone before. Loveena couldn't deny it—she was falling in love with him. The thought of him dying made her panic. She must save him, doing whatever necessary, even if it meant stitching him up. Whether he felt the same way about her didn't matter, as long as he would live.

Standing up, she looked around the room. *Maybe there's a sewing kit somewhere. Do men do those things? Do they sew? I barely know how to do that myself.*

Quickly opening drawers and searching through cabinets, she noticed things in the cabin that defined Troy. A desk in the corner held a stack of thumb drives with scientific journal names, engineering magazines with earmarked pages were piled high. In another corner of the room stood a rack of fishing rods and hunting gear; a cross bow, and an orange hunting jacket hung on the coat rack next to the door. Next to the jacket, hung a gray sweater; with nothing covering her but the lacy bra, she grabbed the sweater and put it on, pushing the long sleeves up to her elbows.

Loveena ran to the small kitchenette behind the couch, surveying the countertop. *Nothing here.* She opened the cabinet under the sink, finding a ball of string and grabbed it. *No, too thick; he's not a turkey.* She threw it back, slamming the cabinet door shut. Walking the few steps into the living room to the fireplace mantle, she noticed the displayed pictures of a young boy and two older people with a dog. *His son, Tommy? His parents?*

Turning around with a frustrated sigh, Loveena's eyes scanned the room one more time. Seeing a tackle box on a shelf next to the door, she grabbed a kitchen chair, dragging it across the floor. The box was heavy as she pulled it down. *There's got to be something in here.*

Loveena carefully sorted things around in the box with her fingertip. There were colorful lures throughout, all containing sharp hooks of different sizes hiding within them. She saw the one she wanted, a small, plain hook with no fancy lure attached. She grabbed a spool of thin fishing line and closed the lid. Snatching the bottle of Scotch whisky from atop the desk, she thought, this will have to do.

Loveena was done running from her feelings.

Hurrying back to the couch, she prepared the make-shift needle, threading the line through the hook and washing it with whisky over the water bowl. Loveena poured some whisky over her fingers, and to calm her shaking hands, she took a swig, then two. Holding up the hook, she tipped the bottle so a dribble of the alcohol would run down the length of the fishing line. With tears welling up in her eyes, she whispered, "This is so crude. I'm sorry, Troy."

As she poured a small amount of whisky onto the wound, Troy let out a rough groan, stirred, but didn't awaken. Loveena steeled her nerves to make the first stitch, holding the point of the hook poised just above the top of the wound. When the tip pricked his skin, his hand flew up and grabbed her wrist. His sudden movement made her freeze in place. His eyes blinked as he slowly pulled her hand away from his chest. Seeing the fishhook, his brows shot up and his eyes opened wide.

"Please tell me you weren't going to stick me with that!"

Loveena stammered. Speechless, she watched as his wound began to heal on its own.

"I...I thought you were dying and you...you were bleeding...a lot."

The more alert he became, the faster the wound healed, until it disappeared in front of Loveena's eyes. She sat back, placing the hook down on the coffee table. Troy rubbed his hand over his chest. Reaching out, she touched him where the wound had been. His skin was perfect again, tan, and warm beneath her fingertips. No sign of any injury remained at all.

Looking up at Loveena, Troy took her hand in his, resting it on his chest over his now-healed heart. Beneath his skin, she could see the glowing outline of the flame of Faith his Grief Master had placed there. Beside the two keys, giving off a strong steady beat, a third key materialized on another strap around his neck. It was blue, and the twinkling light from it reflected in his eyes.

Leaning closer, she whispered with amazement, "You have another key."

"Yes," he smiled. "Hope."

"But how did you...."

He interrupted her. "I'll tell you later."

Loveena was done running from her feelings. This time, she would not send him the wrong signal. She bent down and kissed him. His lips met hers with equal desire. She felt his hand move to caress her hair, pulling her closer, down into his passionate embrace. Kiss after kiss was answered with tenderness and an intense truth neither had experienced before. They sensed a deep connection between their souls. It went beyond physical attraction, beyond sexual intimacy; their auras combined and encircled them with a blend of sparkling color, a melding together of everything that was good, trustworthy, and promising between them.

Turning on his side, Troy pulled Loveena's legs up onto the couch and she snuggled along beside him. They smiled, embracing each other tightly, wanting more, and promising more as they gazed into each other's eyes. Protectively rolling on top of her, he turned his head toward the fireplace.

"Vincent, I know you can hear me. Go take a break."

Chapter 31

Security Chief Michaels leaned back, stretched out in his chair, with his feet crossed and propped up on his desk. He casually scanned the day's headlines of the regional tabloid projected in the air on a floating laser screen. His peripheral vision caught sight of attorney Adams approaching the closed glass door to the chief's office. He didn't like attorneys; they always seemed to demand things. This particular one had dogged him all week on the SamWong murder case. *What the hell does he want now? The two suspects are already serving their judgments. What more does he want?*

Sitting up, he sighed heavily as he turned off the tabloid screen, snuffing out the butt of his cigar in the ashtray next to him.

Adams peered through the glass of the office door, knocking hard. The chief wanted to tell him to go away. "Door's open, Mr. Adams."

Pushing open the door, Adams gave a slight nod and a half smile. Standing in front of the chief's desk with his hands clasped behind his back, he rocked back and forth on his heels. Attorney Adams enjoyed putting on a demeanor of the intimidating SWI General Counsel.

"Good morning, Chief Michaels. Sorry to disturb you. Do we have any final results yet?"

"No, Mr. Adams. As I told you yesterday, these things take time." The chief picked up a file folder from his desk, flipped through it, and rocked back in his chair, trying to look busy to keep the conversation as brief as possible.

"Why does it take so long? I don't understand. If two people are guilty, as these two obviously are, why isn't it over in the first 24 hours?"

"Well," looking at the attorney over the rim of his reading glasses, the chief pursed his lips. "Maybe they're not guilty. That kind of case can really drag out in the VRC."

Adams sat down in the guest chair opposite the chief's desk and put his hands in his lap, his fingers woven. "Ridiculous. They're as guilty as the day is long. I know, I saw the police reports, and I judged both cases myself."

Michaels tossed the folder back on his desk with irritation and took off his glasses, laying them down on top of the folder. He was annoyed Adams had made himself comfortable, and figured it would now take longer to get him out of his office. "Yeah, well, that could be the problem."

"Chief Michaels, may I ask you a question?" Adams put his elbow on the arm of the chair, tapping his index finger against his lips.

Oh, here we go, thought the chief. *Now he's going to interrogate me.* He leaned forward, crossing his arms on the desk and gave the attorney his full attention.

"What's your question, Mr. Adams?"

"Do you administer treatments on innocent people very often?"

"No, we try very hard to avoid such a situation. Of course, it depends on the decisions of the judges."

"If that's the case, then why would you assume the judges on these two cases would send innocent people to your facility? You might be implying the integrity and ethical standards of the judging panels are questionable. Are you...implying that...chief?" Adams leaned forward in his chair, arrogantly thrusting out his clenched chin and furrowing his brows over his beady eyes.

Michaels sat back, turning his chair from side to side, looking up at the digital clock on his office wall and wondering how long this could go on.

"No, that's not what I think at all. Our corporate sponsors, such as your very own SWI, do a wonderful job providing the best attorneys. We are all grateful for the ethical job they do, even when, with little to no evidence, they find two completely different people guilty of the same murder."

Michaels didn't care if the humorless attorney detected his note of sarcasm. He didn't like this case, or the guilty judgments found by this particular judging panel. But it would be his only opinionated remark on it. He would still do his job regardless of how he personally felt.

He picked up a pen and began tapping it on the desk. A long moment of awkward silence between them ensued as the chief looked up at Adams and politely smiled. *Why is this guy's face always so red? He must have blood pressure problems.* Then, something flashed and caught his eye. Adams wore a fancy ring; an expensive ring; with three diamond letters, SWI, set in gold. *Attorneys make way too much money.*

Adams didn't smile back. "What do you mean by that, chief, insinuating little to no evidence?"

The chief shuffled a small stack of file folders on his desk and stood up. Walking around to the door of his office, he opened it wide.

"Forget it. My opinion is not important."

Adams got up from the chair. "At least we can agree on that."

"I think you're just too involved with this case, Mr. Adams. You're too close to it. The victim was a friend of yours. You represent the victim's company, and you personally judged these cases." The chief put his hand on the attorney's shoulder, casually guiding him through the door. "Now you just need to step back and let the system do its job." Patting Adams on the shoulder, he ushered him out of his office.

"Perhaps you're right. I'll go back to my office and wait for your call."

"Good, you do that," the chief said as he closed the office door and turned the lock.

Adams spoke loudly through the glass.

"And they'd better be dead in the next 24 hours."

Staring at Adams, the Security Chief pushed a button on his side of the door, turning the clear glass to black.

****

Xavier Adams had a back-up plan. He would not leave it to the system to determine the fate of Troy Vincent and Loveena Baptista. He just wanted to confirm whether they were still alive. Now, he'd put Plan B into action.

Walking across the large atrium toward the elevator going to the lower levels, he casually glanced down at the large ring on his finger. He needed to tie up the loose ends of this mess so he could go on to more important matters, like taking over SWI; and then getting elected as CEO of the WBoD. He never expected his meeting with Hoy to end up like this, but it all worked out to his advantage. Hoy SamWong was dead and two people Adams hated would take the blame.

That bitch should've never rejected me; she slept with everyone else. Throw coffee in my face, will you? Now you're getting what you deserve, you little slut. And that pompous inventor, Troy Vincent...I didn't like him from the start. Eliminating him will end those pesky patent lawsuits against SWI real quick. The Board will definitely appoint me CEO. Let's see if you die the way your old man did – with a little help from me.

The events of a week ago replayed in his mind. Hoy intentionally held up the last two payments on their agreement. Hush money, Hoy called it. Adams told him the monthly amount just wasn't enough, and he needed more money to keep Hoy's dirty little secret quiet.

But Adams wasn't really going to divulge it and Hoy knew it. He couldn't, not without implicating himself in the murders the two of them had committed. The rest of the world thought the elderly Dr. Vincent committed suicide, when in reality, SamWong's murderous madness and Adams' jealous ambition befell him.

That night, Adams had demanded more money, much more to stay quiet. Hoy refused. They argued, and he left Hoy's office, stomping through the outer office in anger and returning to his suite of offices down the hall. *If I hadn't gone back to insist he pay me now, things might have turned out differently. I didn't expect to find him lying unconscious on the floor.*

At first, Adams thought he was dead. When he looked closer, he saw Hoy still breathing. A strange green mark appeared on the breast pocket of Hoy's suit jacket, looking almost like smoldering fabric. There were no signs of a struggle. For all he knew, maybe Hoy tripped and fell, dropping hot coffee on himself. He didn't know what happened, and frankly, he didn't care. Adams had no compassion for the little bastard. He saw the diamond SWI ring and took it in place of the missed payments.

"I'll take this for the last two payments you owe me," and he pulled it from SamWong's limp hand. "If you decide to give me what I want, I might consider returning it."

As he left, he saw Loveena's security card on the floor next to the door. Picking it up, he paused, contemplating an opportunity to kill two annoying birds with one stone, both Hoy and his little errand girl. Carefully wiping his prints from her security card, he laid it next to Hoy's body. Then, grabbing a pillow from the couch in the room, he smothered Hoy with it, holding his body down until the twitching stopped. To make sure he was dead, Adams grabbed an electrical cord running along the floor and wrapped it around Hoy's neck, pulling it tight. He went around the room wiping off his fingerprints from everything he previously had touched. Finally, he removed the cord from Hoy's neck, taking it with him to dispose of it.

The next morning, Adams watched as an innocent by-stander, feigning surprise at the police activity in the building, and demanded justice at the emergency WBoD meeting. He cooperated with the police, dropping hints about Hoy's involvement with Loveena and the names of his enemies, emphasizing Troy Vincent's. Monitoring the progress of the investigation, he made sure he scheduled himself for the judging panel on the two cases. Everything was going smoothly, and now he would finish the job.

Adams stopped beside a janitorial door on the far side of the atrium and looked around, slipping into the unlocked closet unobserved. He pulled a small duffle bag containing a maintenance uniform from the top shelf, having placed it there on his way in to see Chief Michaels. Removing his suit, he slipped on the tan shirt, khaki pants, and black boots worn by the facility's work crews. Putting on a brown ball cap completed the uniform, and he stuffed his suit back into the bag, replacing it on the shelf. He would pick up the bag on his way out. With a portable box of plumbing tools in his hand, he blended in with the dayshift staff of the facility. Only the diamond ring he wore looked out of place. Not wanting to lose it, he decided to keep the ring on.

Adams was the lone rider in the elevator as it went down. He pulled a small aerosol can from his pocket and examined it. The contents of the little vial inside the small container became a discovery of a lifetime, and SamWong Industries secretly obtained all the rights to it. Commonly known as the Demon Hormone, it was a natural occurring hormone that remained dormant in the body. But in laboratory tests, it could become fatal under certain conditions. The discovery, isolation, and alteration of the natural hormone captivated and worried the medical community.

If the hormone was altered with a specific enzyme, it would release a poisonous toxin, which could kill its host within minutes. Unlike slow growing cancers taking time to manifest and debilitate its host, this 'demon hormone' acted similar to endorphins, releasing quickly to manage pain, only it did just the opposite. As its name implied, the symptoms observed in the lab included high body temperatures, hallucinations of a bizarre and demonic nature, and extreme pain prior to the death of the subject. Being such a new discovery, there was no known antidote or cure.

SamWong wanted a way to remove people, but make it look like death by natural causes. After all, the hormone left no traces behind for autopsy detection. Using his own private lab and a loyal technician, they experimented with Hoy's own blood sample, having found it carried a higher than normal count of the natural hormone. In secret, the lab enhanced the hormone by injecting the enzyme into it, making it instantly toxic. Delivered as an aerosol, instead of requiring an injection, it became a portable weapon, just what Hoy wanted. Adams thought the design of the dispenser quite clever, appearing as an ordinary inhaler, with the deadly agent delivered as a mist. *Such an innocent-looking murder weapon; how ironic it came from SamWong's own blood.*

The aerosol delivered a two-part agent. Part one, consisted of the harmless Demon Hormone that would circulate among the blood cells. Part two, was the time-activated amino acid enzyme embedded in the hormone, combined with a steroid which would enhance the 'demon-like' symptoms. Once released, it would seek out and destroy blood cells, setting off the fatal reactions: hallucinations, pain and death. The lab work remained so secret, only Hoy, Adams, and the technician knew of it. The technician later disappeared; the body never found. That was only part of their secret.

The other part of the secret involved Dr. Vincent. Hoy SamWong felt publicly humiliated and left angered by the deal he made in acquiring VSA. Discovering the twelve androids could become potential nuclear bombs made him the laughingstock of the WBoD. Word spread fast of the deal with VSA going sour, and SamWong left holding the bag. When Dr. Vincent's team refused to find a way to disarm or destroy the androids, Hoy became enraged and sought revenge.

Adams, viewed by many to be next in line to take over SWI, was only too eager to appease Hoy. He knew this tiny, lethal weapon might someday serve him, as well. Together, they planned a meeting to discuss the androids' work with Dr. Vincent at the doctor's house. There they tried out the new SWI Demon Hormone on the unsuspecting doctor. Adams held him down while Hoy administered the drug via an inhaler. They did not expect it to work so quickly, or be so successful on a human. When the doctor immediately expired, they panicked. Adams suggested they make it look like a suicide, and hung the elderly Dr. Vincent from a rafter in the garage.

One squirt of this into their VRC and it's all over. Slipping the small inhaler back into his pocket, he patted it with satisfaction, as the elevator door opened.

The android had Troy and Loveena. Adams didn't know the exact location of Vincent's workroom, but he knew the section he was assigned to. The attorney made his way to the security station on the lowest level.

Fast asleep in a chair, Amon snored with his feet propped up on the security desk. Terry's nose was buried in a collectors' edition of a comic book with his back to the counter. Neither man heard the attorney approach. Adams stood at the security counter in front of them for several moments before banging his fist on the surface. Both attendants jumped up from their chairs.

"Yes, sir?" Terry quickly responded, rolled up his comic book and stuffed it into his back pocket. Noticing the maintenance uniform, his attitude became dismissive. "Oh, maintenance. What do you want?" he quipped.

"We got a call to check out the air filtration system in this section," said Adams.

Terry was apprehensive. "Well, we didn't call you. What's the problem?"

"Gotta do an air treatment."

"We didn't get any notice of an air treatment...."

Adams interrupted, "It's an emergency; not enough time to send out a notification."

Stepping up to the counter, Amon asked, "What do you gotta do?"

Adams held up the inhaler. "Inject this into the VRC air filtration system."

"What is it?" Amon looked closer at the little tube in Adam's hand.

"It's...an antibiotic."

Terry reached for the tiny canister, but Adams pulled it back.

"Something that small?" Terry shook his head. "There's no guarantee it will go through the system. It might hit a few of the chambers, but...."

"Will it hit the two chambers the robot is monitoring?" Adams asked with some exasperation.

The two attendants puzzled over the question, raising their shoulders in uncertainty.

Amon responded. "I guess it will. Why? Is there a problem with his?"

"We received a report his chambers are highly contaminated."

Terry didn't like the unusual protocol. "We'll have him clean the chambers with a special decontaminant before the next candidate uses it."

Adams raised his voice. "No, no, it must be done now, and it has to be done through the air filtration system."

Terry looked at him with suspicion. "Is this some kind of security test? Are you from Human Resources?"

Deciding to play along, Adams thought he should do anything to get these two idiots to cooperate with him. Smiling, he held out his hand to shake Terry's.

"You're real smart, you caught on quick. Congratulations, you passed the test."

Terry shook Adams' hand, noticing the fancy ring. "They must pay you guys in HR quite a lot."

Amon smacked Terry in the side. "Well, we're on top of things down here in this section. We got it covered here." Both attendants then beamed with pride.

Adams came prepared. *I'll have to sweeten the pot or I won't get much further with these two morons.* "So as a reward, you two are getting a bonus—right here and right now. How does five thousand dollars sound to you, boys?"

"Not very much," Terry snorted. "But we'll take whatever we can get, right Amon?"

"Then, let's make it ten thousand—a piece." Reaching in his pocket, Adams pulled out a fat money clip. He counted out twenty separate one-thousand dollar bills, placing them in two piles on the counter. The eyes of the two attendants lit up as the money was plunked down, one bill at a time. When he was done, they eagerly reached for the bills, stuffing them into their pockets.

"Now, we still need to fix the air filtration system," Adams said.

"No problem. We can take care of that right now," Terry said. Turning to Amon, "Hey, buddy, watch the desk." He stepped around the counter and out of the security station, smiling at Adams. "Ya see? We got it covered. Follow me."

Terry walked down the hall toward the locked air filtration room with Adams right behind him, the inhaler securely tucked in his hand.

Chapter 32

The night sounds of the forest filtered through the open window of the loft. Troy and Loveena lay beneath the soft down coverlet of the suspended bed, their bodies entwined and exhausted. Her head gently nestled against his chin as he held her, his right arm bent back behind the pillow. From somewhere outside, Troy heard the romantic strings of a Spanish guitar softly and slowly drifting across the lake, playing Ravel's intoxicating *Bolero*.

Loveena rested her hand upon his chest, drawing circles with her index finger over the spot where his chest injury had been. Neither of them spoke, there was no need, content to just hold each other for a while.

Staring up at the stars through the roof-top window above them, Troy contemplated the beauty of the dense Milky Way. The bed hung by cables under the big window and anchored to the ceiling rafters. With the touch of a button next to the bed, he could open the sliding section of roof covering the glass. He often wished he could be out among the stars, like the android travelers were supposed to be; but not this night, gazing down at Loveena.

Listening to the forest outside, the peace and tranquility of his lakeside cabin brought balance into his life. Now lying with her in his arms seemed the most natural thing in the world, as though they had always been meant for each other. For a few hours, he would allow himself to relax and languish in this happiness. He knew Tommy was alive, and he knew Loveena felt as he did. Troy pushed aside the thought it could all end at any time, though in the back of his mind, he did wonder how it would end.

"You didn't tell me how you got this key," said Loveena, as her finger traced over the top of the blue-colored key of Hope around Troy's neck.

Turning on his side toward her, he looked into her dark brown eyes. *Her eyes are so beautiful.*

"When I was injured, I thought I might die. I felt sad because I would lose Tommy all over again." He ran his finger down the side of her cheek. *Her skin is so soft.* Playfully touching the tip of her nose, he softly chuckled and teased, "And I was also extremely worried I wouldn't see you again."

Loveena grinned, pinching his chin and placing the palm of her hand on his cheek. Troy kissed her palm, and she ran her hand over his broad shoulder, down his arm, before cupping it over his.

"I tried to make my peace with the Maker."

"You mean, God," she whispered. "Please, call him God."

"With...God." He felt odd calling the Maker by his forbidden name. "Then a Grief Master appeared, asking me in a rather terse manner, if I had a reason to live."

"And what did you say?"

"I have a son who needs me, so he can live again." Leaning closer to her, Troy felt her sweet, warm breath just beneath his lips. "And I have a woman who needs me...so I can live again."

The steady beat of the exotic *Bolero* rang in his ears and smoldered in the twin fires of her eyes. His mouth covered hers, tasting the passion of her kiss and receiving as much in return. Moving his body against her, the feel of her damp skin next to him heightened his desire once more. Her arms wrapped around his neck and firm breasts rose against his chest. They surrendered to each other again. Locked in the rhythmic movement of their lovers' embrace, the world would have to wait.

As the mysterious melody moved through the loft, it surrounded their bodies with chords building toward a sensual crescendo, blending with the sound of their lovemaking, intensely connected; igniting; explosive; and all-consuming; until exhausted. The music of love floated on the crisp night air across the serene lake.

Outside, moon glow reflected on the ripples of the water, and the forest noise became quiet. Their world was at peace for the moment.

****

The early morning sun filtered through the trees. Troy emerged from the shower behind the small kitchen, having left Loveena asleep in the loft. Pulling on some clean clothes from a basket, a pair of jeans and a gray t-shirt, he walked barefoot to the sink and rinsed out a coffee cup. The coffee maker signaled a freshly brewed pot was ready to be poured. He savored the taste, feeling totally parched, realizing they hadn't anything to eat or drink since before entering the VRC. Loveena told him Vincent had provided the iced tea at the beach house, and now, probably this coffee, too, hoping to keep their bodies alive with a simple, satisfying illusion.

With the cup at his lips, he peered out the kitchen window. A solitary doe stealthily crossed the yard, stopping long enough to taste the late fall berries of a bush. She trotted off into the forest, and Troy waited for the buck to show himself. He bent down to slip on a pair of socks and his boots. When he stood up, he saw the 13 pointer creep out of the shadows and cautiously advance across the clearing to the trees, following the doe.

"There you are, you big son of a gun," Troy whispered. He had caught a glimpse of the big male once before. He knew it must be rutting season for the buck to come near the cabin in daylight. Being so comfortable here in the cabin, Troy reminded himself it was only a VRC illusion. The safe house would soon be gone, and he needed time to think about their next move.

I think better outside, he thought, crossing the room to the front door. Spotting his crossbow on the wall, he grabbed it, along with the quiver, and quietly closed the cabin door behind him.

Taking in a deep breath of cool fresh air, he filled his senses with the richness of fall, his favorite time of year. It came as no surprise that the safe house in the VRC turned out to be the cabin he loved. Troy spent weeks alone here after Tommy disappeared, retreating from life, taking refuge among the only things he still believed in, himself and Mother Nature. He never returned after it burned to the ground from the lightning strike. He sat down on the steps of the porch and took another sip of coffee. It was good to be back here one last time.

Laying the crossbow across his lap, he pulled a small rag from the quiver to wipe it down. At least, now he held a decent weapon in his hands to defend the two of them. Troy worked while he tried to unravel who might be after them, to put the pieces of the puzzle he knew together.

SamWong Industries is behind our convictions. They want Loveena dead because she's the daughter of some corporate resistance leader. She knows too much about Hoy SamWong. They want me dead because...I don't know why they want me dead; because I threatened him? It could be the patent lawsuits.

He adjusted the range on the scope of the crossbow. *Or maybe my ex-wife has something to do with it,* he mused. Picking up his coffee cup, he took another sip. *I know our own demon hormones are creating these demons.*

"Four demons came at me in my memory center; there should only be one left," he said out loud. "Not sure about Loveena's count."

I didn't kill SamWong. Loveena didn't kill him. Vincent and Adams were both in the room. But Loveena saw Adams leave.

Troy sighed; he didn't want to think Vincent would kill a human, though he was physically capable of it. Non-military androids weren't supposed to kill humans, but working in the VRC every day, The Brethren certainly knew how to do it.

Vincent never said how he stopped SamWong from choking Loveena. Could an android decide on its own to commit murder?

Troy shook his head with distaste. Vincent had been created for the expansion of humanity, programmed to represent the best mankind could offer. Instead, it may be possible he ended up learning the worst man is capable of. After all, Vincent wanted to be more human-like.

Vincent and the Grief Masters

Pulling out one of six auto-loading magazines in the quiver, Troy checked the label: *Liquid Magnesium Bolt Arrows – Quantity 15 per bolt.* He clicked it on top of the crossbow over the arrow track, snapping it into place directly under the scope. The crossbow, a self-loading automatic weapon, dropped one thin arrow from the bolt of fifteen into the flight groove and drew the string back into the latch. Also self-cocking, it could rapid-fire as quickly as he could pull the trigger.

The unique arrows were Troy's own invention. Hollow inside, each arrow contained a small quantity of the liquid magnesium that ejected out the end of the arrow upon impact. Contact with oxygen made it burn so hot, it vaporized anything within a ten-foot radius of the target. When the magazine bolt emptied, it automatically ejected and another bolt could be quickly snapped in place. His quiver held up to six bolts, a total of 90 magnesium arrows. He intended it for use on construction sites, but the SWI corporate militia commandeered the design. It was one of his patent lawsuits pending against SWI. Troy used his unique arrows to remove tree stumps and debris outside the cabin. Now other targets came into his mind.

Loveena said she heard Adams and SamWong arguing. Adams said he wanted more. More what? Money? Was Hoy paying Adams under the table? Or was Adams blackmailing him? What were they hiding?

Troy knew Adams could be tenacious. *Maybe he came back to the office; maybe Adams murdered his buddy, SamWong.* "Boy, that would be poetic justice, wouldn't it?"

Putting the crossbow to his shoulder, he looked through the scope, taking aim at a tree stump at the end of the dirt path. As he placed his finger on the trigger, Vincent's hologram suddenly appeared in the crosshairs of his scope. Jerking the crossbow up, the arrow fired into the trees, hitting a large branch. The liquid magnesium flared up, vaporizing a section of the wood, and the rest of the branch came crashing down to the ground. Troy stood up, securing the safety on the trigger, and pulled the quiver across his shoulder. Carrying his crossbow with him, he walked down the path toward Vincent.

"It wasn't you was it, Vincent? You didn't kill SamWong. You couldn't. You're programmed to help humans, not destroy them. It was Adams."

"It appears so," Vincent replied. "I stunned SamWong enough to release his hold on the girl. However, the electrical shock I delivered only rendered him unconscious."

"Adams is next in line to take over the corporation and possibly, the World Board," Troy speculated. "He must have found Loveena's security card in the room; the perfect setup for him." However, Troy puzzled over why all the pieces didn't quite fit together.

"I don't understand. What were the two of them hiding? Possibly, covering up something?"

"Yes."

Once again, Troy realized the android knew more than he chose to reveal. "What?"

"You must maintain an even temperament no matter what your emotion tells you. A demon can feed off your negative energy."

"Spit it out, Vincent. Why was SamWong paying Adams on the side?"

As the wind picked up, Troy looked over his shoulder at a dark cloud in the distance appearing over the lake.

"SamWong's computer remained on, with an accounting ledger open. I took the liberty of tapping into his files. A record of payments to Adams came up."

Leaves blew across the path. Troy glanced back at the storm clouds gathering. "Go on."

"The recorded payments began the same day your father died."

"I don't get the connection."

"Two other files dated the same day appeared to be linked to a report from SamWong's lab, one on the development and toxic enhancement of a new hormone. According to the file, the blood type used in the test came from SamWong's own blood, already containing a high amount of the natural demon hormone."

A low rumble of thunder echoed in the distance. The sky darkened.

"Ok; what does that have to do with my father's death?"

"The other file consisted of scanned notes written in SamWong's own hand, detailing a test of the poisonous altered hormone on an unsuspecting human. A report labeled, *'Test Results of the Demon Hormone,'* described the test as 'very successful,' and the victim died. The victim was Dr. Vincent, your father."

A loud crack of lightning flashed above the lake. Troy's stomach jumped into his throat as the thunder rumbled across the land.

"Are you saying," Troy stumbled over the words, "they...murdered him?"

It wasn't suicide? His mouth went instantly dry as he tried to swallow, absorbing the shock. *It wasn't suicide.* He never believed the death certificate, but here existed the hard evidence proving the real truth of what happened. It was tough to take.

Vincent continued, "One more record completed the file, a copy of your father's autopsy report. SamWong noted, while the demon hormone had disappeared from the body, an echo of the altered enzyme remained. A scribbled notation on the file showed a cash payment to the mortician to seal the autopsy records. I couldn't stay to review more. Other people were in the building and I needed to remove Loveena from his office as quickly as possible. I copied the files to my databank." He held up his index finger to indicate he simply touched SamWong's computer to make the copy. "I later forwarded the files to Don Tyler."

Feeling the shock travel to his very core, Troy could feel hatred begin to well up inside of him. SamWong and Adams murdered his father and made it look like a suicide. Hate was an uncomfortable, consuming emotion, but one he justified to himself.

"Why? Why would they do that? They already owned his company."

"Because he would not destroy what he created, what he loved. He would not destroy me."

Hate, pure hate pumped through Troy's brain. The goodness he found within his three Grief Master keys turned dark. Nothing more powerful existed in the human psyche than hate, except love, and Troy felt none for either man, especially the one who condemned him to the VRC. He held his crossbow out in front of him, glaring at it with murderous contemplation.

"It's a good thing SamWong is already dead. But Adams isn't, not yet anyway."

Vincent spoke with a quiet firmness. "You must remain calm. Do not become brash while still inside this VRC."

Troy looked at him with pain of this deep wound reflected in his eyes, wondering if the android felt anything about this revelation. His father created him, and Vincent spoke of loyalty to him. Troy challenged him, speaking in a harsh tone.

"Doesn't it bother you, Vincent, what they did? In a perverted way, he was your father, too. Do you feel *anything*? I know you said you couldn't help us, but even an AI such as yourself, at some point, has to take a side!"

Vincent paused to process the question. "If human emotion were to dictate the outcome of this situation, it could result in the murder of attorney Adams. However, that being negative and *uncivilized*," emphasizing the last word, "more consequences would arise. Dr. Vincent preferred logic to resolve conflict. I honor his memory by performing in the manner in which he taught me."

Staring at the ground in silence, Troy realized the android had a way of quietly disarming him. He paced back and forth, rubbing his hand across his eyes until he dropped his arm to his side with a subdued resignation, unleashing the pressure valve on his outburst at the android.

"Damn it, Vincent," he said. "Why do you have to be so pragmatic? Do you not feel for one second like seeking revenge? Seeing Adams dead? You are...." Troy stopped, sidelined by the android's words about honoring his father's memory. With a heavy sigh, he continued, "You are more like my father than I ever was."

He knew Vincent was right. They were still in the VRC and there would be time later to confront Adams and 'resolve the conflict,' as the android put it. With storm clouds billowing and climbing into a towering thunderhead, Troy realized their time in the safe house might be about to end. He needed to get back to Loveena.

Turning to Vincent, he added, "You'd better go. We're not free of this place yet." Another arrow had automatically loaded; he took the safety off of the trigger.

"I came to warn you," Vincent said. "The demon hormone with the toxic enzyme has been detected in the air filtration system. I diverted your air supply to an outside duct and rerouted fresh oxygen to both of your chambers from an emergency system. However, I am unsure if I successfully blocked all of it in time."

Troy could see Vincent appeared concerned about this turn of events. "What does that mean?"

"It means the next demon you face may not be from either of you."

Chapter 33

Loveena awoke, stretched her arms high into the air as happiness filled her heart from the night before. Knowing Troy felt the same and relishing in the afterglow of his tender and passionate love making, made her body tingle all over again. She pushed the thoughts of the dangers of the VRC temporarily from her mind and climbed out of bed, looking forward to a hot shower.

She wrapped a towel around her, feeling refreshed. Loveena exited the shower and noticed a basket of clean clothing sitting on the floor. Her camisole top had been destroyed when she tore it up to make a bandage for Troy's chest wound. So she decided to wear a shirt of his instead. Rummaging through the basket shed found a sleeveless white t-shirt. Holding it to her nose, she sniffed the fresh, clean scent, then slipped it over her head and pulled on her jeans.

As a cool breeze blew through the cabin from the open kitchen window, she also grabbed a flannel shirt from the basket, rolled up the sleeves, and tied the front ends of the shirt into a knot. Slipping on her boots, Loveena glanced in the bathroom mirror at the round-necked t-shirt and loose, unbuttoned flannel shirt, knotted at her waist. "It will have to do."

Following the smell of coffee into the kitchen, Loveena found a mug and poured herself a cup, wrapping both hands around it to keep them warm. She savored the taste of the strong, black coffee, feeling thirsty and hungry, too. Looking out the window above the sink, she saw storm clouds gathering over the lake. Loveena hadn't noticed the man seated at the end of the couch until he began to speak. Chills went down her spine like icicle daggers.

"So you think he loves you?" Hoy SamWong asked with a sadistic sneer.

Vincent and the Grief Masters

Loveena dropped the mug in the sink breaking the handle, as coffee slopped over the edge of the counter. She knew that voice without turning around to see who spoke.

"What are you doing here?" she whispered, barely able to get the words out.

"Well, I'm not sure. One minute I'm in my office, and the next, I'm staring into the face of that disgusting robot, Vincent, I think his name was. One thing I am sure of Loveena, you and I have unfinished business." His voice sounded cold.

He stood up, stepping to the fireplace, and leaned his forearm on the mantle. His square face, darkly tanned, sported ruddy, red cheeks and wide-set eyes as gray as the storm clouds gathering outside. Thin lips smiled at her. "I asked you a question," he said.

Loveena, tried not to stammer, wiping the puddle of coffee back into the sink with a dish towel. "I ...I guess I didn't hear your question, Hoy."

Outwardly, she would act nonchalant, as if his presence didn't bother her; but inside, she was overwhelmed with terror that he had returned. Hoy would take any opportunity to belittle and bully her. *SamWong could intimidate a monk. How can he be here? Troy, where are you?*

"I said, so you think he loves you?" First looking at his manicured nails, he then, stared at her, peering down his nose with contempt.

"I don't know who you're talking about," Loveena stalled. *If only Troy would walk through the door.*

"Of course you do—Troy, isn't it? The ignominious son of Dr. Vincent. One of my enemies, as you well know." He chuckled. "A dead enemy, to be exact."

"Oh, him. What about him?" Her knees began to shake. *Hold onto your courage, girl, don't let him manipulate you.*

Picking up the fireplace poker, he bent down, stabbed at the ashen log, and the embers reignited, flaring up. The log resumed burning as a small flame spread across it. While he was stirring the embers, she quietly pulled the flannel shirt together and buttoned it over the Grief Master keys hanging around her neck, so they would not be visible. She didn't want to lose the courage, faith and hope discovered inside herself, but didn't want him to notice their keys either.

"You're fooling yourself, Loveena. He's only after one thing, and you, my dear, know exactly what that is. After all, you are so good at it."

Hoy stood up sporting the cruel smile she was so used to seeing when he was alive. It conveyed a message he never failed to show her: he disapproved of her, he was better than her, and he could destroy her anytime he wanted. Hoy walked slowly across the living room toward the open kitchenette behind the couch, the hot poker in his right hand.

Loveena needed to stand up to him and not let him control her as he had in the past. She turned to look him straight in the eye. "You wouldn't know love, Hoy, if it rose up and bit you in the ass." Backing out of the kitchen area into the living room, she moved toward the door on the opposite side of the room from him.

"You are nothing to him, you are less than nothing. You can't even keep yourself out of trouble. Look where your antics have gotten you?" He spread his hands out, waving the hot poker carelessly around. "Yes, yes, I know where we are."

He moved around the back of the couch stopping by the small kitchen sink, as she paused by the opposite end of the couch.

"The VRC is such a useful invention. Sanctioned eliminations approved by society and right under their noses. Oh, what mindless cattle they are." He picked up the broken cup from the sink, looked at it and laid it on the counter.

"Tsk-tsk. You broke it, Loveena. You're such a screw-up. No one's going to miss you, my dear, not even your latest lover boy."

Loveena was as tall as he, but the man could always make her feel small and worthless within seconds of being in the same room. She didn't want her new found strength and courage to disappear, but she could feel it slipping away with his intimidating words.

"In fact, I would be doing the world a favor by ridding it of low class street-walking vermin like you. It will be such fun to destroy you." Raising the poker above his head, he smashed it down on the counter, pulverizing the cup.

Loveena shrank back against the wall, as the shattered pieces flew across the room, scattering along the floor. He was coming for her, only steps away. Her Patience, aka Courage, came forward, sending an adrenaline surge and her wits re-awakened. She knew self-defense, even if it was just a college class in the past. The moves burst out of her in a sudden fountain of self-preservation. She kicked, punched and forced him back across the small space toward the sink.

Hoy was now the one on the defensive, swinging the hot poker at her. She kicked it from his hand and it flew across the living room, tangling in the drapes and setting them on fire. Hoy turned toward the poker, stretched out his hand and the lethal piece of iron detached itself from the burning drapes, flying back through the air and into his waiting grasp.

Loveena darted for the cabin door, but now the poker he held morphed into a black whip. Cracking it across the room, it wrapped around her wrist before she could grab the door knob, yanking her back, and down to the floor.

Hoy now crossed the small room with large strides, grabbing her by the hair with his free hand. With her firmly captured in his grasp, the whip retracted from her wrist and turned back into the solid poker.

She was losing her courage, her hope. The keys hidden under the flannel shirt began to lose their colors, turning grey. Disappointment grew in her soul as she became unable to cling to the momentary strength to stand up to him.

"No one has you but me, do you understand?" he shouted. Black clouds swirled and rumbled, thunder echoing across the sky. With his fist tightly wrapped in her long hair, Hoy dragged her up and across the floor away from the door.

Loveena hated Hoy SamWong, but her hate seemed to make him grow stronger. Her Grief Masters whispered encouragement to stay calm. The louder they spoke, the louder the wind rushed through the cabin from the open window until their voices were drowned out. Hoy's lust for power, to control and possess her, was too consuming. Recognizing this as the demon of Hate, she realized it would be hard to fight such a powerful human urge. She and Troy were truly in danger of being consumed. How could they defend themselves from that which destroyed civilizations and mobilized masses to kill each other?

"You'll see who wins at this game—at every game!" Laughing maniacally, Hoy pointed the poker toward the loft window. Charged electrons from the tip of the poker shot up, shattering the large window as shards of glass rained down from the loft ceiling. The stream of electrons spread through the storm clouds above. A lightning bolt manifested from the storm, cracking with an ear-shattering sound. Feeling the floor beneath her rattle, Loveena's knees buckled, she collapsed to the floor and covered her ears with her hands. She resumed struggling against the grip on her hair to no avail, as he turned and pointed the poker at the fireplace. A tongue of fire from the log jumped out attaching itself to the end of the poker, burning red hot. As he swung it back through the room, everything it touched caught on fire. With the back of the cabin now engulfed in flames, he pulled Loveena to her feet and shouted at her above the noise of the storm and fiery chaos.

"I hate the Vincents! I have always despised them! But I also envy everything about them! Frankly, I might have paid a fortune to have you feel about me the way you do about your precious boy toy. But now you, my dear, will see him die before you do!"

****

All three of Loveena's Grief Masters, Patience, Faith and Hope, appeared before Troy and Vincent at the end of the path in front of the cabin.

"You must help her!" Hope said.
"What's happening?" Troy asked.
"She is not alone." Faith responded.

"Hoy SamWong is with her," Patience added. "She is losing us."

Vincent turned to Troy. "This is the demon I spoke of. It has manifested in the embodiment of SamWong. Extreme caution, as this one will not hesitate to kill you both. You must find a way to defeat him." Then his hologram faded out.

Troy turned around and saw smoke pouring out of the back of the cabin. He ran up the path followed by a blur of color from Loveena's Grief Masters. Before he could reach the porch, a bolt of lightning flashed across the sky, hitting the tin roof. A thunderous crash lit up the clearing as its electric fingers split across the roofline, running down all four corners of the cabin. The cabin exploded, shooting pieces of wooden structure in all directions, throwing Troy backward several yards through the air. Flames raged, as black smoke filled the clearing. Troy lay unconscious, with his crossbow on his chest.

****

The loud explosion left a ringing in Troy's ears, like his head was inside a giant bell. Fighting his way back to consciousness, he slowly sat up. The blast simultaneously knocked his three Grief Masters from his own body. They lay a few feet from him, all struggling to recover. On his right, Courage sat up, shaking his head to clear it. To his left, the golden Faith and teal-blue Hope helped each other to their feet.

Courage stood up, helping Troy to his feet. "Are we all right?" Troy asked.

Wiping the dirt from his eyes with the back of his hand, he looked around at all three, who appeared stunned but steady, and they all nodded. All wore the same clothing as Troy, tinted in their own hue. Each one was at once an independent Troy, with a common connection to his soul. They would stand and fight for him separately, but they would act and think as one.

Troy looked with dismay at the cabin. Nothing remained except a partial stone structure, the fireplace. Pieces of the roof and logs from the walls littered the clearing, landing as far away as the shore of the lake. Flames had spread to the pine tree forest and smoke filled the air, billowing up to the storm clouds above. The surrounding grass was incinerated and the dirt left blackened. Near the edge of the forest, Troy saw the smoldering dead body of the doe. A howling sound from the injured buck echoed from somewhere in the burning forest.

A rancid smell welled up from holes opening in the scorched earth, releasing columns of sulfur into the air. Troy figured the demon hormone Vincent mentioned became the catalyst changing his peaceful safe house into the next VRC chamber. This one included the burning fires of hell.

As the smoke blew back toward the lake, Troy saw Hoy SamWong standing in the middle of the cabin rubble, unscathed. He held a red-hot fireplace poker in one fist and clutched Loveena's hair tightly in his other. Black soot streaked across her face and covered her clothing, but she appeared uninjured by the explosion. Held closely by SamWong, Loveena stood unable to move, but her eyes honed in on Troy.

SamWong lifted the poker, swinging the transformed, burning whip in circles above his head. Snapping it around, it swung down and stung the back of Loveena's knees. Troy heard her cry out as she fell to her knees once more, followed by SamWong's taunting voice.

"Is that hate I smell in the air, boy? Your hate, or mine? Or maybe, it's hers. It all fuels the same storm."

The black tumultuous clouds swirled above them, lightning flashing inside the billows, sending rumbles of thunder echoing across the sky. SamWong's words traveled on the air, as though his voice came from the storm clouds above. He railed at Troy with a vengeful reverberation filling the air.

"Hate drives this world! It feeds the greedy and devours the weak! Hate is what we love to do! You and me, boy, we have the same evil running through our veins. We want what others have.

We lust for it. We lie and steal to get it. We seek revenge when we can't have it; and then we hate ourselves for all of it!"

Troy and his Grief Masters stood steadfast as the wind changed direction, sending waves of smoke against them. Troy yelled back, "Hate may drive you, but I only want to destroy it—and you with it. It won't rule me as it has you."

SamWong's eyes shimmered with treacherous glee.

"Don't fool yourself, for your hate is great, Troy Vincent. It grew strong when I stole your wife, followed by the takeover of your company; and even stronger when I commandeered your little invention that stole your boy's life. I found that quite amusing!" SamWong's voice turned serious as he glared at Troy. "And how does it feel now knowing I killed your father?"

Troy's jaw stiffened, his eyes narrowed and veins in his temples pulsed. He most certainly did feel a great deal of hate. Inwardly, he was fighting the urge to kill, trying to control the rising volcanic reaction to SamWong's words pounding in his ears. Knowing his reaction was exactly what the demon wanted Troy still couldn't keep it from flooding over him. *Forgiveness is not an option here; I'm vowing an eye for an eye.*

His Faith Grief Master stood to his right and put a warning hand upon his arm. "Do not listen to him. Hate does not heal, it only promotes more hatred. Your faith has healed your heart. Now only faith and thoughtful resolve can fight such evil."

Pulling her by her hair, SamWong forced Loveena to her feet as he stepped from the rubble. Loveena struggled and his whip wrapped around her waist and arms like a boa constrictor.

"And this little play thing," the demon taunted, pointing the end of the hot poker close to her face. "How is your hate, knowing that I, the one true reason for all of your misery, took this little whore over and over—and she loved it."

Troy held his crossbow up to his shoulder, taking aim, but his Hope Grief Master stepped up to his other side, laying a hand upon the top of it.

"You know he is lying. He is manipulating you. Do not give in to him. Your hate will only fuel his evil energy. There is hope to defeat him on your terms, not his."

Troy looked at Loveena, but her head hung down in despair. He whispered to her. "Loveena, do not lose hope." Looking up at him, he thought she may have heard him. As much as he wanted to see SamWong dead, he couldn't pull the trigger, knowing he could risk losing her to the liquid magnesium.

Her three Grief Masters suddenly appeared in front of him.

"She has sent us to fight with you on her behalf," said Patience.

"She believes in you," her Faith added.

"She can hear you," her Hope confirmed.

Troy offered them reassurance. "I will not let her die."

"She knows this," her Faith replied.

SamWong, unable to see the heavenly Grief Masters, could not tell who Troy was speaking to. He turned his attention toward the sky, retracting the whip bound around Loveena, causing her arms to bleed. He whirled it into a circle high above his head, the long, flaming tip stretching into the clouds. Acrid rain began to beat down on the burnt ground. Turning his face skyward and letting the rain pelt down upon him, steam rose up from his body. He began to howl, raising the poker higher, pumping it in the air in a posture of mad power.

His face twisted, contorting into demonic features. His eyes sunk back into dark hollow cavities; his ears grew into thin, pointed spikes. His mouth opened extremely wide, displaying decaying rows of sharpened teeth, and his hair turned into a white-hot flame, tinged with orange colored tips. The skin fell from his face, neck, and hands, revealing layers of reptilian scales, glowing like orange embers in the bottom of a fireplace. His black suit and red tie remained unchanged and unburned, creating a striking look, a true personification of Corporate Rule displayed by the contrast between business attire and the evil lurking underneath it. And the demon of Hate, the CEO of the World Board of Directors, who emerged from SamWong himself, was birthed by his own demon hormone into the Devil Incarnate.

Chapter 34

SamWong relaxed his grip on Loveena's hair and she took off running toward Troy. The demon scowled as he realized his mistake. He pointed his finger at the landscape in front of her and it started to move, lengthening to a distance of one hundred yards.

It didn't slow Loveena's Olympian pace. She stumbled when the ground shifted under her feet, but kept running. She hurdled over boulders pushing up from the earth which made her run even faster. Her eyes were fixed on Patience, who stood next to Troy.

Patience turned to him. "She wishes you to know, no matter what happens to her, she wants you to live, and save your son."

SamWong was not done with her yet. He whirled the whip around and released it. The black snake-like leather sailed after Loveena, wrapping around her neck and jerking her to the ground. Grabbing at the whip, she managed to wedge her fingers between it and her skin to stop the stranglehold, loosening it enough to gasp for air.

SamWong stomped the ground with one of his black crocodile boots, and two cracks in the earth traveled from his boot across the yards running along either side of Loveena. Tall, jagged rocks sprang up from the cracks separating her from Troy.

Troy cocked the crossbow, loaded a magnesium bolt arrow and took aim at the towering rocks. Pulling the trigger, the arrow sped to its target, exploding and dissolving them into dust. The automatic reload allowed him to keep repeating the action until the rocks disappeared.

SamWong opened his mouth and two drooling bats emerged, spread their wings and flapped to her side before Troy could cross the remaining twenty yards to Loveena. When they touched the ground, each one became a man-sized demon, with gruesome facial features similar to SamWong's, black lifeless eye sockets, narrow pointed ears, and decaying teeth, but they wore no suits. Their half-naked, deformed bodies bore heavy scars and the tops of their heads oozed black tar. Quickly grabbing the loose ends of the whip, each ghoul placed an end in its mouth, clenching their teeth down on it.

Transforming back into large bats, they flew Loveena back to him, her body dangling between them. She grasped desperately to hold on with one hand to the leg of one bat, while keeping the other hand between her neck and the whip to stop it from strangling her. They flung her at SamWong's feet, and morphed once more into the half-naked demons. They stepped behind him, standing like grotesque body guards. The whip around her neck mutated into a choke collar with a chain hooked to SamWong's wrist.

"This collar is forged by your hate and fear, my dear. It will keep you bound to me forever."

Troy had seen enough. He assumed there wasn't enough evil in the entire VRC System to manifest such a demonic world. Neither he, nor Loveena, could harbor a level of hate that could produce such a hellish landscape. It could only be coming from SamWong. He turned to the six Grief Masters now flanking him. They were all he had to fight with, and Troy's and Loveena's only hope. "You are messengers who saved us. But do you fight? Will you fight? I see no other way out but to fight fire with fire."

Troy's Faith spoke first. "There is one true way, which will come to you."

His Hope spoke second, "But good doesn't triumph over evil by being passive."

"So in the meantime," said his constant companion, Courage, "we are Masters *over* Grief, and we will fight it with you." He placed his magenta hand on top of Troy's crossbow, and one by one, the other five Grief Masters placed their hands upon the weapon, as well. A prism of color appeared in the rain surrounding it. Each one repeated, "We fight." As they pulled away, a full quiver of bolts hung across their shoulders and an identical crossbow appeared in the hands of each one of them, locked and loaded.

SamWong pointed his index finger toward the sky and then pointed it at Troy.

"Kill him!" he commanded.

Lightning shot from the angry storm, splintering into multiple fingers and marching across the ground. A platoon of hideous looking creatures, like the two who dragged Loveena away, sprang from the mud in each scorched spot. They bore scars of torture, grotesquely disfigured, some missing limbs, eyes or teeth. Growling and snorting, some beat their hairy fists against their shields. Armed with archaic weaponry, they held spiked clubs, two-headed axes, and long pikes. They embodied an ancient evil underworld of darkness, and SamWong fueled their lust for violence with his own hatred.

Troy and the Grief Masters advanced. The army of demons stood between them and Loveena. They aimed their crossbows at the evil front line and fired. Each time a liquid magnesium bolt fired, it exploded, taking out several rows of demons at one time. Firing the bolts repeatedly as they pushed forward, ten, twenty, fifty yards, they vaporized dozens of the enemy. Advancing further into their demonic ranks, scores of Hate's fighting footmen fell in behind the courageous group, but the seven fighters continued to eliminate them.

"Regroup!" Troy shouted.

Troy and the Grief Masters formed a circle of menacing crossbows facing outward, back to back, protecting their flanks. Moving as a tight group, they crossed the yards of soggy landscape. Rivers of rain carved trenches in the mud beneath their feet. The trenches opened, releasing small plumes of sulfur and steam. Patches of blue flame burned across the landscape, sending acrid smoke into the air. Troy choked on the hellish smell and his eyes burned, but nothing was going to stop him from reaching Loveena.

However, the fighting conditions worsened. For every few steps forward Troy's fighting unit made, they lost half the gain, forced back by the rain, the flames and smoke surrounding them. The wet magnesium bolts became less effective in the rain, exploding with less incinerating impact and flaming out too quickly. Their quivers were drawing down fast. Troy knew they would run out of ammunition before they could cross the remaining distance.

"I'm out," yelled Courage. With Troy's magazine and quiver now empty, too, the demon army began closing in.

When their ammunition was totally depleted, Troy's small unit engaged in hand-to-hand combat, swinging their crossbows as weapons. Troy's Grief Masters fought as he did, as soldiers, having trained unseen beside him during the war. Loveena's Grief Masters fought with skills they learned while silently accompanying her in the college self-defense classes. Flashes of color lit up the crowded mass of moving bodies. They fought for Troy and Loveena's survival; they fought for good against evil; they fought for the one true Maker who created them against a Devil Incarnate who vowed to destroy them. But the demon army kept coming.

A frustrated SamWong wondered why the fight was taking so long. He could only see Troy on the battlefield, wielding his crossbow against his ghoulish army. "How can one man defeat so many?" he sneered. He noticed Loveena looking away from the battle, praying under her breath. He jerked hard on her chain, grabbing her chin and forcing her head toward the battle scene.

"Open your eyes. Watch! See him be destroyed! Your prayers will not save him," he said ruthlessly.

The keys around her neck pulsated rapidly, catching his eye. SamWong stared at the colors—magenta, gold, blue; the same glimpse of colors flashing across the battlefield where demons fell and disappeared. Releasing his grip on her chin, he grabbed up all the straps to her keys in one hand. "What witch's sorcery is this, Loveena?"

He pulled them off one at a time, snapping each leather strap from her neck, and scrutinized each one with a scowl. Dropping them into the mud before her one at a time, the demon ground each into the mire with his boot. As he did, Loveena's Grief Masters began to fall on the battlefield.

Troy saw Loveena's Hope fall first, sinking into the ground. Then Patience took a blow to the chest and fell. As a demon lifted his ax to destroy her, she dissolved into the mud. Troy swung his crossbow into the jaw of an advancing tar-headed ghoul. Turning around, he saw Loveena's last Grief Master, Faith. She repeated Loveena's transmitted thought to him, "Live and save your son."

Then she, too, was struck, dissipating into the mire. Troy's adrenalin dwindled, replaced with fear for Loveena. Still fighting fiercely, he glanced toward the spot where he last saw her. Neither she, nor SamWong were there.

His heart sank as the demon army closed in on top of him.

****

The rain had stopped. Troy bent down on his knees in the mud, his hands tied behind him, his head forced toward the ground by the grubby fist of a hairy beast. He could neither raise his head nor see in front of him. His three Grief Masters assumed the same position on their knees. As Troy was a prisoner, so now were they. The demons could not see them, only the colored prism hanging in the air around Troy. Courage knew Troy needed to stay positive. Speaking for the three, he told Troy, "We stay strong."

Hearing something like a whisper, the demon next to Troy forced his head lower. "Shut up!"

Troy could see his Grief Master keys hanging down below his chin. All three pulsed in unison and he found strength in it. "We stay strong," he whispered back.

His thoughts went to Loveena. Whatever happened, he would keep her alive in his mind, hoping it would help her. And if any harm had truly befallen her, he would honor her request. He would find a way to live and save his son. In his heart, he made her these two promises.

A commotion stirred the crowded demon army in front of Troy. He could see their ugly feet shuffle and move aside. His knees slipped in the mud, as he repositioned himself for a better look. All he could see were two black crocodile boots stopping several feet away, the black poker tapping the side of the pants leg.

"Get up," SamWong ordered.

Troy lifted his head and sat back on his heels. He moved his head and shoulders to loosen the pressure from his forced position of submission, but the beast beside him grew impatient and grabbed Troy, yanking him to his feet.

Pacing in front of him, SamWong spoke with smug superiority.

"You can't win, Troy, only the powerful win."

"Don't tell me I can't win; that only makes me try harder."

SamWong noticed the same keys around Troy's neck as Loveena had worn. He stepped forward grabbing them together and pulled them off with such force it left lines of blood across the back of Troy's neck. Troy glanced over at his three Grief Masters as they disappeared.

"We are always with you," Faith said. Troy knew he would never be without them again.

SamWong called for a box. A demon came forward, got down on one knee, opening a small box. He dropped the keys into it and closed the lid.

"Destroy these," he shouted, thrusting the box back at the bearer, who bowed and backed away. Turning back to Troy, the demon of Hate smiled. "Now I have you both." Stepping aside, the body guards behind him moved apart. Loveena stood behind them; her hands bound in front of her, and wide tape covering her mouth.

Troy sucked in a breath of relief. Their eyes locked onto each other.

"You thought you could survive the VRC, but in the end…I win," said SamWong.

"What do you want from us?" Troy asked him, not taking his eyes from Loveena.

"I want you to die. But," tapping his finger against his chin and looking back and forth between the two lovers, he continued, "I want you to decide who will go first. Yes! That will be fun."

Troy didn't respond, and Loveena couldn't answer. They would share their last few moments immersed in each other's love. They could feel it join, surround, and uplift each other's hearts, even though they were separated and about to die.

"No volunteers?" SamWong asked. "Then, I'll choose."

Raising his hand, he pointed to the ground beneath Loveena's feet, turning it into a soft quicksand quagmire. Loveena's eyes widened as the ground gave way, making her sink down to her hips. The two demons beside her tried to run but were swallowed up and disappeared beneath the quicksand.

"Stand still!" Troy shouted, "Don't struggle!" He took a step forward, but was forced back down to his knees by two foot soldiers on either side of him.

The cruel demon laughed. With a mocking tone, he shouted to the ugly crowd. "I'm going to enjoy this! Two lovers destroyed, not by hate or the VRC, but by their own selfless love!" His army laughed loudly with him, their shoulders shaking jovially.

Troy pulled with frustration at the ropes binding his hands behind him. Still tight, a small prism of color surrounded the rope, and loosened it. His Grief Masters whispered to him, sending a message loud and clear in his mind.

Courage, faith, hope, love...and the greatest of these is love!

Troy watched Loveena sink down to her chest, unable to grasp anything around her. The voices of the Grief Masters filled his head, swirling in his heart, repeating the message.

Look for a key; find the key! It will save you both, whispered Courage. Then Vincent's deep voice pierced Troy's ears. "Look within your heart, Troy, the key is IN your heart!" Now Troy understood. Vincent did not speak in metaphors; he meant the key would literally be hidden within Troy's own heart.

Troy startled SamWong as the ropes dropped from his wrists to the ground. Now freed, he lurched sideways; smashing his shoulder into the demon on his right, then turned and planted a solid right cross to the chin of the demon to his left. The color of his Grief Masters returned, surrounding him with a bright aura which scared the rest of the army. They slowly backed away from him.

"There is something more powerful than all the hatred of your kind in the world, Hoy," Troy shouted. "But you'll never understand what it is."

SamWong, also stepped back from Troy, and asked disdainfully, "And what is that?"

Troy held up his right hand as the flame of Faith burned an opening in his shirt. He thrust his hand deep into his own chest and into the eternal flame within his heart. Pulling out a shimmering white key, he held it up tightly in his fist as his chest re-closed.

"Love," Troy replied.

Bluish-white beams of light shot out between his fingers and across the clearing, blinding and vaporizing the demons around him. As Troy turned slowly around, the bright beams spread across the landscape, destroying every foot soldier. Then pointing the key toward the darkness above, the light dissolved every trace of storm clouds in the sky.

As the beams retracted, a new Grief Master revealed herself, bathed in a luminescent, white glow. This one, unlike his other three, didn't resemble him, but appeared as an angelic entity all its own. Tall and floating on a cloud enveloping her feet, she spread sparkling white wings out behind her. Her skin radiantly shimmered, and brilliant rays of light emanated from her robed body. She spoke in a quiet voice only Troy could hear. "I am a Grief Master, Troy. I have been sent here on behalf of both you and Loveena. My name is LOVE."

The powerful, cosmic energy exuding from her presence made SamWong shrink back. He could not see her, but he felt a strong, unsettling shift in the balance of power from him to Troy. As the demon became weaker, he retreated to a position next to Loveena, who continued to sink slowly into the quicksand. She held her arms in the air, trying to keep her head above it.

The Grief Master stretched out her hand as a long, golden spear appeared in her grasp. She handed it to Troy. "Find your mark. You must destroy any anger or hatred left within you that threatens to destroy everything in your future. Rid yourself of these once and for all, and claim the peace and love promised to you." Then she disappeared.

Taking the spear in his hand, Troy had no hesitation in bringing destruction down upon this evil in the form of SamWong. He knew this was not a man, but a demon, which embodied not only SamWong's hatred, but also the hatred left lurking in Troy's own heart. Destroying this demon could mean killing himself along with it. Either way, it would finally release Troy from Hate's deadly hold. In a final effort to save Loveena, he felt a healing and cleansing of his soul sweep over him.

SamWong watched as a golden spear appeared in Troy's hand out of nowhere. His eyes narrowed and his lips sneered in defiance. Placing his black boot upon Loveena's head, he pushed her down into the quicksand, and her head disappeared from view. Her arms and hands, still visible above the ground, fell limp.

Troy lifted the golden spear above his shoulder, taking aim at his decade-long nemesis. "This is for my father." He threw it as hard as he could.

SamWong raised his whip, ready to swing and deflect the spear. Vincent's frightening unmasked holographic face suddenly appeared and loomed large before the demon. The sight of the terrifying chrome skull brought back memories to SamWong of the night he died in his office. His demonic features disappeared as his face returned to its human form. With eyes wide and terrified with fright, he dropped the whip from his hand.

The spear sailed through the air, piercing Vincent's hologram, and finding its mark deep in SamWong's right eye. The spear point protruded through the back of his skull. He fell backward into the mud as worms emerged from the ground around him, covered his body and carried it down below the surface. The demon of Hate, the Devil Incarnate in the embodiment of SamWong—disappeared forever and was devoured into oblivion.

Troy immediately crossed the distance to Loveena, grabbed her hands and pulled her out of the muck. She fell limp against his chest as he picked her up and moved her lifeless body to solid ground. He wiped the grime from her face, frantically running his hands across her eyes and down her cheeks, and removing the tape from her lips. Tears stung his eyes as he cradled her against his chest, wrapping his arms protectively around her. He bent his head to hers, taking her hand in his, and kissed her lips. "Don't leave me, Loveena! Please, don't leave me," his voice commanded with desperation.

The Love Grief Master reappeared floating behind them. Troy looked over his shoulder at the shimmering Grief Master and pleaded, "Please, don't take her." Turning back to Loveena, he whispered, "She needs me; she loves me—and I need her," he held his face close to her, "because I love her."

His words breathed life back into Loveena and she stirred. The muddy quicksand disappeared from her face and the smoky soot vanished from her clothes. She opened her eyes and smiled up at him. Troy helped her to her feet and embraced her tightly. They stood holding each other as their original street clothes reappeared on them.

The Love Grief Master with her blue-white light beaming all around rose toward the sky. Holding her palms up toward a dark blue heaven, her powerful light traveled up among the stars. All six of the other Grief Masters returned, encircling the couple in a protective cocoon of color, blending together in a radiant aura surrounding them and whispering: *Courage, Faith, Hope and Love. We are here; we are strong; and we are with you always.*

Troy and Loveena, now safe in each other's arms, heard the distinct click of doors unlocking.

Chapter 35

Troy and Loveena stumbled out of the two open VRC chambers and stood just feet apart from each other. They both gasped for fresh oxygen to refill their lungs and tried to regain their stability on shaky legs. Never having met in the real world, but falling in love in a surreal one, Troy was unsure if she would still feel the same. Looking at Loveena, he wanted to reach for her, but hesitated. *Would she remember?* He swallowed hard. "I'm Troy."

Crossing the short space between them, she launched herself into his arms and kissed him. He grinned, burying his face against her hair. Still in his arms, she leaned back and smiled up at him. "I'm Loveena."

They wore the same clothes as when they entered the VRC system, Troy's were intact without holes or bloodstains. Loveena's clothes also bore no damage. The only evidence remaining of their life and death struggle were the keys hanging around their necks.

The glass chamber doors of both VRCs remained wide open as wispy white curls of iridescent mist spilled out. Halogen ceiling lights glared down casting an eerie glow on the dissipating fog. Exposed pipes and the oil-stained concrete floor replaced the hellish landscape. All of the demons threatening to destroy them were now gone.

"We're free," Troy whispered. He leaned his forehead against hers, running his hands down her arms. They turned, looking at the open chamber doors, no longer intimidated by them.

"Did all of that just happen?" Loveena asked.

Troy looked at the new Love key she wore, shimmering with a sparkling white glow against her skin. It pulsed in sync with his. They knew the experience was all too real. Feeling the qualities the Grief Masters had awakened in them, they both realized the importance of their message. The keys represented courage, faith, hope, and love, the essential elements to protect, sustain, and rebuild their souls, renewing their lives, and above all, they would remain within them. Without these life lines, they would surely perish.

Loveena ran her fingers over Troy's keys.

"They saved us." As she spoke, the four keys around Troy's neck faded under her fingertips, with hers disappearing as well. Loveena tried to grasp the vanishing keys.

"No, no, wait!" The keys dissipated into their skin, leaving a momentary sparkle behind.

Troy stopped her, and clasped his hands over hers. "They are always here; that's what they were trying to tell us. They're a part of who we are; and we must continue to believe in them."

Troy kissed her hands, and Loveena leaned her head against him. Turning away from the chambers, they saw Vincent gliding toward them on his nanobits foot board. He held two bottles of electrolyte fluid in his mechanical hands, one for each of them.

"Here, drink this, all of it." The drink relieved the extreme thirst they both felt after several days of confinement. The android handed each of them a small white tablet. "Take this."

"What is it?" Loveena asked.

"Protein food tablet; it will restore your systems until you can get sustenance," Vincent replied.

"Yeah, we're starving," Troy said. He looked at the tablet, wishing it was real food, but swallowed it and gulped the rest of the drink down. "How do we escape this place?"

"Follow me." Vincent turned and glided toward a dark hallway.

"And my son?" Troy asked as they followed quickly behind the android.

"He will join you in your escape. The presence of SamWong's demon means Adams wanted to guarantee your deaths. I have recorded your death certificates in the system and provided body bags for disposal. The deception may work, or it may not. We must hurry."

Troy worried as they made their way down the empty hall. "How are we going to get out of here without being noticed?"

"Through here."

A locked metal door blocked the exit at the end of the hallway. Placing his mechanical hand on the digital lockbox, tiny nanobits moved from Vincent's hand through the lock, decoding the pin number and turning the tumblers. Unlocking the door, he opened it and led them into an abandoned trucking garage.

The lights flickered on as he waved his hand in front of an electrical panel. Standing on an elevated platform once serving as a delivery area, Troy could see only a dead end. The cement block walls were sparsely strung with webs and sprigs of weeds under the dirty windows, and dust lay in little piles throughout the cracked cement floor. The large garage doors at the far end appeared rusted and locked down. It was apparent no one had been in this docking bay for a while.

A stairway from the platform led down to the floor of the garage. Looking over the metal handrail, Loveena watched a rat scurry along the floor and disappear through a hole in the wall.

"Where can we go where they can't find us?" she asked.

"I am sending you to planet D1. Your father awaits you there," Vincent replied.

Troy's brooding eyebrows drew together. "Just how are we going to get there? We can't exactly go through your wormhole without it killing us."

Vincent held his arm out in front of them, motioning for them to step back as he pushed a large red button on the platform wall. Two horizontal metal plates on the platform floor moved, each jerking with rusty squeals. As the plates opened vertically, a freight elevator rose through the darkness from below.

Vincent turned to Troy. "This may look familiar to you."

Troy watched curiously as the squeaky elevator came to the surface. The old hydraulic lift pushed its load up into the light. Troy's expression changed from concern to recognition as he watched his prize invention, the Human Transporter Pad, come into view. It was all there—the four position pads, the control panel, the server, and trajectory plotter. As the freight elevator came to an abrupt stop, Troy stepped onto the lift, inspecting the old HTP.

Shaking his head in disbelief, "How did you get this?"

"You removed critical software before SamWong took possession of it. His technicians did not know what this was and ordered it to be destroyed. Samuel Baptista took possession and hid it until The Brethren could study it. We replaced the missing software."

"Is it safe?" Troy asked.

"Yes. We copied your design and used them in other hidden locations to send people and supplies to D1. However, this one is your original."

Troy turned to the NTB. "And Tommy?"

Vincent pointed to the left front transporter pad. "This position is for him. I will transmit his particle stream onto this pad once the sequence has been activated. He will rematerialize and be transmitted to the planet with you."

The HTP hummed as Vincent turned it on. "Please take your positions."

Loveena hesitated, and shook her head. "I don't know about this, Troy."

Troy guided her to one of the rear pads. "It will be fine. Besides, you've been through worse, remember?" He stood on the pad directly in front of her as Vincent programmed the trajectory plotter on the control panel.

"It is a six-minute transmission. You will not experience any sensation." Looking at Loveena, the android tried to reassure her. "It is quite safe."

Troy now became concerned for Vincent's safety. He stepped off the pad and over to Vincent. After everything the android had done to help them, Troy didn't want any harm to come to him. "You have to come with us. There's still another pad here."

Vincent shook his head. "I must stay and securely hide this HTP. No one must discover your location or how you traveled there. And...all pads will be occupied."

Vincent pointed his hand to a recessed corner of the freight platform. He levitated a small carrier containing his feline companion. Moving it across the area, he grasped the handle, holding the cage up in front of his mask. The little cat meowed, sticking her paw out to touch his chin one last time. "Take care of my friend."

He walked over and placed it on the fourth unoccupied pad next to Loveena. Looking at her he added, "She likes fish."

Walking back to the control panel, Troy was adamant with Vincent.

"You and The Brethren must follow us. They'll know you helped us. You'll be in grave danger."

"I must be the electrical conduit for their wormholes in order for them to leave this planet," he answered. "If I must stay to help the others escape, then that is my mission. When Samuel Baptista finds a way to reverse the flow of energy in a wormhole, then I will follow."

Troy knew he could not dissuade the android, but he felt a kinship toward him and a genuine concern for his safety. They shared more than a name. They shared the same DNA, and oddly, the same parents. Vincent was the closest thing Troy had to a brother.

"We will find a way, I promise you." Emphasizing his words, Troy repeated, "I will find a way."

Vincent held out his hand to Troy to say goodbye. Troy gripped the NTB's mechanical elbow instead, pulling him into a brotherly arm embrace, forearms entwined, leather to metal; a symbolic gesture of brotherhood between man and android. They nodded an acceptance of each other and of Vincent's decision to stay. Then Troy stepped back onto the HTP pad.

The electron generator of the machine began increasing in volume. Vincent pointed his finger toward the left HTP pad to restore Tommy to human form. A green laser stream shot from the tip of his finger to the center of the pad, forming a rapidly rotating ball of electrons. It stretched vertically, up and down, then horizontally, from side to side. A shadowed shape emerged. Troy stood on the pad next to Tommy's, watching his son's body rebuild. The boy became a faint image of himself, turning to solid form. Once fully restored, Tommy saw his father on the pad next to him.

"Daddy!" he exclaimed.

"Tommy, don't move!" Troy urgently responded.

All three of their bodies faded, along with the cat, dematerializing into green vertical streams that condensed into tiny balls of light. Then they were gone.

****

Samuel Baptista thought six minutes was equally short as an instant, and as long as a lifetime. When Vincent transmitted a message that the VRC judgments were complete and his daughter free, his heart jumped for joy. He immediately called together the scientific team on D1, and they gathered as a welcoming committee in one of the facilities' transporter rooms.

Baptista thought how Dr. Vincent would have been so proud of his son's achievement. Several HTPs existed on the planet, all patterned after Troy's original design. They constructed a larger version to transport animals and supplies from Earth. Without the invention, populating the Brethren's incredible outpost on D1 would have been impossible. The Resistance would have remained segmented pockets on Earth. The fate of some of the world's best scientists would have ended in the VRCs. Unknown to Troy, his invention gave mankind a chance for a new future.

The scientists, technicians and some outpost personnel filed into the transporter room to greet the space travelers. Dr. Casey Devony, chief scientist of Dr. Vincent's original team, was in the group. Samuel had developed a great respect for her work in biomechanics, and over the years they had developed a close personal relationship. She knew every detail of each one of the twelve NTBs and was as anxious as Samuel to have them leave Earth. However, they had not found a successful method to reverse the energy of a wormhole in order to retrieve Vincent. His unique metal alloys, not available on D1, remained tightly controlled by corporate securities on Earth, making replication of an android such as Vincent impossible. And using an HTP to transport him was out of the question, as the deconstruction could trigger a nuclear explosion. It appeared the Brethren could be less one member in order for the group to survive.

During the six-minute wait, Samuel Baptista reflected on how life was flourishing on D1. The small population worked hard to expand the outpost. Dr. Devony's daughters, Katelyn, a biologist, and Hailey, a dietician, created hydro-farms and food synthesizers with the help of several androids. It allowed a greater variety of cuisines to develop.

The one mechanical engineer, Austin Samuels, and his incredible crew, learned how to work with certain natural elements found on D1, to build more structures. Experimentation with the materials available on the planet also allowed for simple manufactured goods.

Even physical fitness programs were individually designed by their chief medical consultant, Dr. Allison, to strengthen each person's endurance in the thinner atmosphere. Their small population included some of the brightest minds, finding ways for some comforts of modern living to emerge. But the addition of Troy Vincent would bring an innovative visionary so badly needed for D1 to progress.

Everyone contributed, and as far as Baptista could tell, everyone seemed happy. The first mission outpost, against all odds, appeared to be working. Even the different cultures and religions brought together under a one-roof worship center encouraged and practiced tolerance, respect, and peace. The more they worked together, the more they became one united people. *This is a new world in more ways than one*, he thought.

He knew Loveena would love the weather here. Temperate, balmy, sunny days, and clear, star-filled nights, were reminiscent of Ramona Cove. However, the water in the planet's ocean was not so blue – more aqua; and swimming was discouraged until they could document the indigenous oceanic creatures. The dwarf triple-sun solar system produced spectacular golden sunsets, and when the third sun went down in the evening, the nights became comfortably cool, under the planet's single pink-colored moon. *She will love the beauty of this place.*

Samuel started building a house on a small inlet just down the beach from the main buildings. Patterned after the blue beach house with a wrap-around veranda, it still needed some work. He decided to call it, Loveena's Lagoon. It would be a gift to her as a small way to make up for the terrible wrong he inflicted on her by his disappearance.

When the four space travelers began to materialize on the HTP in front of him, beads of sweat dotted his forehead. *Will my daughter be glad to see me? Or will she not speak to me at all?*

He took out his handkerchief and nervously wiped his brow as the silhouette of his daughter darkened one of the pads. Her face came into view and her dark, shining eyes fell upon him for the first time in years. No longer the little girl he carried on his shoulders along the beach, he saw a stunning beauty, smiling back at him with tears in her eyes. The HTP had safely transported her and its other three passengers to the control room on D1.

Samuel could say nothing but his daughter's name as he opened his arms to her. She flew off the platform and flung her arms around her father's neck, weeping softly into his shoulder. Samuel repeated, "My darling, Loveena! I'm so sorry...I am so sorry."

****

For six long minutes, Troy held back the urge to grab his son and hug him. Emerging out of the blackness of space into the brightly lit transporter room of D1, Troy and Tommy reached for each other simultaneously. Tommy jumped into his father's arms, and Troy tightly held the little boy he thought he had lost forever.

They stood on the platform, repeating each other's names as tears spilled down Tommy's face. After a long moment, Troy noticed the many people in the room. They clapped at the happy reunions between Loveena and her father, and Troy and his son. Troy stepped off the platform, still holding his son in his arms, as Tommy clung to his father.

Samuel Baptista greeted him, holding out his hand to Troy.

"We have long awaited your arrival. Thank you doesn't express the full gratitude I owe you for helping my daughter." Loveena kept her arm around her father's waist, smiling up at him, not wanting to take her eyes off of him.

"You're welcome." Troy put Tommy down, his son staying close by his side. Looking around at the faces in the room, he recognized one, though her hair now appeared gray.

"Dr. Devony, I remember you."

"Troy," she took his hand in hers. "It's been a long time." She placed a piece of candy in the palm of his hand, as she had always done when he was a boy. Troy laughed, "Thank you! We're famished." Then she offered one to Tommy, who eagerly took it.

"Come this way," she said. "We have plenty of water and food to offer after your confinements."

Troy noticed a thin, gold chain around her neck. Three charms hung from it, three tiny keys, each one a different color. She saw his gaze fall upon the keys.

"We make them here. I wear mine to remind me of the lessons I learned in the VRC," she said.

Looking around, he saw others wearing similar gold chains with small colored keys.

"You are among many friends here," she added.

Tommy held his father's hand as Loveena joined them. "My name's Tommy. Are you a friend of my dad's?"

Troy raised an eyebrow at her, wondering how she would respond.

"Yes," she smiled. "We are good friends, Tommy. I hope to be yours, too." The little boy smiled, taking her hand in his.

Troy turned to Dr. Devony. "What can we do about Vincent?"

"We need your help with that," she responded.

D. L. Farrar

Chapter 36

Attorney Adams pushed the receiver button of his earpiece. The audio-com announced, "Incoming call from Security Chief Michaels."

"Accept the call." Adams wiped the corners of his mouth with a napkin and pushed his takeout dinner off his desktop into the trash can. The chief's face appeared in the air above the desk, as Adams sat back in his over-sized leather chair.

"Good evening, Chief. You have news, I presume?"

"The judgments are done. They both expired moments ago at exactly18:05 hours," said the glum-looking chief.

"Good," Adams said with a slight smile. "I appreciate the call."

"You're welcome." The chief moved to end the transmission, but Adams interrupted him.

"Oh, one more thing," the attorney said. "I'm wondering, did you visually confirm their deaths?"

"There's no need," Michaels explained. "The death certificates have already been filed."

"Yes, but in this case, I would feel better if we had an extra confirmation," Adams politely urged.

The chief pursed his lips and looked perturbed by the request. "I trust the NTB has done his job. It's not necessary to go digging around in body bags."

Adams sat up with a stern look and crossed his arms in front of his chest. "I insist. If you don't mind, I'd like to personally identify the bodies."

"Well, it's an unusual request...."

"I'm on my way," Adams clicked off the transmission. Opening his desk drawer, he removed a six-inch sheathed dagger with an ornate handle. Contemplating its intended use, he tucked it into the inside breast pocket of his suit and left his office.

****

Security Chief Michaels paced by the door of the facility's Crematory room. Looking through the wall of windows into the large white brick room, he watched the process of a VRC candidate's final journey. Inside the room, a wall of five small iron-plated doors opened intermittently to conveyor belts leading into each of the five separate crematory ovens. Carts with closed body bags from the VRC floors lined up in front of the five oven stations.

A timer on the wall above each iron door displayed a red and green light. When the red light came on, the oven was working. Once it switched to green, the worker would open the door, load another body bag onto the moving conveyor belt and lock the cast-iron door after the body entered. The worker then turned to a digital screen and recorded the bag tag number, date and time of disposal, and pushed a start button to initiate the cycle.

Workers in the room wore portable oxygen tanks on their backs with protective masks to avoid breathing in the fumes. Wearing a clear, protective mask over his mouth and nose, the chief blocked out most of the chemical stench permeating the area. He was agitated with Adams' request to see the body bags. His mood was further angered by the smell and the heat of the room, still seeping into the adjacent hallway where he waited. Perspiration ran down the sides of his face as he watched the crew work. It was rare he came down to this part of the facility, which he avoided, as much as possible.

Chief Michaels stopped his pacing when he saw two security attendants escorting Mr. Adams to the Crematory. Fed up with the attorney's interference, he let loose his aggravation instead of greeting him.

"Mr. Adams, do you know what is so damned irritating about you? You just won't leave a man to do his job, will you? I'm in charge here."

Adams shot back, "Then you've got nothing to worry about, do you?" A security attendant handed the attorney a mask to wear.

Michaels continued. "There's nothing to find down here and the last time I checked, dead bodies tell no tales."

He could tell Adams' temper was also short. The burly man's fists tightened by his side and a vein popped out on the side of the attorney's temple. Glaring at the chief, Adams pulled the mask on, yanking hard on the chin strap to tighten it.

"Someone is helping convicted criminals escape. And that someone is connected to the Resistance sabotaging Corporate Rule. I want to know who it is and who is working on the inside."

"I trust my crew," the chief said emphatically through his mask.

"We'll see. Where are their body bags?"

Chief Michaels motioned for the Crematory Supervisor to lead them into the brick room. Giving the supervisor two prisoner numbers, they watched him pull up a roster on the digital screen displaying the bag numbers collected that day and their corresponding pick-up locations. Scrolling down the list, he found the two tag numbers and pointed to a cart on the left.

"Over there, fourth door cart."

Walking over to the cart, the three men approached the crewman standing next to the assigned cart of body bags. Pull out tags 924 and 818," the supervisor ordered.

The crewman used an automated hoist above the cart which he attached to a large, metal ring belted around the middle of each bag. One at a time, he pulled several bags off the top of the cart, lowering each onto the floor. When he came to the two tag numbers, he repositioned the hoist, hooked it onto the larger bag first, and moved it to the floor near the chief. Tag 924 appeared attached to the zipper. Unhooking the hoist, he then attached it to the next bag on the cart. He lowered the smaller bag marked 818, onto the floor beside the first.

"Open them," Adams demanded. The crewman partially unzipped each bag. The faces of Troy Vincent and Loveena Baptista lay lifeless. With eyes closed and discolored skin, the bluish-grey faces peered out from the zippered openings.

A look of suspicion crossed Adams' face, his eyes narrowing. He scratched at the strap around his chin. Bending over, he yanked the heavy zipper down on each bag, pulling them wide open. The bodies appeared stiff with rigormortis as he poked each body with his finger.

Chief Michaels sighed. "Satisfied?"

"Not quite," said Adams.

Kneeling down by bag 924, he pulled the dagger from his breast pocket, throwing the sheath across the floor. Before anyone could stop him, he stabbed the forehead of body 924 up to the hilt of the knife, pulling the blade down through the face. The blade cut easily through a gelatin-like form, splitting it open to expose only a gel mold, not obstructed by any hard bone or muscle. He pulled the knife out and stepped over body 924 to body 818. Straddling the body, he stabbed into the neck of 818, cutting it straight down through the chest. The gel mold split apart like the first, exposing a second manufactured body.

"Fake bodies!" Adams spit out.

Chief Michaels sucked in air, his nostrils flaring. *Deception! Damn! Damn it to hell!*

"Do you trust your crew now?" Adams yelled, standing up with the dagger clinched in his hand. He wagged the tip of it at Michaels.

"I want that robot!" Adams shouted and walked away, tearing off his mask and throwing it across the room. "Now, Chief!"

Mortified, the chief bent down to touch the solid gel substance, weighing and looking like a real body. Anger crept into his face, turning red from both embarrassment and humiliation as he bit his lip and pounded his fist into the palm of his opposite hand. He hated the fact Xavier Adams' suspicions proved right. But more than that, his pride was stung by a betrayal he hoped would never happen, from someone he thought very highly of. He had no other choice but the one he must now make. Standing up, he turned to the supervisor.

"Call Vincent to my office. If he doesn't come, have a full security detail search for him…and arrest him."

****

The crackling sound from the old speaker system bounced off the walls, echoing through the empty truck garage. Vincent listened to the page calling him to the Security office, then turned back to the control panel of the HTP. From the trajectory plotter, he deleted the programmed coordinates to planet D1, removing the digital blade containing the transmission history. Even if someone discovered the machine hidden below the platform, they would not be able to trace the location of D1 or know the identity of its galaxy travelers. Once again, the android pushed the red button on the wall and the HTP disappeared into the dark depth below the platform. The steel doors closed on top of it, hiding the secret inside. Vincent dropped the digital blade to the floor and vaporized it with a short laser zap from his fingertip.

Time was of the essence. He now turned his attention to The Brethren. Although they shared a common consciousness link, he needed to send an encrypted transmission which would reach not only them, but Don Tyler and Samuel Baptista. Knowing he risked discovery by transmitting on a radio frequency, the immediate circumstances outweighed the risk. The time had come for them to leave, and it needed to be done quickly. He sent the communiqué to all of them at once:

Our preparation stage is complete. Stop all work and leave now; discovery is imminent. I am activating the energy wormholes for your journey. We must begin Phase II of our mission, colonization.

A collective response came back to him: *Understood.*

They agreed to leave no one behind, but the urgency of Vincent's message implied the importance of protecting The

Brethren. The sacrifice of one unit to save the group was now unavoidable. They also knew, once on D1, they would try to retrieve Vincent.

Vincent turned off his mask and stood with his arms wide open, emitting a powerful surge of electrons that spanned thousands of miles between each wormhole. He had to draw on enough energy to create a level capable of reaching the NTBs incarcerated on the other side of the globe. The amount necessary to send all of them at once required Vincent to draw on resources well outside the VRC complex. Multiple bolts of electron streams shot from his body to the electrical panels on the walls, through electrified rails in the old subway tunnel, and out to lines of power plants miles away. Branching further, he drew on electrical towers, hydroelectric dams, and massive generators. He took control of the global power grid with all of its generating facilities and transmission lines.

One by one, each NTB turned from his or her work and stepped into an emerging green wormhole. Those who were in isolated VRC rooms left their monitoring assignments, opened the chamber doors to free their prisoners, and vanished quietly into the swirling vortexes. NTBs, in the proximity of other facility employees excused themselves politely, walked to isolated hallways or closets, where they also stepped into wormholes and disappeared.

Lights throughout the region dimmed, buzzing off and on, with power shortages spreading across the continents during Vincent's massive power surge. Some entire cities went dark as he redirected their electrical supply. He remained the constant conduit until all eleven Brethren safely traveled to the surface of their galactic oasis on D1, in the constellation, Scorpios. They traveled beyond the speed of light by fusing their molecules with the dark living matter of space, becoming one with it, and relocated faster than the normal six minutes required for humans. It was almost instantaneous.

When his job was complete, the electron streams shut down and left electrical generators, connections, and boxes everywhere scorched and burned. Most of the global power grid returned to normal within minutes. However, Vincent stood bent over and motionless. For the first time in his existence, he needed to recharge himself. Vulnerable and unable to move from the empty garage, he didn't know exactly how long it might take.

The Brethren's journey, though brief, allowed Vincent's global energy boost to be noticed and traced by the VRSM Security. The rusty locks on the wide garage doors in the truck bay cracked. They exploded open as the heavy double doors slowly cranked up. The doors squeaked as dry, rusted chains struggled to hoist them. Still standing on the freight platform, Vincent finally regained his mobility and turned toward the opening doors. It was too late to leave and he couldn't teleport away without being seen. He switched on his facial mask as the outside light beamed in, lighting up the garage bay.

Two large vehicles flashed bright headlights directly on him. The front grills of the armor-plated trucks had blast-resistant shields mounted on them. Within the shields were small viewing windows made of triple-plated glass, allowing the drivers to see Vincent. More armed vehicles drove up behind them and into the loading dock. Exhaust fumes spewed into the confined space as personnel vehicles also arrived, parking everywhere outside the entrance, blocking all access to any escape route.

Security attendants dressed in protective combat gear jumped from the vehicles and ran into the garage, as others rushed from the adjacent hallway to surround the platform. The armed guards lined the parameter, cautiously maintaining a distance from Vincent. Wearing thick helmets with dark face guards, each attendant held a rectangular blast shield with one hand and a laser weapon in the other. The laser beams were all targeted on the android. No one approached Vincent as he stood alone in the middle of the loading platform.

A bull horn clicked on from one of the armor-plated trucks. "Robot, you are under arrest. Put your hands up where they can be seen and do not move. Do not activate any weapon, including your internal nuclear device, or you risk immediate annihilation."

Vincent raised his hands as the sleeves of his cloak slipped down and exposed his metallic, skeletal arms, scorched in spots from the electrical surge he had generated.

"You will not be harmed if you cooperate. You must remove the nuclear fusion device you have and lay it on the platform in front of you."

Vincent did not move. *VRC Security has no understanding of my complex anatomy,* he thought. Using his telepathy so they could all hear him, he explained, "It is not a part that can be removed like a battery. It is only an internal program, which I will deactivate."

The voice within the vehicle did not respond right away. No one in the garage moved, least of all Vincent, who was quite sure they would blow him and the entire VRC complex to pieces if he did.

"How do we know if you have deactivated it?"

"You don't."

A sigh of frustration came through the bullhorn. Several long moments passed as both sides considered the situation. The bullhorn clicked back on.

"Look, we're only doing our job here. Give us your absolute word you will not use any force against us. No one needs to get hurt, human or...robot."

"May I lower my hands?"

"No! Do not move from that spot and do not activate any of your morphing nanobits."

Vincent complied with their request. "I will not use force against you," he promised. "Unlike humans, I place a high value on all life."

An hour passed. Trucks backed out of position, allowing a remote-controlled crane to roll into the docking bay. On the end of its long arm hung a four-sided clear, thick blast-proof box, suspended by a hook from the top of the crane. Specifically designed to withstand bomb blasts, Vincent recognized its purpose, but thought it insufficient for their protection if he activated the internal fusion program. However, he would be true to his word and not use force against humans. That was how Dr. Vincent had programmed him.

The crane rolled up to the platform and positioned the blast box next to him. As the side of the box opened, Vincent was instructed to remove his cloak and step inside. Obeying the command, he did as they asked, and his uncloaked, skeletal form stepped into the box. The side closed behind him, sealing him in.

A hose positioned inside the box sprayed his arms and legs with a chemical compound containing a freezing agent. Droplets of spray disrupted his mask application, and it flickered off. He turned his head away, holding it up to keep it dry, but the freezing agent saturated the nanobits in his limbs, and they became frozen solid.

A few minutes went by and the side of the box opened again, allowing two small, mobile construction bots to enter and position themselves, one on each side of him. Each raised a reciprocating saw on a flexible arm. When they were done cutting, Vincent lay on the floor of the box, his head and thorax intact, but his four frozen limbs severed from his body now lay scattered around him. The construction bots exited and a retrieval bot entered, gathered up the limbs and removed them from the box. The frozen appendages made up of millions of nanobits, were dropped into another bomb disposal vehicle and taken away for immediate destruction.

Chapter 37

The night sky on D1 shone clear and bright. Millions of stars dotted a black heaven above the first colony on New Earth; at least, that's what Samuel Baptista was calling it. "Like New Plymouth or New England, we'll pay respect to our origins, our Mother Earth."

A gentle tide lapped at the shoreline as reflective starlight floated on the waves of a quiet ocean and bounced off tiny crystals in the sand. Lights from the windows of the buildings illuminated the cliff-top outpost and cast a glow on the beach below.

The peaceful solitude of the planet's beauty drew Loveena outside to the stone veranda. Looking over the railing at the beach, she saw more glistening crystals wash ashore, sparkling like tiny diamonds. The night air smelled different here, sweet and clean. A light breeze felt cool on her skin as she pulled a small shawl up around her shoulders. The memories of her troubled life seemed far, far away. She touched her neck, hoping to find her Grief Master keys still there. Instead, she heard their voices within her mind: *we are with you always.*

Her father walked out and joined her at the stone railing, watching her gaze up at the planet's only moon. Turning toward the night seascape, he struck a match and lit the tobacco in his pipe. He took several puffs to draw the smoke through it before he spoke.

"It's a beautiful place, is it not?" he asked.

Loveena smiled at him and glanced across the buildings. "What you have done here is incredible; truly, a new beginning." But her smile faded.

He noticed her expression change as he turned the smoking pipe in his hand away from her. "You are safe here. But you are troubled. Why?"

Loveena looked up at the stars and wondered where Earth was in the vast night sky.

"Our home, our planet, what happened to it, Daddy? How did it become so cruel?"

Samuel sucked on his pipe, contemplating an answer. "I have asked that question quite often. I arrive at the same conclusion each time."

"Which is?" Loveena asked, looking at him with curiosity.

"When the edict of others separate man from his moral beliefs it creates a hunger, a loss, leaving only emptiness. So he tries to fill it. He grabs at anything: money, land, power, revenge, whatever fuels his greed. It soon replaces honesty, humility, happiness, and any empathy for his fellow man. And still he remains unsatisfied. Eventually, it spreads like a cancer, destroying everything around and inside him."

A puff of smoke escaped his lips, floating toward the starlit night. "For Earth, it happened on a global scale, subtly, and all too quickly. In half a century, the darker nature of mankind, which always lurked in the shadows, took control." Raising his bushy, gray eyebrows, he said with a sigh, "No Grief Masters existed on that scale to save mankind from itself." He looked down at her. "They seem to be more of an individual experience. Influenced by childhood teachings, perhaps? Many lessons get lost as children turn into adults. Some remember them; I dare say many do not."

He placed his hand on the railing, and Loveena put her arm through his. "For me," she said, "that loss led to fear, loneliness, and sorrow."

He put his arm around her shoulders and squeezed her reassuringly. "But you survived, my sweet girl, and I thank God you survived. You remembered lessons your mother taught you long ago. I'd like to think that's what saved you."

Loveena looked down and shook her head. "No. I was saved by forgiveness."

Samuel nodded, "Ahh," wagging his finger in the air, "Now that would be the saving grace of our Maker. He has the only effective way to deal with our darker side."

Loveena turned toward her father. She felt forever grateful to have the chance to be with him again and tell him what had been on her mind for a while. "I want to thank you...*you* and Mommy."

"I do not deserve it, Loveena. I wasn't there for you most of your life."

"Yes, you do," she leaned on the railing. "I was lucky to have heard of those virtues, about courage, faith, hope, and love through your stories and books. You read them to me as a child. And Troy and I, we were both lucky to have parents who lived those values in their everyday lives. We at least learned what many others never have the chance to. We wouldn't be here if it wasn't for the Grief Masters unlocking those things already buried deep within us."

A contemplative silence fell between them. Samuel puffed on his pipe. Loveena remembered the smell of the sweet, woody smoke. It reminded her of when she sat beside him at the beach house and he would read to her from his special library, stories of ordinary people with courage against great odds, finding hope in the most humble of places, and of love that softened hearts and healed wounds. Every story left a deep impression on her.

Looking out over the calm ocean, she looked at him, wanting to know more of his own story. "Tell me about the Resistance. How did you become this leader they speak of?"

He exhaled another small puff of smoke, holding his pipe in front of him. "The discontent growing on Earth is not just for the loss of a spiritual relationship. It is also for the disappearance of certain freedoms," he replied. "There is a yearning for just and fair rights of individuals to be restored and for a leadership which respects and protects the rights of all, not just a select group. It's imperative that we return to elected leaders chosen by the people; not leaders only appointed by the wealthy. Corporate Rule is devouring itself with its own incestuous corruption and greed. Soon the voices of the many that were silenced by the power of a few will take back what belongs to all."

Loveena saw the seriousness in his faraway stare. She wondered how much he had already done to fight for the freedom of others. The father she once knew would not sit back and simply enjoy a new life on a distant planet. *He's planning something for Earth. And I want to be a part of it, to help in whatever way I can.* She felt a renewed sense of self-worth awaken in her, a calling and a new direction for her life. She would pursue this discussion with him later. For now, however, she decided to bring his attention back to the current crisis at hand. "Do you think they'll find a way to help the android?"

Samuel tapped the hot ash from his pipe over the edge of the veranda railing and cocked his head toward the glass door behind him. "The most brilliant minds I know are in there working on it. I have every confidence they will find a way."

With a twinkle in his eye, he peered at his daughter with a sly smile. "By the way, one of those brilliant minds is that young man, Troy Vincent. Remind me to thank him again for bringing you back to me. Or have I lost your heart to him already?"

As they walked toward another door leading to the living quarters, Loveena slipped her hand in the crook of his elbow. "There's room for both of you," she smiled.

****

Through the glass doors at the opposite end of the veranda, Troy listened as Dr. Devony and The Brethren worked around a large conference room table. Maps of Earth and galaxy quadrants projected in the air above numerous keyboards, scribbled with notes and formulas along the margins. Two of the androids were conferring with the chief scientist. The other NTBs sat around the table, studying different trajectory plots on computer screens.

Dr. Allison, the medical supervisor, entered the room, and Troy anxiously walked over to her. "How are the test results on Tommy? Is he ok? Will he be all right?"

Vincent and the Grief Masters

"All of his lab tests and vital signs show no adverse effect," she reassured him. "His blood samples are normal; his muscle and organ tissues are good. He appears to be perfectly fine. It's amazing, having been in such a deconstructed state for so long. But we'll keep an eye on him."

Troy sighed with relief. "Good; that's good," he repeated nervously. "Thank you, Doctor."

She chuckled at his fatherly concern. "Really, don't worry, he'll be ok," she patted Troy's arm. Looking over at Tommy asleep on the couch, she asked, "Do you want me to take him to your new quarters? He'd sleep better in a real bed."

"No, I don't want him out of my sight," Troy said protectively. He shrugged, "At least, not just yet."

"I understand." She walked toward the door to leave. "Just let me know if you need anything."

Troy gazed at his sleeping son snuggled under a blanket, with Vincent's cat curled up beside him. He gently touched the top of Tommy's head. He just couldn't take his eyes off the comforting sight. How many nights he wished he could have tucked his son into bed, and here Tommy was, living and breathing again, right next to him. Troy felt he had only one being he could thank for it—a selfless android who was himself in trouble on Earth.

Troy left his son sleeping and joined Dr. Devony and the androids at the holographic blackboard. He watched how each android studied the problem, doing volumes of calculations that would take him days. He was unsure what he could contribute, if anything. Rubbing his hands together, he hesitantly turned to her. "I don't know how I can be of help. You have all of these amazing AIs here."

She nodded. "Yes, but they don't think outside the box, Troy, not the way humans do." Noticing his reluctance, she added, "We need forward-thinking minds like yours to take over when they leave."

Troy looked at her with surprise. "Leave? Why would they leave? Where are they going?"

"The Brethren are adamant about fulfilling their original mission to go out into the galaxy. They never planned to stay on D1. In fact, they already have a new destination in mind, one among a list of possible planets chosen before their program was canceled." She pulled up a small section of a galactic map on the screen and pointed her pen at a star system. "An M-class exoplanet called K2-18b, hydrogen-rich atmosphere, possible water oceans on its surface; and in the habitable zone of its star; approximately 124 light years from Earth."

The chief scientist looked at Troy and shrugged with a sigh. "But a long way from D1; so you see, we really do need you. Anything you can glean from them while they are here helps, of course, but know this, Troy—it is *your* inventive mind, *your* capability to envision the impossible as being possible, that brought us here. Your HTP saved every human being on this planet. Your father was brilliant. I admired and adored him; but so are you." Giving him a nod and a reassuring smile, she stepped away to speak with one of the androids.

Troy now understood what his role in this strange world might be. He realized he could still be of value; still contribute something to help others. His usual lack of self-confidence melted away, replaced with a spark of self-worth and a growing motivation to look to a new future for himself and Tommy.

He went straight to work. Troy stood with his arms crossed, studying the largest projected screen suspended over the conference room table. He took time to review every calculation written on it, some of which were crossed out, others appearing incomplete with question marks. One end of the screen displayed an interactive map of the galaxy where D1 was located. A lengthy pen mark stretched across to a spot marked, Earth.

He wanted to ask a question, but was unsure how to approach the androids, so he turned to Dr. Devony. "How do I talk with them? Do they have names, like Vincent does?"

"Oh, yes," she replied. "When we were building them, we had to be able to tell them apart. Each one of us adopted an android and gave it a name, either our own family name, like Vincent has, or the name of someone we admired, or who was important in our work." She pointed to several androids. "That's Galileo; that one is Stephen Hawking; over there, the Asian android, he's Michio Kaku, after the astrophysicist. We just call him Kaku. The female at the computer there is my adopted android, Katherine Johnson. She's like one of my own daughters. Just ask them their names, they'll tell you."

Troy turned to the android at the board next to him. "It's Galileo, right?"

"Yes, and you are Troy Vincent," he replied.

Troy nodded, now feeling a bit more comfortable in a room full of Vincents. "I have a question. If wormholes are time-based, the amount of energy to sustain it depends on the time needed. Can it stay open indefinitely until you find Vincent?"

Galileo shook his head. "It is imperative we locate his signal first. But we have not been able to find it." The android further explained, "The wormholes used to travel between Earth and D1 were of short durations and between two known points. Only our brother, Vincent, could generate enough power to create one and keep it open for the time required."

Dr. Devony added, "Each android has the power to create limited energy, but not on the scale Vincent could. One idea could be to combine their power, but I am not sure they can collectively create anything to go this entire distance, let alone keep it open for long." She pointed across the long axis. Hawking moved next to Troy at the board, marking a numeric formula on the screen. "It would be difficult to plot a trajectory without knowing a destination," he said. "It would require a wormhole too big to be sustained."

Galileo added, "It would collapse, if not parts of it, all of it."

Troy paced, assessing the situation, while learning more about space travel from the androids. There were so many questions he wanted to ask them, but he would hold those for later, concentrating on Vincent's situation.

"Doesn't he have an automatic transponder?" he asked. "They must have him confined where he can't transmit, or it's being blocked somehow."

Dr. Devony laid her pen down on the table. "We have to assume we will not get an exact location until the moment his signal is detected, assuming he maintains that position."

"Then we'll need to have a recovery plan ready to launch," Troy said. "Look, we know the coordinates of his last known location." He turned to the other androids in the room. "Would some of you please take a sector of airspace, start with that spot and search in an outward radius, scanning for his signal? When it appears, if it appears, we must be ready to act."

Troy turned to Hawking and Galileo at the board. "We will work together on combining your energy into a sustainable wormhole. Dr. Devony, if you would please, work with Katherine and the others to determine what level of energy would be required for a recovery from any of the sectors."

Half of the NTBs sitting around the table divided up the worldwide VRSM Complex and projected its different locations onto smaller screens in front of them. Each android began analyzing the thousands of wireless signals appearing and disappearing from their screens, like tiny traffic control lights.

As she looked at the countless signals, Dr. Devony turned toward Troy. "I would say this is the proverbial needle in a haystack." Troy put his hands on his hips, scanning the busy screens in the room. "Ain't that the truth?"

After talking with the two androids to better understand the intricacies of wormhole construction, Troy had an idea. "The Brethren are each capable of producing not only nuclear fission, but nuclear fusion as well, right? So from fusion, we can create a concentrated, controlled beam. If it rotates quickly enough, it could expand into a wormhole and create the same type of directional movement Vincent does." The three got to work on it.

Hours later, Dr. Devony had gone back to her quarters to take a sleep break. The Brethren remained steadfast at their screens, still scanning for Vincent's signal. Troy had also taken a break earlier, carrying his son to bed, in what would now be their new home. It was a nice suite of rooms: two bedrooms, a living room, bath, and kitchen between them. A large patio looked out onto a secluded lagoon. A monitor in Tommy's room would signal Troy when his son would awaken.

Back in the conference room, moonlight began to fade into dawn. Troy swirled lukewarm coffee around in his cup. He set it on the table, rubbing his eyes with the heels of his hands, feeling the need for sleep himself. *I have to keep working the problem.* Getting up, he walked the length of the holographic board, reviewing it once again. What was he missing? The problem didn't lie in sending the energy in one direction to Earth, but in reversing it to make it return to D1. Usually the energy flowed in a circular fashion, to and from Vincent. But they needed to pull Vincent back to them. He repeated the question over and over in his mind, searching for...he smiled to himself...searching for a *key*.

He wandered around the back of the holographic board and read the same calculations in reverse, appearing as in a mirror. *What force is great enough to reverse the stream of energy and make it flow in the opposite direction? Sending energy forward is easy; pulling it back again is the hard part.*

Like Newton's apple falling from a tree, the 'key' hit him. Turning to the androids, he asked, "What is a fundamental force that can repel itself?"

Hawking responded, "Magnetism."

"Yes!" Troy said decisively. "After we pick up Vincent, we bounce the wormhole off a repelling energy of equal or greater force."

Kaku looked up with an understanding nod. "Use the Earth's magnetic poles, the geomagnetic field, to deflect the wormhole back to us."

"Yes!" Troy excitedly responded. "The repelling force of the Earth's magnetic field may be more than enough to bounce the flow of energy back to D1."

"And how does he get from the planet's surface to the geomagnetic field?" asked Dr. Devony, returning to the room.

Kaku suggested, "We use nanobits from The Brethren embedded inside the wormhole to direct it to a spot on the magnetic field. Then the nanobits' polar magnetism will be repelled by Earth's geomagnetic field."

"Bouncing him back to D1," Galileo said.

"It would be like grabbing a return train back home," Troy added as he sat down at a computer to work out the math. He brought up a 3D graphic image of the rotating Earth with its magnetic fields.

The three androids stood behind Troy, looking over his shoulder. "The angle of return has to be precise or he could fly right past D1. All we need now is his location."

Katherine had been working on calculations involving different longitude/latitude locations on Earth with lightning speed. She looked up from her screen. "The energy level needed to produce a wormhole from a controlled fusion beam to Earth falls within the limits The Brethren can collectively produce."

Troy felt the old scientific thrill he loved whenever he hit on a viable solution. He flexed his fingers and started working the numbers. "Vincent, you've got a ticket to ride, buddy."

Chapter 38

The pitch-black space surrounding Vincent did not bother him. However, the fact he could not move did. VRSM Security told him his arms and legs had been removed from his body to prevent him from controlling the surrounding environment. They claimed his nanobits could morph and provide an escape. They left the rest of him untouched, fearing he would release his nuclear fusion program. That was still intact, along with all of the other programs residing in his head. He could have resisted, but his intellectual choice remained steadfast, to not harm those who were instructed by others to dismantle him.

The isolation of the blast box, his prison cell, was welcome. No one would harass him here. No one would question him about the Resistance, or accuse him of treason against Corporate Rule. And no one would threaten to destroy him or his brothers. All of that was left in the courtroom where he was projected onto a screen miles from the five-attorney panel who judged and pronounced him guilty. Attorney Adams, whom Vincent met only once, apparently was on the panel, as he recognized the man's voice, threatening once more to send him to the bottom of the ocean. The angry man spoke like he couldn't wait to administer a guilty verdict. Vincent gave little defense in his responses. He knew Adams, and the others had already determined his fate before the trial began.

Vincent spent the hours reviewing his original data logs of music, art, and literature. He played operas and symphonies, reading the full orchestration of George Gershwin's *Rhapsody in Blue*. While listening to the music, he read famous works from *The History of Rome* to classic novels by Falkner and Hemmingway, but shied away from Stephen King, whose novels disturbed him.

Being an expert multi-tasker, he simultaneously viewed museum works from the Louvre to the Guggenheim, with art images flashing across his mask. Vincent thought so much talent came out of man's brief existence on Earth. However, the second half of the 21st Century did not produce many artisans in any of these areas. The many types of bans and restrictions on what could be created caused humans to have little desire for the arts now; and not able to afford any of it, they paid little attention to it. He pitied the planet's loss of such valuable and expressive mediums.

He knew he was in the belly of an empty oil tanker, having seen it during the night as a helicopter lowered the blast-proof box with him in it through an open hatch. When the hatch slammed shut above him, he didn't speculate further on his fate.

When arrested, he had turned off his transponder, not wanting The Brethren to jeopardize themselves for his sake. *Better for Troy, Loveena, and all of them this way,* he thought. Vincent was making a choice, one that made him feel more human. Unsure why it seemed important, he only knew he valued the freedom to choose.

Another human feeling he didn't expect, nor cared for, was one of absence. Vincent missed his cat. She appreciated him, with no earthly expectations other than a piece of food or a small bowl of milk. He felt the same way about her, enjoying her company, listening to her purr as he worked. Remembering a musical work called, *Cats*, in his database, he turned on his audio and listened to the soundtrack. He particularly liked the song, "Memory." The little, scrawny cat who sang about longing for someone's touch, or the first light of another day to live, reminded him of his tiny companion who spent much of her day scrounging the alleyways outside. At night, she would return to the protection of his hidden workroom. Vincent envisioned her jumping into the broken air vent that led to the outside world. She always turned to say goodbye. A shaft of sunlight beaming through the old vent would skip across her tiny body as she slipped away.

As the aging feline sang the last line of the song, *Look, a new day has begun,* a sliver of sunshine broke through the inky blackness and the hatch high above him opened. The net around the blast box rose, taking him up to the small patch of blue sky visible through the opening. The noise of the tanker's crane chugged away reeling up the cable. As the cargo net broke through into the sunlight, its contents were swung out over the side of the ship to a small barge floating next to the larger oil tanker. Vincent could see piles of trash bags covering the entire top deck of the barge. The cargo net was lowered just above one of the piles, untethered it, and let it fall free of the cable. While the crane's cable still held the blast box, a mechanical arm removed the net.

The box then descended within a few feet of the garbage pile, where it abruptly stopped and Vincent heard a click. The bottom of the box opened, dumping him out. His back slid down the surface of the slick garbage bags, but the ragged edges of metal left when his limbs were removed caught on some ropes holding the bags in place. Lying face up on the bow of the ship he slipped again, but this time his thorax wedged under another rope and he was bound to the floating beast. It made him think of Captain Ahab bound to the white whale, Moby Dick.

A familiar voice came over the loudspeaker. Security Chief Michaels said, "Hello, Vincent. Do you know where you are?"

Vincent could not see him beyond the mounds of garbage. "I am on a trash barge."

"Yes. You are bound for the Puerto Rico Trench, the deepest spot in the Atlantic Ocean. There you will remain…" the chief paused. Vincent noted there was an emotion in the chief's voice as he spoke. The android wasn't sure if it sounded like human sadness or human regret. "There you will remain and submerge to a depth which will destroy your circuitry and crush you. This is the judgment the court has given you."

Standing in the wheelhouse with the small crew of the barge, Chief Michaels gruffly cleared his voice and clicked on the loudspeaker again. "I have been ordered to visually confirm that this judgment is carried out. Do you have anything you wish to say, Vincent?"

The android was silent. He watched a seagull circle above him, analyzing its aerodynamic movement. He never had an opportunity to spend time outside and watch a bird in flight. It fascinated him. After a long, silent moment, the loudspeaker clicked back on a third time.

Michaels turned away from the crew and spoke quietly into the hand mic. "If it means anything at all to an android like yourself…well, I'd like you to know…I personally think highly of you, Vincent. You always reminded me of a Hindu slave who served the British Army and died saving a wounded soldier. Despite being mistreated, he wasn't afraid to face the danger of the battlefield. You are very much like him. The last line of that poem went something like, "Tho' I've belted you and flayed you, by the livin' God that made you, you're a better man than I, Gunga Din."

Vincent heard an audible sigh come through the loudspeaker.

"Anyway…that's all I wanted to say," the chief straightened. "Goodbye, Vincent." The loudspeaker clicked off.

Goodbye, Chief Michaels.

****

The chief clicked off the microphone and placed it back in its holder. The Barge Master readied to launch away from the dock. As Chief Michaels watched him in the wheelhouse, he glanced out the window and saw a taxicab fly up the dock, stopping by the pier to the barge. Attorney Xavier Adams exited the cab carrying an overnight bag.

Michaels turned, and taking large strides to the door, he opened it and ran down the companionway from the upper deck as fast as he could. Once on the lower deck, he ran to the top of the gangplank and arrived just in time to stop the attorney from boarding. Moving to the middle of it, Chief Michaels blocked access to the barge with his large body. He filled the width of the plank, causing Adams to step back down to the pier.

"I've come to witness this," yelled Adams over the noise of boats in the harbor.

"No, I don't think so. He deserves someone who cares about him, and that's not you."

The Barge Master, watching what was happening, pushed the button to retract the gangplank. Michaels stood his ground, riding on it as the gangplank moved backward. He jumped onto the deck at the last second as the ramp disappeared, sliding into its hold. Pushing the throttle forward, the Barge Master eased the old iron lady slowly away from the pier.

Adams followed it, hurrying down the dock, shouting to the Security Chief. "You have a weakness for these lifeless tin cans, Chief. They're dead inside. They have no souls to cry over."

Chief Michaels saw a bullhorn hanging on a rack on the outside wall. He grabbed it, clicked it on, and addressed the attorney. "I think you have that backward, Mr. Adams. No one will cry over yours. By the way, I received an anonymous file containing a handwritten ledger by Hoy SamWong. It showed a record of multi-million-dollar payments to you. It couldn't have come from the android; he's been with me the whole time. Someone else is on to you, Mr. Adams. And now, the authorities are on their way to your office to ask you some questions. They're curious how you came by that unusual diamond ring you wear. They tell me it belonged to SamWong. You know, Mr. Adams, I'm really looking forward to the day I can personally escort *you* to a VRC."

The barge turned toward the harbor entrance. Chief Michaels gave a casual one-finger salute to the stunned attorney, who stood speechless, mouth agape, at the end of the dock.

****

Garbage barges made weekly runs south across the point where the Atlantic Ocean flowed into the Caribbean Sea. The blue-green water of the Bahamas blended into azure just north of Puerto

Rico. Here the ocean floor sloped from two miles to three, then plunged over five miles deep into the ocean bottom. For decades, the Puerto Rico Trench became the dumping ground for trash from all over the Western Hemisphere. The deepest trench in the Atlantic Ocean stretched for several hundred miles from west to east.

Ocean trenches around the world shared a similar fate. As land became scarce, with rising seas and sprawling urban development, society left its dirtiest problem to the slow subduction process of the Earth's crust. Fill the deepest terrain with trash, and it would be consumed inch by inch, into the submerging folds of the planet's plate tectonic process. However, the growing mounds were close to a mile high in spots on the ocean floor and would take centuries to succumb to the process. The ocean and its marine inhabitants suffered greatly at the hands of humanity.

For three days the barge traveled across calm waters. Ocean white caps broke low, disappearing against the blue cloudless sky of the horizon. Vincent lay positioned at an angle, with his head higher than his chest, against a hill of garbage. At night, he had a front-row seat to a spectacular view of billions of stars in the galaxy; a destiny he no longer claimed. During the day, a light ocean breeze blew across him as the ship sailed along. He could tell the temperature from his internal thermostat was a balmy ninety-eight degrees; a cool day for just north of the equator. Aware the decaying heaps of garbage would be giving off obnoxious gases, this was one time he was content to not have the sensory implant for 'smell' in his program.

He had never been to the ocean and, although having knowledge of its environment, this would be the first time he could actually experience it. He wondered what it might be like to be submerged. His system didn't require air, but as his brothers, they were all equipped to colonize on land, never in liquid. He concluded being submerged would damage him beyond repair and decided to make an internal backup of his operations program, storing it in an airtight section of his head.

****

Chief Michaels spent most of the trip confined to his quarters with repeating waves of seasickness. He ventured topside as they approached their destination. Standing in the air-conditioned wheelhouse, he still held a towel to his face to block out the stench while he watched the young boatswain at the ship's wheel. The Barge Master stood nearby giving him directions. Observing how uncomfortable the chief was, the young man smiled at him, missing a top front tooth and a couple of bottom teeth. "Ya get used to it, the smell; ya don't notice it after a while," he said.

The chief thought the salty sea air aged the young man, making him appear much older than he probably was, with deep wrinkles carved into his tan, leathery face. Michaels' voice was muffled by the towel. "How long have you been working the barges?"

"Ten years, maybe longer. Cap'n here, he's been on this run for decades. Forty years, sir?"

The Barge Master nodded. "Forty-two years, seven months, and nine days. Two and a half more years, and I be retired." Removing his captain's hat, he brushed his arm across his balding head, wiping the sweat on his sleeve. His white, stubbly beard made him appear much older, too.

The chief removed the towel, using it to wipe the perspiration off of his face and neck. *Life near the equator is just too damn hot. Gotta give credit to these guys for what they do.* "Do you plan on going somewhere cooler when you retire? Somewhere that doesn't smell quite so bad?" He chuckled.

"Got a small place in Jamaica…upwind from here." They all laughed.

After a short time, the boatswain announced, "Comin' to the drop zone." He spun the wheel to bring the side of the barge around into position. Cutting the engine, he let the ship glide, rolling with the waves seven miles above the deep trench.

"So how do you make all these bags sink to the bottom?" asked Chief Michaels.

"Well, come with me," the Barge Master replied. "I'll show you how we prepare a dump."

The two men left the wheelhouse. The chief returned the towel to his nose, coughing at the putrid smell as they went out on the companionway. Descending the ladder to the lower deck, he followed the older man to the stern of the ship. A large control panel housed behind a thick wall of Plexiglas faced the stern, looking out onto the surface of the ocean behind the barge.

The old captain pointed to a row of switches lining the panel. "Each of these switches transmits a wireless signal to small explosives embedded in this here trash. Ya see, those bags float when they hit the water. It's the air pockets in 'em. The explosives act like cans of shot, big shotgun shells. When I throw the switches one at a time, they explode and send shot through the bags lettin' 'em take on water and sink. Got it?"

"Hmm. How far away are you when you do this?" The chief frowned with concern about Vincent's nuclear weapon potential.

"Oh, we'll be turned around and on our way back by then."

Starting back toward the wheelhouse, a glint of bright sunshine bounced off Vincent's metal chest, temporarily blinding the chief. He stopped, raising his hand up in front of his face to shade his eyes. The Barge Master, unaffected by the bright sun, continued up the ladder to the companionway on the upper deck.

The gold on the cross of Vincent's torso reflected the sun so brightly the chief could not look toward the bow of the ship. Squinting, he turned his head toward the wall, fumbling for the railing at the base of the ladder. On the bulkhead before him, he clearly saw a sun ray cast the reflected shape of the long cross on Vincent's chest. The outline of the cross danced in the light, looking as if it was burning, etching itself into the gray paint of the wall. Removing the towel from his nose, Chief Michaels dropped his arm from the railing, staring at the shadow of the shimmering cross. It wasn't just the trash smell that disgusted him, it was also this judgment. "I wish I could help you," he whispered. "But I'm just doing my job. I can't change the system, Vincent." He balled up the towel and with frustration, threw it down to the deck. His shoulders slumped as he hung his head down and continued up the ladder.

The barge came equipped with large electronic platforms the Barge Master referred to as sleds. Back inside the wheelhouse, the captain pushed three buttons, and the sleds began moving. The three sleds rose slowly, pushing up from the center of the ship toward each side, causing the piles of trash to slide and spill over into the water.

Vincent felt the bags underneath him give way as he slid with them, falling over the side with the trash. When the sleds reached a fifty-five-degree angle, they stopped moving and locked into place. A wide hydraulic plate at the back of each sled pushed forward like an arm, sweeping any garbage left on the sled into the water. The captain pushed the three buttons again, and the sleds retracted down to their original positions, locking in place.

D. L. Farrar

Chapter 39

The old captain started the engine, wheeling the barge around for the return trip to port. Moving in a large curve away from the floating trash debris, the resulting wake in the water pushed the piles of bags further apart. Vincent landed upright, floating on an enormous pile of bags, bobbing up and down. The rope around his torso kept him tethered to the bags. At first, he was riding above the water, then the bags shifted, and he started to sink. Still attached by the rope, his head remained above the water as it lapped midway up his chest.

A mile from the trash dump, the barge slowed without coming to a full stop. The boatswain and Chief Michaels went back down to the stern and the control panel.

"This clear blast panel here will make sure we ain't hit with nothin'," the younger man said.

"Would it really blow this far?" asked Michaels.

"Well, ya never know what might be in a load a' trash. Could be sumpthin' dangerous, like bullets or grenades. I even saw a load a' fireworks explode once," he laughed. "That was real excitin'!"

The chief, still worried about Vincent's internal weapon, tried to estimate how far away they were from the debris, and moved to a spot well inside the protective blast panel.

"Here goes. Do ya wanna do the honors? Throw the switches?"

Nervous sweat ran down the chief's face. "No, you go ahead."

The young man pushed the first switch down on the panel with his thumb. In the distance, a blast went up from a section of the floating trash. Bags flew into the air, along with several fleeing seagulls and a shower of water. Going slowly down the line, he threw each switch, dispersing buckshot throughout the bags. As bags filled and sank, the water concealed sections of garbage until nothing was left visible on the surface.

Chief Michaels let out a pent-up sigh, running his hand across his closed eyes. He pulled out a handkerchief and wiped the sweat once again from his forehead and the back of his neck. A stressful weariness made his entire body ache.

"I'll be glad to get back to shore," he muttered.

****

Sunrise on New Earth crept over the ocean's horizon. Yellow rays of sunshine bathed the stone veranda on the eastern side of the compound, overlooking the ocean. In his new apartment, Troy rose early, showered, dressed, and made coffee before waking Tommy. Samuel Baptista had enlisted the boy's help on a building project. Troy was so relieved his son was physically doing well, fitting into life here, and, more importantly, happy. However, Troy could not let himself feel the same until he either resolved or knew of Vincent's fate.

Troy and The Brethren had constructed a plan, one he thought to be a good one. However, he also realized the odds of succeeding were probably against them. A week had passed, days of waiting, scanning for Vincent's signal. Dr. Devony explained, because the daily rotation of D1 took 36 hours, instead of the normal 24 hours on Earth, more days had passed for Vincent. The difference in time was closer to a two week equivalent. They may have to conclude the android had been destroyed already and call off their search.

Troy spent the days reading computer logs of the early development of the compound, while the NTBs continued the search for Vincent's signal. He studied the documentation on the local geography while learning how the androids chose a strategic coastal location near a water source on a protected inlet. The resident biologists wrote assumptions of what natural vegetation may be edible or non-edible. One entry he read discussed whether artifacts found were of an alien origin, who may have visited the planet once, or perhaps evidence of an indigenous species that had long since disappeared. So far, there was no sign of land-dwelling creatures, other than small rodents, insects, and fish varieties.

The team determined the environment stable and safe for human habitation. It was a lucky find in a huge galaxy and the next great step for mankind, even though mankind, as Troy knew it, would now have to change and adapt to a new world. He hoped it would be a better place, one in which the foundation for humanity would define success as unlimited growth with diversity and unity, and not growth stagnated by greed and division.

However, the logs urged caution, underscoring that a sizable portion of the planet remained unexplored. The probability of unknown danger was high. One particular log recorded unstable weather appearing regularly to the north, accompanied by dangerous fluctuations in temperature. A manned expedition there had yet to be attempted.

Around noon his earpiece buzzed. Loveena waited for him on the veranda. Since they arrived, they could only steal a few minutes during the day to meet, joining each other for dinner with Tommy in the evenings. He ached to hold her and spend another night in her arms, but they both knew it would have to wait. Walking to the glass doors of the conference room, he saw her standing by the railing, her dark hair shining in the sunlight reflecting a halo above her head.

She smiled as he approached and took her by the hand, leading her to a darkened doorway. Before she could utter a good morning, he pulled her close and kissed her. Making up for time apart, they embraced, tightly holding each other, neither one wanting to let go, but knowing their brief meetings would have to do for now.

"Any news yet on Vincent?" she asked.

Troy shook his head. "I'm not sure we'll be able to find him."

Loveena's concern for the android showed in her eyes. "Don't give up."

"I won't. How can I?" he half-smiled. "He's my brother."

"And where's Tommy this morning?"

Troy chuckled, "He's with your father learning how to swing a hammer at your new beach house. He's soaking up the attention he's getting from everyone."

She laughed, tapping her finger on his chest. "And it's long overdue. He deserves it. Such a helpful little guy probably gets it from his father." Glancing down to avoid his eyes, she stifled a smile and said with a whisper, "You know, that beach house is going to be too big for just me."

Raising his eyebrows, Troy responded, "I think your father might have something to say about that." He gave her another kiss. "Let's give him and Tommy some time to get used to the idea. It doesn't mean I won't be over for dinner every night."

"Oh, will you be cooking?" she teased.

Troy's earpiece buzzed again, calling him back to the conference room. After another tight embrace and a lingering kiss, he left her side.

****

Later that afternoon, Troy was seated in a chair at the conference room table, having been lulled to sleep by the warmth of the triple dwarf suns. One of the female androids, Sally Ride, turned up the audio on a section of map in front of her. Filtering out all the extraneous white noise, she narrowed in on a low-pitched ping, beeping out a constant rhythm. The repetitive sound broke through Troy's sleepy subconscious. As he opened his blurry eyes, Kaku was leaning down in front of him. The android's stare startled him as he blinked awake.

"We have located our brother. His transponder has been isolated."

Rising from the chair, Troy rubbed the sleep from his eyes, lifting away the grogginess of his nap. Following Kaku, he walked over to the monitor, pinging out the steady beat. Dozens of blinking lights moved across the map. "Where is he? Which one?"

She waved her hand across the monitor and all of the lights dimmed except one. Sally isolated the one light, using her finger to highlight it with a red circle off the northeastern coast of Puerto Rico. "There...that is him."

Troy became rejuvenated as energy flowed back into his brain and his head cleared. They were ready to initiate their recovery plan. "Ok, let's go get him."

"There is a problem," Galileo announced, as all the Brothers nodded at once. They already shared the disturbing news with each other through their common consciousness.

"What problem?" Troy looked around at the unexpressive faces.

"He is underwater," Hawking replied.

"And advancing with moderate speed toward the ocean bottom," added Sally.

"What?" Troy asked with surprise.

Hawking explained, "Wormholes are designed to work through space and solid substances, but not through liquid. The surrounding uneven pressure of liquid on the outside would be greater than the air and energy on the inside. The wormhole would collapse."

"And a traveler must be able to step into a wormhole. It has no way to pull him out of the water," Galileo said.

Troy felt the weight of a ton of bricks hit his shoulders. He exhaled a heavy sigh, walked to the glass doors, and stood looking out at the afternoon sunset over the ocean. Turning back to the eleven quiet NTBs in the room, he ran his hand through his tousled hair. *They need to know humans don't give up when the odds are against them.*

He put his hands on his hips and bit his lower lip with a look of determination. "Ok, ladies and gentlemen, tell me some options."

No one spoke. Vincent had been the natural leader of the group. Baptista said they didn't seem to function as well without a leader. Troy assumed that's what was missing. So, he would need to step up and be their leader in Vincent's absence.

"Come on, you guys, we can do this. There's gotta be another way. Let's be creative; think outside the box."

Hawking ran calculations in his head. "In every scenario, the wormhole collapses if submerged in liquid. The water pressure on the outside of the tunnel destabilizes the opening's equilibrium. However...there is one outcome with a higher probability of success."

"Let's hear it," Troy said.

****

The first explosion had rocked the garbage bags Vincent was entangled with. Jarred by the vibration, his transponder was switched back on. He bobbed around until his weight on the bags caused him to turn face down in the water, still tethered by the rope. The second explosion went off closer and the floating bags surrounding him began taking on water, lowering him down. As the weight of the descending garbage equaled his own, his body rotated back up toward the water line above him. The rope dislodged from the bags, finally freeing him. The cavity inside his torso still maintained air pockets, slowing his descent, as bag after bag sank past him on a downward path. He could see the bright rays of sunshine beam through the water as tiny fish surrounded him, cleaning the spattered garbage from the lenses of his mask. He appreciated their attention and a purely human thought flashed through his mind. *Perhaps this is what a kiss feels like.*

In the sunlight, he saw marine creatures he had never encountered. Besides the schools of colorful fish and jellies floating nearby, a pod of playful bottlenose dolphins encircled him. Swimming at great speed toward him, they then changed direction and swam away, only to return again. Each one slowed in front of the sinking android, chattering with clicks and whines, as though they were trying to converse with him. Two swam up, jumped together from the water and splashed back into it, straight down to him. They accompanied Vincent on his languid descent for another hundred meters or so. Wishing there was a language in his databank which could convert what they said, he sent a generic audio wave of greeting out to them. After all, he was programmed to make contact with any new species.

It apparently worked, as more dolphins joined in, swimming next to him. They circled and nudged him back toward the surface; but each time, he sank again. Vincent thought their efforts quite valiant, and he thanked them. With a final passing, each one swam by him with one pectoral fin up in his direction. Then the pod moved on.

As the sunlight from above diminished to a dim blue, Vincent continued to observe numerous marine species, making notes in his log. In the distant water, he could see a shadow, the dark form growing larger and larger as it approached. Behind it, a smaller shadow accompanied it. A deep rumbling sound echoed through the water, announcing its presence to him. The form became distinct as it closed the distance between them, and the rumbling song of the humpback whale called to her calf, swimming beside her.

As she approached Vincent, he could see her large eye was drawn to the shiny golden cross on his torso, reflecting the last threads of sunlight. She looked into his face, releasing another deep note that resonated through the water, surrounding him with reverberations. He felt sadness in the tiredness of her sound. He assumed she bore the heavy burden of being one of the last of her kind. It was well known the great whale populations in much of the oceans had died away; a significant loss that could not be reversed.

Several other large family members followed behind her, all moaning an acknowledgment to Vincent as they traveled to cooler waters. Her calf accompanied him down another few hundred meters, before being called away by the distant echoing clicks of her mother.

Vincent bumped along a rocky ridge, where sea anemones displayed their vibrant colors and crabs and starfish appeared locked in a slow-motion battle. The ridge gradually descended to a much darker ocean, and he felt the pressure of the deep on his chest. Tumbling along a flatter plain, his internal compass told him the edge of the Continental Shelf lay not far ahead. In front of him would be a steep plunge into the Puerto Rico Trench, the deepest point of this ocean. Without appendages, he would be at the mercy of the moving ocean currents. He thought it preferable to not go over the edge, but it was looking unavoidable.

In his VRC assignments, he observed situations where the end of life became inevitable. Often he heard the human candidate engage in a conversation, called a prayer. Sometimes the results were unexpected and made a difference.

In his continual search to discover what it must be like to be human, Vincent chose the human action: he chose to pray. Unsure what a prayer was, or what he should say, or even who to say it to, he remembered the man in the white robe he mentioned to Troy and Loveena. So, he prayed to him.

The ocean current slowed, and Vincent came to rest against a large rock. The current pushed him into a crevice on the side of it and he became tightly wedged. His head remained upright as his thorax was squeezed, slowly crushing inward. The rock was all that kept him from drifting another fifty feet to the edge of the drop off and into the dark abyss. He continued to pray, and only asked for a little help.

In the dark water, a tiny light floated toward him. He watched it come closer as the light grew. Stopping above him, it took the form of a key. It emitted a gold and white shimmer that lit up the area surrounding the rock. Floating out from the key, a leather strap appeared. It encircled his chrome head, coming to rest on the top portion of the golden cross on his chest. The water along the muddy plain brightened with golden sparkles.

The deep-water current flowed against Vincent's thorax with increasing pressure. His head, made of thicker metal, protected his databases and remained unaffected. As his chest cavity beneath the golden etched cross finally collapsed in upon itself, a new software application uploaded. He wasn't even aware this program existed inside of him. Redirecting it to the database server in his head, Vincent scanned its contents as it streamed.

In the distance, he saw men and women walking across the sandy plain toward him in a single line. Each one appeared dressed in clothing that represented different periods of time in human history, going back thousands of years. Some wore or carried symbols and Vincent wondered about their meaning, as each one was distinctly different. As he watched them approach, the history of hundreds of religions of the world educated him, giving recognition to the ancient civilizations each represented and the deities they worshipped.

Vincent began to understand who these people were. Cave paintings, clay tablets, hieroglyphs, scrolls written in old languages streamed across his mask. He instantly deciphered them, reading and comprehending their messages. Sacred texts of many cultures represented by the individuals now walking in front of him unlocked the important role each played in creating the world's civilizations.

A growing awareness of a common thread was developing in the android's central core. It was the enduring belief by humans across the millennia in the existence of something greater than man—a higher power that could not be seen. Hope and trust developed into a reliance on it, becoming an integral part of humanity's development. A devotional desire turned into 'faith,' and many different faiths formed, reflecting the values of different cultures. These faiths bloomed into a 'love,' bonding humans to an eternal longing to be with this unseen power.

It caused man to exist with two constant soul-searching questions: why are we here and who created us? Whether it was an actual being, or the vast awesome power of the cosmos, Vincent wasn't sure, but it was present throughout the entire human history, giving purpose and meaning to life itself. Vincent now felt he knew what the unspoken, intangible piece of *being human* meant.

The text of the Bible's New Testament was the last segment of the hidden program that streamed across his mask. The emergence from the dark into the sparkling water of the man in the white robe accompanied the end of the lengthy, multi-cultural parade of spiritual leaders. With the upload now complete, all of those who had a part in the extensive religious history of mankind had walked past him, and continued walking across the sandy plain toward the darker ocean abyss. However, the last man in line, the one in the white robe, stopped and stood in front of him.

Chapter 40

"I know who you are," the android said.

"I have been sent here on your behalf, Vincent."

"Are you the Maker? Are you God, the ultimate Grief Master?"

"I am His Son, Jesus."

"And the others?" Vincent asked.

"We are all sons and daughters of God, calling Him by different names, following the laws set before them within their own culture and time. Some have many followers, as do I. Your maker, Dr. Vincent, believed in me, worshipping my Father through me. Just as the good doctor wanted to share his faith with you, because he loved you, I now come with the love my Father has for you."

"Then you are the Christ?"

"To the Christian world, I am the Good Shepherd. I am the Way, the Truth and the Life, and no one comes to our Father except through me." Jesus sat down beside the rock next to Vincent, his legs crossed and his hands folded, casually resting his elbows across his knees.

"To you, Vincent, my name is Compassion. As you have shown compassion to your human charges, my Father is compassionate toward you."

"I have seen you in the VRCs," Vincent said. "Why do you come for some and not for others?"

Jesus pointed to the crushed cross on the android's chest. "Just as you carried my message beneath that cross you bear, you didn't know it until now. Others do not know my message. They either have not heard it or choose to take another path. You see, our Father created free will; the ability to choose. So, many follow me, some follow the other sons of God; and still, some follow none." Jesus smiled at Vincent.

"You see, Vincent, if you do not know my Father, then He doesn't know you. But rejoice! He knows your name, as you now know His. Your selfless actions have been noted, and your search for a human soul has given you one."

"But I have done bad things. If what you teach is the way, I must be excluded."

"Recognizing those things which humans all have, is called sin. True, the Father does not allow sin in His presence. But, I was sent to take on the sins of the world, so that those who believe in me can reconcile with Him."

Jesus touched the white key around Vincent's neck. "Forgiveness is the key, the way; and it comes only by the Grace of God. Ask for it, and it shall be given. Then, you must sin no more."

Vincent thought Jesus spoke to him as a friend, and he appreciated that. There was a comfort deep inside him coming from the words he heard, both foreign and yet familiar; things Dr. Vincent also said to him.

"I know you think because you are not human you do not belong within the family of God. But there are human qualities in you, Vincent, which many men fail to possess. You laid down your life, your existence, to save the lives of others. One, who gives his life for another, gives the greatest sacrifice of all."

"As you gave your life upon a cross for the sins of others?"

"My Father sent me into the world, not to destroy it, but to save it."

Vincent looked down away from Jesus. "I am only a machine."

Jesus picked up a tiny starfish from the base of the rock and held it in his hand. "Look at all the creatures of the world. He cares for the smallest of them, the most helpless of them. There is room at His table, and in His heart, for whoever wishes to be there." Laying the starfish down gently in the sand, he took a moment to watch it move away.

Then he continued. "His love brings life to the lifeless. His comfort sustains us. His grace saves us. Just as a Grief Master's message brings renewal to someone who needs it, my Father sends me with this message for you: He loves you."

Vincent turned off his mask and looked up, displaying his naked, skeletal face to Christ, with all of his imperfect frailties and inhuman shortcomings. Jesus reached out and gently touched the android's head. The silver chrome covering the mechanical body silently turned to gold. Vincent felt a warmth he had never known flooding through him. It went to a depth he could only imagine must be where the soul resides, to a heart within his brain; not a circuit or a gigabyte, but an indescribable spot that felt *alive.*

"I have seen you take those who did not survive the VRC. Will you take me with you?" the android asked.

Jesus stood up as the sparkling water surrounded Him. "Where I go, you cannot go. Not yet. You have more work to do. But I can help you." He spread his arms wide and a golden radiance surrounded both of them.

Vincent did not want Him to go, hoping this man and his comforting words could stay beside him forever. "Please, stay."

"You can talk to me anytime, anyplace you like. Remember me in your travels, Vincent. Share my words with all those you meet." He stepped back and motioned with his hand for an approaching shy sea creature to come closer. Speaking one last reassurance, Jesus said, "And know this, my friend…I am with you always." Then He turned and walked across the watery plain, following the line of the other spiritual leaders into the dark ocean and was gone.

The sparkling water remained as the elusive white octopus approached Vincent. He realized that Jesus had directed the sea creature to help him, so he would comply with whatever it decided to do. The octopus reached out with one arm, exploring the rock into which Vincent was securely wedged. When his chest caved in, it pushed him deeper into the crevice, tightly wedging his torso. Several more arms wrapped around Vincent's body, pushing hard against the rock with two of them. However, Vincent did not move.

The octopus paused, as if evaluating the situation. Looking at the android with its two eyes on top of its head and its giant bell laid back in an unthreatening manner, it gently caressed the golden head with the tip of one arm, as if it wanted to show Vincent some empathy. Skimming around Vincent's shoulders, it perched behind the android, wrapping itself around his torso and placing half of its arms on the rock. With its suckers sticking tightly against the metal, the creature turned red pushing and pulling with all of its might, but still no progress.

Vincent quickly scanned his database for information on this species and discovered they were highly intelligent. He sent an audio wave through the water, hoping it would understand his message. *Take my head; I do not need my body. It can be rebuilt. Just take my head.*

The creature understood. Floating to the top of Vincent's head, it repositioned itself. It wrapped four arms around his head and under his chin, being careful not to cover the android's eye sockets. Bracing two arms against his shoulders and two more against the rock, it pulled and pulled, not letting go until Vincent's head finally came free, detaching from the cables and connections to his body.

The octopus cradled the golden head in four arms and raced from the ocean bottom. As they ascended, Vincent looked back and saw what was left of his battered, abused body. His missing arms and legs were savagely severed off, and his torso mangled. The top portion of the golden cross on his chest remained visible until the murky darkness filled in below him. Wherever the creature intended to take him didn't matter, as long as it was up.

The octopus used the other four arms to propel them along. The sticky suckers held its precious cargo firmly in place. Vincent was sure he wasn't in any danger of being accidentally dropped. The inky blackness of the lower depths gave way to dark blue water. He could feel the pressure change within his head and knew he was going up a lot faster than he had come down.

Hearing the haunting calls of the humpbacks approaching, the octopus seemed nervous, having risen into a different watery environment. Being a bottom dweller, it was apparent to Vincent the creature felt in danger being out of its normal realm. In fact, he interpreted a confusing message from her, stating she needed to get back to her 'broken pipe' of tiny eggs.

The shadows of the humpback family came into view. As if the octopus knew it climbed as far as it dared, it whirled, hurtling Vincent toward the approaching shadow. Vincent's head twirled around in an upward motion, as he caught glimpses of the tiny octopus retreating back toward the safety of deeper water.

The motion of his head slowed and the large mother humpback rose up beneath Vincent. She caught him with her extremely broad nose and lobbing her immense tail up and down, she created an inertia that pinned him to her. Up through the dark blue world, meter after meter, her huge body cut through the water. Her calf clicked behind her, as the other family members accompanied them, moaning songs, sounding almost cheerful.

Vincent sent the matriarch a message of hope, promising her he would come back someday and help her and all the others of their kind. He assured her their lineage would endure and made a promise to her young calf. As if she understood every word, the great whale let out a bellow of bubbles, circling her head and brushing against his metal cheeks. She returned an audio wave in such a low register, it was almost undecipherable. All he could understand was a whale's version of the words, 'grateful' and 'thank you.'

The blue water became spiked again with long beams of sun rays as the whale slowed her upward progression. Slipping from the spot on her nose, Vincent started to descend. Without his air filled torso, his head fell through the water like a ball of lead. The humpbacks swam away, and he could do nothing but watch them leave.

Then he heard the constant chatter of the playful dolphin pod surrounding him. Diving down beside him on either side, they stopped his free-fall. He bounced up and down on the snout of one dolphin, and was passed to another. They tossed him through the water, turning him upside down and right side up, among the different dolphins. It seemed to be a game for the entire pod as they rose closer and closer to the surface. Vincent became convinced they must be the happiest creatures in the ocean and certainly, the most talkative. He would make it his mission to help them, too.

He didn't know where they were taking him, but through the last few feet, the water became clear, and he saw it. It was a greenish, swirling entrance to a wormhole, hovering just feet above the surface of the water. *The Brethren must have picked up my signal after the explosions,* he thought. Then he realized, Jesus knew.

The Good Shepherd had said, "Remember me in your travels." Vincent wondered at the time why Jesus would say that when he was pinned at the bottom of the ocean. Now he had no doubt Jesus already knew The Brethren would find him. *In fact, he probably pre-arranged it.*

Vincent would not question the validity of it…ever.

However, one problem remained—how to get into the wormhole. He knew it would collapse if the water surrounded it on the outside, so it could not descend into the water. As the dolphins crowded around him, supporting him in the waves with their snouts, he looked up. It was only a few feet above him; far enough above to avoid the larger waves, but not close enough for the dolphins to push him into it.

The swirling motion of the opening inched closer. As it did, the water began churning in the same direction. The dolphins remained steadfast, holding Vincent partially above the water, but the swirling movement beneath them turned into a whirlpool. One by one, each dolphin was forced to pull away from him. When the last two dolphins could no longer stay in position, they had to swim away and Vincent's head fell into the maelstrom, swirling around and around.

However, instead of the rushing water descending into the depths, the center of the whirlpool started to rise. As the edge of the wormhole closed to barely an inch above the water, Vincent realized the transforming phenomena. A waterspout was forming from the centrifugal force of the swirling wind. The rising water moved up into the wormhole, taking Vincent with it. The structure would not collapse if the water was *inside its walls*, but be strengthened by the water's pressure within it. Tons of water streamed upward, filling the inside funnel and supporting the wormhole's whirling walls.

Vincent surfed along the inside of the wormhole on the front edge of a continual wave of water. So energized by the creative rescue, he searched for an appropriate piece of music to play from the new database of sacred music that had uploaded. The inside of the wormhole joyfully resounded with an arrangement of the *Hallelujah Chorus* from Handel's *Messiah,* complete with full orchestra and choir! He sent a message to his Brethren. *Well done...and thank you!*

New Earth, Day 730
Epilogue

On the beach, a half mile from the main outpost buildings, the eleven androids stood in a circle with hands joined. Their eyes closed, they focused all of their mental capacity on generating a combined nuclear fusion energy beam, created together by the group, and tethering the tenuous wormhole from D1 across a quadrant of the galaxy to Earth. Stray electrical bolts zapped here and there, running continuous streamers around their circle until it generated enough energy to continue up the main beam. The pulsing energy stream ascended into the stratosphere and beyond, leaving the planet's surface through a backdrop of clear blue sky and puffy white clouds. As it traveled through space, the swirling fission energy would create a hollow wormhole shape. Melding with the dark energy of the galaxy, it would lengthen as it propelled instantaneously toward its destination. The magnetic nanobits embedded in the stream from the eleven androids would eventually bounce off Earth's magnetic field and lead the wormhole back to D1—at least, that was the plan.

Troy and Loveena stood by the railing on the wide stone veranda, watching The Brethren try to retrieve 'a needle in a haystack,' as Dr. Devony called it. She and the rest of the scientific team were also gathered on the veranda, anxiously awaiting any news. Samuel Baptista walked out from the doors of the conference room to join her. He kissed the soft cheek of the worried doctor.

"Nothing yet," she told him. He took her hand, patting it with reassurance. Then the older couple joined Troy and Loveena at the railing.

"I just got a communiqué from Don Tyler," Samuel said. Troy and Loveena looked over at him, waiting for him to continue. "It seems you are now the most wanted man on Earth." He broadly smiled at Troy. "Corporate Rule has charged you with escaping and absconding eleven of the most dangerous NTBs ever built. The highest reward is offered to whoever discloses your whereabouts."

"Nice to be wanted," Troy said sarcastically. "What about Loveena?"

"She wasn't mentioned," Samuel replied. With a more serious expression, he added, "And I hope it stays that way." He reached over and put his hand reassuringly on her shoulder.

The four stood in silence, contemplating the news from Earth and watching as the galaxy travelers on the beach did all they could to rescue one of their own.

Troy's watch signaled an incoming message, projecting a small screen into the air in front of the group. It was Hawking, sending a message from the circle on the beach.

"We have him. He's on the way. However, he is not alone."

Troy and Samuel looked at each other with concern and expressions of alarm. "Who's with him?" asked Troy anxiously.

"It seems he is traveling with some companions he promised to look after."

"Companions?" Loveena asked.

"Yes," Hawking continued. "As Vincent has put it, he is accompanied by a large pod of chatty dolphins, eight lovely whales, a countless number of fish, and one tiny, but very brave, octopus and her 'broken pipe' of eggs. They will arrive momentarily."

Troy grabbed Loveena's hand, and they headed for the steps leading down to the beach. Samuel remained with Dr. Devony, as everyone else joined them at the railing, searching the sky for the swirling opening of a green wormhole.

Partway down the beach, Tommy played with Vincent's cat, dragging a large blade of beach grass through the sand. The cat followed close behind him, pouncing on the grass as he pulled it along. A loud thud made Tommy stop and turn around. Lying face down in the sand was a golden head. The little feline immediately ran over, sniffed it, and began purring loudly, rubbing her head all over it.

The wormhole, having dropped Vincent first, moved the short distance from the beach to the ocean and hovered just above the waves. Widening at the base, the opening gently deposited tons of water along with dolphins, whales, numerous fish of all types, and the little octopus family. The whales breeched, blowing water high into the air, while the dolphins swam and jumped, poking their heads up, and chattering incessantly before disappearing into their new home. They would find it flush with sea creatures similar to schools of sardines, millions of shrimp, and tons of krill.

Ever curious, Tommy bent down and picked up the golden head. He turned it over to inspect it and brushed the sand from Vincent's face. The android popped on his holographic mask, creating a dual digital picture of Tommy on the lenses.

"Why do you look like me?" asked Tommy.

A deep, raspy voice responded, "Because I have your DNA, Tommy Vincent."

Troy and Loveena came running toward Tommy, calling out Vincent's name. Tommy turned to his father with the android's head in his arms. "Look Daddy, a golden robot."

"No, Tommy, he's not a robot," Troy said with a laugh. "He's your Uncle Vinny!"

Taking Vincent into his hands, Troy held him up to his eye level. With a broad smile he said, "You have no idea how glad we are to see you!" Loveena stood next to Troy and put her hand on Vincent's head, noticing his chrome was now gold. "You're part of our family now," she insisted.

Troy planted a big kiss on top of the metal skull, and Vincent projected a line of yellow laughing emojis moving across his mask.

Teleporting from their position down the beach, the Brethren appeared behind Troy and Loveena, nodding their silent android greetings to Vincent. Their original mission group was now complete.

Troy held up the android's head to see all of his brothers, sisters, and the extended D1 family cheering from the veranda. "Welcome to the galaxy, Vincent!" Troy shouted.

Vincent flashed into the air a big, holographic happy face emoji with a heart, so that Dr. Devony and her team, and Samuel Baptista, could see it. Some of the staff set off celebratory fireworks from the veranda. For the first time in his existence, Vincent felt a genuine emotion of his own—human joy! Like Troy and Loveena, he was given a second chance, and it included the miracle of a soul granted to him by the Ultimate Grief Master. And on top of that, he now had a real human family of his own.

With a party atmosphere ready to go all evening, Vincent decided to play his favorite mid-20th century rock music, starting with one that just jumped to the top of his playlist, *Livin' on a Prayer,* by Bon Jovi. Vincent's brothers joined in as background singers with the deep-throated introduction, while his sisters played holographic guitars, organ, and drums. Troy danced with Loveena, and Tommy danced with the cat on the sandy beach. The scientific team and residents of New Earth partied on the veranda.

A swirl of Grief Master colors surrounded Vincent's head, lifting it onto a projected holographic body. They fastened a monk's cloak around him and draped the hood loosely across his skull. Then the colors morphed into the six Grief Masters, the three of Troy's, and the three of Loveena's, and they all danced on the beach among the others.

A microphone appeared in Vincent's skeletal hand, and he sang!

Vincent and the Grief Masters

Coming Soon!

'FORBIDDEN FRUIT'

By D.L. Farrar

The sequel to

'Vincent and the Grief Masters'

Find out what happens to our trio, Troy, Loveena, and Vincent when they must travel back to Earth in search of Samuel and Tommy. Discover who now runs the World Board of Directors as the most powerful, and most dangerous, CEO in the world.

CREDITS

Musical selections referenced in this book or used as chapter backgrounds provided on the website, played through links to Spotify on https://dianalfarrar.wixsite.com/dlfarrar

Website Banner Page: *Rey's Theme,* from *"Star Wars: The Force Awakens,"* Artists: John Williams, Anne-Sophie Mutter, The Recording Arts Orchestra of Los Angeles; Composer: John Williams; Album: *Across The Stars,* 2019; Producer: Bernard Guettler; Source: Deutsche Grammophon (DG) Berlin

Chapter 1: *Eye of the Tiger,* Artists: Survivor; Composers: Frankie Sullivan, Jim Peterik; Album: *Eye Of The Tiger,* 1982; Producers Frankie Sullivan, Jim Peterik; Source: Volcano; License: Spotify (4:03)

Chapter 3: *Bring Him Home, (Instrumental)* Artists: The Piano Guys; Composer: Claude-Michel Schonberg; Arranger: Steven Sharp Nelson; Album: *The Piano Guys,* 2012; Producers: Steven Sharp Nelson, Al van der Beek, Jon Schmidt; Source: Portrait/Sony Masterworks; License: Spotify (4:15)

Chapter 3: *(Alternate w/lyrics) Bring Him Home,* from *"Les Miserables,"* Artist: Colon Wilkinson; Written and Composed by: Alain Boublil/Alain Albert Boublil/Claude Michel Schoneberg/Herbert Kretzmer; Album: *Cameron Mackintosh presents Les Meserables, 1987*; Produced by: Alain Boublil, Claude-Michel Schoneberg; Source: Verve MC; License: Spotify (3:17)

Chapter 6: *Jail House Rock,* Artist: Elvis Presley; Composers: Jerry Leiber, Mike Stoller; Album: *Elvis Golden Records,* 1958; Producers: Jerry Leiber, Mike Stoller; Source: RCA Records Label; License: Spotify (2:26)

Chapter 8: *Survival,* Artists: America; Composer: Gerry Beckley; Album: *Alibi,* 1980; Producers: Matthew McCauley, Fred Mollin; Source Capitol Records; License: Spotify (3:16)

Chapter 10: *Iron Man,* Artists: Black Sabbath; Written and Composed by: Black Sabbath, Bill Ward, Geezer Butler, John Osbourne, Terence Butler, Tony Iommi; Original Album: *Paranoid,* 1970, Album: *Iron Man 2012 ReMaster*; Producer, Rodger Bain; Source/License: Rhino/Warner Records; License: Spotify (5:55)

Chapter 13: *All Along the Watchtower;* Artist: Jimi Hendrix; Composers: Bob Dylan, Jimi Hendrix; Album: *Electric Ladyland,* 1968; Producer: Jimi Hendrix; Source: Legacy Recordings; License: Spotify (3:58)

Chapter 16: *Claire de Lune,* Artists: The London Symphony Orchestra; Composer: Claude Debussy, 1890; Album: *Firelight, 20 Classical Masterpieces,* 2018; Source: The Music Factory; License: Spotify (2:03)

Chapter 16: *In the Mood,* Artists: the Glenn Miller Orchestra; Rendition by Glenn Miller, Composers: Joe Garland, Andy Razaf; Album: *Glenn Miller, Ultimate Big Band Collection,* 1939; Producer: Glenn Miller; Source: Masterworks Jazz; License: Spotify (3:36)

Chapters 20 & 21: *One (Is The Loneliest Number),* Artists: Three Dog Night; Written and Composed by: Harry Nilsson; Album: *The Best of Three Dog Night,* 1968; Producer: Gabriel Mekler; Source: Geffen*; License: Spotify (3:02)

Chapter 23: *The Green Leaves of Summer,* Artists: The Brothers Four; Written and Composed by: J. E. Cason, McGayden; Album: *The Brothers Four Greatest Hits, 1960*; Source: Columbia; License: Spotify (2:54)

Chapter 27: *Ticket To Ride,* Artists: The Beatles; Composer: John Lennon, Paul McCartney; Album: Original Single 1965, *Help, ReMastered 2009*; Producer, George Martin; Source: EMI Catalogue, MPL Sony Music Publishing; License: Spotify (3:09)

Chapter 28: *Stairway To Heaven;* Artists: Led Zepplin; Composer: Jimmy Page, Robert Plant; Album: *Led Zepplin IV (Delux Edition),* 1971; Producer: Jimmy Page; Source: Atlantic Records; License: Spotify (8:02)

Chapter 30: *When I Fall In Love,* Artist: Julie London; Arranged and conducted by Andre Previn; Written by Edward Heyman and V. Young; Album: *Your Number Please,* 1959; Producer, Bobby Troup; Source: Capitol Records; License: Spotify (3:23)

Chapter 32: *Bolero,* Artist: Michael Fix; Composer: Maurice Ravel, 1928; Album: *Lines & Spaces,* 2014; Source: Acoustic Music Records; License: Spotify (4:14)

Chapter 34: *Time In a Bottle,* Artist: Jim Croce; Written and Composed by: Jim Croce; Album: *Photographs & Memories: His Greatest Hits,* 1974; Source: BMG Rights Management (US) LLC, BMG Publishing; License: Spotify (2:08)

Chapter 38: *Rhapsody in Blue,* Artists: Columbia Symphony Orchestra, Piano and Conductor, Leonard Bernstein; Composer: George Gershwin; 1924; Orchestration by Ferde Grofe; Album: *Rhapsody in Blue and an American in*

Paris, 1959; Producer: John McClure; Source: Sony Classical; License: Spotify (16:27)

Chapter 38: *Memory,* from *"CATS,"* Artist: Andrew Lloyd Webber, Sarah Brightman; Written by: Andrew Lloyd Webber, T. S. Eliot, Trevor Robert Nunn; Album: *The Andrew Lloyd Webber Collection,* 1997; Producer: Andrew Lloyd Webber; Source: Polydor Records; License: Spotify (3:56)

Chapter 40: *Hallelujah (chorus),* from *"The Messiah,"* Artists: The Mormon Tabernacle Choir at Temple Square; Composer and Lyricist: George Frideric Handel, text compiled by Charles Jennens, 1741; Album: *The Essential Christmas,* 2002; Producer unknown; Source: Sony Music Entertainment Inc. Columbia; License: Spotify (3:56)

Chapter 40: *Livin' On A Prayer,* Artists: Bon Jovi; Composed and Written by: Desmond Child, Jon Bon Jovi, Richie Sambora; Album: *Slippery When Wet,* 1986; Producer, Bruce Fairbairn; Source: Island Records, Universal Music Publishing; License: Spotify (4:09)

****

Written works referenced in this book:

Chapter 22: *The Sound And The Fury,* Author: William Faulkner; Publisher, Jonathan Cape and Harrison Smith, 1929.

Chapter 22: *Through The Looking-Glass, and What Alice Found There,* Author: Lewis Carroll; Illustrator: John Tenniel; Publisher: MacMillan, 1871.

Chapter 38: *Gunga Din* (from *The Barrack-Room Ballads)*, Author: Rudyard Kipling, 1892.

Chapter 38: *Moby Dick/The Whale,* Author: Herman Melville; Publisher, Richard Bentley, 1851.

****

Please note: some chapters in this book mention suicide. If you are struggling, or know someone who may be in emotional distress, do not hesitate to call the National Suicide Hotline – just dial 988. A confidential, professional provider can give immediate assistance. <u>You are not alone.</u>

D. L. Farrar

ABOUT THE AUTHOR, D. L. FARRAR

Diana Farrar grew up looking at the stars. Her first published work appeared in a nationally syndicated newspaper column, an inspirational poem about the Gemini 4 mission and the first historic spacewalk. She was fourteen. Her father, a brilliant scientist contracted to work with JPL and the NASA Apollo Space program, taught her to think outside the box. Her childhood imagination was shaped by the stories of Mary Shelley, Jules Verne, Orson Welles, Rod Serling, Gene Roddenberry, and other such minds that introduced her to 'what's beyond.' Her favorite Saturday matinees featured creatures that 'thrilled and chilled' her. It is no accident that the main characters in her first novel were named for her favorite matinee villain, Vincent Price.

As a young adult, she spent time reading articles from her father's magazines, such as *Scientific American, Popular Mechanics, the AIAA Journal* (aeronautics and astronautics), *National Geographic*, as well as history books. While not understanding everything she read, it broadened her mind to think about possibilities beyond man's current place in the universe. It also taught her to always try and learn something new.

Physics and chemistry turned out not to be Diana's strong suits, but writing, music, and composition were. She soon discovered her most successful pieces combined inspirational themes with stories of ordinary people. This set her work apart from the science fiction worlds she drew her own inspiration from. Articles such as a human-interest series on women's shelters earned her a Wall Street Journal award. In 2022, she won a first-place award for the true story of a military man's crossroads that led him to a crucial life changing decision.

Realizing her work might help someone in a personal crisis or in relationships with others, or perhaps, with God, Diana has authored inspirational works such as short stories, poetry, a musical with eighty pages of original music and a Hollywood screenplay with a future option from HBO. Large churches have sought her out to write holiday stage plays that have drawn thousands of people to hear devotional inspiration through her imagination. But her unique ability to successfully combine science fiction and faith has produced a story of interest to fans of multiple genres and age groups.

Diana's professional career spanned over forty-five years in the business side of book and magazine publishing, where she once again had a chance to revisit earlier interests. She worked for such magazines as *Smithsonian/Air & Space* magazine, *Caribbean Travel & Life*, Colonial Williamsburg's *Trend & Tradition* magazine, to name a few. Now retired, she's concentrating on writing novels. She is currently working on a sequel to *Vincent and the Grief Masters*, entitled, *Forbidden Fruit*, and a third book of personal short stories called, *Who Comes to the Table*? And occasionally, Diana still picks up a science journal or astronomy magazine just to learn something new.

Author D. L. Farrar, star gazer, soul searcher

Made in the USA
Middletown, DE
28 February 2025